THEY CAME
TO KILL

THEY CAME TO KILL

A PREACHER & MacCALLISTER WESTERN

WILLIAM W. JOHNSTONE

and J. A. JOHNSTONE

PINNACLE BOOKS
Kensington Publishing Corp.

www.kensingtonbooks.com

PINNACLE BOOKS are published by

Kensington Publishing Corp.
119 West 40th Street
New York, NY 10018

All Kensington titles, imprints, and distributed lines are available at special quantity discounts for bulk purchases for sales promotions, premiums, fund-raising, educational, or institutional use. Special book excerpts or customized printings can also be created to fit specific needs. For details, write or phone the office of the Kensington sales manager: Kensington Publishing Corp., 119 West 40th Street, New York, NY 10018, attn: Sales Department; phone 1-800-221-2647.

PINNACLE BOOKS, the Pinnacle logo, and the WWJ steer head logo are Reg. U.S. Pat. & TM Off.

ISBN-13: 978-0-7860-4418-4
ISBN-10: 0-7860-4418-7

First printing: July 2020

10 9 8 7 6 5 4 3 2

Printed in the United States of America

Electronic edition:

ISBN-13: 978-0-7860-4419-1 (e-book)
ISBN-10: 0-7860-4419-5 (e-book)

CHAPTER 1

Somewhere west of El Paso, 1850

The sweating men, pale under their sunburns, were about to die, and they knew it. They crouched in a shallow gully that ran along a sharp sandstone rise too steep to climb. Twenty men now, because two of their number lay out there some thirty yards in front of the gully, their corpses baking in the blistering midday sun. Numerous arrows stuck up from the backs of their blue uniform jackets. They had been the slowest of foot when it came to running for cover, and they had paid the price.

Lieutenant Damon Charlton sat with his back against the side of the gully and worked the cork out of the neck of his canteen. He tipped his head back and took a long swallow of the tepid water. No point in worrying about saving it now.

"Lieutenant, w-what are we gonna do?" one of the men asked.

Charlton thought his name was Weatherbee, Wellington, something like that.

What are we going to do, Private Weatherbee or Wellington or whatever in bloody blue blazes your name is? We're going to die, that's what we're going to do. Quickly and relatively painlessly if we're fortunate. Screaming in agony if we aren't.

But of course he couldn't say that, so Charlton responded, "This is a good defensive position, Private. We'll continue to hold it until the hostiles tire of this and depart."

"But . . . but our horses, sir. Our horses ran away. The Apaches must have 'em by now. We're at least eighty miles from El Paso. We'll never make it back there on foot."

Knowing what he did of the Apaches, Charlton thought it likely most of those army horses would wind up in the savages' stewpots. They were a nomadic people but didn't travel much by horseback. He had been told by an old-timer that the Apaches trusted their own legs not to give out more than they trusted those of horses. They could run all day when they needed to.

Trying to keep his voice level and calm, the lieutenant said, "We'll deal with that when the time comes, Private. Right now, the most important thing is to hold our position, as I said."

He heard grumbling along the line and knew some of the men were angry with him. To their way of thinking, he had led them into this deathtrap, and they weren't wrong.

But he'd had no choice. His orders had been to take this patrol into the wasteland west of the western tip of Texas, into what had been the Mexican territory of Nuevo Mexico until the Treaty of Guadalupe Hidalgo a couple of years earlier, following the end of yet another war.

Officially it was New Mexico Territory, owned and controlled by the United States, although the boundaries were fuzzy. Some Texans thought it should be part of that state. The Mexicans still claimed territory in the southern part of the region. But those were just words in documents and lines on maps that could not be pointed to out where the sun beat down and rattlesnakes and red savages lurked behind every rock.

The politicians in Washington, Mexico City, and Austin squabbled over those words and map lines, while soldiers rode out into the harsh landscape to meet death.

Charlton corked the canteen. He had no idea how long the Apaches would take in getting around to killing all of them. He supposed he might have time to get thirsty again later, so he might as well save some of the water after all.

He heard a low, monotonous sound and realized that one of the men was praying. He almost snapped then, almost shouted at the man that prayer wasn't going to do any good, that there was no one to hear it in this desolation, but Charlton swallowed the words at the last second. Losing his temper wouldn't do any real harm—after all, their situation couldn't get any worse, could it?—but it wouldn't accomplish any good, either. So why waste his breath?

He leaned his head back against the sandstone and closed his eyes. The sun was so bright that didn't make much difference, but his eyelids cut the glare a little. As soon as he did that, however, the same images played out in his mind's eye.

The patrol had stopped to rest the horses, when suddenly arrows began to come seemingly out of nowhere. Several of them struck horses and the animals went down screaming. Charlton had spotted the gully and recognized it as cover, so he ran toward it, knowing that they didn't have time to mount up. Besides, where would they go? It seemed like the hostiles were everywhere around them, judging by the way so many arrows filled the air, coming from every direction . . .

Even though he hadn't shouted any orders, the rest of the men had streamed after him and followed his example in leaping into the gully, all except the two who didn't make it and lay there feathered with arrows. Shots blasted, the echoes rolling across the arid landscape, although the men had fired blindly, unable to contain the reaction to being attacked by invisible foes. The gunfire died away as the arrows stopped coming . . .

It seemed as if hours had passed since then, although Charlton knew that in reality it was more like half an hour. He didn't see any reason to pull out his pocket watch and check the time. It hadn't taken him long to understand what a bad fix they were in. The horses that hadn't been killed in the ambush had run off, spooked by the gunfire and the smell of blood. What kind of army mounts were those, he had asked himself bitterly. On foot, unable to venture out from the scant cover, all the patrol could do was wait. Maybe . . . maybe there *would* be a miracle. Maybe the Apaches would tire of this standoff and leave. Maybe another patrol would come along. Maybe—

With a harsh, incoherent yell, one of the soldiers suddenly scrambled up out of the gully and sprinted across the flats. Another man cried, "Come back here, you fool!"

The running man jerked his head around and called over his shoulder, "I'll get the horse—"

An ugly, guttural sound interrupted that declaration of vain hope as an arrow skewered the man's neck from right to left. He stumbled, twisted, turned all the way around so he was facing back toward the gully. Crouched there, the men saw the torrent of blood that flooded from the soldier's open mouth. Another arrow struck him from behind and drove all the way through his body so the flint head erupted from his chest.

That was wasteful. The neck wound was already fatal. That wild thought careened through Lieutenant Damon Charlton's mind, then he told himself it didn't matter. No doubt the Apaches would retrieve all their arrows once every member of the patrol was dead— which might not be much longer.

Shrill, yipping war cries came from left and right. The Apaches who had crawled up, unseen, until they were within a few yards of the gully leaped up and charged. Brandishing knives, they dived into the gully.

Earlier, Charlton had taken his Colt Dragoon revolver from its holster and placed it on the ground beside him so it would be handy. That saved him the few seconds it would have taken to withdraw the weapon from the flapped holster. He dropped the canteen, snatched up the Dragoon, and eared back the hammer. With the blood thundering through his veins, he didn't even notice the Dragoon's cumbersome weight as he aimed it at the closest Apache and pulled the trigger.

The cap-and-ball's heavy boom hammered Charlton's ears. Powder smoke gushed from the muzzle, and for a second he couldn't see the charging Indian. Then the view cleared enough for him to spot the Apache, stumbling as blood welled from the hole in the middle of his chest. The man's momentum carried him a couple more steps before he pitched forward and landed facedown on the very lip of the gully. His arm hung over the edge. His hand still clutched the knife he'd intended to bury in Charlton's flesh, but as the lieutenant watched, the man's nerves stopped working, the muscles relaxed, and the knife slipped from the Apache's grip, dropping to the sandy ground.

All that happened in a heartbeat. Charlton cocked the Dragoon again as he shifted his aim. Another Apache came in from the left. Charlton fired. He was a little high this time. Instead of striking the Indian in the chest, the .44 round blew away a fist-sized chunk of his head. That dead man landed on the ground beside the first Apache Charlton had killed.

Elsewhere in the gully, several soldiers had managed to fire their muskets, but the weapons were unwieldy and not well suited for close work. They were actually better as clubs when it came to hand-to-hand fighting so the men used them that way as they battled frantically for their lives. A few of the Apaches went down with shattered skulls.

But there were too many of the savages. They plunged their knives into the soldiers again and again. Men screamed as blood darkened their already dark blue uniforms even more. Some had their throats cut, causing crimson fountains to geyser out from the gaping wounds. The gruesome melee spread along the gully.

Lieutenant Charlton twisted to his right. A few feet away, one of the Indians had hold of a soldier's throat with his left hand while he used the knife in his right to stab the luckless trooper in the chest. The Apache was enjoying this brutal murder too much. He didn't notice Charlton aiming at him until it was too late. The Apache turned his head toward the lieutenant just in time to receive the bullet through his open, yelling mouth. It threw him backward in a lifeless sprawl.

Instinct turned Charlton back to the left. The Dragoon roared again, and a savage doubled over as the slug punched deep into his guts.

The revolver's cylinder held two more rounds. Charlton had an extra, loaded cylinder in his pocket, but he knew he would never have time to switch them out. He started to tremble with the knowledge of his impending death. But he still had those two rounds, he reminded himself. It took two hands to control the weapon, but he cocked and lifted the Dragoon and shot another savage in the chest. The man flew backward with arms and legs flailing.

Five shots, five dead hostiles, Charlton thought. He probably would have gotten a medal for this, if anyone had ever known about it. If he hadn't been destined to have his bones bleach in the pitiless sun, his fate unknown and therefore not mourned.

The Apaches were notorious for torturing captives, he reminded himself. He had one round left in the Dragoon, and the time had come for him to put it to its best use.

He pressed the muzzle against his throat, under his chin. His thumb fumbled for the hammer.

Something crashed into him from the right, and the Dragoon flew out of his hand. As he lay on his side, he cried out and reached for the revolver where it landed on the ground a few feet away, but strong hands pulled him away and rolled him onto his back. A dark shape loomed over him, blotting out the sun. The man drove a knee into Charlton's belly, sickening him and pinning him to the ground. His pulse boomed inside his head like a drum as he watched the Apache lift a knife above his head. The weapon hung there for a second, poised for a killing stroke.

In that heartbeat, which seemed to stretch out for an eternity, Charlton tasted the dirt in his mouth, felt its gritty sting in his eyes. He heard the shrieks of his men as they were slaughtered. He saw the sun reflect off the knife blade, took note of the brass hilt, the bit of bone handle showing where the Apache's sinewy fingers weren't wrapped around it, the round brass pommel on the end.

That wasn't a crude knife fashioned by some primitive, he thought. It was a white man's blade, doubtless taken from some corpse. And it was going to claim another life.

Instead, the Apache suddenly reversed the knife as he brought it down, and the brass pommel struck Lieutenant Damon Charlton between the eyes rather than the blade sheathing itself in his heart. The impact was like an explosion in Charlton's brain, a burst of red that flared brighter than the sun before fading quickly into an all-encompassing black.

CHAPTER 2

MacCallister's Valley, Colorado, 1852

Jamie Ian MacCallister brought the Sharps rifle smoothly to his shoulder and squeezed the trigger. The rifle's thunderous boom blended with the big cat's scream as it launched itself toward Jamie from the rocky knob above him.

The heavy-caliber bullet caught the mountain lion in the chest, but even though it was a killing shot, it wasn't enough to deflect the beast's flight. Jamie was a big man, but not big enough to withstand the impact of well over a hundred pounds of killer cat. The hurtling body crashed into Jamie and knocked him backward off the ledge.

Claws ripped through Jamie's sheepskin coat and raked his flesh. Dying jaws snapped together well short of his throat, instead of ripping it out as the mountain lion had intended. As man and cat both tumbled down the rocky slope, Jamie got his hands against the beast's bloody chest and shoved it away from him. He rolled a few more yards before he was able to grab hold of something and stop his out-of-control plunge.

It was a good thing he did. Less than ten feet away, a cliff dropped off sheer. The mountain lion's body slid over the brink and plummeted a hundred feet to crash through the pine branches below.

Breathing a little hard, Jamie clung to the rock he had grabbed, looked around for a second handhold, and got a grip on another outcropping. The slope was steep, but once he caught his breath, he climbed it without much trouble, heading up toward the ledge he'd been moving along when the big cat jumped him. He ignored the burning from the scratches the claws had left on his broad, powerful chest.

His Sharps had caught on the rough ground not far from where he'd dropped it when the mountain lion knocked him off his feet. He was glad to see that. He wouldn't have to climb all the way around to that lower level to retrieve it, as he would have if it had gone over the cliff. A fall from that height might well have damaged the rifle beyond repair, too.

Would have damaged *him* beyond repair, for sure, he thought with a grim chuckle.

Then he sobered. He'd caught only a glimpse of the mountain lion as it dived at him, but he had seen that it was a magnificent creature and a part of him regretted having to kill it. It never would have attacked a human being if it hadn't been hungry from the hard winter not long past, the same sort of hunger that had led it to go after the herd of cattle Jamie had been building up for several years. He had himself a good ranch in what had come to be called MacCallister's Valley, and he wasn't going to let anybody—man or beast—take it away from him.

Jamie spotted his broad-brimmed, brown felt hat

and was glad he hadn't lost it, either. He gathered up
the rifle and the hat and clambered the rest of the way
to the ledge. As he stepped onto it, he looked up at
the knob where the big cat had been lying in wait.
He'd been tracking the mountain lion all day, and he
knew the cat had been tracking him, too. But the
deadly competition had come to its end.

Jamie slapped the hat against a buckskin-clad thigh
and put it on. He reloaded the Sharps, sliding one of
the long .52 caliber cartridges into the breech, then
checked to make sure the Walker Colt was still in its
holster on his right hip and hadn't fallen out during
his tumble. The revolver was there.

With the important things taken care of, he pulled
his coat aside and lifted the buckskin shirt to take a
look at the wounds on his chest. There were four
scratches, each a few inches long. They were still bleeding, but not much. Jamie made a face, but the grimace
was inspired more by the damage done to a perfectly
good shirt than by the wounds themselves. Scars were
scattered all over his tall, muscular body. A few more
added to their number didn't matter.

He took a bandanna from his pocket, pressed it
over the claw marks, and held it in place with his right
arm as he turned and started making his way back
down the mountainside. To his left, MacCallister's
Valley opened in a broad, impressive sweep. The slopes
of the surrounding snowcapped mountains were
dark with evergreens. Down in the valley, the snow was
gone and lush grass was starting to rise. Wildflowers
dotted the meadows. It was the sort of view to take a
man's breath away, and it still affected Jamie that way,

although he and Kate had been settled on their ranch for a good number of years.

Raised a good number of kids, too. All were grown and out on their own except for the youngest, Falcon, and despite barely being a teenager, he already had the wanderlust in his eyes. Jamie knew that because he had seen it in all the others as they started to come of age. If anything, it was even stronger in Falcon, and he was such a strapping youth that Jamie knew he and Kate wouldn't be able to hold on to the boy for much longer.

Jamie had set out from the ranch this morning on horseback and picked up the cat's trail at the last place it had attacked the herd. Not surprisingly, that trail led to the high country, and eventually Jamie had left the horse behind and continued his tracking on foot.

It took him the better part of an hour to reach the spot where he had left his mount. The horse was still there and bobbed his head up and down as he let out a whicker of greeting when Jamie stepped close. Then it shied away as it caught the scent of the big cat or the blood from Jamie's wounds, or both.

"Take it easy there, old hoss," Jamie said. "Nothing to worry about. That critter's dead, I'm all right, and we're going home."

He slid the Sharps back into its saddle scabbard, untied the reins from the sapling he'd knotted them around, and swung up into leather. He wanted to be home by dark. At this time of year, it could still get mighty cold at night.

By late afternoon, he came in sight of the sprawling log and stone ranch house and the several outbuildings and corrals around it. He also saw something that made his eyes narrow under the bushy, graying brows. Four horses he didn't recognize were tied up at the hitch rail in front of the house.

The presence of strangers didn't necessarily mean trouble, of course, but even so, Jamie reached down and slid the Walker Colt up and down slightly in its holster, just to make sure it moved freely.

Everything looked peaceful. He drew up alongside the horses and saw the *US* brand on their left shoulders. Those were army mounts, he realized, increasing his puzzlement. He didn't know of any reason why the army would be paying him a visit.

The front door opened and Falcon came out while Jamie was dismounting. Despite his young age, Falcon was almost as tall as his father, and the width of his shoulders indicated that they might well be as wide as Jamie's someday. He had an unruly thatch of blond hair.

A grin spread across his face. "Soldiers inside lookin' for you, Pa."

"I can see that," Jamie responded as he leaned his head toward the horses. "What do they want?"

"They ain't sayin'."

"Your ma would correct you if she was out here. They *aren't* saying."

"That's what I just told you," Falcon said. "Anyway, Ma's set 'em down in the parlor and given 'em coffee and insisted that they stay for supper. They want to talk to you, so I reckon you'll soon find out what they're after."

Jamie handed the reins to his son. "Here. Put this horse up for me."

"Aw, I want to go in with you and find out what this is all about."

"You'll find out soon enough, if it's any of your business. Now take the horse on to the barn, rub him down, and give him some grain."

"All right." Falcon started to turn away but paused to look over his shoulder and ask, "What about that mountain lion? I almost plumb forgot to ask about that."

"He won't bother our herd anymore."

Falcon grinned, clearly proud of his father. "I knew you'd get him."

Jamie didn't mention how close the big cat had come to getting *him*.

"One more thing, Pa," Falcon called as Jamie started into the house. "One of those fellas isn't a soldier. At least, he ain't dressed like one."

Jamie didn't bother correcting his son's language this time. He was too interested in satisfying his own curiosity about the visitors.

After all the years of being married to him, Kate knew his step, of course. When he went into the house, she called from the parlor, "In here, Jamie."

Jamie took off his hat and coat and hung them on a hook. As he moved into the parlor doorway, his keen-eyed gaze quickly took in the four visitors. Two of them, both in uniform, sat on a divan. A colonel and a major, he noted, so whatever this was, the army was taking it seriously.

Another soldier, a lieutenant who was probably an aide to the other officers, was in a straight-backed chair to the side, while a gray-haired, middle-aged man in a brown tweed suit occupied an armchair near the fireplace. His face was instantly familiar to Jamie, although the name didn't want to come right away.

Kate was in a rocking chair she favored, but she stood up quickly with a look of concern on her beautiful face when she laid eyes on Jamie. He knew she had spotted the rips in his shirt and the bloodstains around them.

"Jamie," she said as she took a step toward him. As always, she nearly took his breath away with her beauty, even with that worried expression on her face. "Are you all right?"

"Yeah, I just tangled a little with that big cat I went looking for. It's nothing to worry about."

"Nothing to . . . Let me see." Without waiting for his permission, she lifted his shirt, which he found rather uncomfortable with strangers in the room. "Why, that bandanna is so bloody it's stuck to the wounds! You come into the kitchen. That needs tending to, right now."

"But Kate," he said with a vague wave toward the four men, "we've got company."

"Their business can wait," she said crisply. "Can't it, gentlemen?"

The familiar-looking civilian smiled and said, "Certainly it can, Mrs. MacCallister." To Jamie, he went on. "Now that I've met your wife, Jamie, after hearing so much about her, I'd advise you not to argue with her."

The man's voice prodded Jamie's memory, and a name popped into his head. "Owen! Owen Charlton."

"That's right. I didn't know if you'd remember me or not. But you go on with Mrs. MacCallister. It's not as if the fate of the entire nation depends on the errand that brought us here, or anything like that."

One of the soldiers said, "Actually, sir—"

Owen Charlton stopped him with a curt gesture, then smiled and nodded again at Jamie, who allowed Kate to lead him out of the parlor.

As they went out to the kitchen, he couldn't help but think of Owen Charlton's comment about the errand that had brought them here and the fate of the nation.

Jamie had an unsettling hunch that despite what Charlton said, maybe those two things *were* related.

CHAPTER 3

Kate sat him down at the big table in the kitchen, dipped a cloth in a basin of water, and got to work soaking the bandanna loose from the bloody wounds. "I thought you were going to find that mountain lion and shoot it. From a distance."

"Well, that was the plan," Jamie responded dryly, "but the cat had ideas of its own. We don't have to worry about him going after our stock anymore. I came out on top in that fight."

"From the looks of these claw marks, the mountain lion was on top, at least for a while."

Jamie changed the subject by saying, "When did Owen Charlton and those officers show up?"

"About two hours ago. I've been keeping them entertained. The others seem rather stiff and worried about something, but Mr. Charlton is a charming man, or at least pretends to be. Where do you know him from, Jamie?"

"Last time I saw him, he was in uniform, too. A colonel. I did some scouting under his command seven or eight years ago, over in the Missouri Territory. Reckon he's either retired since then, or else he's on some sort of special assignment that's got him in civilian clothes."

Jamie winced as Kate peeled the bandanna away from the wounds. She had loosened it enough with the wet rag to make it let go.

"Somebody could be carving on you with a bowie knife and you'd never make a sound or show it," she said with a smile. "But let your wife do something that stings a little and you make a face like that."

"Well, it stung more 'n a little," Jamie said defensively, then grinned at her.

"It's going to sting even more. I need to clean those scratches with whiskey. None of them look deep enough to require any stitches. I'll just put some dressings on them and bind them in place. Considering all the other scars you have, these won't even be that impressive."

"That's what I was thinking."

As Kate continued working, she said, "I noticed something about this man Owen Charlton, Jamie. Like I told you, he's very easygoing and charming, but I could see something in his eyes, some sort of pain that's haunting him. Do you know anything about that?"

Jamie shook his head. "Not a blasted thing. You reckon he's sick?"

"Not physically. This strikes me as something that hurts him differently. Something in . . . well, his soul."

Jamie didn't say anything to that, but he took Kate's words seriously. She was as perceptive a person as he had ever met, and the best judge of character, to boot.

By the time he walked into the parlor again, with bandages tied around his chest and wearing a clean, homespun shirt over them, Falcon had come into the house and was straddling a chair he had turned around.

Owen Charlton smiled and said, "I've been telling your son about the advantages of a military career, Jamie. I hope you don't mind."

"Nope, but I'm afraid the boy may be too head-strong and fiddle-footed to suit the army."

"But they get to wear uniforms and carry sabers," Falcon protested. "That sounds mighty excitin'."

Charlton said, "Unfortunately, if you're an officer, you wind up sitting in a great many dull meetings, as well. Like the one I'm about to have with your father."

Jamie took that as a hint and told Falcon, "I'll bet you can find some more chores to do. Probably won't even have to look very hard."

"But, Pa—"

"Come along, Falcon," Kate said briskly. "I need you to bring in some firewood."

Falcon looked like he wanted to argue, but he knew better than to disobey his mother. He sighed and followed Kate out of the parlor.

"Now we can get down to business," the colonel said.

Charlton said, "Jamie, this is Colonel Jedediah Hargrove and his aide, Major Aaron Bolton. And Major Bolton's aide, Lieutenant Henry Parkhurst."

Jamie nodded, said, "Gentlemen," and shook hands with all three officers. "Welcome to MacCallister's Valley." He looked at Charlton. "You retired now, Owen?"

Charlton cleared his throat, looked a little un-comfortable, and said, "As it happens, I'm a general. But I'm in civilian garb because I'm here as a special representative of the White House."

"President Fillmore sent you?" Jamie asked with a frown.

"That's right."

News from back east was sometimes slow in reaching MacCallister's Valley, but Jamie knew Millard Fillmore occupied the White House at the moment, with an election coming up later in the year to see if he would continue to do so. He didn't have any particular opinion about Fillmore, politics never having interested him that much, but he wasn't aware of anything bad about the man. It was a complete mystery to him, though, why the President would send Owen Charlton to talk to him.

Jamie settled himself in his own rocking chair and said, "This sounds like sort of a deep tale. You'd best start from the beginning, Owen."

Charlton sat down, leaned forward, and clasped his hands between his knees. "Are you familiar with the transcontinental railroad?"

"I know such a thing doesn't exist."

"Not yet, but there's been a great deal of discussion in Washington about the building of such a road. As you can imagine, an undertaking like that would be very expensive, with a lot at stake."

Jamie nodded. "Not just money. There'd be a lot of power and influence riding on it being a success, too."

"Exactly!" Charlton said, ticking off the points on his fingers as he went on. "Money, power, and influence . . . You start talking about those three things, and people in Washington sit up and take notice. It doesn't take them long to stake out their positions, either. The discussions about a transcontinental railroad have centered around two prospective routes."

"Each one with its own supporters, I imagine."

"That's very true. Some believe that the country would be best served by the railroad taking a northern route across the plains and through the mountains. Others are firmly convinced that a southern route through Texas and then across the territory acquired from Mexico by the Treaty of Guadalupe Hidalgo would be better. Not only that, but it's also thought that Santa Anna would be willing to sell the United States even more land across the southern border. Mexico has been financially strapped ever since he became president again."

Jamie scowled. "Santa Anna." The name sounded like it tasted bad in his mouth. "That fella has more lives than a cat. How he keeps winding up back in power down there south of the border is more than I can figure out."

"That's right. You were at the Alamo, weren't you?" Charlton said.

"For a while, before it fell. Good thing I got out when I did, or we wouldn't be sitting here today. But a lot of good men *didn't* get out, and as far as I'm concerned, their blood is on Santa Anna's hands."

The barrel-chested Colonel Hargrove spoke up. "You wouldn't allow your justifiable resentment toward the Mexican president to affect your service to your country, would you, Mr. MacCallister?"

"So far, nobody's said a blasted word about how you figure I can serve my country this time," Jamie snapped. "No offense, Owen, but you're just talking around it with all this palaver about railroads."

"No, that's really the main reason I'm here," Charlton said. "At the moment, a southern route isn't really feasible because the territory between Texas and California, even with that already officially under United States control, is mostly unexplored and . . . untamed."

Jamie had been rocking slightly in his chair. He stopped, peered intently at Charlton, and said, "You're talking about the Apaches."

Grim-faced, Charlton nodded. And for a second, Jamie saw what Kate had mentioned earlier—pain flaring to life in the man's eyes. Jamie's mention of the Apaches seemed to be the spark that had set it off.

Charlton's mouth was a thin line as he said, "That's right. Other than the trail up to Santa Fe and the few settlements that have developed along it, Mexico never really brought the area under control. And traffic along that trail has been disrupted many times by raids carried out by the hostiles. There is no trail running from east to west. What it comes down to is that anyone venturing west of El Paso del Norte is risking his life . . . and in great danger of losing it."

"What about the army?"

Major Bolton said, "We've tried to establish regular patrols—" He stopped short at the look Charlton gave him.

Deep trenches had appeared in the older man's cheeks. His blithe, charming manner had disappeared completely.

"The Apaches *must* be pacified, at least to a certain extent, before an adequate investigation and survey of the area can be made," Charlton said. "President Fillmore has placed me in charge of this effort and instructed me to see it through to a success, no matter what is required."

"What's that got to do with me?" Jamie asked. His voice was as hard and grim as Charlton's.

"There's no better fighting man west of the Mississippi . . . or east of there, either, for that matter. Jamie Ian MacCallister is one of the best-known frontiersmen in the nation, spoken of in the same breath as Kit Carson and Jim Bridger."

Jamie held up a hand to stop his visitor. "Why don't you go ask those fellas to get rid of the Apaches for you, then? That's what you're after, isn't it? You want me to take on the whole blasted Apache tribe?"

"There's something else—" Charlton broke off and turned to look at Hargrove, Bolton, and Parkhurst. "If you gentlemen wouldn't mind, I'd like to speak with Mr. MacCallister in private."

Colonel Hargrove frowned. "With all due respect, General, the President made us part of this delegation, too."

"I'm aware that, but . . . I'm asking you, Jedediah. Not as one soldier to another, but man to man."

Hargrove looked at him for a long moment, then got to his feet and jerked his head toward the door. "I believe I'll go smoke a pipe on the front porch. Come along, Major, Lieutenant."

The three officers left the room.

Once they were gone, Charlton lifted a hand that trembled slightly and passed it over his face. "I came to you, Jamie, because I know you, and I don't know Carson or Bridger. I know your capabilities, and I know I can trust you."

Jamie leaned forward and said harshly, "Spit it out, Owen."

"My son is out there . . . somewhere in that wasteland west of El Paso . . . and I want you to find him."

CHAPTER 4

For a long moment, Jamie didn't say anything. Owen Charlton's head drooped forward as he sighed. He stared at the floor, but he seemed to be seeing something else.

Finally, Jamie said quietly, "I don't remember you talking about a son when we knew each other before, Owen."

"Well, we never talked that much about family. We were there to do a job, and we did it." Charlton forced his head up so he could meet Jamie's gaze again. "I have a son. His name is Damon. He was . . . he *is* a lieutenant in the army. He was posted to the fort that was established a few years ago just across the Rio Grande from the Mexican city of El Paso del Norte."

"I've been there," Jamie said. "Quite a settlement growing up around it. Some call it Franklin, others just call the whole place, on both sides of the river, El Paso."

"Yes," Charlton nodded, "and now that so much of the land west of there belongs to the United States, it's going to be the gateway to the West . . . but only if that territory can be at least partially civilized."

"Which brings us right back to the Apaches. What do they have to do with your son?"

"More than a year and a half ago, Damon led a patrol out there into the badlands to try to gauge the enemy's strength and position. They never returned to the post." Charlton's hands knotted together again, so tightly this time that the knuckles turned white. "Eventually, a stronger force was sent out to search for them. They found the patrol . . . or what was left of it. The mutilated remains of twenty-one mounted infantrymen. When the patrol left the fort, it numbered . . . twenty-two men. A lieutenant, a sergeant, and twenty enlisted men."

"Your son's was the body they didn't find?" Jamie guessed.

Charlton nodded. "That's right. You understand, the elements . . . and the scavengers . . . had not been kind to the men. But none of them wore a lieutenant's uniform. This makes me believe that Damon was captured by the Apaches."

"You know it was an Indian attack responsible for what happened to them?"

"The bodies were full of arrow wounds," Charlton said. "There's no other conclusion to draw."

Jamie sat back in the rocking chair and rubbed his chin. "If the Apaches were able to tell that Damon was the leader, yeah, they might've taken him prisoner rather than killing him outright with the others."

He didn't say the other things that were going through his mind. The Apaches might have captured Damon Charlton so they could take him back to their village and take their time torturing him to death. They were experts at making a man's death take a long, agonizing time. It was great sport for them.

But the chances that Damon might still be alive after more than a year and a half—which was obviously what his father was hoping—were practically nonexistent.

"So you can see why I came to you," Charlton hurried on. "I can't ask the army to search for him as a personal favor to me. It just wouldn't be proper."

"But you can ask *me* to do that."

Charlton flushed. "I'll *beg* you to do it, if that's what it takes. I'm not too proud for that, Jamie. I'll do anything to find my son and rescue him from those savages, even if it means getting down on my knees and pleading with you."

"Stop that," Jamie snapped. "I wouldn't ask any man to do that, and sure as blazes not an old friend." He paused. "But I'm still a mite confused about all this, Owen. You've got an army post, what, a hundred miles or so from the area you're talking about? If the army hasn't been able to deal with the Apaches, how in the world do you expect me to?"

"It's because you're *not* in the army, Jamie. You don't have to worry about rules and regulations. You're acquainted with frontiersmen . . . top-notch fighting men . . . and you can recruit any of them you want, as many as you want. I have access to funds that can be used to not only to outfit them but also to pay them for their services. It's our hope that a small, fast-moving force of seasoned Indian fighters can succeed where the army has, at least so far, failed." Charlton shrugged. "As you might expect, there's considerable opposition to *this* idea, too. Colonel Hargrove and the others are here because the president insisted that they accompany me and present a united front, but they don't like it. They consider it a slap in the face to the army. And as a military man myself, I have to admit, it goes against the grain to believe that civilians can do the job better. But that's what we intend to find out."

"And find your son at the same time."

"Yes. The Good Lord willing, you'll locate Damon while you're out there."

Jamie didn't believe there was any possibility of that. But what if it was one of his boys . . . what if it was *Falcon* who was missing? He would cling to any shred of hope, too. He would never stop thinking there was a chance his son might come home.

"You say I can ask anybody I want to come along with me?"

Charlton's face lit up at that question. "Does that mean you'll accept the job?"

"Depends on the answer to the question I just asked you."

"Absolutely. Anyone you want. I have complete faith in you, Jamie, and as long as I do, so does the president."

Jamie nodded slowly and said, "All right, then. I'll have to see if I can find the fella I'm thinking about. If I can, and if he agrees to help me round up some other men and will come along himself, I'll give it a try."

"That's wonderful! Who is this man you're thinking of?"

"They call him Preacher."

CHAPTER 5

Santa Fe

The streets, or so the old saying went, were laid out by a drunkard on a blind mule. They twisted this way and that, with no apparent rhyme or reason, and many of them were so narrow that the second-floor balconies of the Spanish-styled adobe buildings on either side almost touched. A man who was athletic enough could leap easily from one balcony to another—as many hombres fleeing from cuckolded husbands had proven over the years.

The man called Preacher wasn't the sort to mess with married women, but he was being pursued through the streets of Santa Fe anyway. At least, the men on Preacher's trail *thought* they were pursuing him.

In reality, he was just leading them on, waiting for the right moment to spring his trap.

Earlier in the evening, he had spotted them watching him in the cantina where he'd been drinking and enjoying a game of dice. The gods of chance had been kind to the mountain man, and he had walked away from the game with a goodly number of gold coins in his poke.

That had increased the interest of the three *bus-caderos*, who sported fancy sombreros and gaudily embroidered jackets and had pistols and knives thrust behind the colorful sashes they wore around their waists. Preacher would have been willing to bet the trio had never done a lick of honest work to pay for those things.

He'd downed one more shot of tequila at the bar after stepping away from the game, and the glass had rattled a little against the hardwood as he set it down.

As he wound through the streets, he gave some thought to what had led to the chase.

He swayed slightly and announced to the chubby bartender, "Reckon I'll go and turn in for the night."

"Señor Preacher, perhaps you should avail yourself of one of the rooms upstairs," the bartender suggested. "You appear to be a trifle unsteady on your feet."

"I'm fine," Preacher said loudly. "Got me a fine hotel room a few blocks from here. But I appreciate the sentiment, Pancho."

"I worry because there could be bad hombres abroad in the night—"

"Can happen," Preacher broke in. He leaned on the bar for a second, then pushed away from it and turned toward the entrance. He pushed through the strings of beads that hung over it like a curtain and stepped out into the chilly night.

He walked about a block, weaving a little and singing "By the Sad Sea Waves," which he had heard Jenny Lind perform at a concert a year or so earlier during a trip back east. When he paused and looked behind him, he caught a glimpse of

*three figures silhouetted for a second against the light in the
cantina door. They were after him, all right.*

*"You ought to be ashamed of yourself, ol' son," he muttered
to himself. "Baitin' them poor fellers on like this. Been a while
since you had much excitement, though, and there's a hunch
a-percolatin' in this ol' brain that those boys have done this
sorta thing before. Prob'ly left more 'n one poor son of a gun
bleedin' to death in an alley. So I don't 'spect to lose a heap o'
sleep over what might happen here in the next little spell."*

*While he was talking, he turned a corner into an even
narrower street. His keen ears picked up a faint whisper of
boot leather on hard-packed dirt behind him. His stalkers
were still there.*

Since then, Preacher had led the three would-be
robbers on a merry chase, in and out of alleys and
cramped streets. Several times, he'd figured he was in
a good spot for the varmints to jump him, but they
held back for some reason. Up ahead, the alley he was
following opened up into a plaza, and it wasn't likely
they would attack him there. Maybe they had thought
better of the idea of robbing him. If they decided to
just fade away, he would let them go and head back
to his hotel after all.

Loud, angry voices coming from the plaza ahead of
him took him by surprise. They were in English, too,
which in Santa Fe was normally less than a fifty-fifty
chance.

"—away from him, Clementine, or I'll—"

"—filthy hands off—"

"—let her go!"

Fellas arguing over some soiled dove, Preacher
supposed. None of his affair, whichever way you
looked at it. But tempting those three *bandidos* to
come after him hadn't really been his business, either,

and he'd done that. With them behind him and this
fresh trouble up ahead, he didn't hardly know which
way to turn.

The would-be thieves settled that for him with a
rush of footsteps from behind. *Now* they decided to
make their move, he thought as he whirled around,
any semblance of a drunken state vanishing in a heartbeat.

Torches flickered in the plaza. Enough light from
them filtered into the alley for Preacher to spot the
three figures hurtling toward him. He ducked as the
first attacker reached him, rammed a shoulder into
the man's midsection, and straightened and heaved,
throwing the hombre right over his head. The would-be
robber let out a startled yell as he flew through the air,
a cry that was suddenly cut short as he crashed down
on his back.

Preacher heard something whipping through the
air at him and weaved aside. The club thudded against
the ground, and the man wielding it grunted as he
stumbled forward, thrown off balance by the missed
blow. Preacher backhanded him in the head and
knocked him against the wall of one of the buildings
flanking the alley.

The third man lunged at Preacher, who spotted a
tiny glint of torchlight from the long, heavy blade of
a knife. He jerked his belly out of the way but felt the
razor-sharp edge rake along his buckskin jacket. He
reached down and clamped a hand around the man's
wrist. He tried to twist it enough so the hombre would
let go of the knife, but the man resisted. At the same
time, he fumbled with his other hand at the mountain
man's throat and got hold of it. They staggered back
and forth as they wrestled with each other. Preacher

grasped the wrist of the hand choking him and tried to pull it free, but the varmint was too strong.

Preacher understood. This fella was the biggest and most powerful of the trio, but he had hung back a little, letting the other two jump him first in order to gauge just what they were facing. If those two were able to knock him unconscious or kill him, so much the better. They could have stolen his poke and been gone. When they failed, though, the third man stepped in, figuring that the intended victim had been softened up a mite, anyway.

That hadn't worked according to plan, so Preacher and the leader were left to battle it out on equal terms. Even worse, the first two were recovering and would be rejoining the fight any moment.

Preacher stopped trying to loosen the hand gripping his throat and instead used that fist to punch where he figured his opponent's face was. The blow landed solidly, and Preacher felt the hot spurt of blood across his knuckles. It came from either the man's nose or lips—Preacher wasn't sure exactly where he had hit the son of a gun.

But he heard the grunt of pain and felt the man's head rock back under the impact. Preacher hammered another punch home. He pushed hard with his feet and drove the man backward. There had to be a wall behind him somewhere—

There it was! Sour breath laden with tequila fumes gusted in Preacher's face as he rammed the man into the adobe wall and pried the hand away from his throat. Just in time, too. Preacher's pulse had been thundering inside his head and a red haze seemed to drop in front of his eyes, all because of the lack of air.

He gulped down a breath, twisted hard with his other hand again, and the crack of bone rewarded him, accompanied by a cry of pain. The knife clattered to the ground.

Footsteps sounded behind him. The other two thieves were trying to get back into the thick of it, just as he'd expected. He grabbed the front of the third man's shirt and wheeled around, pulling the stunned hombre with him. A hard shove sent him floundering right into his partners in crime. Skulls rapped together, legs tangled, and the whole bunch went down in an ungainly sprawl.

Preacher's throat hurt as he tried to get enough breath in his lungs. His hands dropped to the pair of .44 caliber Colt Dragoon revolvers holstered on his hips. He could have hauled out those hoglegs first thing and ended this robbery before it really got started, but that wouldn't have been sporting.

Realizing he didn't care about sport anymore, he leveled the guns at the three men who were struggling to regain their feet and eared back the hammers. That ominous metallic sound was enough to make the thieves stop moving around.

"This has gone on long enough," Preacher said. "You fellas savvy what I'm sayin'?"

Panting from exertion and pain, one of the men answered, "We speak your language, *viejo*."

"You can call me old if you want, *cabrón*, but I'm the one on my feet with guns in my hands. You boys are wallerin' around on the ground like a bunch o' babies."

They spat more curses at him until Preacher's sharp voice cut them off.

"Listen here. Back there in the cantina, I found out

your names." That was a lie, but they didn't have to know that. "I know where to find you, too. If I hear anything about you robbin' any more poor folks, I'll hunt you down, and there won't be no playin' next time. I'll just kill you, one by one. No mercy, no talk . . . just death."

"That is bold talk for one so old! Who are you?"

A faint smile curved Preacher's lips in the darkness, under the drooping, gray-shot dark mustache. "In the mountains up north, the Blackfeet call me *Asesino Fantasma*. That name mean anything to you?"

One of the men couldn't contain a gasp. "The Ghost Killer!" he said to his friends, confirming that Preacher's notoriety had made it that far south. "They say he has slain thousands of Indians!"

"And my share of white men and *Mexicanos*, too," Preacher said. "So you know I mean what I say, and you know I can do it. If you don't want to wake up some mornin' with your throat cut from ear to ear, you best not stray off the straight and narrow from now on, *comprende*?"

The biggest of the trio sat up and asked in a surly voice, "Why does the famous Ghost Killer not go ahead and slay us?"

"Oh, I'm sure you boys deserve it. Tell you the truth, that's how I figured this little dustup would end. But I guess I'm just feelin' generous tonight. And I've already killed so many no-good skunks this month, I reckon it gets old after a while." Preacher gestured with one of the Dragoons. "Now *vamanos* while you got the chance."

He kept them covered as they got up and scuttled away along the alley. He really should have killed them, he mused. As he'd told them, they no doubt had it coming for past crimes. But nobody had appointed him judge, jury, and executioner, and he'd drifted into Santa Fe to enjoy himself, not to clean up all the crime in its narrow, winding streets. Although, he thought as his eyes narrowed, that might be an interesting chore for another time . . .

He had just holstered the Colts when a scream came from the nearby plaza. During the scuffle in the alley, he had lost track of the squabble going on in the plaza. Obviously, it had escalated. The woman screamed again as Preacher wheeled in that direction.

"Dadgummit!" the mountain man said. "One fracas don't hardly get over with 'fore the next one breaks out."

It had always been that way, so he didn't know why he should expect anything different. With his hands resting on the butts of the Dragoons, he strode toward the plaza.

CHAPTER 6

It was late enough in the evening that the young girls no longer strolled about the plaza with their *dueñas*, trying to catch the eye of any young *caballeros* who happened to be around. In fact, the open square was deserted except for half a dozen people who were clustered at one side. The young woman who had screamed was backed up against a wagon with two mules hitched to it. She was quiet because her hands were pressed to her mouth in horror.

A few yards away, a young man struggled in the grip of a much larger hombre who had his arms pinned behind his back. The youngster was trying not only to get loose, but also to avoid the fists of another man who stood there slugging away at him. Two more men stood to the side, grinning and letting out little whoops of encouragement from time to time.

Preacher had never laid eyes on any of those folks, but he knew four-to-one odds when he saw them—and he didn't like that at all.

Luckily, Preacher could make those odds even. Himself—plus two fully loaded Colts. He slid the guns from their holsters as he stalked across the plaza.

The two spectators saw him coming first, and one of them yelled, "Clete, look out!"

The one who'd been thrashing the youngster broke off the beating and turned to see what was going on. Like the other three, he was tall and broad-shouldered, with just a little bit of a gut to keep him from being as brawny as he might have been. All four wore buckskin trousers and homespun shirts. Two had broad-brimmed felt hats, while the other pair sported coonskin caps.

Hill men, Preacher decided. Tough, with plenty of bark on them. Probably from the Smokies or the Ozarks, he guessed.

The one who'd been doing the beating leveled an arm and pointed a finger at Preacher. "Look here, old-timer!" he rasped. "You better put away them guns and skedaddle outta here 'fore you get hurt. Those Dragoons weigh too much for your old muscles. You're liable to let one of 'em droop and shoot your own foot off."

Preacher's eyes narrowed. He raised the right-hand gun a little and squeezed the trigger. The booming report rolled across the plaza and the girl by the wagon cried out involuntarily. The big man's hat flew off his head and sailed several yards through the air. He ducked, stared at Preacher in shock for a couple of seconds, and then started to claw at the butt of the pistol stuck in his waistband.

Preacher had already cocked the Dragoon again. He aimed it at the man while he kept the left-hand gun pointed in the general direction of the two spectators. "It won't be your hat that gets ventilated next time. Now step away from those folks and their wagon.

You there, the one holdin' the boy, let go of him and move away."

The owner of the hat with a brand-new bullet hole in it straightened and glared at Preacher. "This ain't none of your business," he said through clenched teeth. "And in case you ain't noticed, there's four of us and one of you."

"And I've got nine rounds left in these Dragoons," Preacher snapped back at him. "That's more 'n enough to kill all of you twice over."

"Not if you miss some of those shots when we rush you. You ain't fast enough to drop all of us."

"You'll never know," Preacher said, "because I'm blowin' your maggot-ridden brains out first thing."

One of the bystanders said, "I think maybe you better listen to him, Clete. The old coot looks crazy enough to do it."

"There you go, callin' me old again." Preacher shook his head. "That's plain annoyin'. Way I figure it, I'm still in the prime of life."

As a matter of fact, he was fifty-two years old, and that *was* getting pretty long in the tooth for most men. But the rugged life Preacher had led had given him an iron constitution and a vitality that men twenty or thirty years younger would have envied. His weathered features and the gray in his hair and mustache were really the only signs of age he displayed.

He glanced at the man holding the youngster. "You still ain't let that boy go like I told you to. Now, I admit I got kind of a narrow angle here, but I'm bettin' I can slip a bullet right past his ear and into that ugly face of yours—"

With a grimace, the man let go of the youngster and stepped to the side.

As the youngster crumpled to the ground, the girl cried, "Fletch!" and rushed to him.

The young man muttered and shook his head as the girl knelt and lifted him so that his head and shoulders rested in her lap. Preacher left it to her to comfort him and motioned for the four older men to stand together, well away from the wagon. As they did, he noticed four horses with their reins dangling, standing at the edge of the plaza, and assumed the varmints had ridden there on them.

He noticed something else—the four men all bore distinct resemblances to each other. There were slight variations in height, weight, coloring, and the shape of their features, but when they were grouped together like that, it was obvious they were related, and pretty closely, at that.

Brothers, more than likely, he thought, considering there wasn't a great deal of difference in their ages.

"I don't know what sort of grudge you have against that young fella, and I don't care," he said. "If those are your horses over there, you'd best get on 'em and fog outta here without lookin' back."

"This is family business," the one who'd been throwing the punches insisted. "You got no right to stick your nose in it."

"Family?" Preacher repeated.

"Yeah!" another said. He pointed at the girl and the young man. "That there no-good Wylie done despoiled our lil' sister. It's our bounden duty to kill the skunk!"

The girl looked up from where she was stroking the youngster's battered and bloody face and shouted, "Fletcher didn't despoil nobody, you mush-mouthed idiot! He's my husband! We're married!"

"In the eyes of the law, maybe," said the one who seemed to be in charge. "But not in the eyes of the Mahoney family, and that's the only law you need to abide by, Clementine!"

So they *were* brothers and the girl was their sister, Preacher mused. And they didn't approve of her choice for a husband. Those hill clans were, well, clannish. Quick to take offense and mighty stubborn when it came to holding grudges. Sometimes a minor insult or even a misunderstanding could turn into a long, bloody feud.

But they were in Santa Fe, a long way from the Smokies or the Ozarks or wherever these Mahoneys came from, and ganging up on a fella like that was still unacceptable in Preacher's eyes, no matter what the family history.

So he said, "Shut up and get outta here, like I told you to do. That shot I fired a minute ago is liable to bring the law out, and if I've got to waste half the night talkin' to some puffed-up official, there might as well be some bodies a-layin' on the ground to justify it."

The boss Mahoney glared at him for a long moment, then said, "My name is Clete Mahoney, mister. These are my brothers Lew, Harp, and Jerome. We'll be seein' you again."

"Excuse me 'most to death if I say I ain't particularly lookin' forward to it." Preacher kept one gun steady and motioned with the other revolver. "Light a shuck, boys."

Glowering and muttering, the brothers shuffled off toward the waiting horses.

Preacher turned slowly and kept the Dragoons trained on them as they went. He didn't lower the guns while the men mounted up, wheeled their horses, and rode out of the plaza along one of the darkened boulevards. He slid over closer to the wagon so he could use it for cover, just in case the shadows made the Mahoneys bold enough to try turning around and burning powder at him.

He might should have tried to disarm them before running them off, he told himself, but he didn't know if they would have crossed that bridge or dug in their heels and decided to risk a shooting scrape. This way he'd allowed them to depart with a little of their pride intact.

The hoofbeats dwindled until they had faded away entirely.

Preacher said, "Girl . . . Clementine, was it? . . . Best get your man in the wagon and move on outta here while you got the chance. Them brothers of yours may not stay gone."

"They'll go off somewhere and get drunk and tell themselves how big and brave they are, even though you run 'em off with their tails betwixt their legs," the girl said, spitting the words out in a savage tone. "They'll have to do that before they come after us again." She sighed. "But you're probably right. We don't need to waste the chance you've given us. Come on, Fletch." She stood and tried to help him to his feet.

But he pushed her hand away and said, "I can get up by myself. Just because I'm no match for all four of those animals doesn't mean I'm a weakling."

Preacher could understand him feeling that way, but just as a matter of fact, the boy *was* a mite on the scrawny side. Tall and slender, with a thatch of red hair and an array of freckles across his face. He was fairly well dressed, and the wagon and the mules were of good quality. He might not be rich, but his family had a nodding acquaintance with money.

The girl, on the other hand . . . well, she was enough to make any man look twice if he had eyes in his head to see, and even some blind fellas might instinctively know she was something special. Thick waves of honey-colored hair around a sweet face highlighted by big eyes and a generous mouth. In this bad light, Preacher couldn't tell what color her eyes were, but he guessed either a deep lake blue or a rich brown. Poor illumination from flickering torches or not, he could see the full-bosomed figure just fine, displayed as it was in a white blouse that scooped down and left her shoulders half bare and a long brown skirt that clung to swelling hips. Clementine Mahoney Wylie, to put her full married name on her, was a downright beautiful young woman.

Honestly, too beautiful for a fella like Fletcher Wylie, especially with that surly attitude he was exhibiting. But being chased and harassed by four brutes like the Mahoney brothers was enough to make anybody proddy. Preacher knew that if he'd been in Fletch's boots, he'd have committed mayhem a-plenty.

Preacher finally pouched the irons he held and snagged the mules' reins to hold them while Fletch helped Clementine climb to the wagon seat.

The youngster hauled himself up after her, took the reins from Preacher, and said, "Thank you, mister . . . ?"

"Just Preacher," the mountain man told him. "No *mister.*" Something occurred to him. "You folks have a place to stay?"

"Well . . . no. It was after dark when we got here.

We knew Santa Fe had to be close, so we just kept pushing on."

"We can find a place, can't we?" Clementine asked.

"Maybe. At this hour, though, it might not be what you'd call a decent place." Preacher glanced into the back of the wagon, under its canvas cover. He couldn't see very well, but the bed seemed to be pretty full of household goods and supplies. "Tell you what. I know a good livery stable and wagon yard where you can leave this wagon and it'll be safe. Then the two of you can have my hotel room."

"We couldn't do that," Fletch protested.

"We'd never put you out of your own room," Clementine added.

Preacher shook his head. "You wouldn't be doin' me a disservice. To tell you the truth, I was a mite worried about how I was gonna sleep. I ain't what you'd call accustomed to havin' a roof over my head, but I thought I'd try it for a change. I'd be just fine with seein' you folks get some better use out of it."

"But you've already helped us so much," Fletch said. "Why are you doing this?"

Preacher smiled. "Let's just say I was young once myself."

CHAPTER 7

The owner of the livery stable yawned as he came out to lead the mules into the adobe barn through the big double doors.

While he was doing that, Clementine gasped in fear, shrank against Fletch, and exclaimed, "Is that a wolf?"

Preacher grinned as the big cur that had trotted out of the barn reared up and rested his paws on the mountain man's shoulders. "There might be some wolf blood in him. I don't rightly know his, what you call it, pedigree. But he's mostly dog, I reckon. Fact is, that's what I call him. Dog."

"Those are very . . . impressive . . . teeth," Fletch commented. He had his arm around Clementine's shoulders.

Preacher ruffled the fur on Dog's head. "Yeah, I'd claim his bark's worse 'n his bite, but to tell the truth, he don't bark all that much and he's got quite a bite on him when he wants to. But he's a good trail partner."

This one was the latest in a long line of similar companions, all called Dog, all devoted to Preacher and almost supernaturally smart. Now and then, he wondered about the good fortune that had allowed all of them to find their way to him, one way or another, but he had never been one to spit in the face of luck, so he didn't waste a lot of time pondering the question. Some things just *were*.

"He's stayin' here, along with my horse, since folks at the hotel tend to look a mite askance at the likes of him in their establishment," Preacher went on. "In fact, I'll be comin' back here myself, once I get the two of you settled in at the hotel."

"You're going to sleep in a barn?" Clementine asked.

Preacher grinned. "A good pile of hay's the height of luxury, if you don't mind maybe sharin' it with a critter or two."

"I still feel like we're putting you out," Fletch said with a shake of his head.

"Not a bit. Grab your gear and come on."

Fletch hefted the bag he had taken from the wagon. "You can at least let us pay the liveryman—"

"No, I told you, I won a good deal of *dinero* earlier this evenin'. This'll keep some of it from weighin' down my poke as much."

They walked around the corner and a couple of blocks along the street to the hotel, a two-story adobe building with a wooden balcony along the front, which faced another plaza. The balcony with its wrought-iron railing formed an awning over the flagstone gallery that ran the length of the hotel. Decorative gourds hung on ropes from the bottom of the balcony.

Preacher led the young couple inside and informed the clerk at the desk that they would be taking his room for the night. The man started to frown and say something about two guests instead of one maybe costing more, but he fell silent at the hard look Preacher gave him.

With a bob of his head, the clerk swallowed and said, "Yes, sir, that'll be fine. Just fine."

Preacher turned to Fletch and Clementine. "You said you pushed on after dark to get here. Does that mean you ain't had supper?"

"Well . . ." Fletch said.

"I figured as much." Preacher jerked his head toward an arched door to the side of the hotel lobby. "Dinin' room's still open. Let's get some food in you."

"You're not going to pay for *that*, too," Fletch insisted.

"All right." Preacher grinned. "Shoot, you can even buy me a cup of coffee."

"That's a deal."

The dining room was almost empty, only a few guests making use of it so late.

A Mexican waitress came over to the table where they sat. "There's not much left in the kitchen. Beans and tortillas and maybe a little *cabrito*."

"That'll do," Preacher said. "Bring it for these fine young folks, and bring me a cup of coffee."

"*Sí, señor.*"

While they waited, Clementine said, "I really don't understand why you're being so kind to us, Mr. Preacher."

He raised a finger. "I told you about that *mister* business." His grin belied the stern tone of the words. "I wouldn't go so far as to say that Fletch here reminds me of me—"

"I can't even begin to imagine that anybody would think *that*," Fletch said.

"For one thing," Preacher continued, "I left the farm my family had and lit a shuck for the frontier when I was mighty young, little more 'n a boy. I had me a right strong hankerin' to see the elephant, or at least some real mountains. I wound up seein' 'em, all right, and plenty more besides."

He paused because the waitress arrived with coffee for all of them. He waited until he had taken a couple of sips of the strong, black brew before he said, "I was still pretty young, though, not even Fletch's age, I'd say, when I met a gal who took my fancy."

"Oh," Clementine said, then asked eagerly, "What was her name?"

"Jenny," Preacher said. His mind drifted back to those long-ago days. Jenny had been beautiful, no doubt about that, but the image of her in Preacher's head was a dim one, blurred by time even though she had been Preacher's first love. Things between them had ended badly, but these two didn't have to know that.

"And we remind you of what you and Jenny had?" Clementine asked.

"Sort of. But come to think of it," Preacher said, "you remind me even more of another young couple I once knew. Ran into 'em many years ago, so they ain't young anymore, but they were at the time. About the same age as you two, and fresh married, so they was just startin' out, too." He sipped the coffee again. "Jamie and Kate MacCallister. Remember those days almost like they was last week."

"What happened to them?" Fletch asked.

"They went on to have a passel of kids and start themselves a big ranch up Colorado way. Mighty nice place, and mighty nice family."

"They're still together?" Clementine wanted to know.

"They sure are, last I heard. And it was only a year or so ago that I saw Jamie last."

The waitress set platters of food in front of them, and from the way Fletch and Clementine dug in, Preacher knew they were hungry.

With satisfaction, he watched them eat for a few minutes, then said, "I ain't over-fond of talkin' about myself. Let's hear about the two o' you. Where are you from?"

"Tennessee," Fletch answered. "A little town in the Great Smoky Mountains."

Preacher nodded, pleased that his hunch about their origins had been confirmed.

"Fletch's father owns the store there," Clementine said with a note of pride in her voice.

"What about your folks?"

"We just have a farm outside of town," she said with downcast eyes.

"Nothin' wrong with farmin'," Preacher told her. "I don't hardly see how the country could get along without farmers."

Fletch nodded. "That's what I've tried to get her to understand."

"Well, there are farmers," Clementine said, adding with a sigh, "and then there are *farmers*"—she made a face—"like my brothers. Raising crops has always been too much work for them. They'd rather spend their time drinking in taverns or getting into fights or roaming around the mountains looking for something to shoot. They're wastrels and layabouts, and they've always been a pure vexation to my ma and pa."

Having met the Mahoney brothers, Preacher could understand that assessment of them.

"They always caused trouble when one of us girls wanted to get married and leave home," Clementine continued. "I have two older sisters."

"Clementine's the youngest in the family," Fletch put in.

She nodded. "That's right. So it was only a matter of time until the boys . . . got around to me."

Preacher narrowed his eyes at her. "Are you gettin' at what I think you're gettin' at, Miss Clementine?"

"If it's something filthy and disgusting, then yes, unfortunately I am. But I knew, from seeing everything that had happened before, what I needed to do, so I never let any of them corner me anywhere alone, and when they tried to . . ." Her shoulders rose and fell. "I've always been a fast runner. Faster than those pig-gutted boys."

The tone of disgust in her voice had him shaking his head. "I'm startin' to think maybe I should've invested some powder and shot in dealin' with 'em."

"No," Clementine said quickly. "They're still my brothers. I . . . I wouldn't have wanted to see them killed. I just want them to leave us alone and let us go on to California."

"That's where you're headed? California?"

"That's right," Fletch said. "Far away from Tennessee . . . and the Mahoneys."

"I never really thought they'd come after us," Clementine said. "They . . . they threatened Fletch when we announced that we were getting married. They told him to leave me alone and forget about me if he knew what was good for him."

"I'd never do that," Fletch declared.

Clementine went on. "They said they would kill him if he defied them. But they didn't actually do anything because Mr. Wylie—Fletcher's father—is good friends with the sheriff and the magistrate. Clete and the other boys didn't dare do anything except threaten and bluster, and that wasn't enough to stop us."

She reached over and rested her hand on Fletch's. He turned his hand so he could grip hers tightly and smile at her as their fingers intertwined.

The two of them really were in love, Preacher thought—although he wondered if some of what Clementine felt came from wanting to get away from her brutish brothers.

"Once we got away from there," Fletch said, "I suppose they weren't as afraid of what might happen to them if they came after us. We knew they were dogging our trail . . . we'd caught glimpses of them from time to time . . . so that's one reason we kept pushing on so hard. But now . . ." He sighed. "Now they've caught up to us. I'm not sure what we're going to do. Try to get ahead of them again somehow and stay ahead of them. We probably shouldn't have stayed here in Santa Fe tonight, but the mules are just too exhausted to go on." He squeezed Clementine's hand again. "And although she probably won't admit it, I'm sure Clementine is, too."

"I'll do whatever I have to," she said. "You know that, Fletch."

He nodded, and again they exchanged a heartfelt glance.

Preacher felt a little like he was watching a play performance, and he remembered his highly educated friend Audie speechifying about some old Greek fella who claimed that life imitated art as much as art imitated life. Some of those old Greeks knew what they were talking about, and some of them were full of bullfeathers, Preacher had found.

He shoved aside such philosophizing to take a more practical approach. Leaning forward, he said, "With you two travelin' in that wagon and Clem's brothers mounted on what looked like good horses, there ain't no way in Hades you can get ahead of 'em and stay ahead of 'em."

Clementine looked a little devastated by that blunt statement. "Then what can we do?" she asked. "I know my brothers. They . . . they really will kill Fletch and drag me back to Tennessee if they believe they can get away with it."

"There's only one thing for it," Preacher said. He looked back and forth between them and gave in to the impulse that had sprung to life in him. "Been a while since I've been out yonder to California. I'll just mosey along with the two of you and see to it that those boys leave you alone."

CHAPTER 8

Preacher didn't think the Mahoney brothers would bother Fletch and Clementine while they were staying in a respectable hotel in the middle of Santa Fe, so he left them there and returned to the livery stable where he had made arrangements with the proprietor to spend the night in the hayloft. That meant he still had a roof over his head, but it was nowhere near as fancy as the hotel, so he felt more at home.

The two young people had been hesitant at first about accepting his offer to accompany them to California, but Preacher had a hunch they reacted that way because they felt like they ought to, not because it was what they really wanted. But they had seen how the mountain man handled Clementine's brothers and had to realize that their chances of reaching their destination safely were better with him along.

On the other hand, they had just met him. How did they know they could trust him?

In the end, they had agreed to his proposal. Under the circumstances, they couldn't do much of anything else.

Preacher fell into a light, dreamless sleep and woke

up refreshed as gray predawn light began to filter through the cracks around the hayloft door high on the rear wall of the building. Preacher heard the hostler moving around down below, busy with early morning chores.

A man's voice spoke up, the tone harsh and unfriendly. Preacher couldn't make out the words, but something about them alarmed him. He rolled out of the hay, grabbed one of the Dragoons from the coiled shell belt he had left close at hand, and came up on his feet, wearing only socks and his buckskin trousers. A couple of steps took him to the ladder, and as he reached it, he heard the liveryman exclaim, "Watch out for that dog, mister!"

Only one dog was around here as far as Preacher knew. He heard snarling, a surprised curse, and a gunshot.

Preacher went down the ladder about as fast as a man possibly could. When his feet hit the ground, he whirled toward the entrance and saw that both big doors were open, letting in more of the gray light. Dog stood poised in the entrance, stiff-legged, hackles raised as he growled—but thankfully unharmed as far as Preacher could see.

Just outside the livery barn, an odd-looking figure stood silhouetted in the street. Preacher kept his gun ready as he tried to figure out what it was. The thing was big and bulky and kind of waving around in the dim light.

After a minute or so, Preacher realized he was actually looking at *two* men. A smaller one in the grip of a much larger one was being held from behind with a brawny arm around the neck so that the captive's feet were off the ground. The man flailed his arms and legs, but he couldn't get loose.

"Preacher!" a booming voice said as the mountain man moved forward.

Preacher's eyes widened in surprise. "Jamie?"

Jamie Ian MacCallister let go of the man he'd choked a considerable distance along the road to death and gave him a shove that sent him sprawling facedown in the dusty street. The man gasped and tried to scramble up, but Jamie planted a heavy, booted foot in the middle of his back and pinned him to the ground. At the same time, he pulled the Walker Colt from its holster on his hip and aimed the revolver at the man's head as he thumbed back the hammer.

"I caught this fella trying to shoot Dog," Jamie said. "Want me to go ahead and show him across the divide?"

Preacher grinned. He knew his old friend wasn't a cold-blooded murderer, but the man squirming under Jamie's boot wouldn't be aware of that. As far as he knew, he was about to get a .44 caliber trail blazed through his brainpan.

Preacher recognized the man as one of the Mahoney brothers. Not Clete. Preacher didn't know which name went with which of the other varmints, but it didn't matter. Clearly, the brothers hadn't given up their quest to kill Fletch Wylie and reclaim their sister Clementine, and this fella must have traced Preacher to the livery stable in the hope of picking up their quarry's trail.

"It'd be a mighty good use of powder and shot if you was to do so," Preacher said in response to Jamie's cold-blooded question, "but I reckon you can let him up and boot him on his way. He didn't hurt Dog, did he?"

The big cur turned and nuzzled Preacher's free hand. There was more light now, and he couldn't see any wounds on the animal.

The liveryman spoke up, saying, "No, that shot went wild, thank goodness. I tried to warn him. If that big hombre hadn't grabbed him when he did, I reckon Dog would've ripped his throat out about half a second later."

"More 'n likely," Preacher agreed. "Seein' that Dog's all right, don't kill the rapscallion, Jamie."

Jamie grunted, removed his boot from Mahoney's back, and stepped to the side. He kept the Colt trained on the man as he said, "I don't know what your problem is, mister, other than being ugly as sin and addlepated to boot, but you'd better take it somewhere far away and don't slow down while you're doing it."

Mahoney reached for the gun he'd dropped when Jamie grabbed him, but Preacher wagged the Dragoon and said, "You can come by here later and get that hogleg, when we ain't around. And you'll be derned polite about it, too, if you know what's good for you. If you ain't, I'll find out about it, and you don't want that."

The man rubbed his neck, scowled, and scuttled away like the oversize rat he was. Remembering what Clementine had mentioned the night before about the brothers' filthy habits, Preacher gave serious consideration to shooting him anyway but finally lowered the Walker when the varmint went out of sight around a corner.

He set the gun on a barrel and went over to throw

his arms around Jamie. The two big men hugged and pounded each other on the back. Dog reared up and tried to lick Jamie on the face, but the towering newcomer was just a little too tall for that.

Preacher stepped back and regarded Jamie with a puzzled frown. "I suppose it's possible, but I'm thinkin' you didn't just happen to come strollin' along this street at exactly the right time to grab that varmint."

"Well, comes down to it, that part of the affair really *was* just a coincidence, but you're right. I didn't just happen to be here. I was looking for you, Preacher."

"I thought as much," Preacher said with a nod.

"I rode into town mighty early this morning and started paying visits to all the places I thought you might stay. Came on a hotel clerk who told me you'd had a room there but had given it up for a young couple. Said he overheard you telling them you'd sleep here at the stable. So I legged it over here and walked up at the right time to take a hand in that little fracas."

The liveryman spoke up. "You saved that hombre's life, whether he knows it or not. Like I said, Dog would've killed him."

"I wouldn't hold my breath waitin' for the varmint to appreciate that little gesture," Preacher drawled. "He's a pretty sorry specimen, and so are his brothers."

"What's the story on them?" Jamie asked with a frown.

Preacher waved that off. "I'll tell you later. You've said you were huntin' me. What for?"

Jamie pointed at Preacher's bare chest and suggested, "Why don't you get some clothes on, then we'll get ourselves on the outside of some grub and coffee and I'll explain the whole thing." He paused and drew in a breath. "It's not a pretty tale."

They went to the hotel where Jamie had picked up Preacher's trail. It was busier than it had been the previous evening but not crowded yet. Preacher didn't see Fletch or Clementine and assumed that they were still asleep. He wasn't surprised. The two young people had looked purely worn out the last time he'd seen them.

Over coffee, steaks, fried potatoes, eggs, and biscuits, the two frontiersmen traded stories. It didn't take long for Preacher to fill Jamie in on the problems Fletch and Clementine had been through. It was a fairly simple, if sordid, yarn.

Jamie's story was more complicated, filled as it was with political intrigue, high finance, family tragedy, and decisions that would almost certainly play a momentous part in the development of the country. Preacher listened with great interest. He had never had much book learning, only a few years before he took off for the tall and uncut, plus what he had picked up from years of on-and-off associating with former college professor Audie. But he had a keen mind and quickly grasped the stakes of all the details Jamie laid out.

"So this General Charlton wants you to go down to the border country and clean out the Apaches." Preacher sipped his coffee, cocked his head, and gave Jamie a quizzical look over the cup. "Seems like a mighty big job for one man when the whole army ain't been able to handle it so far."

"Well . . . I don't think he figures I'll handle it by

myself. He said I could recruit anybody I wanted to help me out."

Preacher's puzzled look deepened into a frown. "Then I got a hunch I know why you came lookin' for me."

"You're the best fighting man on the frontier," Jamie said.

"Some would say *you* are."

Jamie dismissed that with a wave of the hand. "That's for other folks to argue about, if they've got the time for such things. All I know is that I'd feel better going into any fracas with you at my side, Preacher. Not only that, you know plenty of other fellas who are usually itching for trouble, as well."

A grunt of laughter escaped from Preacher's lips. "Sure can't argue with that statement."

Jamie cradled his coffee cup in big hands and leaned forward a little. "So I thought that if you and I put together a force of a dozen or so men, we could fight the Apaches in their own style. Hit 'em hard and fast when they aren't expecting it and stay on the move. I reckon if we did that, it wouldn't take long before *they* would come looking for *us*, and all we'd have to do is take care of them as they show up."

"Yeah," Preacher said dryly, "all we'd have to do is live through a few hundred 'Paches huntin' us, wantin' to peel the hide off us an inch at a time. And find out what happened to Charlton's son while we're at it. That's all."

Jamie nodded slowly. "It'd be a right stiff challenge, I suppose."

"And to be honest, it's one I might not mind acceptin', except for one thing. I got one of those . . . what you call it? Prior commitments."

"To those two young folks?" Jamie asked.

Preacher nodded. "I promised I'd see 'em through safely to California. Fletch seems like a nice enough young fella, but he ain't no match for those no-good brothers of Clementine's, and he never will be."

"If that fella I ran into at the livery stable is a good example of them, I'd have to agree they're no good."

"The one called Clete, who appears to be the oldest and the boss of the bunch, is even worse, I'd say." Preacher leaned back in his chair, scraped a thumbnail along his grizzled jawline, and then tugged at his earlobe as he pondered. "On the other hand, if what you're tellin' me is right, this whole business of tryin' to decide where the railroad's gonna run could turn out to be mighty important for the whole country."

"It could," Jamie agree.

"Does the whole idea of a railroad runnin' from one end of the country to the other sit as poorly with you as it does with me?" Preacher asked bluntly.

Jamie didn't answer for a long moment, then said, "From everything I've heard and read, we'll never bring civilization to the frontier without it."

"I don't know about you, but it seems to me like civilization ain't always all it's cracked up to be."

Jamie had to laugh at that. "I can't disagree with you about that, Preacher, but not everybody feels the same way about the frontier that we do. Most folks never saw it the way it used to be, when everything was clean and new. The country needs room to grow. *People* need room to grow. That's coming, no matter what old-timers like you and me think about it." He drank some more of his coffee. "And to be honest, having started a family and a ranch, a little more civilization doesn't always seem like such a bad idea to me."

"I can see how a man 'd feel that way, even if I never have. So I'd like to help, Jamie, I really would, but—" Preacher stopped short as he glanced toward the arched entrance into the dining room. "You can take your own measure of Fletch and Clementine. Here they come now."

CHAPTER 9

Wary looks appeared on the faces of the young couple as they approached the table. Clearly, they were expecting to see Preacher but hadn't known anyone would be with him. As both men rose out of courtesy to Clementine, the couple's eyes widened when Jamie's height became apparent.

"Mornin'," Preacher greeted them. He gestured toward Jamie. "This big galoot is an old friend of mine. Remember how last night I mentioned Jamie and Kate MacCallister? Well, this is Jamie his ownself, in the considerable flesh."

Jamie stuck out a big paw and said, "Pleased to meet you, Fletch. Preacher's been telling me about you and Mrs. Wylie and the problems you've been facing."

Fletch looked a little hesitant about shaking hands with Jamie, but he did. Jamie's hand practically swallowed up Fletch's, but Jamie didn't bear down, just gave the young man his normal firm grip. Even that was enough to make Fletch's eyes widen more. Preacher could tell he was relieved when Jamie let go.

Jamie turned to Clementine and nodded politely. "Ma'am. It's an honor to make your acquaintance."

"Thank you, Mister . . . MacCallister, was it?"

"That's right, ma'am."

"Wait a minute," Fletch said. "Preacher told us about you and your wife just last night, and this morning you turn up in Santa Fe?"

"That's the workin's of fate for you," the mountain man said. "This ain't the first time I've knowed somethin' to happen that'd make a man's eyebrows go to climbin' his forehead."

"Maybe Preacher sensed somehow that I've been looking for him," Jamie said, "and that's what brought me to his mind last night."

Preacher glanced at his old friend. "How'd you track me down, anyway? You ain't explained that yet."

Jamie grinned. "Started riding and asking questions every time I came to a place where there were some old mountain men. Didn't take long before I ran into somebody who said they'd heard you were planning to drift down toward Santa Fe. You know how the frontier is, Preacher—for all its vastness, it can be a pretty small place."

"Folks are just plumb nosy and like to meddle in other folks' business, is what you mean. But I'm glad you found me, Jamie, even if it does put me in sort of a pree-dicament."

"What do you mean?" Fletch asked.

Jamie waved a hand at the table. "Why don't you two sit down and join us for breakfast? I'm buying."

"You don't have to do that—" Fletch began.

"I'm happy to. Consider it a very belated wedding present for the both of you."

Clementine said, "But you don't even know us. Why would you give us a wedding present?"

"Any friends of Preacher's are friends of mine, too. Now, let's sit down."

They did so, with Fletch holding Clementine's chair. The waitress brought over coffee right away for the two young people and hurried to the kitchen to fetch food for them.

While they were waiting, Fletch said, "You mentioned you've been looking for Preacher, Mr. MacCallister. Is it all right if I ask why?"

"Actually, the answer has something to do with you fine folks. I asked him to give me a hand with a little chore, but he explained to me that he's already promised to help you get to California."

Fletch looked quickly at Preacher. "If there's something else you need to do, we won't hold you to the arrangement you made with us."

Clementine added, "It wasn't a business deal or anything like that. You agreed to come along just out of the goodness of your heart." She smiled. "And it's a very good heart, I'm thinking."

"What sort of chore is it you were talking about, Mr. MacCallister?" Fletch asked.

Jamie and Preacher glanced at each other. The assignment Jamie had accepted from General Owen Charlton was government business, after all, and not something to be discussed with just anybody.

But Preacher shrugged and said, "I reckon they're trustworthy. That's what my gut tells me, anyway."

"All right. You folks have probably heard about how someday, there's going to be a transcontinental railroad . . ."

For the next few minutes, Jamie explained the task he'd been asked to do, pausing when the waitress arrived with plates of food for Fletch and Clementine. By the time he was finished, Fletch was nodding.

"I've heard my father talking about this," he said. "As the owner of a store, he knows how important the transportation of goods is to business. He believes the railroads are going to have to be expanded a great deal if the country is ever going to prosper as it should."

"That's what all the politicians in Washington seem to think, too," Jamie said. "The wrangling comes in on the question of how they're going to do it."

"Then what they've asked you to do is vital," Fletch said solemnly. He turned to Preacher. "And you could help Mr. MacCallister a great deal."

Preacher shrugged. "More than likely, but I already gave you my word—"

"I have an idea," Clementine said. "Why don't you help Mr. MacCallister, and Fletch and I will come along, too?"

The three men at the table just stared at her, unable to find the words to respond to her suggestion. Finally, as she started to look annoyed at their reaction, she said, "Well? What's wrong with that idea?"

"Derned near everything," Preacher said.

"I don't reckon you know exactly what you're suggesting, ma'am," Jamie said.

"It sounds really dangerous," Fletch said.

Clementine chose to respond to her husband's comment. "We've been living in terrible danger ever since we left Tennessee, Fletcher. Do you really think these Apaches that Preacher and Mr. MacCallister are talking about are worse than my brothers?"

Jamie answered that question. "No offense intended, Mrs. Wylie, but I'm afraid they are. A lot worse."

"And there are a lot more of 'em," Preacher added. "Back east where you come from, all the Indian troubles have been mostly over for a long time. There are hundreds of Apaches down there in the area we've been talkin' about, and just about every single one of 'em hates white folks and would like nothin' better than to kill all of us."

"My brothers want to kill Fletcher," she said stubbornly. "And when they do, they'll drag me back to Tennessee and make my life pure misery." She shook her head, making the thick waves of blond hair swing back and forth around her face. "I'm sorry. I'd rather take my chances with the Apaches."

"You say that now," Preacher told her, "but you don't know what it's really like out there. It ain't just the Apaches you got to worry about down yonder. It's so hot and dry, you'd think you wandered into the Devil's parlor, and there's a rattlesnake or a scorpion under every rock. Get too close to the cactus that grows there, and you'll wind up with what feels like a hundred little knives stickin' in you. It hardly ever rains, but when it does, there's liable to be a flash flood comes along that'll wash you away. Or else a dust storm that'll dump a whole bucket full o' dirt down your throat. I've heard it said there's a million ways to die in the West, and you'll find most of 'em down there along what's now the border betwixt us and Mexico."

Preacher's recitation of the perils that would be

waiting for them if they came along left Clementine looking a little abashed, but determination still shone in her eyes. "If Fletch and I stay here in Santa Fe, we're doomed. If we try to go on by ourselves, we're doomed. Isn't it fair to say that?"

Preacher didn't answer, but his grim expression made it clear that he agreed with her.

"But if you help Mr. MacCallister, and we come along with you, we'll at least have a *chance* to make it to California safely, won't we?" she pressed.

"A mighty slim one," Preacher said.

Fletch swallowed hard, clearly made nervous by what Clementine was suggesting, but he said, "Slim chances are better than none. The only other option is for you to refuse to help Mr. MacCallister, and I don't want to be responsible for something bad happening that could affect the entire nation."

"Neither do I," Clementine said quickly.

"Besides," Fletch mused, "didn't you say you were going to assemble a larger group, Mr. MacCallister? So we wouldn't be traveling with just you and Preacher."

Jamie nodded and admitted, "That's true. I figure there'll be at least a dozen of us, maybe more." His voice took on a harsher note. "But we'll be going down there to fight Indians, not to nursemaid a couple of pilgrims. Sorry to be so plainspoken about it, but that's the truth."

"Well . . . maybe we could help you fight the Indians," Clementine said. As Preacher and Jamie started to look skeptical, she hurried on, "Fletcher is a good shot. He really is."

Fletch shrugged in vague agreement.

"And I'm even better," Clementine continued.

"A better shot than Fletch?" Preacher asked.

Clementine's chin lifted defiantly. "And why shouldn't I be? Fletch grew up in town. I was raised on a farm, but we hunted for a lot of our food, too. I could knock a squirrel out of a tree at fifty yards by the time I was ten years old." She looked back and forth between Preacher and Jamie. "You don't believe me?"

"We didn't say that—" Jamie began.

"Both of you own rifles, don't you?"

"Sure we do." Preacher said.

Clementine scraped her chair back, the bit of breakfast still remaining on her plate forgotten. "Come on. I'll just show you!"

CHAPTER 10

The three men stared in silence at Clementine.

After a long moment, she said, "Are you afraid to take me up on it?"

Fletch said, "I, ah, didn't know you could shoot . . ."

"Well, you never asked me about it, did you?" She turned back to Preacher and Jamie. "I don't mind demonstrating how I can shoot, if one of you gentlemen will let me borrow a rifle."

"We each carry a Sharps," Preacher said. "That's a mighty heavy weapon for—"

"For a girl to handle?" Clementine finished for him. "I'll admit, I've never used one before, but I'd certainly like to try."

Preacher looked at her for a moment, then said, "Dadgummit, you've gone and got me curious."

"Me, too," Jamie admitted. "I worry that you'd break a shoulder if you tried to shoot one of those Sharps, though."

"Not if you tell me how to do it," Clementine said. "I'd really like to see how I can do."

Fletch started to shake his head. "I don't think this

is a good—" He fell abruptly silent when Clementine glared at him.

"We'd need to find a good place somewhere out of town for you to shoot," Preacher mused. "But I reckon you could hitch up your wagon and follow me and Jamie."

"Or rent some saddle mounts from that liveryman," Clementine suggested. "I can ride, too, you know. I was riding almost before I could walk."

"Somehow that don't surprise me." Preacher looked at Jamie and shrugged. "I'm game if you are."

"Let's see if the little lady can back up her brags," Jamie said.

Clementine crossed her arms over her chest and looked confident, but Preacher thought he saw a hint of uncertainty lurking in her eyes, which now, in daylight, he saw were a rich, dark brown, just as he'd thought they might be.

Jamie paid for the meals, and the four of them left the hotel and walked toward the livery stable. The sun was well up and the streets, narrow and crooked though they might be, were full of people, horses, wagons, and buggies. Preacher kept a sharp eye out for any of the Mahoney brothers. Even though he had seen them only by feeble torchlight the night before—and one of them in predawn shadows this morning—he thought he would recognize any of the varmints if he laid eyes on them.

He was confident that the brother he and Jamie had had the run-in with that morning had already told the rest of the clan that Preacher was staying at the livery stable. They were probably keeping an eye on the place, hoping he would show up again and lead them to Fletch and Clementine. In that case,

Preacher was putting the young couple right back in the sights of Clementine's vengeful brothers—but at the same time, the Mahoneys would see that their quarry had not one but *two* brawny frontiersmen as allies.

Under normal circumstances, that ought to have been enough to persuade them to give up their pursuit. As obsessed and ruthless as Clete and the others seemed to be, Preacher didn't hold out much hope of that happening.

When they reached the livery stable, Fletch and Clementine once again warily eyed Dog, who ignored them for the most part. Preacher asked the hostler to saddle a couple of mounts for the two young people, while he slapped his own hull on Horse, the rangy gray stallion who, like Dog, was the latest in a long line of Preacher's trail partners sporting the same name as his predecessors. Jamie's big bay was still saddled from earlier.

With a frown, the hostler looked at Clementine and said, "Uh, I don't have a sidesaddle for the lady."

"That's all right," she said without hesitation. "I can ride astride. Just let me fix this . . ." She pulled up the long skirt she wore and tied it so that it functioned roughly the same as a pair of trousers. That left her legs bare up to a scandalous height, which caused Fletch to turn a bright red but didn't seem to bother her much.

When the hostler had her horse ready, she took the reins from him, gave him a sweet smile, and said, "Much obliged, sir."

His Adam's apple bobbed up and down. "Uh, yes'm. You're welcome."

Clementine put her left foot in the stirrup and swung up into the saddle. "Let's go," she told the men.

Jamie and Preacher were trying not to grin as they mounted up.

"Get a move on, son," Preacher said to Fletch.

They rode into the nearby foothills of the mountains surrounding Santa Fe, and once again Preacher watched to make sure they weren't followed. He noticed that Jamie was doing the same thing.

They stopped in a fairly flat meadow with a cluster of pine trees on the far side, maybe fifty yards away. Preacher reined in first, and the others followed suit.

The mountain man pointed across the open space and said, "See that tree where the first big branch forks and one side of it hangs down a mite? There's a good-sized clump of cones on it. You reckon you could hit that, Miss Clementine?"

"With my old squirrel rifle, I could," she said. "No doubt about it."

"A Sharps is a good bit different from a squirrel rifle. You can bring down a buffalo or a grizzle' bear with one of 'em if you hit it right. Want to give it a try?"

"I sure do."

Preacher pulled the heavy rifle from its saddle sheath. "Best get down from the horse first."

When Clementine had dismounted, Preacher handed her the Sharps. She took hold of it with both hands and her arms sagged under the weight.

"Are you sure you want to do this?" Fletch asked her.

"I'm certain. I just have to get used to how heavy it is, that's all." She hefted the Sharps. "See? I can manage it."

She might think so, but Preacher could tell by the way her muscles stood out how much of a strain it was.

He swung down from Horse and pointed to a nearby sapling. "Rest the barrel in the crook of that tree," he suggested. "Nothin' wrong with usin' a rest to steady a gun before you fire, if you need to. You can find a rock for that or sometimes put the barrel over the saddle of a standin' horse." He squinted at Clementine. "You ain't tall enough for that, though."

She stepped over to the sapling and lifted the Sharps so that the barrel was sitting in the crook Preacher had pointed out. Then she looked over her shoulder and said, "I should have asked you earlier. Is it loaded?"

He nodded solemnly. "All you got to do is cock it, draw your bead, and squeeze the trigger. Plant your feet and brace yourself good before you do, though."

Clementine had to use both thumbs to pull back the hammer. While she was doing that, Jamie and Fletch dismounted.

Fletch went over to her and said, "You really don't have to do this."

"I think I do," she replied without looking at him. She nestled her cheek against the smooth wood of the rifle's stock. She kept her right hand clasped around the stock while she reached forward with her left and raised the sights. Then she took hold of the rifle with both hands again as she began aiming at the clump of pine cones across the pasture.

Preacher crooked a finger at Fletch, and when the young man came over to him, he said, "Leave her be, boy. She needs to concentrate on what she's doin'. Her bein' able to shoot could come in mighty handy for the two of you."

"What about me?" Fletch asked with a slight note of

resentment in his voice. "Isn't it important that I can shoot, too?"

"Maybe we'll see how well you can do, here in a spell. Ladies first, though."

They stood and watched while Clementine lined up her shot. At one point, as the moments crawled by, Fletch opened his mouth to say something, but Preacher silenced him with a lifted hand.

Finally, Clementine drew in a deep breath and held it, and Preacher knew from that action that she did indeed have some experience at shooting. A second later, the gun's boom rolled over the foothills like a peal of thunder.

Almost lost in the sound was a squeal of dismay as Clementine flew backward and the Sharps fell to the ground in front of her. She sat down hard, luckily not on any cactus. Fletch might not have minded picking needles out of her if that had happened, but it wouldn't have been an enjoyable experience for Clementine.

Fletch rushed over to her, calling her name.

As he bent down to help her up, she said irritably, "I'm all right, I'm all right. I just wasn't ready for how hard it was going to kick." She glared at Preacher. "You should have warned me more about that."

The mountain man shrugged. "You know it's a heavy-caliber weapon. Figured you'd know it has a pretty hard kick."

"I hit the pine cones, though, didn't I?"

"See for yourself." Preacher pointed across the meadow to the tree where the cluster of pine cones still hung from the low branch. "I was watchin' 'em. They never budged."

Jamie added, "Looked like your shot went well high."

Clementine dusted off her bottom. "I want to try again."

"Sure." Preacher withdrew one of the long cartridges from his pocket. "You load it this time."

"Are you going to tell me how, or do I have to figure it out for myself?"

"Give it a try," he suggested. "We'll see how well you do."

She snorted and took the cartridge from him, then went over to the rifle. Fletch hurried to pick it up for her. She looked like she was going to scold him for doing that, but instead she took it from him and studied it for a few moments before levering the trigger guard down, which opened the breech where the cartridge went and ejected the empty brass.

When Clementine had reloaded the Sharps and closed the breech, she lifted it with a grunt of effort and rested the barrel in the forked branch again. This time she spread her feet a little more and braced herself better. She didn't take as much time to aim, either. After only a couple of minutes, the Sharps blasted again.

The cluster of pine cones exploded as the heavy round ripped through them. Clementine stayed on her feet, too, even though the recoil made her rock backward a little.

"I did it!" she cried as she peered through the smoke that had gushed from the muzzle. "I hit them!"

"You did," Preacher told her. "And in the time you took to do it, only a few dozen Apaches would've gotten to you and made sure you never fired another shot."

CHAPTER 11

Clementine stared at him, first in confusion, then in disbelief, and finally in anger. Her face reddened and her eyes blazed. "I'm just learning how to shoot that rifle! I hit the target on my second shot! I think that's pretty good."

"It is good," Preacher agreed. "But you got to be a lot surer on your aim and a lot quicker handlin' whatever gun you're shootin'. Where we're goin', if there's trouble, you likely won't have much time to get your shots off."

Fletch said, "Then we *are* coming with you and Mr. MacCallister? You've made up your mind?"

"I didn't say that," Preacher responded with a shake of his head. "What I should've said was, *if* you go down there with us. Luckily, it'll take a while to round up the rest of the fellas who'll be part of the bunch. That'll give both of you a chance to practice and think about whether you really want to do this." Preacher took the Sharps from Clementine and handed it to Fletch. "Let's see what you can do."

Fletch looked nervous as he took the heavy rifle, but he reloaded without any trouble, having watched

Clementine do it. He said, "Should I use the tree to brace the barrel, too?"

Preacher nodded. "Sure, go ahead."

"What should I shoot at? Clementine already knocked down those pine cones."

"Aim for the branch where they were hangin'."

Fletch settled the rifle's barrel in the tree fork and spread his feet wide to steady himself. He pressed his cheek against the stock and took aim. Clementine called encouragement to him, but he didn't seem to hear her. All his attention was concentrated on what he was doing.

Preacher and Jamie stood together and waited for Fletch to fire. Quietly, Jamie said, "The girl did better than I thought she would."

"Yeah, but shootin' at pine cones ain't the same thing as shootin' at Apaches."

"Not hardly," Jamie agreed.

The Sharps boomed as Fletch squeezed the trigger. The recoil didn't knock him down, but no splinters flew from the thick branch that was his target, either.

He looked around at Preacher and Jamie and asked, "I missed, didn't I?"

"You did, for a fact," Preacher replied.

"Can I try again?"

"Sure." Preacher handed him another cartridge. Fletch reloaded and drew another bead.

"You have enough cartridges for these two to practice?" Jamie asked under his breath.

Preacher chuckled. "Can always buy more," he said.

Fletch's second shot was a miss, as well. His growing frustration was apparent on his face. Clementine offered him comforting words and rubbed a hand on his arm, but that didn't seem to do much good. In fact, Fletch looked even more upset after that. Preacher could understand how it might rankle a fella for his wife to be better at something like shooting a rifle than he was.

Fletch buckled down to try harder but missed the target twice more. "I give up," he said disgustedly. "I thought I could shoot at least a little, anyway, but I'm terrible!" He pressed the fingertips of his left hand against his right shoulder. "And that Sharps has a mighty powerful kick."

"It does," Preacher said. "I've got an idea, though. Give me the rifle."

Fletch handed over the Sharps.

Preacher pulled one of the Colt Dragoons from its holster, turned it around, and held it out to the young man, butt first. "Try this instead," he suggested. "There's a little flower bloomin' on that bush over yonder. Try hittin' it."

"That's a really small target," Fletch protested.

"And you're a heap closer to it than you are to that tree," Preacher pointed out. "It ain't more 'n twenty feet away. You don't want to be usin' a handgun at ranges much longer than that less'n you just have to."

"Give it a try," Clementine urged her husband.

Fletch looked down at the revolver in his hand for a moment, then shrugged and nodded. He squared up to the bush Preacher had pointed out and thrust the Colt out in front of him, extending his arm as far as he could.

"Don't stick it out there that far, and don't stand so stiff," Preacher told him. "Nothin' wrong with usin' both hands to steady the gun, either. Try it that way."

Fletch nodded and adjusted his stance. He held the Colt with both hands and cocked it. After aiming for a moment, he squeezed the trigger. The gun boomed and bucked against his palms.

The bullet ripped through the bush about a foot below the bloom that was Fletch's target.

While the echoes were still rolling away, Preacher said, "Not bad for the first time. You got four more rounds in there. Keep tryin'."

Fletch blew out his breath and nodded.

As he lined up his second attempt, Jamie leaned over to Preacher and said, "That's not an easy shot, you know."

"I know," the mountain man said. "I just got a hunch about the boy."

Fletch squeezed the trigger again, and the flower disintegrated from the bullet's impact.

"I did it!" he whooped.

Preacher gathered up several loose rocks about half the size of a normal man's hand and lined them up on a tree branch.

"Try shootin' them offa there. Don't take a lot of time, and don't think all that much about what you're doin'. Look at what you want to hit, and point the gun where you're lookin'."

Fletch took another deep breath and nodded again. He raised the Colt, still using both hands, and squeezed off the three rounds as fast as he could cock the revolver. The first two shots missed, but with the third one, the rock at the far right of the trio flew off the branch.

Clementine clapped her hands. "Fletcher, that's wonderful!"

"Some fellas just have more of a knack with a handgun," Preacher said to Jamie. "I took a chance that maybe Fletch is one of 'em."

"He still needs a lot of work, though," Jamie replied.

Preacher nodded. "Yep. And we're gonna give it to him."

He showed Fletch how to reload the Dragoon and set up more targets. As he continued practicing, Fletch managed to hit two out of the three rocks and finally knocked all three off the limb with three shots. He seemed to have a natural eye with the Colt that he didn't have with the Sharps.

"That's enough," Preacher said as he called a halt to the practice session. "Your arm's already gonna be sore tomorrow from handlin' that hogleg, Fletch."

The young man handed the gun back to Preacher. "I ought to get one of my own."

Preacher nodded toward the revolver holstered on Jamie's hip. "The Walker's a better design. These Dragoons are what I'm used to, though. Next time we come out here, you can try the Walker, if that's all right with Jamie."

"Sure," Jamie agreed. "I'm looking forward to seeing what you can do with it, Fletch."

Both members of the young couple seemed happy with the way this outing had gone.

Then Preacher said, "You claimed you're a good rider, Miss Clementine. Looked like you sat the saddle all right on the way out here, but what if you have to ride a mite harder than that?"

"Like this?" Clementine asked.

She pulled her mount's reins loose from the bush where they were tied and swung up into the saddle. With her heels nudging the horse into a gallop, she leaned forward over the animal's neck and rode hard toward the other side of the meadow. The wind made her blond hair stream out behind her head.

As she pounded toward the trees on the far side of the meadow, Fletch began to look worried, but then Clementine reined in, barely slowing the horse as she pulled the animal in a tight turn and raced back toward the three men. As she brought the horse to a sliding stop near them, an abrupt halt that kicked up some dust, she called, "How's that?"

"Not bad," Preacher replied. "Especially considerin' you never rode that horse until today."

"You did a fine job, young lady," Jamie added. "Of course, it's not quite the same as if you were being chased by Apaches."

Clementine persisted. "But between the way we both shot and this demonstration of how well I ride, you have fewer misgivings about taking us along with you, don't you?"

"We'll think about it," Preacher promised. "Thing of it is, none of us have to make up our minds right now. It's gonna take some time to get the bunch together, so you'll have more chances to practice your shootin'. No matter how things turn out with this job of Jamie's, the better the both of you can handle a gun and ride, the better your chances of makin' it to California like you planned."

The others mounted up, and they started back toward town. Preacher scanned their surroundings, wondering if any of the Mahoney brothers had trailed them and watched what they were doing. If that was the case, maybe Fletch's burgeoning prowess with the Colt Dragoon would make them think twice about their vengeful pursuit.

Again, though, Preacher doubted if that would actually turn out to be true.

"Did you have anybody in particular in mind for

joinin' up with us?" Preacher asked Jamie as they rode side by side.

Fletch and Clementine were a short distance ahead of them.

"Well, we know quite a few of the same fellas," Jamie replied. "I thought you might have some ideas on the subject. I trust anybody you'd want to have with us, that goes without saying."

Preacher rubbed his gray-stubbled chin for a moment. "Yeah, I know a heap of fellas who like a good fight better 'n just about anything in the world. Even have a pretty good idea where most of 'em are. But there's a good chance I won't be able to get in touch with all of them."

"Well, find the ones you can," Jamie said. "And tell them that if it's a fight they're looking for, we've got a dandy for them!"

CHAPTER 12

They spent the next month in Santa Fe. Preacher and Jamie each wrote letters and also spread the word by telling acquaintances drifting through town who they were looking for. The mail was undependable, of course, so there was no way of knowing how long it would take for those letters to reach the ones they were intended for, or even *if* they ever would. Passing the word in person was also slow, with no guarantee of results.

But as Jamie explained, General Charlton hadn't given him any sort of deadline. The government was more interested in how well this chore was carried out, instead of how fast.

And the good thing about the delay was that it gave Preacher and Jamie plenty of time to work with Fletch and Clementine on their shooting and riding. The young couple had no timetable for reaching California, either.

As the days went past and turned into weeks, they saw no sign of Clementine's brothers. However, Preacher didn't take that to mean that the Mahoney brothers had given up and gone back home to

Tennessee. He figured they were just laying low, waiting for a chance to kill Fletch and grab Clementine. He and Jamie didn't plan on giving them that chance. One or both of them were always nearby except when the young couple were alone in their hotel room.

Every day, the four of them rode into the foothills. Jamie bought Clementine a pair of canvas trousers for riding so she wouldn't have to tie up her skirt anymore. He offered to get her a sidesaddle, which would have been a lot more ladylike, but Clementine refused.

"I grew up riding astride," she explained. "If I tried to use one of those fancy sidesaddles, I'd probably just fall off and break my neck."

She continued to improve her shooting eye, although Preacher wasn't sure she would ever be strong enough to handle the heavy Sharps without a strain.

"You need somethin' with more punch to it than a squirrel rifle," he told her, "but lighter than that Sharps. We'll look around and see if we can find somethin' better suited for you to use."

Fletch took to the Walker Colt even better than he had to the Dragoon. Preacher bought him one of his own, along with the holster to carry it.

That prompted Fletch to say, "You and Mr. MacCallister keep buying things for us. You're even paying for the hotel room. I can't help but think that we're taking advantage of you."

"Nothin' of the sort," Preacher assured him. "I'm still usin' that money I won the same night we met, and Jamie's done well for himself with that ranch up in Colorado. We ain't hurtin' for funds."

"Besides," Jamie put in, "I remember what it's like

being young and just starting out in a marriage. You and Clementine will need money when you start your new life in California, so you might as well hang on to what you have." He thought for a second and went on. "Not only that, but the government's authorized me to pay the men who go along with me on this mission. The two of you aren't really part of that, but you'll probably lend a hand along the way, so it's only fair that you get some of the wages, too."

Preacher and Jamie had discussed their plans for trying to keep the two young people safe during the inevitable hostilities. The group would need a base camp of sorts, and the Wylie wagon could provide that, as well as carrying some of the necessary supplies. Preacher hoped to put together a large enough group that one or two men could stay to guard the camp at all times, while the others ventured out in their forays against the Apaches.

But at least to a certain extent, Fletch and Clementine would have to be responsible for their own protection, and to that end, Preacher and Jamie continued working with them on their shooting.

They practiced for several hours almost every day. Fletch progressed to the point that he could whip out the Walker Colt with a fair degree of swiftness, and he hit what he aimed at most of the time.

Clementine's accuracy improved, too, especially after Preacher found her a lighter-weight Mississippi rifle and presented it to her. The only drawback was that it was a muzzle-loading percussion weapon instead of a breechloader, so he had to teach her how to handle that chore. It was slower to reload than the Sharps, but Clementine was a better markswoman with it. After a few days, she was well on her way to stripping the pine trees of all their cones on the far side of their favorite practice spot.

The four of them were having dinner in the hotel dining room one evening when Preacher suddenly lifted his head, sniffed, wrinkled his nose, and frowned.

Jamie saw the reaction and asked, "What is it?"

"I know that smell," the mountain man replied. "See if you get a whiff of it."

Jamie drew in a deep breath, made a face, and said, "Phew."

"Exactly," Preacher said.

Clementine looked a little queasy as she smelled the strong, distinctive aroma, too. "What is that?"

"Not what," Preacher said with a smile. "Who."

He turned in his chair, spotted a man in filthy buckskins standing in the dining room's entrance, and raised a hand to catch the newcomer's attention. The man's grimy face lit up with recognition. He grinned as he started across the room toward them. Guests at the tables he passed leaned back away from him and looked dismayed as he went by. The smell he carried with him washed out in front of him like a wave.

"Preacher!" the man exclaimed. "Boy, howdy, it's good to see you again."

Preacher was on his feet and grasped the hand the newcomer thrust out at him, and then they pounded each other heartily on the back.

"Good to see you, too, Pugh." Preacher turned and gestured toward the others at the table. "You know Jamie Ian MacCallister."

"We ain't ever met, as I recollect, but I sure do know of him," the man called Pugh said. "Howdy, Jamie."

Jamie stood up and shook hands. "Glad to meet you. Pugh, was it?"

The man cackled with laughter. "That's my name, but ever since I went to the mountains and started trappin', nigh on to thirty year ago, folks been callin' me Phew. I answer to either of them monikers."

"And this is Fletch Wylie and his missus, Miss Clementine," Preacher went on.

"Howdy, Fletch," Pugh greeted the young man. Then he swept off his stained, battered old hat and made a creditable bow toward Clementine. "Miss Clementine, it's a plumb honor and a privilege to make your acquaintance."

"Yes, uh, I'm . . . I'm glad to meet you as well, Mister . . . Pugh," Clementine said tentatively.

"I apologize for the smell, ma'am. It seems to follow me around for some reason."

Preacher said, "The reason is, you plumb hate water and don't never take a bath less'n you happen to fall into a river or a lake."

Pugh frowned. "Bathin' ain't natural. Iffen the Good Lord had meant for man to have much truck with water, He'd 've given us gills, like He done with fish."

"You can argue about what the Good Lord did or didn't intend with Audie when he gets here."

"Audie's comin' along on this here jaunt?" Pugh's face showed excitement and interest again.

"I ain't heard from him yet, but I'm hopin' so. Him and Nighthawk both."

"Well, sure, iffen Audie shows up, Nighthawk will, too. Them two are always together. I reckon Nighthawk's as big a talker as ever?"

"I wouldn't be surprised," Preacher said. "Have you heard from any of the other boys?"

"Nope. Soon's I got your letter, I lit a shuck for Santa Fe. Truth to tell, the relatives I was visitin' seemed a mite glad for me to dee-part, although I sure can't figure out why they'd feel that way."

Preacher noticed the clerk from the lobby had entered the dining room and was making his way toward them hesitantly. "Is there a problem?" he asked the man.

"No, no, not at all," the clerk answered hastily. "Some of the other guests approached me and asked if, ah, this gentleman was going to be stopping here at the hotel . . ."

Preacher felt a flash of annoyance. Pugh's smell was pretty potent, all right, but he had as much right to be here as anybody else. Preacher might have said something along those lines, if Pugh hadn't responded first.

"Naw, naw, I ain't stayin' here, if that's what you mean, little feller," Pugh said. "Never could stand to be cooped up inside four walls for very long at a time. Figured I'd make camp somewheres out o' town."

"That's a good idea," Preacher said. He told Pugh how to find the meadow where they had been practicing riding and shooting. "As the other fellas show up, they can stay out there, too."

"That's fine, mighty fine. I'm lookin' forward to seein' all of 'em. And then we'll all go off and—"

Preacher held up a hand to stop him. He and Jamie hadn't said much around other folks about Jamie's mission. Preacher didn't really believe it would be a problem if people in Santa Fe knew that they would be setting off to fight Apaches, once the rest of their force got here, but just as a general rule, both frontiersmen believed in playing their cards pretty close to the vest. It was better to ensure that extra problems didn't crop up, since later on they'd probably have plenty to deal with that arose naturally.

After a few minutes of reminiscing with Preacher, Pugh left the hotel to head out to what would be the campsite for the group.

As Preacher sat down at the table again, Fletch said, "Well, Mr. Pugh certainly seems like, ah, a colorful character."

"Smells to high heaven, don't he?" Preacher said with a grin. "You kinda get used to him, but you don't ever get so's you don't notice when he's around. Tell you what, though, he's a fine fightin' man who won't never let you down. I'll be glad to have him on our side."

"So will I," Jamie agreed. "I've heard plenty about him. Didn't the two of you fight off more than a hundred Blackfeet one time?"

Preacher made a face and said, "I don't know how them crazy stories get so blowed up like that. There weren't no hundred Blackfeet that time Pugh and I had a little dustup with 'em. Couldn't've been more 'n seventy or eighty of the varmints."

"Seventy or eighty Blackfeet," Fletch said. "And the two of you fought them off."

Preacher shrugged. "For a while. Then a few more of our friends showed up and we chased them Blackfeet back where they come from."

Jamie chuckled and asked, "How many more of your friends are we talking about, Preacher?"

"I don't rightly recollect. Three or four, I'd say."

Fletch began, "So five or six of you chased eighty Blackfeet—", but then he stopped short and looked at the dining room's entrance.

The young man's expression made Preacher glance around. A dark-faced stranger stood there wearing a sombrero, a fancy charro jacket, tight trousers, and a pair of low-slung guns that his hands hung menacingly near as he started toward the table.

CHAPTER 13

Preacher and Jamie came to their feet and turned so that they faced the newcomer. The aura of potential danger was so thick in the air that everyone else in the dining room looked nervous and began glancing around as if searching for some place to dive for cover if bullets started flying.

The stranger didn't make a play for his guns, though. He stopped and said in a faintly accented voice, "I am looking for Jamie MacCallister."

"You've found him," Jamie said, his own tone flat and hard. "What can I do for you?"

"It is said in certain places along the trail that you are looking for men. Men with special skills."

The stranger's attitude made it clear that he considered himself to possess those skills.

Jamie and Preacher glanced at each other. They had known when they put the word out that it might reach men other than those for whom it was specifically intended. The frontier, as Jamie had said, was a small place in many ways.

"Maybe I am," Jamie said in response to the

stranger's comment. "You've got the advantage of me. You know who I am, but I don't know who you are."

"I am called Ramirez." The man said the name as if that was more than enough to tell them all they needed to know.

Jamie shook his head and said, "Never heard of you, amigo."

That response—or lack of response—to the name made anger flare in the man's dark eyes. "If you ever spent much time around the Rio Grande, señor, you would have heard of Ramirez."

Jamie hooked his thumbs in his gun belt. "So you're a big he-wolf down in the Texas border country. That doesn't mean anything where we're going."

Ramirez scowled. His hands moved slightly toward his gun butts as he rasped, "Perhaps this will mean something—"

"Don't do it, son," Preacher said. "To start with, the chances of you outdrawin' Jamie MacCallister are mighty small, and even if you manage to do it somehow, you ain't fast enough to get both of us. I'm plumb sure of that. And that's what you'd have to do to walk out of here alive."

Ramirez stood there stiffly, his hands still curved clawlike above his guns as his gaze flicked back and forth between Preacher and Jamie.

"Listen," Jamie said, breaking the tense, momentary silence. "Why don't you stop trying to impress us and just sit down and talk to us? We're done with our supper. You can join us for a cup of coffee."

Ramirez hesitated for several seconds longer, then said, "I will not be disrespected."

"*Earn* my respect and you'll get it. I can promise you that."

"Same goes for me," Preacher added.

Fletch said, "I think maybe Clementine and I will go on up to the room . . ."

For the first time, Ramirez acknowledged their presence. He turned to Clementine, took off his sombrero, and said, "My apologies for interrupting your dinner, señorita."

"It's *señora*," Fletch said, having picked up that much Spanish somewhere. "This is my wife."

"My apologies again," Ramirez murmured. He didn't leer at Clementine or even show any undue interest in her, but it was clear that he recognized a beautiful woman when he saw one.

"That's, uh, that's all right," she said, a little flustered by this stern, prickly gunman. She stood up, Fletch jumping to help her with her chair, and then the two of them left the dining room, casting glances back over their shoulders as they went.

Preacher said, "I'm goin', too, just to make sure them pesky brothers o' hers ain't laid any traps upstairs."

"Good idea," Jamie said with a nod. They hadn't seen hide nor hair of the Mahoney brothers for quite a while, but it was always a good idea not to let your guard down.

As Preacher left the dining room, Jamie waved a hand toward one of the empty chairs at the table. Ramirez waited a second, then shrugged, put his sombrero on a chair, and sat down on the one next to it. Jamie signaled to the waitress for coffee.

"All right," he said to Ramirez, "tell me why you want to go along on this trip."

"You go to kill Apaches, do you not?"

"Nobody ever said anything about that in the word we put out," Jamie replied.

Ramirez waved that away. "What else would you be doing in that part of the territory? There is very little else down there, señor. But someday, there could be, and that is why it is important to eliminate the threat from those savages."

Ramirez had a canny streak about him, Jamie realized. He had formed a theory from pretty sparse information, and he was on the right track.

Jamie said, "Maybe that's what we've got in mind."

"I have killed Apaches," Ramirez declared. "Also Yaquis, and Mexican soldiers, and gringos."

"Well, you're just a one-man army, aren't you?"

Ramirez leaned forward and glared, and he might have replied hotly if not for the waitress's arrival at that moment with his coffee. He nodded curtly to her and muttered, "*Gracias.*"

"You mentioned fighting Mexican soldiers," Jamie said. "Are you a bandit, Ramirez?"

"I am a fighter for freedom. Santa Anna may call himself *presidente*, but he is a tyrant, a monster!"

"We're in agreement on that," Jamie said, nodding. "I don't have any use for the varmint, myself. But you should know that what we're setting out to do may have some benefit for him, at least indirectly. How's that going to sit with you?"

"I hate Santa Anna . . . but I am one man, and he has an army at his beck and call." The *pistolero*'s shoulders rose and fell in an eloquent shrug. "His soldiers have made the border country along the Rio Grande too hot for me, but they pay little attention to what goes on this far west. So perhaps it is time for me to explore this region and see if it is to my liking. The work will be satisfactory, if it involves killing Apaches."

Jamie leaned forward, and his face was like granite as he said, "One more thing you've got to understand . . . I'm in charge of this bunch, and when I'm not around, that other fella who was here a few minutes ago is the boss."

"The old man?" Ramirez smirked.

"That old man is called Preacher."

Recognition flickered in Ramirez's eyes. Even south of the border, they had heard of the legendary mountain man known as Preacher.

"Very well," he said after several seconds. "That is understood. You are *el jefe.*"

For a long moment, the two men sat there looking at each other, and then Jamie nodded slowly. "We'll see how it works out. I'll provide supplies, ammunition, and whatever else we need for the job. I can advance you a little *dinero* if you want some, but the real payoff comes when the job is finished."

"That is agreeable," Ramirez said. "When do we leave?"

"When all the others get here," Jamie said.

Over the next few days, more of the men Jamie and Preacher sought showed up in Santa Fe. The camp at the meadow grew. Jamie had let the clerk at the hotel know to send anyone who was looking for them out there. Preacher introduced Jamie to his friends from fur trapping days as they arrived.

Deadlead and Tennysee were both lean, buckskin-clad men of indeterminate age, but they weren't young. Tennysee was quick with a laugh or a joke.

Deadlead was more serious, and according to Preacher, he had gotten his name because he was a crack shot with a pistol.

"Best and fastest I've ever seen with a handgun," Preacher declared. "I figured I'd set him to workin' with Fletch, see if he can improve the boy's natural-born pistol-handlin' skills."

Graybull was a mountain of a man, bigger even than Jamie. Fellows of that size often tended to be slow and lumbering, but Graybull could move quickly and nimbly when he had to, such as when somebody was trying to kill him—or when somebody *needed* killing. Luckily for everybody around him, Graybull was slow to anger, although he was an unstoppable force when his ire was roused.

When Preacher performed one of the introductions, Jamie shook hands with the newcomer and said, "Powder River Pete. I've heard of you."

"No, no," Preacher said. "This ain't Powder River Pete. That's a whole other hombre. This here is Powder Pete, so called because he's better at handlin' blastin' powder than just about anybody. Name's got nothin' to do with the Powder River. You need somethin' blowed up, Powder Pete's your man."

"I'll try to remember that," Jamie said, squeezing Powder Pete's hand, "the next time I need something blown up."

The next arrival brought a fiddle, a French accent, and a merry attitude with him. "Dupre is what they call me," he said to Jamie. "And I, of course, have heard of the famous Jamie Ian MacCallister. It will be an honor to ride with you, *m'sieu*."

"Wait'll you hear him go to scrapin' on that fiddle of his," Preacher said. "Even if you ain't the dancin' kind, it'll make you want to get up and shake a leg. Miss Clementine's gonna be kept busy, because all the fellas'll be linin' up to dance with her."

"Not Phew, I hope," Dupre said with a look of alarm. "Never would I subject a lady to such a fate as to dance with that malodorous one!"

From halfway across the camp, Pugh called, "I heard that, you derned Frenchie, and I think you're tryin' to insult me!"

"Are you saying my words are untrue?" Dupre shouted back.

"Well, maybe not, but that still don't mean I'll put up with any loose talk from the likes o' you!"

Jamie asked Preacher, "Are those two liable to wind up trying to kill each other?"

Preacher grinned. "Naw, they're good friends. They just like to hooraw one another."

"Good. We'll have enough trouble fighting the ones we're supposed to, without battling among ourselves."

It might still come down to that, though, Jamie thought, especially with Ramirez in camp. The Mexican gunman was surly most of the time, as if looking for something to be insulted about. These old mountain men didn't put up with any guff, so sooner or later Ramirez's attitude was liable to rub them the wrong way.

The fireworks that might explode if that happened wouldn't be pretty.

CHAPTER 14

It wasn't only Preacher's old friends who showed up to join the group. One day a stocky man in late middle age rode in on a rawboned mule. He wore canvas trousers and a buckskin jacket. A black hat with an eagle feather stuck in its band was pushed back on a mostly bald head with jug-handle ears sticking out on both sides. His strong chin had a little tuft of silvery beard sticking out from it.

Jamie greeted him with grinning enthusiasm and introduced him to Preacher. "This is Edgerton. We scouted together a few times and have backed each other's play in plenty of trouble."

Preacher shook hands with the man, whose face was so solemn it was hard to imagine him ever smiling. But Edgerton's voice was friendly enough as he clasped Preacher's hand and said, "Heard a-plenty about you, mister. I'll be happy to call you friend."

"Friends it is, then," Preacher declared.

Less than twenty-four hours later, two men rode in together. At first glance they looked more like farmers than Indian fighters, wearing uncomfortable-looking shoes instead of boots, trousers that were a little too short for their long, gangly legs, and white shirts and black coats that hung on their scrawny frames like clothes on a scarecrow. Their lantern-jawed faces were pale under round-crowned black hats. Their hair wasn't just fair, it was pretty much colorless.

"Lars and Bengt Molmberg," Jamie introduced them to Preacher and the others. "They were with a wagon train I helped guide out to the Oregon country a while back, but they decided they weren't interested in settling down after all, once they got a taste of excitement on the frontier."

"Are they twins?" Clementine asked in a half-whisper.

"Yes, ma'am, I believe they are, but to tell you the truth, I never really asked them, and they don't talk much."

"They speak English," Preacher said, "or just Scandahoovian?"

"Everything I've ever told them in English, they seemed to understand," Jamie replied. "Like I said, they're not exactly talkative."

Preacher shook hands with the Molmberg brothers anyway and told them, "Glad to meet you boys. If Jamie says you're fine fellas, that's plenty good enough for me."

Lars and Bengt nodded but said nothing. Preacher glanced at Jamie.

"Like that all the time, are they?"

"Yep."

When trouble came, it involved Ramirez, as Jamie had suspected it might, but the clash wasn't between the Mexican gun-wolf and any of the men who had joined the group previously. It erupted between Ramirez and another newcomer who rode up to the camp.

This man wore a flat-topped black beaver hat that looked completely out of place above his coppery, hawklike face. It didn't go with the rest of his outfit, either, which consisted of a beaded leather vest, no shirt despite the chill still in the air, buckskin trousers, and high-topped moccasins. He had a gun belt strapped around his waist, with a Walker Colt in the attached holster and a sheathed bowie knife on the other side.

Ramirez was sitting cross-legged beside a small fire, but as soon as he saw the newcomer, he came to his feet like a snake uncoiling. *"Comanche!"* he spat. His hands darted toward his guns as he stepped forward.

The newcomer reacted with blinding speed, diving out of his saddle and tackling Ramirez before the Mexican could complete his draw. Both men went down. The stranger's momentum sent them rolling through the fire, scattering ashes and burning bits of wood. They writhed and wrestled, Ramirez still trying to pull iron while the other man yanked the bowie from its sheath and raised it high, ready to plunge it into Ramirez's chest. At the same instant, Ramirez cleared leather with his right-hand gun.

By that time, the commotion had attracted attention all over the camp. Preacher and Jamie were close enough that they reached the two fighters before any actual killing commenced. Jamie's powerful fingers clamped around the wrist of the newcomer's knife hand, making sure the blade didn't descend, while Preacher planted a boot on the wrist of Ramirez's gun hand, pinning it to the ground.

"Stop it, you blamed idjits!" Preacher roared. "What in blazes are you fightin' about?"

"You let a Comanche ride into your camp!" Ramirez yelled. "Those savages live only to kill! I have seen what they do—"

"He's not full-blood Comanche," Jamie interrupted. "His ma was white."

The man's lips drew back from his teeth in a snarl as he leaned over Ramirez. "But I still live to kill, as you said," he told the Mexican gunman in English. "Especially puffed-up little popinjays like you."

"Take it easy, Dog Brother," Jamie said. "If I let go of your wrist, you promise not to plant that bowie in Ramirez?"

Preacher said, "You know this hombre, Jamie?"

"We've crossed trails a few times," Jamie said. "How about it, Dog Brother?"

"I will not kill the *Mejicano*," Dog Brother said with surly reluctance. "Unless he tries to kill me. Then I will show him no mercy."

"Fair enough," Preacher said. "I'm gonna move my foot. You pouch that iron, you hear me, Ramirez?"

After a few seconds, Ramirez nodded with the same reluctance Dog Brother had displayed in agreeing to call a halt to the fight.

Jamie and Preacher stepped back. The two battlers watched each other with extreme wariness as they got to their feet and put away their weapons. Dog Brother picked up his beaver hat, which had gone flying off when he dived from his horse, knocked the dust from it, and settled it on his head without ever taking his eyes off Ramirez.

"A filthy half-breed is no more worthy of trust than a full-blooded cur of a Comanche," Ramirez said.

"A Mexican is a fine one to speak of trust," Dog Brother returned. "They are all sneaking thieves."

"Both of you settle down and shut your mouths," Jamie told them harshly. "Neither of you is important enough that we won't boot you out of this bunch right here and now. We can't have any fighting amongst ourselves."

"That's right," Preacher added. "We'll have plenty of fightin' with other folks where we're goin'."

Dog Brother turned his head to look at Jamie. "Your letter said there would be fighting, but not with who." He cast a sneering glance in Ramirez's direction. "Mexicans?"

"Apaches."

Dog Brother thought about that for a second, then nodded. "They are ancient enemies of my father's people. I hate my father and all the Comanche . . . but I would not mind killing some Apaches."

"You hate the Comanch'?" Preacher asked in surprise.

Dog Brother gave him a haughty look but didn't bother answering otherwise. Instead he looked around at the crowd of men who had gathered and said, "All these men are going to fight the Apaches?"

"That's right," Jamie said.

Dog Brother jerked his square chin in a nod and thrust out his hand to Jamie. "I will go, too, if you are their leader, MacCallister."

"I am," Jamie said as he shook hands, "and I'm glad to have you along."

Ramirez didn't look at all happy about that, but he picked up his sombrero and walked away as he slapped the hat against his thigh.

Some of the other men started to move closer, as

if they were going to introduce themselves to Dog Brother, but the half-breed turned his back on them, went to his horse—a big gray, not an Indian pony— and grasped the reins to lead it away.

"Well, he ain't friendly a-tall," Tennysee drawled.

"He said he hates the Comanch'," Powder Pete added, "and he sounded like he don't cotton to the Apaches, neither. Does he just hate *all* Injuns?"

"Nope," Jamie said, shaking his head. "Dog Brother hates *everybody.*"

A couple of days passed, and it began to look as if everyone who was going to show up in response to the summons already had. That bothered Preacher, because there were two more men he'd been hoping to see and he would feel a lot better about venturing down into Apache country if they were along.

Then he spotted two riders approaching the camp from the direction of Santa Fe, moving along at a deliberate pace. One of the riders was big, that was apparent even at a distance, but his companion appeared to be a child perched on a small, spotted pony. A big grin stretched across Preacher's face as he recognized them.

"These are the fellas I told you about," he said to Jamie. "And I'm mighty glad to see 'em. These ol' boys have been to Hades and back with me more times than I can count."

Everyone gathered to greet the newcomers, even Ramirez and Dog Brother—although the Mexican and the half-breed stood apart from the others *and* from each other, one on either side of the main group.

As the riders came closer, it became obvious that the larger of the pair was an Indian. His lined, weathered face appeared ancient at first glance, but it was difficult to determine an Indian's age. Even Preacher, who had known this man for decades, wasn't sure how old he was.

The second man was white, as old as Preacher or perhaps even older, but he had a sprightly air about him that made him seem younger. His eyes sparkled with a keen intellect. When he stood up, he was three and a half feet tall, and his broad shoulders and sturdy body made him seem almost that wide. Preacher had heard him described as a large amount of trouble in a very compact package, and truer words were never spoken.

The big Indian was a Crow warrior named Nighthawk. His diminutive constant companion was called Audie. He had a full, distinguished name that he had gone by, back in the days when he was a college professor, but since he had left that life behind him to head west and become a fur trapper and adventurer, he had never used it again. The two of them were just Audie and Nighthawk, the best friends Preacher had ever had.

After they had reined in, Nighthawk dismounted first and then lifted Audie from the pony's back to set him on the ground. Preacher hurried forward, pumped Nighthawk's hand, and then went down on one knee to pound Audie on the back and shake hands with him, too.

"You two are a sight for sore eyes, and I ain't jokin'," Preacher declared. "I was about to give up on you."

"As if we'd ever pass up the opportunity to partake of an adventure with you, Preacher," Audie said.

"You'd probably like to know what you're gettin' into—"

"No need for that. The only knowledge required is that you're involved, and when that's the case, it's a veritable certainty that excitement will abound!" Audie looked around at the men who had gathered and went on. "Now, other than the ones with whom Nighthawk and I are already acquainted, who are all the members of this ladies' sewing circle you've assembled?"

Some of the men started to bristle at that, but Preacher quickly put them at ease by introducing Audie and Nighthawk.

Jamie shook hands with both of them and said, "I've heard a heap about you fellas. It's nice to finally meet you."

"The feeling is certainly mutual," Audie said. "The name Jamie Ian MacCallister is renowned from one end of the frontier to the other."

"Umm," Nighthawk said. The big Crow warrior hardly ever said anything else.

Audie continued to Jamie. "You've probably known Preacher longer than anyone here except Dupre."

"Yeah, I was just a youngster the first time we ran into each other. And we've been crossing trails ever since."

"Usually when all hell's about to break loose," Preacher said dryly. "Let me introduce you to the other fellas."

That went well except for Ramirez and Dog Brother, both of whom walked off before any introductions could be made.

"Don't mind them," Preacher told the newcomers.

"They're surly as old 'possums, but as long as they do their jobs, I reckon that's all that matters."

"Indeed," Audie agreed. He smiled. "It appears that Nighthawk has already made some new friends."

Nighthawk stood with his arms crossed, solemnly regarding Lars and Bengt Molmberg, who stood a few feet away looking equally somber. After a long moment of silence, Nighthawk said, "Ummm." The Swedish brothers returned grave nods.

"Aw, shoot!" Tennysee exclaimed. "Now we're never gonna get any peace and quiet around here with them three jabberin' away like that!"

CHAPTER 15

Now that Audie and Nighthawk had arrived to join the group, Preacher was ready to get the expedition started, but he supposed it was a good idea to wait a few more days, just to make sure no one else showed up. Jamie agreed. Also, they could use that time to finish buying supplies for the journey.

Preacher and Jamie were at one of the stores fronting on Santa Fe's main plaza, along with Fletch and Clementine, who had brought their wagon from the livery stable so it could be loaded. The young people were still inside the store as Clementine picked out a few last-minute things she wanted to take along for their new home in California.

Jamie and Preacher stood out on the high porch and loading dock as clerks carried crates and bags out of the store and placed them in the back of the wagon.

Jamie frowned and commented, "I'm not sure we can get everything we need in there. We've got fifteen mouths to feed—seventeen if you count Fletch and Clementine—and that many folks go through a lot of food."

"I figured we'd do some huntin' for fresh meat while we're down there," Preacher said.

"Hunt what? Rattlesnakes? Lizards? Might be a few scrawny javelinas roaming around, or some bighorn sheep in the little mountain ranges that pop up here and there. It's not a country rich in game animals."

"We can get some pack mules," Preacher suggested. "You can carry a lot of supplies on a mule."

Jamie rubbed his chin in thought and nodded. "That's a possibility—"

"Mr. MacCallister?" a man's voice interrupted him.

Jamie and Preacher turned to see two men standing there. They wore town suits and hats and looked out of place in a rough-and-ready frontier settlement like Santa Fe. Their pale, unlined faces testified that they hadn't spent a lot of time out in the sun, either.

The man who had spoken went on. "My name is Noah Stuart." He was the younger and larger of the pair, probably in his late twenties, with dark hair and a friendly, handsome face. A pair of spectacles perched on his nose.

"Son, you say that name like you expect it to mean something to me," Jamie responded. "No offense, but we haven't met, and I don't reckon I've ever heard of you."

"You didn't get Mr. Charlton's letter?" Noah Stuart asked as he cocked his head slightly to the side in apparent surprise.

Jamie shook his head. "I haven't heard anything from Owen in weeks."

The second stranger, small, in his mid-thirties, with a squinty look about him, plucked at Stuart's sleeve and said, "Perhaps we should try to contact

Mr. Charlton ourselves and find out if there are any later orders for us."

"If Mr. Charlton wanted us to know anything, I'm sure he would have gotten in touch with us, Chester," Stuart replied.

"But he may have tried, and his message simply hasn't reached us yet. We should go to the territorial governor's office and make sure. He did say that he would contact us through the governor's office, didn't he?"

"That's true," Stuart admitted. "I suppose it wouldn't hurt—"

"Hold on a minute," Jamie said. "Before the two of you go gallivanting off, how about explaining why you were looking for me in the first place?"

"Oh. Of course." Stuart nodded. "Chester and I— this is my assistant, Chester Merrick—we've been sent to join your expedition."

Jamie and Preacher looked at each other, then back at the two men.

Jamie said, "You *do* know why we're heading down into the border country, don't you?"

"Of course," Stuart answered without hesitation. "You're being sent to establish peaceful relations with the primitives who live in the area."

"Welllll . . ." Preacher said, "I reckon that's one way of puttin' it."

"We're going to kill Apaches and run out the ones we don't kill," Jamie said, not softening his tone or the words he spoke.

"And you boys just don't look like Injun fighters," Preacher added.

Stuart said, "We were made aware that there might

be some, uh, some *resistance* from the natives but that they would come around once the facts of the situation were explained in the proper manner—"

"The only explanations Apaches listen to come in calibers," Preacher said.

Chester Merrick swallowed hard and said, "That sounds very dangerous."

"Surely it won't be *that* bad," Noah Stuart said with a slight frown.

Jamie said, "Preacher's right. There's going to be a lot of fighting, and I can't figure out why Owen Charlton thought you two gentlemen ought to come along."

"Not to fight," Stuart said firmly. "I'm a surveyor and cartographer, and as I told you, Chester is my assistant. Neither of us are . . . mercenaries."

"You're not in the army, either, I'd wager."

"Certainly not, although we do work for the United States government, specifically the Office of the Interior and Secretary Thomas Ewing."

Jamie nodded. "But at least I understand now why Owen gave you this job. You're supposed to make a survey for a possible railroad route through the southern part of the territory, aren't you?"

"Precisely," Stuart replied. "Before further discussions can proceed in Washington, it has to be determined whether it's even feasible for a railroad to be built through the region. Not only that, but there's also the question of whether following the best route will require acquiring more land from Mexico, or whether the territory already ceded by the Treaty of Guadalupe Hidalgo will be sufficient." Stuart's voice was firmer and more confident now that he was talking about something within his area of expertise. "You understand, it may be years before any actual work begins on the railroad, but all these preliminary investigations must be done first."

"Something's got to start the ball," Preacher muttered.

"What? Oh, yes." Stuart shrugged. "I suppose one could phrase it that way."

"I understand what you're telling us, Mr. Stuart," Jamie said, "but I'm not sure *you* understand just what you're getting into. There's a mighty good chance some of us won't be coming back from down there."

Merrick said, "You mean we may be *killed*?"

"That's what Apaches do," Preacher said. "Killin' white folks is one of their favorite things."

Jamie knew Preacher was overstating things a bit just to make sure the very real dangers of the situation soaked in for Stuart and Merrick. The pallor on the faces of the two men had deepened during the conversation.

Stuart summoned up a look of determination as he said, "Nevertheless, this is the assignment we've been given, and we intend to carry it out. Isn't that right, Chester?"

Merrick didn't answer for a long moment, and when he did, it was with obvious reluctance. "Yes, I . . . I suppose so."

Preacher asked, "How'd you boys get here?"

Stuart turned and pointed to a large, sturdy-looking covered wagon parked up the street in front of the hotel. A team of six mules was attached to it.

"That's our wagon."

Preacher rubbed his grizzled chin and wanted to know, "How much room you got in it?"

Stuart looked surprised by the question. "Well . . . some, I suppose. Of course we have all our surveying equipment, along with some supplies and personal belongings, but all that doesn't fill up the wagon."

"I know what you're thinking," Jamie said to Preacher.

The mountain man shrugged. "We're gonna be usin' Fletch and Clementine's wagon for our camp anyway. That other one ought to give us enough room for supplies for everybody."

"Wait a minute," Stuart said. "Our wagon belongs to the United States government—"

"And we're going to be on government business," Jamie told him. "Here's another thing you need to consider if you want to come along with us, mister. Preacher and I are in charge of this bunch. We'll be giving the orders, and you'll be following them. How does that sit with you?"

"You'll allow me to conduct the surveying and mapping activities I've been assigned?"

"If at all possible," Jamie said. "But there may be times when I tell you to sit tight, and you'll need to sit tight. You'll be expected to help out around camp, too."

"That sounds reasonable," Stuart said. "What do you think, Chester?"

"I suppose," Merrick replied, but again he sounded definitely less than enthusiastic about the whole affair.

Jamie nodded and said, "All right. I reckon you can come along if you're bound and determined to do it, as long as you know what you're getting into. Go get your wagon and bring it over here so we can load some of our supplies in it."

Stuart turned to Merrick. "You can do that, please, Chester."

Muttering to himself, Merrick walked away, heading toward the wagon parked at the hotel.

"Something else I just thought of," Jamie said. "I know you're not fighters, but did you fellas bring any guns with you anyway?"

"As a matter of fact, we did. It was thought we might need weapons for self-defense, or in case we decided to do some hunting. We have a pistol—it looks rather like the one you're carrying, Mr. MacCallister, so it may be the same type—along with a rifle and a shotgun."

"Ever actually *used* any of them guns?" Preacher asked.

"We've done a bit of target practice along the way." A note of pride entered Stuart's voice as he added, "And now and then I shot a few rabbits that we roasted over a campfire. So you see, we're not complete novices when it comes to surviving in the great outdoors."

Jamie and Preacher managed not to laugh at that. While they were trying not to grin, Fletch and Clementine emerged from the store. Fletch was carrying several paper-wrapped bundles of whatever Clementine had picked out to buy. They both stopped short when they saw Jamie and Preacher standing there talking to a stranger.

Jamie beckoned them over and said, "Fletch, Clementine, this is Mr. Noah Stuart. He's a government surveyor and mapmaker. He and a friend of his are going to be coming along with us. Stuart, this is Mr. and Mrs. Fletcher Wylie."

"Wait a minute," Stuart said. "You're taking a *woman* along with you?"

"That's right," Jamie said.

"Yet you balked about Chester and me accompanying you and acted like it was an insane idea. But you'll take a *woman* into Apache country."

"Just a minute, mister," Fletch said. "You haven't even said hello yet, and you're already talking like you don't want my wife around."

"I'm sorry." Stuart quickly swept off his hat, held it in front of his chest, and nodded politely to Clementine. "My apologies, Mrs. Wylie, and I assure you, it's an honor and a pleasure to make your acquaintance." He held out his hand to Fletch. "And I'm glad to meet you as well, Mr. Wylie."

Still frowning a little, Fletch shifted the packages in his arms so he could shake hands with the surveyor.

"I have no objection to the two of you coming along on this expedition," Stuart went on. "I was surprised, that's all."

"Because I'm a woman," Clementine said. "It just so happens that I'm a crack shot and have been riding horses practically my entire life, so I'm perfectly capable of taking care of myself, Mister . . . Stuart, was it?"

"Yes, ma'am. Noah Stuart. I assure you, I meant no disrespect."

"Good. Keep it that way." With a curt nod, she turned and headed for the wagon.

Jamie couldn't help but notice the way Stuart's eyes followed her for a second, although the surveyor moved his gaze away before it became too blatantly improper. Clearly, though, he found Clementine attractive.

Fletch must have noticed, too, because he gave Stuart a narrow-eyed stare, then followed Clementine. He threw a few suspicious glances back over his shoulder.

Stuart cleared his throat, put his hat back on, and said, "I should go help Chester with our wagon. Those mules can be awfully stubborn at times." He went down the steps at the end of the porch and cut across the plaza toward the hotel.

Preacher watched him go and said quietly, "Seems to me we might have a little problem brewin' there."

"You mean the way that hombre looked at Clementine?" Jamie said. "I saw that, too, and so did Fletch. Stuart better make sure it *doesn't* become a problem, or he and Merrick are liable to find themselves headed back to Santa Fe on their own."

"I don't reckon you knew anything about some surveyor comin' along with us?"

Jamie shook his head. "Owen Charlton didn't say anything about it to me, but I'm not surprised. Politicians always have to study on everything for a long time before they ever make a move. They never want to rub too many people the wrong way. Might cost 'em votes when the next election rolls around."

"The way that young fella was talkin' about how it might be years and years before anything ever gets done on that railroad makes another thought occur to me."

Jamie looked over at Preacher and said, "That maybe Owen had another motive for sending us down there that's just as strong as getting a look at the territory?"

"Yeah. He admitted he wants you to find his son . . . or at least find out what happened to him."

Jamie nodded slowly. "I think maybe that's more important to Owen than the government part. And he has to know, whether he'll admit it or not, what a slim chance there is that his boy Damon is still alive."

"So if he can't be rescued, his father wants him avenged . . . by us killin' as many of the varmints as we can."

"I reckon that's about the size of it," Jamie said. "He gets his vengeance, and the Office of the Interior gets a survey."

"Two birds with one stone, as the old sayin' goes. Or in this case . . . two Apaches with one stone . . . and likely a whole bunch more."

CHAPTER 16

While the rest of the supplies were being loaded into the two wagons, Fletch and Clementine went to the hotel to gather up the few things they had left there. When finished, they would move out to the campsite, so they would be ready when the time came to depart on the expedition the next morning.

It had been so long since they'd seen any sign of Clementine's brothers that Fletch worried they would let their guard down. Preacher and Jamie hadn't been sticking as close to them as they had at first, and it just seemed unlikely that the Mahoneys would make a move when there were so many people around. Because of that, Fletch resolved to be even more wary, so they wouldn't be taken by surprise.

"Imagine the nerve of that man, saying that I shouldn't come along just because I'm a woman," Clementine was saying as they went down the second-floor corridor toward their room.

"Well, I don't think that's exactly what he said," Fletch pointed out. "He was just upset because Preacher and Mr. MacCallister didn't want him and that other surveyor to join the group. But if he *had* objected because of, ah, who you are, you have to admit that it's not an uncommon attitude."

"I set him straight, though, didn't I?"

"You certainly did," Fletch said.

You also impressed him, he thought, *and I'm not sure I like that.* He had caught some of the other men looking at Clementine with a little too much interest, most notably that Mexican gunfighter, Ramirez, but all of them had treated her courteously and there hadn't been any real problem. Fletch knew quite well that Clementine was a beautiful young woman, and it was going to be impossible to keep men from looking at her. She had never shown any tendency to return that interest, though, and as long as that was the case, he figured they were all right.

But Noah Stuart was much different from those grizzled, scruffy, and in some cases filthy old mountain men. Stuart was younger, probably less than a decade older than he and Clementine. And despite clearly not being an outdoorsman, he was well-built and even handsome, Fletch supposed. He really wasn't a good judge of such things, but he had no doubt that Stuart was better-looking than *he* was. Anybody with eyes could see that.

"Does what we're about to do scare you, Fletch?"

The question caught him a little off guard. He said, "Ah . . . well . . . sure, a little. I mean, we're going into an area where there'll be a lot of danger. We'll have to be alert all the time, and there'll probably be some fighting. But I trust Preacher and Mr. MacCallister to do all they can to keep us safe, and sometimes you just have to take a risk. We talked about this when we decided we wanted to go along."

"I know. And I'm not backing out, not at all. It

would be even more dangerous for us to stay here or try to go on by ourselves." She opened the door of their room. "Even though they haven't been around, I know Clete and the other boys haven't given up—"

"That's right. We sure haven't," a harsh voice said as the door swung back.

Clementine cried out as someone grabbed her and jerked her farther into the room. Fletch's first instinct made him charge into the room after her. He dropped the packages he was carrying and clawed for the holstered Walker Colt on his hip.

But even as his hand closed on the revolver's grips and he started to lift it from the holster, something slammed into the side of his head and sent him spiraling down into darkness.

While the store clerks loaded the rest of the supplies into the surveyors' wagon, Jamie and Preacher explained the plan to Noah Stuart and Chester Merrick.

"We'll all travel together up to a certain point," Jamie said, "and then find a good spot to make our main camp. Once we've done that, you and the Wylies will stay there while the rest of us scout around for Apaches."

"You mean we'll be by ourselves?" Merrick asked with a look of dismay.

Jamie shook his head. "No, a couple of the men will stay with you."

Stuart said, "Two men won't be enough to fight off an Apache war party."

"Thought you figured those 'Paches 'd listen to reason, once everything was explained to 'em," Preacher drawled.

Stuart flushed. "Perhaps I was being a bit naïve. I don't mind admitting that I'm quite inexperienced when it comes to such things. But I'm trying to understand the reality of the situation."

"If there's trouble, you fellas may have to pitch in and fight," Jamie said. "I know Fletch and Clementine will. That'll be six well-armed defenders, and most small bands of warriors won't want to tangle with something like that. They like to have the odds on their side, and if they figure they'll have to pay too big a price, they'll leave you alone."

"But what if it's a bigger war party?" Merrick asked.

Jamie shrugged. "We'll find a place to camp where you ought to be able to hold off any attackers for a while, at least until the rest of us get back."

Stuart shook his head. "That isn't going to work. In order to conduct a proper survey and map the area, we'll have to move around quite a bit. Every day, in fact."

"That probably won't happen," Jamie said bluntly. "But we'll shift our camp as often as we can, and some days maybe you can take your wagon out and three or four of the boys will go with you while you do your surveying. I reckon we'll just have to wait until we get down there before we find out what's going to work and what isn't."

Stuart sighed and said, "I suppose. Honestly, though, this seems almost like an impossible task for all of us."

"Not impossible," Jamie said. "It'll just require a lot of hard work and guts."

"And more than a little luck," Preacher added. He was looking across the plaza as he spoke. From where he stood, he could see up the alley that ran alongside the hotel where Fletch and Clementine had been staying.

His eyes narrowed as he spotted movement at the far end of that alley. A man was back there, swinging up onto a saddled horse. There was nothing alarming about that, but the skin of the back of Preacher's neck suddenly prickled anyway.

The man turned his head a little and Preacher could see his profile, and that was enough for him to recognize the hombre.

"Blast it!" he exclaimed. "That's Clete Mahoney!"

Preacher jumped down from the porch, ignoring the steps at the end of it, and started running across the plaza. Pounding footsteps behind him told that Jamie was following him.

Preacher didn't yell. He didn't want Clete to know that he'd been spotted. That would just cause the man to flee sooner. So far, Clete was just sitting back there on his horse, saying something to somebody. He gestured for emphasis. Preacher figured the others were behind the hotel, too, and wherever the Mahoney brothers were, no matter what they were doing, they couldn't be up to any good.

Realizing that he couldn't run along the alley without attracting Clete's attention, Preacher veered toward the hotel entrance. As he bounded onto the gallery, Jamie caught up with him.

"You spotted the Mahoneys?" Jamie asked.

"Behind the hotel," Preacher replied as he flung open the door. He charged into the lobby with Jamie right behind him. The clerk at the desk gaped at the two big frontiersmen as they rushed through the room and headed toward the back of the hotel.

Not exactly sure where he was going, Preacher ran into the hotel's kitchen and asked the surprised Mexican cook, "Where's the back door?"

The wide-eyed man pointed without saying anything. Preacher started to draw his Dragoons, then realized that if the Mahoney brothers had grabbed Clementine and Fletch, he couldn't start throwing lead around without knowing what was going on. The risk was too great that his shots would hit one of the youngsters.

He slowed his rush and held up his hand in a signal for Jamie to do likewise. He grasped the knob and eased the door open a few inches, just enough to peer out into the alley behind the hotel.

What he saw made his jaw tighten with anger.

CHAPTER 17

Two of the Mahoney brothers were struggling to lift a limp Fletch Wylie onto a horse's back. Fletch appeared to be deadweight, so they were having a difficult time of it.

The fact that they were trying to take the young man with them told Preacher that Fletch wasn't actually dead. If he had been, they probably would have just left him in the hotel.

Another brother was already mounted and had Clementine on the horse with him, holding her securely with one arm clamped around her waist. They had gagged her with a bandanna so she couldn't cry out, and her wrists were lashed together in front of her. It looked like the piece of rope that bound her was pulled painfully tight.

That was a mighty sorry way to treat any woman, let alone your sister, Preacher thought, but from what Clementine had said about them, the Mahoney brothers were capable of much worse. That was what she was in for if Preacher and Jamie allowed them to ride away with her and Fletch.

They probably had in mind killing Fletch and

might even be planning to make Clementine watch, so that she would be too terrified to ever defy their will again.

Of course, knowing Clementine, Preacher was sure that would backfire on them and make her hate them more than ever, but he and Jamie didn't need to let things reach that point.

"I'll try to get Clementine away from that varmint who has her," Preacher said quietly. "Reckon you can tackle those two who are busy with Fletch?"

Jamie jerked his head in a curt nod. "Let's move."

Preacher took a deep breath and then flung the door wide open. Several steps led down to the ground outside. Preacher charged through the door and left his feet from the top step in a flying tackle that carried him into the brother who had hold of Clementine. The impact knocked Clementine and her captor out of the saddle and off the horse.

A huge leap landed Jamie behind the two men who had finally just succeeded in draping Fletch's unconscious form over the back of another horse. He grabbed them by the necks and jerked them away from the animal.

The powerful muscles in his arms and shoulders bunched as he rammed them into each other. Their hats flew off, and their heads clunked together with a solid thud. When Jamie let go of them, they collapsed like puppets with their strings cut.

Preacher hit the ground next to Clementine and the brother who'd been holding her. He rolled away so he'd have some room to move around, but as he did, a gun roared and a bullet kicked up dirt only inches from his head.

That had to be Clete shooting at him, he thought

as he rolled again and came up on one knee. He started to draw the right-hand Dragoon, halfway expecting to feel the shock of a bullet slamming into him before he could get the revolver out.

Someone yelled, "Hold it, mister! Drop that gun!"

Preacher glanced toward the alley that ran beside the hotel. Noah Stuart stood at the end of it, pointing a shotgun at Clete Mahoney. The gun in Clete's hand still had a wisp of smoke curling from its muzzle.

"I don't know who you are, boy, but this ain't none of your business," Clete growled at Stuart.

"I'm not a boy," Stuart snapped, "and you appear to be trying to kill an associate of mine, so it *is* my business."

Clete sneered. "You really plan on shooting me?"

"If he doesn't, I will," Jamie said. The distraction had given him time to draw his Walker. He thumbed back the hammer as he aimed it at Clete.

Preacher had his Dragoon out and added it to the array of weapons menacing Clete Mahoney. "I don't believe there's any way Stuart could miss with a scatter-gun at that range, but if he happened to, I reckon me and Jamie could ventilate you just fine, you skunk. You'd best drop that gun while you got the chance."

Even with those odds against him, Clete looked like he was thinking about it for a second or two before he lowered his gun and tossed it to the ground.

"Keep him covered, Stuart," Preacher told the surveyor. As he straightened to his feet, he turned his gun toward the brother who'd been holding Clementine and went on. "Help your sister up, you blasted varmint, and untie her. Get that gag outta her mouth, too. Hurry it up!"

Jamie covered the other two brothers, who were starting to show some signs of regaining consciousness after he'd rapped their heads together.

"You can't steal a girl from her own kin like this," Clete raged. "You got no right!"

Clementine spit the loosened gag out of her mouth and shouted, "I'm not a girl! I'm a grown woman! You're the one who doesn't have any right to me, Clete!"

"You'll be sorry you turned your back on your family," he said as he glared at her.

"I'm just sorry I was ever born into the same family that spawned the likes of you!"

Clete's face was so flushed with outrage that he looked like he was about to pop. He trembled a little, and Preacher knew that he wanted to do something, anything, to strike back at those he considered enemies.

Staring down the twin barrels of a shotgun was enough to give any man pause, though, even a loco varmint like Clete Mahoney, so he just sat there grinding his teeth and glowering.

Clementine turned away from Clete with a snort of contempt and hurried over to the horse where Fletch was draped facedown over the saddle. "Somebody help me!" she cried. "I don't know how bad he's hurt."

"He's all right," muttered the brother who had untied her. "Jerome just walloped him hard enough to knock him out for a spell."

Fletch moaned and shook his head a little, which made him moan even more.

Jamie kicked the other two brothers back to their

feet. They were still half-stunned, but he told them, "Get that young fella off that horse. Handle him careful, too. He's already been banged around enough."

Lew, Harp, and Jerome Mahoney all pitched in, clumsily untying Fletch and lifting him down from the horse. When they set him on his feet, he was unsteady and almost fell.

Clementine got hold of his left arm and pulled it over her shoulders to brace him up. "Come on. Let's get you back in the hotel so you can sit down."

One of the brothers said nervously, "That shot you fired is liable to bring the authorities, Clete. We better get outta here."

"Hold on there," Preacher said. "Maybe you boys ought to be locked up for a spell." That would keep the Mahoney brothers from following them when the expedition left Santa Fe, and that was a pretty appealing prospect.

Jamie must have been thinking the same thing, because he kept his Colt leveled at them and said, "That sounds like a pretty good idea to me, too." To Clete, he added, "Get down off that horse, mister, just to keep you from getting any ideas about taking off for the tall and uncut."

Clete looked like he wanted to argue, but Noah Stuart gestured with the shotgun and Clete climbed down grudgingly from his mount.

"Rattle your hocks over next to your brothers," Preacher told him.

Clete shuffled over to join the others. The four Mahoney brothers stood there looking at Preacher, Jamie, and Stuart as if staking them out on anthills would be too good for them.

A couple of deputy marshals showed up a few

minutes later, checking on the report of a gunshot behind the hotel. Santa Fe was still enough of a frontier settlement, despite having been founded more than two hundred years earlier, that an occasional shot often didn't draw much attention, especially at night. A gun going off in the middle of town in broad daylight was looked into, though.

Although the Mahoney brothers blustered and yelled about being treated unfairly, Jamie dropped hints about working for the government and being in town on official business. His name and reputation were well known to start with, so to protect themselves from potential trouble as much as anything, the deputies disarmed the Mahoneys and marched them off to jail, still grumbling as they went.

"We'll get to the bottom of this, Mr. MacCallister," one of the lawmen hung back and promised. "Will you be around town if the marshal needs to talk to you?"

"Probably not, but I'll be glad to speak with him when we get back," Jamie said.

That seemed to satisfy the deputies.

Once they and their prisoners were gone, Preacher turned to Noah Stuart and said, "We're much obliged to you for givin' us a hand there, son."

"Well, you said if there was trouble, Chester and I might have to pitch in and help," Stuart replied. "The way you and Mr. MacCallister ran off so abruptly, I figured something was wrong and this might be a chance to get started on that. So I grabbed the shotgun out of our wagon and came along the alley to see what was going on back here."

"You showed up just at the right time," Jamie told him. "And the way you threw down on Clete Mahoney with that scattergun was mighty impressive."

"Yes, well, there was one problem with that," Stuart said with a weak smile. He broke the shotgun open and showed Preacher and Jamie the empty barrels. "I was in such a hurry I forgot to load it. I figured that man didn't know that, so I let him think I was going to blow him off his horse."

The two older men just stared at him for a moment, then broke out in laughter. Jamie slapped Stuart on the back and said, "Noah, you just might do to ride the river with, after all!"

CHAPTER 18

Carrying the shotgun tucked under his arm, Noah Stuart went back across the plaza to his wagon while Jamie and Preacher headed into the hotel to check on Fletch and Clementine.

They were sitting on a sofa in the lobby with the solicitous desk clerk hovering around them. Some of the guests had gathered nearby and were looking on curiously. Clementine had a wet cloth and held it against Fletch's head.

"I'm all right, I tell you," he said, sounding annoyed. Jamie couldn't tell if he was annoyed with Clementine or himself.

Clementine took the cloth away from his head. Jamie saw that Fletch had a pretty good lump on his noggin. It had bled some, enough to leave a red stain on the wet cloth, but mostly it just looked like the result of a good walloping.

"I think you need to see a doctor," Clementine said. "There's no telling how bad you're hurt."

"I'm feeling a lot better now," Fletch insisted. "I've got a headache, that's all." He looked up and noticed Jamie and Preacher, then got to his feet in spite of

Clementine's objection. "What happened to Clete and the others?" he asked.

"Some deputies showed up and hauled 'em off to the hoosegow," Preacher replied. "I figure they'll be locked up for a while."

"And that's a good reason for us to go ahead and get out of Santa Fe as soon as we can," Jamie added. "I'd like to put some distance behind us while they're locked up."

Fletch nodded. The movement of his head made him wince a little, but he said, "That's a good idea. We'll be ready to go in just a few minutes."

Clementine stood up. "I'm not sure you're in any shape to travel, Fletcher. You could be seriously hurt—"

"I'm fine." His tone was a little sharper than he intended. As she made a sad little face, he put his hands on her shoulders and went on. "I'm sorry, Clementine. But I really am all right. I can tell. I just want us to be on our way again while your brothers can't cause any trouble for us."

"Well . . . I guess I understand that," she said.

Preacher said, "Hold on a minute. Fletch, look at me. Open your eyes good and wide."

"Why—"

"Just do it," Preacher told him.

"All right," Fletch said. He opened his eyes wide and looked intently at Preacher.

The mountain man studied them with his head cocked a little to the side. After a moment, he nodded in apparent satisfaction.

"Miss Clementine, I believe ol' Fletch here is fine as frog hair," Preacher declared. "His eyes look normal as they can be. I've seen plenty of fellas who got walloped mighty hard on the ol' *cabeza*. The ones who was bad hurt, you could always tell it by how their eyes looked later. I reckon that headache he's sportin' is the worst thing that's gonna happen to him 'cause of this little set-to."

"Are you sure?" Clementine asked him with a suspicious frown.

"I wouldn't lie to you," Preacher said.

"Well . . . all right, then." She added to Fletch, "But I'm going to be keeping a close eye on you."

He summoned up a smile. "I've never complained about that, have I? As long as I can keep a close eye on *you*, too."

Jamie chuckled. "Save your sweet talk for later, both of you. Grab your possibles. Preacher, you mind waiting here until they're ready to go and then coming back to the wagons with them?"

"Nope," the mountain man said. "We shouldn't have let the two of you go back to the hotel by yourselves a while ago, to start with. Might've saved all the trouble and Fletch that clout on the noggin if we'd been a mite more careful."

Jamie left Preacher and the two young people at the hotel and went back across the plaza to the store where the last of the supplies were being loaded into the surveyors' wagon.

"Is Mr. Wylie all right?" Noah Stuart asked as Jamie joined them.

"I think so. He'll be along in a few minutes, and so will Miss Clementine and Preacher. Are you fellas ready to head out to the camp?"

"As ready as we're going to be, I suppose," Stuart replied. He had placed the shotgun on the floorboards of the driver's box at the front of the wagon.

As he reached over and patted the weapon's smooth stock, he added, "I've loaded this gun, by the way. If we need it again, I won't be taken by surprise."

"What about the pistol and rifle you mentioned?" Jamie asked. "Are they loaded, too?"

"They are." Stuart smiled slightly. "I don't think Chester likes that very much."

"Loaded guns can go off," Chester Merrick said. "That worries me."

Jamie told him, "An unloaded gun might as well be a hammer, except you can't drive a nail as well with it. You'll get used to how things are out here on the frontier, Mr. Merrick."

"Perhaps," the man said doubtfully.

To be honest, Jamie kind of doubted it, too.

Preacher helped Fletch and Clementine with their bags. He didn't expect any more trouble since the Mahoney brothers had been hauled off to jail, but he remained alert anyway. Problems could always arise from other sources, and it was also possible Clete Mahoney might have argued the authorities around to letting him and his brothers go.

Nothing happened, though, and a short time later they arrived at the wagons, stowed the last of the gear away, and were ready to depart.

Preacher walked over to the stable to get his and Jamie's horses and rode back with Dog trotting alongside the mounts. Jamie swung up into the saddle and moved into position flanking the Wylie wagon on the right. Preacher was on the left. Stuart and Merrick would bring up the rear in their vehicle.

"Everybody ready to go?" Jamie called.

"We're ready," Fletch declared. Preacher could tell the young man was trying to sound firm and determined, but even so, he heard a hint of a quaver in Fletch's voice. They were setting out on what could prove to be a long, very dangerous journey. Of course, their trip so far hadn't been all that easy.

"Ready back here," Noah Stuart said, holding the shotgun across his knees.

Chester Merrick was beside him on the driver's seat, handling the reins.

"Let's move out, then." Jamie didn't do anything dramatic like wave his arm over his head the way a wagon master would, giving the command to roll the wagons. He just heeled his horse into motion as he spoke.

On the other side of the Wylie wagon, Preacher did likewise.

They headed out of Santa Fe toward the camp in the foothills. Preacher's head was on a swivel as he searched for any sign of potential trouble. That vigilance would only increase once they got into Apache country. Down there, even a moment's carelessness could cost a man his life.

Not for the first time, Preacher wondered if they were making a mistake by allowing Fletch and Clementine to come with them. Unfortunately, this was a true "damned if you do, damned if you don't" situation. When that was the case, all a fella could do was reach a decision and work hard to make the best of it.

Jamie had warned the other men that they would be breaking camp and setting out on their mission when he, Preacher, and the Wylies returned from

Santa Fe, so everyone had their gear packed and ready to go. The addition of Stuart and Merrick to the party came as a surprise. Jamie introduced the surveyors to everyone. The looks of the scruffy old mountain men, the slick Mexican gunfighter, the towering Crow warrior, and the bitter half-breed Comanche seemed to intimidate Chester Merrick and make him even more nervous. Only the gravely silent Swedish brothers didn't appear to bother him.

Noah Stuart just nodded and said hello to the other members of the group. Preacher could tell that he noticed how heavily armed they all were.

After the introductions, Stuart turned on the wagon seat, reached through the opening in the canvas cover, and rummaged around for a minute or so. When he faced forward again, he had the revolver in his hand. He stuck it behind his belt.

Preacher moved Horse closer to the surveyors' wagon and commented, "Now you look like you're armed for bear, too."

"I just want to be prepared," Stuart said. "Chester and I intend to carry our weight and do our part on this expedition. If that means fighting Indians, then so be it."

"You're liable to get your chance to do that, especially if those 'Paches figure out you're surveyin' a possible route for the railroad. They're smart enough to know that such a thing 'd bring more and more white folks into territory they regard as theirs. That'll make 'em madder than they are to start with . . . and that's pretty doggoned mad."

Chester Merrick said, "Savages can't be allowed to hold back the advance of civilization. Have you heard of Manifest Destiny, Mr. Preacher?"

"No, mister," the mountain man said. "And Manifest Destiny is all well and good until you butt heads with somebody who figures *his* destiny is different from yours but just as important. Most times, there's only one way to settle that argument."

Before either of the newcomers could respond to that, Jamie called, "Mount up!" to the rest of the group. He waved to Preacher, who turned Horse and heeled the rangy gray stallion ahead.

The other men formed up around the wagons. Starting out, Audie, Nighthawk, Ramirez, and Dupre flanked to the left. Powder Pete, Tennysee, Deadlead, and Edgerton rode to the right. Pugh, Greybull, Dog Brother, and the Molmberg brothers brought up the rear.

Up at the point, Jamie turned his horse around, sat his saddle as he faced the others, and called, "Everybody ready?"

He got nods and a few affirmative answers. He glanced over at Preacher.

The mountain man said, "Let's go find some Apaches."

This time Jamie wasn't able to resist. He turned his horse, waved his arm over his head, and bellowed, "Move out!"

CHAPTER 19

Jamie's original plan hadn't included Fletch and Clementine or the two government surveyors. He had figured that a group of hard-bitten Indian fighters on horseback could move pretty rapidly. A week should have been enough time to cover the distance between Santa Fe and their destination in what were now the far southern sections of New Mexico Territory, along the current border with Mexico.

With two wagons and four people who weren't accustomed to frontier travel, that plan had to be thrown out the window. The group could only cover about half as much ground each day as Jamie had anticipated. The delay was a mite galling but wouldn't really make much difference in the long run, Jamie told himself. The Apaches would still be there when he and his companions made it to where they were going.

Shortly after the middle of every afternoon, they began looking for a place with good water and grass where they could make camp that night. For the first few days, finding such a spot wasn't difficult. But the farther south they went, the more arid the landscape became. Different shades of brown replaced much of the green of vegetation. Whenever they found a good-flowing creek, Jamie had the water barrels filled before the group pulled out the next morning.

"Closer we get to *mañana* land, the drier it's gonna be," Preacher commented one evening as they sat around the campfire where Audie had a pot of stew bubbling.

Clementine had offered to do all the cooking, but Audie wouldn't hear of that. He'd always been proud of his cuisine, as he put it. Tennysee had asked what sort of critter a *kweezine* was, and whether it was better boiled or fried.

"Do you skin one of them *kweezines* or pluck it?" Powder Pete wanted to know.

"I am surrounded by uncouth bumpkins," Dupre declared. "If we had the necessary ingredients, I would prepare French cuisine for you. Although I'm certain the effort would be wasted on your uneducated palates."

Greybull rumbled, "Well, whatever it is, we know they got them kweezines in France, too. Dupre just said so."

"Umm," Nighthawk said.

The Molmberg brothers nodded in agreement.

After Preacher's comment about the arid climate, Noah Stuart asked, "Where is this *mañana* land you speak of, Preacher? I don't recall ever seeing that name on any of the maps of the region I've studied."

Preacher took a sip of coffee from the tin cup he held and said, "I was talkin' about Old *Mejico*. You ask just about any hombre down there when he's gonna get around to doin' somethin', and he'll tell you, '*mañana*.' That's their lingo for tomorrow."

"Don't get the wrong idea about those folks, though," Jamie added. "Most of them are mighty hard workers when they need to be. They just might not want to admit it all the time. But the farmers down where we're headed . . . *peons*, they're called . . . will work from can to can't to keep their families fed."

"There are farmers in the area?" Chester Merrick said. "Once I heard how bad the Apaches are, I assumed the region was completely uninhabited except for the savages."

Preacher said, "No matter how sorry the land is or how dangerous the place may be, somewhere you'll find a fella stubborn enough to poke some seeds in the ground and hope that a crop'll come up."

"It's been that way since the beginning of civilization," Audie said. "For thousands and thousands of years. I'd go so far as to say there wouldn't even *be* any civilization without those stubborn men."

"And yet the Indians don't farm," Noah Stuart said.

"Some do," Jamie responded. "And I hate to say it, but in the long run, those are the ones who stand the best chance of surviving."

Clementine asked, "Why do you hate to say it?"

Jamie gazed off into the night, his eyes seeming to see into the far, far distance. "Because the Indians who spend their lives hunting and fishing are the ones most like me. I figure Preacher's the same way, and so are most of these other men."

Mutters of agreement came from the mountain men.

"And that means our days are numbered," Jamie went on. "There'll come a time, probably in the next fifty years, when there's no room in the West anymore for the likes of us. The railroads will run everywhere, and the maps that are drawn by men like Noah here will be full of towns and cities. The sort of lives that we've lived . . . and those of the Apache . . . and Dog Brother's people, the Comanche . . . will be nothing but fading shadows then."

A solemn silence hung over the group around the campfire for a few moments, before Clementine finally said, "That's sad, Mr. MacCallister. But I'm looking forward to reaching California. It's civilized, isn't it?"

"Mostly," Jamie said with a smile. "Anyway, most womenfolk are going to prefer that. It's in their nature to want a safe place to bring up their families."

Preacher said, "If it wasn't for the gals, us gents 'd never stop slaughterin' each other till the whole derned bunch was wiped out."

Audie said, "I sometimes wonder what some of my colleagues back at the university would have thought of you, Preacher."

"Most likely they'd 've run screamin' the other way soon as they clapped their eyes on me."

"Umm," Nighthawk said.

"You're right," Audie said. He gave the pot a stir. "The stew does indeed appear to be ready."

A couple of days later, they came to a good-sized stream that followed a twisting path between two rocky bluffs topped by scrubby brush. Preacher scouted out a spot where the northern bluff had fallen in on itself enough to create a trail. The wagons would be able to get down it, although the descent would be a rough, jolting one. The drivers would have to take it slow and easy or risk breaking an axle.

"Hold on," Jamie told Fletch Wylie before the young

man could start down the rugged slope. Jamie lifted a hand to reinforce the order to stop.

Fletch hauled back on the lines and brought the team to a halt. "Don't we have to get across this stream to continue going south?"

"Yeah, but it's not a good idea to start down into a canyon like that when you don't know if there's another way out. Preacher and Dog have gone on ahead to look for one." Jamie hipped around in the saddle and pointed to a low, grayish-blue line on the western horizon. "See those little mountains over yonder? All it would take is a good-sized thunderstorm over there for a flash flood to come rampaging along this river and fill up the whole canyon."

Clementine leaned forward on the seat and peered toward the stream. "I hoped we might make camp down there tonight. I can see some little trees and some shade and grass. It actually looks pleasant."

"It does," Jamie agreed, "but it's not worth the risk until we know more."

She beckoned him closer and lowered her voice to say, "I thought maybe I could go up around that bend and . . . and take a bath in the stream. I feel like I have at least an inch of trail dust on me!"

"Well, you might be able to do that," Jamie allowed. "One person could climb out of there a lot faster than we could break camp and get the wagons and mules and horses out."

"Make that two people," Fletch said. "Clementine's not going to do that without me going along to stand guard."

"We'll see." Jamie wasn't going to make up his mind or even discuss the matter any more until Preacher got back from scouting for a spot on the southern bank the wagons could handle. "For now we'll just wait here."

He didn't have to explain to the other frontiersmen why they were stopping, but Noah Stuart was curious and asked about it. Jamie explained again. Stuart nodded, seeming to grasp the danger of flash floods right away.

Chester Merrick pointed to the distant mountains. "But the sky is clear over there. There aren't any storms."

"They can blow up in a hurry," Jamie said, "and they can dump a lot of rain in just a little while."

Merrick shook his head. "It's so dry around here, you'd think that it never rained."

"It doesn't very often. I reckon that's why it tries to make up for that when it does."

The men loosened their cinches but didn't unsaddle their horses, since they didn't know how long it would be before Preacher returned. Some of them walked down to the stream to fill their canteens. Fletch brought up a bucket of water and let all the animals drink from it.

"If Preacher can't find a way out of the canyon on the other side," Clementine said to Jamie, "what will we do?"

"We'll have to go one way or the other and follow the river until the canyon peters out and we can get across."

"But that could take us miles out of our way, couldn't it?"

"It could," Jamie agreed. "But we don't have to be anywhere at any particular time."

"I know." Worry lines creased Clementine's forehead, and her teeth caught at her bottom lip for a second. "I was just thinking . . . We don't know what happened with my brothers back up in Santa Fe."

"I'm hoping the judge threw them in jail for thirty days for disturbing the peace the way they did."

"But he could have sentenced them to less time than that, or even dropped the charges against them entirely." Clementine turned, shaded her eyes with her hand, and gazed to the north as if she could see all those miles they had covered since leaving Santa Fe. "They could be coming up behind us right now."

"They could be," Jamie said, "but you've got to remember, you're traveling with eighteen armed men. Those brothers of yours would have to be plumb loco to try anything with a bunch like that protecting you."

"You don't know them the way I do, Mr. MacCallister," Clementine said solemnly. "Plumb loco may be the *nicest* way anybody could describe them."

CHAPTER 20

Preacher returned late that afternoon, with Dog trotting along beside Horse. The big cur's tongue lolled out redly because of the heat.

Jamie saw them coming and walked to the head of the trail to meet them. "Have any luck?" he asked the mountain man as he held up a hand in greeting.

Preacher reined the stallion to a halt and turned in the saddle to point toward the west. "There's a place about a mile over yonder where the wagons can get up to the top of the bluff. It'll be even rougher 'n this trail, but they can make it, I reckon. Be a good idea to unload the wagons and hitch both teams to 'em, one at a time, when they go to pullin' up."

Jamie nodded slowly as he considered what Preacher had just told him. "That's a job that'll take a while. It's too late in the day to start on it now."

"That's what I'm thinkin', too," the mountain man agreed.

"We'll stay here tonight and cross the canyon first thing in the morning. We can reach that trail you found on the south side without any trouble?"

"Yeah, the bank's wide enough for the wagons on

both sides, and there's a place part of the way where the river widens out a mite and shallows down. Good solid bed for fordin'. That won't be a problem."

Jamie was glad to hear it. While Preacher dismounted and began unsaddling Horse, Jamie went to inform the others of the plan.

"So we'll make camp right here tonight," he concluded, "and head down into the canyon in the morning."

"You say we're going to unload the wagons before they start up on the other side?" Edgerton asked.

"That's right."

"That means we'll have to carry all the supplies up, crate by crate and bag by bag."

Jamie nodded. "That's about the size of it. You have a problem with that?"

"I didn't sign on to be a pack mule," the jug-eared frontiersman said.

A few of the other men nodded, expressing the same sentiment, and Dog Brother grunted.

"Shoot, don't worry about that," Greybull said. "I don't mind totin' the supplies up the slope. They won't seem so heavy to a fella as big as me."

"Ummm," Nighthawk added.

"Nighthawk volunteers, as well," Audie said.

For a moment, Jamie regarded the group with narrowed eyes. Then he shook his head and a harsh note entered his voice as he said, "Everybody does his part. Nobody's going to sit around while Greybull and Nighthawk do extra shares of the work." He fixed his gaze on Edgerton. "And anybody who doesn't like that is free to turn around and ride back to Santa Fe."

"I never said I wouldn't do my share," Edgerton

responded in a surly tone. "Just said I didn't much cotton to it, that's all. I don't have to like everything that comes out of your mouth, do I, MacCallister?"

"Nope. You've just got to do as you're told."

Edgerton stared coolly at him for a second, then shrugged. "Sure. Never intended otherwise."

Jamie nodded, glad that Edgerton hadn't forced the issue. He wasn't afraid of the man, but where they were going, with the task they were facing, he couldn't afford even a hint of mutiny among the group. It was best that they all understood that now.

They began unsaddling their horses and unhitching the mule teams for the night. Clementine searched among the brush for broken branches that would provide fuel for a fire. She came back with an armful of them and headed toward a cluster of rocks that would make a good location for the fire.

Ramirez watched her go about this chore with open admiration, Jamie noted. The gunfighter admired Clementine too much. That was liable to lead to trouble.

That thought had just passed through Jamie's mind when a gunshot suddenly blasted. He'd been looking in Ramirez's direction but hadn't even seen the man's gun hand move. The Mexican had a Colt gripped in his fist and powder smoke wisped from the barrel.

Clementine had cried out when the shot sounded, and in her surprise, she had flung the armload of firewood into the air. It clattered down around her as the echoes of the shot rolled away.

Instinct caused several of the men to react, as well. Jamie's Walker Colt was in his hand, and Preacher had pulled his Dragoons. Deadlead gripped his revolver, as did Dog Brother. Some of the mountain men lifted their rifles.

"What in blazes!" Jamie barked. "Ramirez, drop that gun!" He trained the Walker on the Mexican gunfighter. "Now!"

Ramirez didn't drop the gun, but he slid it back into its holster. With a sneer, he said, "What you should be doing instead of threatening me, Señor MacCallister, is asking what I was shooting at."

"Well? What *were* you shooting at?"

Instead of answering directly, Ramirez smiled at Clementine and said, "Look at the ground beside you, Señora Wylie."

Clementine looked down, then cried out again and jumped away from the rocks where she'd intended to place the firewood.

Jamie looked, too, and saw the long, thick, scaly shape still writhing there. A couple of strides took him to Clementine's side. The gunfighter's shot had blasted the snake's head away completely, but the rattles on its tail, still buzzing faintly as the body spasmed, identified it clearly.

Pugh reached down, picked up the dead snake, and with a flick of the knife in his hand, cut off the rattles. He held them up and counted to twelve. "Dadgum!" he exclaimed. "This varmint was an ol' grandpa."

"How . . . how can you tell that?" Clementine asked. She was still clearly shaken.

"One year for ever' rattle," Pugh explained. He held out the grisly souvenir. "Here you go, Miss Clementine, if you want it."

She shuddered. "No, I don't think so."

"I'll take it," Ramirez said as he stepped forward and took the rattles from Pugh. "I killed the thing, after all." He smirked at Clementine again. "And saved your life, in all likelihood, señora."

Fletch had been tending to the mules when the shot rang out, but had reached her side. He tried to put a comforting hand on Clementine's shoulder, but she didn't seem to notice that as she stepped over to Ramirez and lightly rested her fingertips on his forearm for a second.

"Thank you, Señor Ramirez," she said. "I don't know how you spotted that terrible creature among the rocks, but I'm certainly glad you did."

"My pleasure," Ramirez said. "It would have been a shame if it had bitten you."

"Yeah, thanks," Fletch put in, but his gratitude sounded pretty grudging.

Jamie figured the young man was relieved and grateful that Clementine was all right but wished that he had been the one to save her instead of Ramirez.

"Rattlers are all over this part of the country," Preacher said. "Keep your eyes on the ground, watch where you're steppin', and don't never stick your hand in a bunch of rocks without pokin' around in there first with a branch or a rifle barrel. A bite from one o' them critters won't always kill a man, but more often than not, it does."

"I suppose I should pick up this firewood I threw all over the place . . ." Clementine began.

"Lemme do that for you, ma'am," Pugh offered. He took his hat off and held it in front of his chest as he volunteered.

"Thank you, Mr. Pugh. You're a . . . a gentleman."

"Well, I may not smell like one, but I got a good heart."

While Pugh was doing that, Dog Brother picked up the dead snake and studied it.

Ramirez, who held the rattles in his left hand, said, "Are you going to eat that, Indian?"

"Rattlesnake's not bad eating," Dog Brother replied, "but I was thinking the skin would make a good band for my hat. Unless you believe it belongs to you as well."

"Take it, savage. I have no use for it."

Dog Brother tensed at the insult. Jamie and Preacher watched as the two men stared coldly at each other. They were ready to step in if gunplay threatened to erupt. They couldn't afford to be killing each other off when they hadn't even found any Apaches yet.

But then Dog Brother turned and strode away.

Preacher watched him go and said quietly, "Them two's gonna get right down to it one o' these days."

"As long as it's after we've done our job, they can shoot each other to doll rags for all I care," Jamie said.

Once the fire was built, Audie got started preparing supper, so Clementine went to Jamie and asked if she could go down into the canyon and take that bath she had mentioned earlier.

"Is Fletch still going with you?"

"Of course."

Jamie nodded. "Go ahead, then. Since we're not camping down there, no need to go around the bend. Just move upstream or down a ways. Don't take a long time about it, though. The sun'll be down in less than an hour, and it'll get dark down there sooner than it will up here."

"All right. Thank you, Mr. MacCallister. I just can't stand all this dirt any longer."

Jamie smiled. "Hate to tell you this, but where we're going, it's liable to be even drier and dirtier."

"Well, I suppose I'll deal with that when the time comes." She went to the wagon, took a clean shirt from one of the bags in the back, and told Fletch, "Let's go. Mr. MacCallister said not to waste any time."

Fletch grinned and said, "Am I gonna wash your back for you?"

She gave him a stern look. "I don't think there's time for that today."

"Well, all right," he said as he shook his head disappointedly. He carried Clementine's rifle as they started down into the canyon, while she took the clean shirt, a towel, and a hunk of soap.

Neither of them were aware that two pairs of eyes were watching them intently, one pair from the camp and the other from the rugged bluff along the southern side of the river.

CHAPTER 21

"Turn around," Clementine said when they had gone a couple of hundred yards downstream.

"Turn around?" Fletch repeated. "I'm your husband. I don't have to turn around!"

"You do if I ask you to," she insisted. "You're supposed to be standing guard, and that means watching for trouble. You can't do that if you're staring at me."

Reluctantly, he said, "I reckon you're right. But like Mr. Edgerton said earlier about toting supplies, I don't have to like it."

Clementine nodded. "That's what every woman wants to be compared to. Toting supplies." She twirled a finger. "Turn around."

Fletch sighed and turned around. He heard slight sounds and knew his wife was taking her clothes off.

"Maybe I'll make it up to you later," Clementine said. Water splashed softly as she waded into the river. "It's cold! How can the water be cold when we're in the middle of this country that's almost a desert?"

"The stream comes from those mountains back to the west, and they've still got snow on 'em at this time of year. That goes into the water as it starts to melt."

"I suppose. I'm getting used to it, anyway."

Fletch stood there looking up and down the canyon as he listened to the splashing of Clementine bathing in the river. He tried to watch the tops of the bluffs as well, but other images kept crowding into his mind. He couldn't stop thinking about how Clementine probably looked right now. He could just imagine the fading reddish-gold light playing over her wet, fair skin . . .

A faint rustling in the brush along the stream about twenty yards away suddenly intruded on those pleasant thoughts. Fletch turned quickly toward the sound and was in time to see a branch moving. Something—or some*one*—was back there, and to Fletch's mind, the only reason for anybody to be lurking along this stretch of river was to spy on Clementine bathing.

He immediately thought of Ramirez and the way the gunfighter had been eyeing her ever since they'd started on this journey, but it could be one of the other men, too. All of them had cast lustful glances Clementine's way at one time or another, or so it seemed to Fletch, anyway.

A part of him wanted to bring the rifle to his shoulder and send a slug whistling through that growth, just to teach whoever it was a lesson, but he knew he couldn't do that. Angry though he might be, he didn't want to risk killing anybody. But he called over his shoulder, "Clementine, get down in the water as much as you can!" and charged toward the spot where he'd seen the brush moving.

He heard her exclaim, "Fletch, what in the world—" behind him, but then he didn't have time to pay attention to anything else she might have said. Holding the rifle at a slant across his chest as he hurried forward, he shouted, "Whoever you are, mister, come on out of there!"

At that moment, his right foot came down on a rock that rolled underneath him. Thrown off balance, he stumbled and leaned far to his right as he struggled to stay on his feet.

That near-mishap turned out to be lucky, because it saved his life. The arrow that whipped out of the brush missed him by only inches as it flew past him on the left. If he hadn't stumbled, it would have driven deep into his chest.

Fletch barely caught a glimpse of the feathered shaft, and it took his stunned mind a second to realize what he had just seen. He finally caught his balance as a wiry, almost naked Apache warrior burst out of the brush and lunged toward him, the knife in his hand upraised to strike.

Fletch had let go of the rifle with his left hand when he almost fell so that he could windmill that arm and try to stay upright. He held the weapon in only his right hand, but he was able to thrust his finger through the trigger guard and fire the rifle one-handed. With no time to aim, it was just a wild shot in the Apache's general direction.

Even so, Fletch's instincts served him well. The bullet struck the warrior in the upper left arm. The impact was enough to stop the man's charge and twist him sideways. He didn't cry out, nor did he drop the knife in his other hand, but the shot stopped his attack long enough for Fletch to drop the rifle and haul out the Walker Colt holstered on his hip.

Fletch had the revolver out in plenty of time, but before he could raise it and fire, his foot slipped again on another rock. This time, his leg shot out from under him and dumped him over backward. He landed at the edge of the stream, and the point of his right elbow struck the ground hard enough that it numbed his entire arm. He couldn't make his muscles work to lift the Colt.

The Apache had righted himself and came at Fletch again, hatred and a killing frenzy blazing in his eyes. In the fading light, he was like a lethal red shadow as he closed in on the momentarily helpless young man.

Three shots roared out, the booming reports coming so close together they sounded like one long, rolling peal of gun-thunder. The bullets crashed into the Apache's back and flung him forward. He stumbled past Fletch and pitched facedown into the river, throwing water up in a big splash around him.

As the splash subsided, the Apache's body rocked a little but didn't move otherwise. The water began to turn red around him from the blood leaking out of the three holes grouped so closely between his shoulder blades that a man's palm could have covered them.

Except for the fading echoes, an eerie silence hung over the canyon for several seconds. Then shouts sounded from the top of the northern bluff as Preacher and Jamie started down the trail to see what the commotion was about. Most of the rest of the group followed them. Dog bounded on ahead.

Fletch lay there stunned at the river's edge. Pins and needles jabbed up and down his right arm as feeling began to flow back into it. He stared at the Apache corpse floating beside him, bobbing gently on the current. The warrior's feet in high-topped moccasins had caught on some rocks, and that kept the body from washing downstream.

Fletch jerked his head the other way to peer wide-eyed toward Clementine. Relief flooded through him as he saw that she was all right. She had done what he told her and crouched as low as she could in the river. Only her head and bare shoulders were above the surface. The water had darkened her fair hair, and it lay plastered to her skin. Her shocked eyes were as big around as Fletch's were.

More sounds from the brush made Fletch twist that way again.

Ramirez stepped out, smiling as he reloaded the gun in his hand. "No need to thank me," he said, ignoring Fletch and looking at Clementine. "I am always happy to assist such a beautiful señorita . . . I meant *señora*, of course."

The gunfighter didn't mean that at all, Fletch thought. Ramirez was deliberately dismissing the fact that Clementine was a married woman. Clearly, he had no respect for that.

But just as clearly, he had saved Fletch's life. Fletch knew he wouldn't have recovered in time to prevent the Apache from killing him.

Still grinning at Clementine, Ramirez went on. "Of course, if you wish to come out of there and express your gratitude to me—"

"Clementine, you stay right where you are!" Fletch called as he struggled to his feet. He fought down the impulse to point his gun at Ramirez and order the man to move away.

Ramirez was holding a revolver, too. If Fletch made a threatening move, the Mexican might shoot him and claim self-defense. Fletch was proud of the progress he'd made at gun-handling, but he knew he was still nowhere near the same lethal level of skill that Ramirez possessed.

Ramirez sneered at him. "You should be grateful to me as well, boy. That savage would have killed you and taken your woman with him back to his village. He would have made her his slave and given her half a dozen squalling Apache brats of her own."

"Shut your filthy mouth," Fletch said through clenched teeth.

"Have a care," Ramirez said. "I don't care whether you thank me, but you will not insult me."

Preacher and Jamie walked up, not rushing since the immediate threat appeared to be over.

Preacher told the big cur, "Dog, search." As Dog bounded off, the mountain man went on. "If there are any more 'Pache hereabouts he'll find 'em and let us know."

"You reckon this was a lone scout?" Jamie asked as he frowned at the corpse floating in the shallow water.

Preacher rubbed his grizzled chin. "Mighty far north for a whole war party. It don't surprise me to see one of the varmints venturin' this far from his usual stompin' ground, though. They're notional folks."

"From here on out, we'd better have even sharper eyes. If there are any more around, they're liable to head back south and carry the word that a bunch of white men with two wagons are headed toward 'em."

"Not all of us are white men," Ramirez snapped as he finally holstered his Colt.

"To the Apaches, you might as well be," Jamie said. "They hate Mexicans just as bad. Maybe even worse."

Ramirez shrugged in acceptance of that statement.

Jamie jerked his head toward the corpse and told the other men, "All right, get him out of there. We'll find a place where we can cave in the bank on top of him. I don't feel like going to any more trouble than that."

"I got the carcass," Greybull said as he stepped forward to lift the dead warrior out of the water. He draped the body over his shoulder as if it didn't weigh any more than a bag of flour.

While several of the men trooped off to take care of that grim chore, Jamie turned to the river and said, "We'll clear out of here now, Clementine, so you'd better go ahead and finish that bath of yours. Then you and Fletch get back up to camp as soon as you can. It'll be dark soon."

"All right," she said from where she crouched in the water.

Fletch figured that position had to be getting pretty awkward and uncomfortable.

"I'm sorry, Mr. MacCallister."

"Nothing to be sorry about," Jamie told her. "Just bad luck. We didn't figure on running into any Apaches just yet. But it could have been a lot worse."

Fletch knew that was true. The words threatened to choke him, but he said, "Ramirez . . . thank you."

"*De nada*," the gunfighter said. "I didn't do it for you." He turned and strode away.

Quietly, Preacher said, "You know the only reason he was down here where he could help you out is because he was tryin' to sneak a look at Clementine, don't you, Fletch?"

"I know," Fletch said. That disturbing thought had already occurred to him.

"Keep a tight rein on your temper, son," Jamie advised. "It won't do Clementine any good if you go and get yourself killed."

"If I tried to shoot it out with Ramirez, you mean?"

Preacher said, "You ain't up to that yet."

"Yet?" Fletch repeated. "You think I ever will be?"

"I'd just as soon we never find out," Jamie said. "Reckon there'll be enough blood spilled on this trip without us doing it to each other."

CHAPTER 22

After the near-tragic encounter with the Apache, everyone was nervous and the camp remained on high alert. Instead of standing guard in two-man shifts, as they had been doing at night, Jamie ordered that three men would be awake and watchful at all times.

Nothing else happened. The hours of darkness passed quietly and peacefully. However, all the members of the party were a little hollow-eyed the next morning, evidence that in spite of the tranquility, sound, restful sleep had been in short supply.

Jamie noticed that Fletch never got very far from Clementine's side as the group had breakfast and got ready to pull out. Thankfully, Ramirez kept his distance and never approached the young couple, let alone make any more leering remarks. Jamie was thankful for that.

It was a solemn bunch that started into the canyon when the sun was about a half hour above the eastern horizon. Preacher, Jamie, and Dog went first to scout out the area. When Dog had returned to the camp the previous evening, Preacher could tell from his demeanor that the big cur hadn't found any more Apaches—but that didn't mean more of them couldn't have slunk into the canyon during the night.

The wagons came next, with the Wylie vehicle taking the lead. Fletch was on the box by himself, at his insistence. He was worried that if the wagon happened to tip over because of the rough path, Clementine might be hurt. Instead, she would ride down double with Audie. She didn't like being told what to do, but Fletch explained that he would be able to concentrate better on the task if he wasn't worried about her safety.

Neither Noah Stuart nor Chester Merrick had any experience handling a wagon and team under such rugged conditions, but one of the Molmberg brothers—Jamie wasn't sure which—volunteered to step in, communicating that with just a few words and gestures. Jamie knew from his previous experience with them, as part of the wagon train he'd led, that they were both excellent teamsters.

The rest of the group followed slowly on horseback as the wagons jolted and swayed down the rough path caused by the bluff caving in at some point in the distant past. In some places, the rocks proved to be too much for the wheels to make it over. When that happened, the men had to dismount, then grunt, heave, and sweat as they moved the barriers out of the way. Without the strength of the massive Greybull and Nighthawk, some of the larger rocks probably couldn't have been budged.

It was slow going, and the wagons didn't reach the sparsely grassed, relatively level ground alongside the stream until past mid-morning. Everyone rested for a short time, grateful for the respite.

Jamie and Preacher were confident that no Apaches were lurking in the area. Jamie leaned toward the idea that the warrior Ramirez had killed the day before had been a lone scout. But sooner or later, the rest of the band that man had belonged to would get curious about why he hadn't returned. Somebody was liable to come looking for him, and not just one somebody, either. It would be a whole war party.

"We'll have to postpone our midday meal today," Jamie said as he addressed the group. "We want to be sure we have time to make it up the other bluff. We don't want night to catch us partway up that rough trail. Let the mules take it easy for a few more minutes, and then we'll get started again."

"Hear that?" Tennysee asked with a grin. "It's the mules that got to rest. Us human beans don't really matter!"

"I know what's important," Jamie said dryly. "Unless you want to be hitched to one of those wagons, Tennysee . . . ?"

The lanky mountain man held up both hands, palms out. "No, sir. I'll do mighty fine without that."

A short time later, they headed upstream toward the ford Preacher had located. Stuart and Merrick were back on their wagon for this part of the crossing. Where the river widened, the water came up only to the wheel hubs, so once the balky mules were persuaded to step out into the stream, getting to the other side wasn't a problem.

When they reached the trail up to the top of the southern bluff, the even more arduous work began. The crates and bags of supplies were unloaded and stacked on the riverbank, along with the crates containing surveying equipment from Stuart and

Merrick's wagon. While that was being done, Jamie sent Audie, Deadlead, and Powder Pete up to the rim to stand guard.

"While you're at it, keep an eye on the sky as well as watching for any signs of Apaches," he told them. "I haven't heard any thunder in the distance, but I don't want to, either. If you see any rain clouds over those mountains to the west, let us know right away."

"Of course," Audie said. "But even if it were to rain in the mountains, any flooding would require some time to reach this point."

"I know. I just want to be able to hurry things along if I need to. Not that I'm planning on wasting any time, to start with." Jamie looked at the bluffs rising on both sides of them. "Never did like spending much time in a place where somebody else had the high ground."

Once Fletch and Clementine's wagon was unloaded, the mules from the surveyors' wagon were brought forward and hitched onto that team, as well. That made eight of the beasts, which Jamie figured would be enough to haul the unloaded wagon to the top, no matter how steep and rough the trail was. Since no one had to ride the box to work the brake on an ascent like this, Fletch joined one of the Molmbergs at the head of the team, grasped the harness, and began leading the mules up the trail.

Again, it was slow going. At times, rocks had to be lifted or rolled out of the way. Greybull and Nighthawk did most of that work, too, being careful not to let any of the small boulders start rolling downhill and cause an avalanche. By the middle of the afternoon, the first wagon was on top of the bluff. The mules were unhitched and led back down to be hitched to the surveyors' wagon.

Grueling task though it was, everything went smoothly. By nightfall, the last of the supplies had been carried up and placed in the wagons again.

"Well, it took all day and everybody's worn out," Jamie said to Preacher as they sat on their horses and looked over the canyon they had just crossed. "I'm glad to be on this side, though."

"And it didn't flood and wash ever'body away," Preacher commented. "Well, we knew it'd be a rare occurrence if that happened."

"Can happen, though," Jamie said.

"Can," Preacher agreed gravely.

Jamie turned his horse to peer southward. "I figure two more days, and we'll be getting into Apache country. That'll be time to start looking for a good base camp."

"Iffen they don't hit us first, between here and there."

"We want them to come to us," Jamie said, "but not before we're ready for them."

Everybody was tired, as Jamie had said, but they were also relieved that the difficult canyon and river crossing had been made without any mishaps. That relief brought a festive air to the camp that evening.

After supper, Dupre brought out his fiddle and began playing a sprightly tune. Tennysee and Powder Pete locked arms and began dancing around in a circle, waving their free arms and jerking their knees high, prompting laughter from most of the others.

Pugh got a laugh, too, when he asked mournfully, "Don't nobody want to dance with me?"

"Ummm!" Nighthawk said.

The big Crow shook his head.

Clementine said, "Well, I want to dance," and took hold of Fletch's hand. They had been sitting on the lowered tailgate of their wagon, but she slid to the ground and tugged Fletch along with her.

Preacher stood with Jamie on the other side of the campfire and watched as Fletch took Clementine in his arms and the two of them began whirling around in the intricate steps of a Virginia reel. Scratching Dog's ears as the big cur sat beside him, the mountain man said quietly, "Now, this could prove interestin'."

"Yeah, I thought the same thing," Jamie replied. "It's only a matter of time until somebody decides they ought to have a dance with Clementine, too."

Tennysee and Powder Pete continued their capering. Some of the men began to clap in time with Dupre's fiddle playing. After the strain of the past twenty-four hours, everyone seemed to enjoy relaxing and letting off a little steam.

Then Edgerton stepped up, tapped Fletch on the shoulder, and said, "I'm cuttin' in here, boy."

Fletch and Clementine stopped dancing. Dupre missed a note but then carried on as Fletch turned to face the dour mountain man.

"I don't—" he began.

"No, Fletch, it's all right," Clementine said quickly. "Mr. Edgerton is a gentleman, and it's just a dance."

Fletch hesitated, then said to Edgerton, "You don't strike me as the dancing type."

"Everybody has memories, boy," the man rasped. "How I am now ain't necessarily the way I always was."

Another second went by, then Fletch nodded. "All right." He stepped back so Edgerton could move in and take Clementine in his arms.

"Appreciate it, ma'am," Edgerton muttered.

They began dancing, and as Jamie watched, he was surprised by how light on his feet Edgerton was. He held Clementine at arm's length, too, and didn't try to pull her closer to him. He actually was acting like a gentleman.

Dupre came to the end of the song. Tennysee was breathing a little hard from his exertions. He leaned over, rested his hands on his thighs for a moment as he caught his breath, then said to the Frenchman, "Play another 'un, Dupre. I'm just gettin' warmed up."

Edgerton took his arm from around Clementine's waist and let go of her hand. Nodding gravely, he said, "Thank you, ma'am. That reminded me of some good times in my life, long ago."

She summoned up a smile and told him, "I'm glad I could help, Mr. Edgerton."

Dupre poised the bow just above the strings of his fiddle. He was ready to launch into another tune, but before he could do so, another figure stood up and stepped in front of Clementine.

"I will dance with the woman now," Dog Brother declared.

CHAPTER 23

Dupre didn't start playing, and everyone else around the campfire fell silent as they stared at the half-breed Comanche standing in front of the blond, beautiful young woman.

Not surprisingly, it was Ramirez who spoke up first. "This is not one of your savage dances where you stomp around or shuffle your feet to make it rain, Indian. Get away from the woman."

The faintest hint of a smile touched Dog Brother's lips as he said, "I am half-white. That means I have twice as much right to dance with her as *you* do, Ramirez."

The gunman came to his feet and stood there stiffly as he glared at Dog Brother. His hands hung near his guns. Dog Brother looked like he was ready to slap leather, too.

Jamie moved forward, getting between them and holding out his hands toward them. "Take it easy, both of you. This doesn't have anything to do with who's white and who's not. I reckon it's up to the lady who she dances with."

"Or her husband," Fletch said. "Clementine's married to *me*, remember?"

"I'm right here," Clementine said. "I can speak for myself." She lifted her chin defiantly. "I'll dance with you, Dog Brother." She looked around. "I'll dance with all of you, if Mr. Dupre doesn't mind playing that long."

"Certainly, madame," the Frenchman said.

Pugh gulped. "Even me, ma'am?"

Clementine smiled at him and said, "Of course. Even you, Mr. Pugh."

"Well, *doggone*! I don't recollect the last time I danced with somebody, and I sure don't reckon I *ever* danced with anybody as purty as you!"

Fletch asked quietly, "Are you absolutely sure about this, Clementine?"

"Of course." Her voice sounded confident, but her smile looked a little nervous to Jamie. "We're just talking about dancing, after all. And fair is fair."

"I suppose." Fletch glared at the rest of the group. "But you'd better *all* be gentlemen, if you know what's good for you."

"Or what, boy?" Ramirez asked with a challenging smirk on his face.

"I *won't* be dancing with anyone who doesn't respect my husband," Clementine said. "That's what." She held out her hands and went on to Dog Brother. "Do you know how to dance like this?"

"Of course I know," the half-breed said. "I have lived with the whites. They are not truly my people, any more than the Comanche are, but I have spent time among them."

As he took her left hand with his right and put his

left hand on her waist, she looked at Dupre and nodded. He began playing again. Dog Brother's steps were a bit awkward as they started dancing, but he seemed to get the hang of it.

Jamie went back to stand beside Preacher.

The mountain man said under his breath, "I worried that it was a bad idea to bring a gal along on a trip like this. Get a woman around such a rough bunch and there's bound to be trouble." He shook his head. "I just didn't see no other way to get her away from them no-good brothers o' hers."

"We've handled it so far," Jamie said. "Once the Apaches are more of a threat, everybody's going to be too busy with them to worry about such things."

Preacher chuckled. "So you're sayin' we ought to look forward to them varmints tryin' to kill us?"

"Well, it'll be something different, anyway."

While Fletch looked on, glowering in disapproval, Clementine danced with all the other men in the group, even Pugh, who said, "Now, ma'am, I won't hold you to what you said . . ."

"Nonsense," Clementine replied, smiling. "Come on, Mr. Pugh." She looked a little green as they whirled around, but she made it through the dance.

Most of the men, who were used to living solitary lives with few, if any, women around, were awkward in their attempts to dance and didn't stay with it long. Chester Merrick's face was bright red with embarrassment and he lasted only a minute or so before gratefully giving way to one of the other men. Even Ramirez didn't try to get too forward with her. Audie seemed to really enjoy it and was the most skillful dancer in the group, despite his lack of stature. Noah

Stuart was also a good dancer but didn't linger after taking a few spins with Clementine.

Preacher and then Jamie joined in at the end, and as Jamie held Clementine, he said quietly, "I appreciate the way you handled that, ma'am. That could have turned into bad trouble, and you kept it from happening."

"Well, I was surprised when Dog Brother wanted to dance," she said, "but it didn't seem like anything worth fighting over."

"Your husband might disagree with you."

"Fletch is just very protective of me. He knows what a bad situation I had to deal with. I'm not as delicate as he sometimes seems to think I am, though."

Remembering the way Clementine could handle a rifle, Jamie nodded. "Yes, ma'am, I expect that's true."

With that behind them, the group settled down for the night. Jamie posted four-man guard shifts. Although he had nothing on which to base it except instinct, he felt like the stream they had crossed was a boundary of sorts, and now that they were south of it, they were already in Apache country. The danger would just grow as they continued heading toward Mexico.

The country became flatter and more arid as they moved on the next day. Vegetation consisted of cactus, scrubby mesquite, and occasional clumps of mostly brown grass. Ranges of small mountains jutted up here and there, but they weren't difficult to avoid. They didn't come across any more streams the size of the one that flowed through the canyon they'd left behind. Most of the creek beds were dry. In some, a thin thread of water flowed sluggishly, but it was still spring. By midsummer, those would be dry, too.

"Why do the Apaches even *want* this country?" Chester Merrick asked from the driver's seat as Jamie rode alongside the surveyors' wagon. "It seems like a terrible place to live."

"It's not very hospitable," Jamie agreed, "but the Apaches are used to pretty harsh conditions. They know where all the waterholes are, and they can not only survive in country like this, they can thrive in it if they're left alone."

"Then why don't we leave them alone?" Merrick grumbled. "Why don't we just let them have it? Then maybe they'd stop killing settlers in other places."

Jamie shook his head. "I don't make those decisions. It's up to the folks in Washington to figure out such things. I'm just doing what an old friend asked me to do."

And that was as much a personal favor as a political one, Jamie reflected—finding out the fate of Lieutenant Damon Charlton.

Noah Stuart said, "This region is important because there may be a railroad running through it someday. Looking around at the terrain, I don't see any significant obstacles to such a thing. Unless there are other canyons like the one we crossed yesterday, and I suppose if there are, trestles can be built across them. Honestly, once the lines begin expanding into different parts of the country, I don't believe anything will stop the railroads."

"Neither do I," Jamie said, "and neither do the

Indians. And *that's* what's going to cause plenty of blood to be spilled in the years to come, I'm thinking."

On that solemn note, he rode ahead to rejoin Preacher in front of Fletch and Clementine's wagon. Dog had ranged on ahead a few hundred yards and was trying to scare up a jackrabbit or two.

As he rocked along in the saddle, Preacher said quietly, "I'm startin' to have kind of a bad feelin', Jamie. Like somebody's watchin' me . . . or diggin' my grave."

"I know what you mean. I started feeling like that a ways back, too."

Preacher turned his head from side to side as he scanned their surroundings. "If there was any high ground nearby, I'd think maybe some 'Paches was sittin' up on it, spyin' on us."

"They've got good eyes." Jamie nodded toward a shallow mesa to the southeast that had to be close to a mile away. "Could be somebody over there."

"Yeah, that's what I was thinkin'." Preacher paused. "Was thinkin', too, that I might take a *pasear* over there and check it out. Have a little better look around."

"They'll see you coming."

"Yeah, but maybe that'll spook 'em into givin' themselves away."

Jamie considered that suggestion, then said, "Take a couple of men with you, just in case you run into any trouble."

"I was already thinkin' the same thing. Audie and Nighthawk. I been ridin' into tight spots with those two ol' boys longer 'n I like to think about."

Jamie nodded. "All right."

"We'll drop back, act like there's somethin' wrong

with one of the horses' shoes, maybe. The rest of you keep goin', and maybe if any of the varmints are over there, they'll watch you and forget about us. Less likely to spot us that way when we start driftin' in that direction."

"Can happen," Jamie said. "Give it a try."

Preacher nodded and pulled back a little on Horse's reins, slowing the stallion. As some of the other men caught up, he spoke to Audie and Nighthawk, and then all three of them slowed down and lingered while the rest of the party continued heading south.

Jamie didn't look back. He didn't want to draw attention to the three men they were leaving behind.

If there were any watchers over there, they would know about Preacher, Audie, and Nighthawk soon enough.

Preacher dismounted and studied the shoe on Horse's left hind hoof for long minutes while Audie and Nighthawk sat nearby on their mounts. Drawing his knife, Preacher pretended to probe at the hoof as if he were trying to work a pebble out from under the shoe.

"See anything over on that mesa?" he asked without looking up at his two companions.

"Not a thing," Audie replied. "I don't doubt your instincts, Preacher, but it's possible there's no one over there."

"Yep," the mountain man agreed. "And it'll be fine with me if it works out that way. I reckon I'll feel better if we make sure, though."

"Umm," Nighthawk said.

"Jamie and the others are almost out of sight," Audie informed Preacher.

"We'll give 'em a few more minutes."

When he judged that enough time had passed, he set Horse's hoof back on the ground and swung up into the saddle. Then he turned the stallion's head toward the distant mesa.

"We'll take it slow and easy," he said. "That way we won't kick up so much dust. Best swing back to the north a ways, too, and circle around a mite."

The three men rode at a leisurely pace as they circled toward the butte. They were still in plain sight, and anyone on top of the rocky tableland couldn't help but see them coming—if they were paying attention. Preacher hoped they were still watching the wagons and the other riders. A glance in that direction showed him the column of dust rising from the group's passage.

"Ummm," Nighthawk said as they came in sight of the mesa's far side.

"I see them," Audie said. "Three Indian ponies tied there at the base, Preacher."

"Yep. I reckon some of the varmints are up there, all right." Preacher leaned forward sharply in the saddle. "At least, they were. They're tryin' to light a shuck!"

He had spotted three figures moving along a trail that angled down from the top. One warrior wore a blue headband, and the other two sported red headbands. Even from where he was, Preacher could see the bright splashes of color.

He didn't want them getting away. He dug his heels into Horse's flanks and the stallion sprang forward in a run. Preacher didn't bother looking over his shoulder to see if Audie and Nighthawk were following him. He knew they were.

The three frontiersmen thundered toward the mesa and the trio of Apaches who were trying to flee.

CHAPTER 24

As he rode, Preacher loosened the Colt Dragoons in their holsters. Dog raced alongside Horse, his legs flashing. At a short distance like this, the big cur could almost keep up with the rangy stallion.

Up ahead, the Apaches made it to their ponies. Preacher saw them hesitate and knew they were trying to decide whether to fight or run. Indians never liked to fight when the odds were even. They always preferred the advantage to be on their side.

They also knew their ponies probably couldn't outrun the pursuers' mounts. The ponies would be faster in their initial spurt, but the bigger horses ridden by Preacher, Audie, and Nighthawk had more stamina. It wouldn't take long to overhaul the Apaches if they fled.

As far as Preacher could see, there was no better place around here for the Apaches to fort up than the rocks at the base of the mesa. He wasn't surprised when they didn't go for their ponies after all but ducked behind the boulders instead.

"Hold on!" he called to his companions as he

raised a hand and signaled for them to halt. As they all came to a stop, Preacher said, "Looks like we got us a standoff here."

"Yes," Audie said, "but in all likelihood, we're much better armed. They probably just have bows and arrows. Maybe an old flintlock musket."

"That's what I was thinkin'," Preacher said as he reached down and hauled the Sharps out of its saddle scabbard.

He pulled his right foot out of the stirrup, threw that leg over Horse's back, and dropped to the ground. He turned Horse and rested the Sharps on the saddle as he took aim at the rocks. His thumb looped around the hammer and drew it back.

"Umm," Nighthawk said.

"I don't see them, either," Audie said. "They've gone to ground among those boulders, Preacher, and they have good cover there."

"I ain't aimin' at the 'Paches themselves," Preacher said. "See where them rocks stick out, up there above their heads?"

Audie squinted in that direction, then said, "Ah. Now I begin to understand."

A moment later, the Sharps boomed as Preacher squeezed the trigger. Stone splinters flew where the heavy bullet slammed into the mesa's side, right under the spot where several slabs of rock protruded, leaning out from the wall.

Preacher began reloading. Horse hadn't flinched at the shot, even in the slightest.

The sound of angry yells drifted through the dry air.

Nighthawk said, "Umm," and Audie chuckled.

"Yes, it appears they've already figured out Preacher's

strategy. But there's not a thing in the world they can do about it."

Preacher had the Sharps ready again. He drew another bead and fired. Again, the slug blasted part of the stone wall into gravel. Outraged howls came from the Apaches concealed in the boulders below.

Preacher slammed two more rounds into the mesa, and suddenly one of the rock slabs, its support chipped away by the bullets, leaned out farther and then gave way. It fell among the boulders at the mesa's base, landing with a crash and throwing up a cloud of dust.

As the dust roiled in a very faint breeze, Audie said, "I wonder if that landed on any of them."

"Don't know," Preacher said as he reloaded the Sharps again, "but I reckon it won't be long until we find out."

It wasn't. Shapes flitted through the dust, then emerged from the cloud and resolved into the three warriors mounted on their ponies. Howling in defiant anger, the Apaches charged toward Preacher and his companions.

"Looks like they decided to put up a fight instead of runnin'," the mountain man drawled. He lifted the Sharps to his shoulder, drew a bead, and squeezed the trigger. As the weapon blasted, one of the Apaches flew backward off his pony as if he'd been slapped off the racing mount by a giant hand—a .52 caliber hand.

But that still left two of them, and they were closing fast. Audie fired and then Nighthawk. A second Apache rocked back on his pony but didn't topple off.

He slowed his charge as bright red blood suddenly appeared on his left shoulder.

The third man came on at full speed, though, and then suddenly was among them, throwing himself off the pony's back in a flying tackle that sent him crashing into Nighthawk.

The big Crow outweighed the wiry Apache by a considerable amount, but the Apache's momentum was enough to drive Nighthawk backward and off his feet. Both men hit the ground hard and rolled over.

Meanwhile, the wounded Apache had gotten close enough to draw back his bow despite his injury and send an arrow whistling toward Preacher. The mountain man darted aside and brought up the Dragoons. The revolvers boomed together. The bullets pounded into the Apache's chest, and he had no chance of staying mounted. He pitched off the pony and landed on his back. Death spasms jerked him over on one shoulder, then the other. His feet beat a tattoo on the hard ground.

Preacher swung around, guns in hands, to see how Nighthawk was doing with the third Apache. Dog stood nearby, watching the struggle with his teeth bared and the hair standing up on his back. Audie was still mounted and clutched his rifle as he watched the fight closely, too. Man and cur both clearly wanted to jump in and help Nighthawk, but he was wrapped up so closely with the Apache as they wrestled that Audie couldn't risk a shot and Dog couldn't get his fangs on the enemy.

Their battle had raised a cloud of dust, too. Preacher saw a knife flash inside the swirling cloud, but he couldn't tell who was wielding it. He heard a sharp snap among the grunts of effort. That was a bone breaking.

A huge shape loomed up out of the dust as Nighthawk rose to his feet. In an amazing display of strength, he brought the Apache with him, gripping the man by an arm and a leg and raising him high above his head. The Apache's other arm dangled at an unnatural angle. That was what he'd heard breaking, Preacher thought.

The Apache shouted defiantly in his own tongue, but there was nothing he could do. He was helpless in Nighthawk's hands. Nighthawk reached his full, towering height, then brought the Apache down hard while at the same time raising his right knee. Again a sharp crack cut through the desert air as Nighthawk broke the Apache's back across his knee. The man's cry cut off abruptly as he passed out from the pain.

Nighthawk tossed him heedlessly on the ground like a child throwing away a broken toy. The Crow straightened again and dusted his hands off dismissively.

Preacher reloaded the Dragoons, pouched the irons, and went over to the unconscious Apache. He drew his knife, bent over the man, and drew the razor-sharp blade across his throat, cutting deeply and stepping back as blood fountained up for a moment. He wiped the knife on the man's buckskin leggings and sheathed it.

"You did him a kindness," Audie said from horseback. "He would have been in agony when he regained consciousness, and he never would have recovered."

"Thought about shootin' him but figured I might as well save the bullet," Preacher said. "Thought about keepin' him alive and tryin' to question him, too, but then decided it'd be a waste of time. Likely he never would've done anything 'cept maybe spit in my eye."

"Umm," Nighthawk said.

"Our friend concurs," Audie said. "We should check the other two, although they certainly appear to be deceased."

Preacher did that, and just as expected, the other two Apaches were dead. "Maybe we should've let one of 'em get away," he mused. "Jamie wants the 'Paches to know we're here so they'll come after us instead of us havin' to hunt 'em all down. It's mighty hard for me to leave an enemy still drawin' breath, though. I ain't in the habit of it."

"They'll be aware of our presence soon enough," Audie said. "I have no doubt of that."

Nighthawk added, "Umm," and the former professor went on. "Yes, we'd better catch up with the others now. I'm sure they heard the shooting and are curious."

They left the Apaches where they had fallen but rounded up the ponies and drove them on ahead as they rode south again. Extra mounts might come in handy, although the Indian ponies were wild enough that they weren't very reliable.

The three men on horseback moved faster than the wagons could, so within an hour they came in sight of the rest of the party. Jamie had been watching for them and rode back to meet them.

As he reined in, he said, "I'm glad to see that all three of you boys look to be all right. Those shots we heard must mean that you found some Apaches."

"They were up on that mesa watchin' us, just like we thought they might be," Preacher said.

"Any of them get away?"

"Nope. Not sure if that's what you wanted, but that's the way it played out."

Jamie nodded. "That's all right. The farther we go, the more of them will be around. Today was just a start, like the one we ran into back at the canyon."

"That's four down," Preacher said. "No tellin' how many more to go."

CHAPTER 25

Chester Merrick had been driving the surveyors' wagon all day while Noah Stuart sat beside him with a large pad of paper on his lap and made sketch after sketch of the landscape, marking every landmark for when it came time to create an actual map of the isolated territory.

They came to a drop-off formed by a low, rugged escarpment that appeared to run for several miles in both directions. Preacher and Jamie, riding ahead, reached it first and reined in.

"This looks like the Cap Rock over in Texas," Jamie said. "Just not as high and rough."

"Don't reckon the wagons'll have any trouble handlin' it," Preacher commented as he leaned forward in his saddle. "I see several places where the slope's gentle enough for them to get down there."

"And maybe a spring or something over that way," Jamie said, pointing to the west. "I see a little bit of green, so there has to be some water."

"Dog and me'll check it out," the mountain man offered. He rode down the slope with the big cur trotting alongside him while Jamie turned his horse and waved an arm for the others to stop.

"What is it?" Fletch asked as Jamie rode up to the lead wagon. "Another canyon?"

"No, just a place where the ground drops off some," Jamie explained. "It shouldn't give us any trouble. Might be a good campsite down there. Preacher's gone to have a look."

Noah Stuart jumped down from the wagon seat and walked ahead to the other wagon. He asked Jamie, "Are we stopping for the day?"

"Maybe longer than that. We're far enough south now that if this turns out to be a good location, we might go ahead and establish our main camp for a while."

Some of the men on horseback had moved in close enough to hear Jamie's comments. Dog Brother grunted and said, "Good. It is time to kill Apaches."

"For once, the filthy savage and I agree," Ramirez said with a cocky grin.

Tennysee nodded. "It's time we had us some good fightin', all right, and that ain't no joke."

"Wait here," Jamie told him, then turned his horse back to the rimrock. As he peered down the slope, he spotted Preacher. The mountain man was already returning.

"It's a good spot, all right," Preacher reported as he and Dog reached the top of the ridge. "A little waterhole with some grass around it for the mules and horses, even a few cottonwood trees. It's between a couple of places where the ridge sticks out, but the rocks ain't close enough on either side to hem in the camp. And the slope at the back ain't so steep that the horses couldn't climb it, although I don't reckon it'd be easy to get the wagons up. Couldn't move the wagons fast, anyway. But the upshot of it is, I don't believe we'd be likely to get boxed in there, and I'm thinkin' the water comes from underground somewhere, so it shouldn't run dry."

"Sounds like we won't find a better place," Jamie said.

"Not likely," Preacher agreed. "Might be some just as good, but none better."

"And this one's right here handy." Jamie turned his head from side to side as he studied the terrain. "We can put a man at the top of the slope to stand guard, and one each on those little promontories you mentioned. The way to the south is wide open, so nobody's liable to sneak up on us that way."

"That'll mean leavin' three men at the camp," Preacher pointed out.

Jamie nodded. "We can do that. There'll be six men in camp, counting Fletch, Stuart, and Merrick, and we can split up the other twelve into two groups of six to scout for Apaches. I'll take one and you take the other."

"Sounds like a good plan," the mountain man said. "We'd best go tell the others."

They turned their horses and rode to rejoin the group. It didn't take long to explain that they would be making camp at the waterhole and likely would stay there for several days.

Clementine was visibly relieved at the news. "Fletch and I have been on the move so much, for so long, that it'll be nice to stay in one place for a while."

"We stayed in Santa Fe for several weeks," Fletch pointed out to her.

"Yes, but that was different. I was always worried that my brothers might show up."

Fletch grunted, looked over his shoulder, and said, "They still might. We don't know where they are or what they're doing. They could be on our trail right now."

"Or after everything that happened, they could have decided to turn around and go home." Clementine didn't sound as if she really believed that.

Jamie knew that he didn't.

They drove the wagons down the ridge, with Fletch and Noah Stuart handling the reins, and then turned west toward the little oasis Preacher had found. When they got there, Jamie saw that the waterhole was about fifteen feet across. The water was clear enough that he could see the bottom, and it filled what appeared to be a natural sinkhole in the rock.

When he knelt beside the little pool, scooped up water in his hand, and took a drink, he found that it was cool and sweet. The water was seeping up from one of the underground streams that could be found even in the desert.

Before letting the horses and mules at it, the men filled canteens and topped off the water barrels, pausing to drink deeply themselves. Some plunged their heads into the cool water, straightening to shake their heads and sling drops from their soaked hair.

As Pugh approached the waterhole, Edgerton said, "Not you, mister. You'll foul it for the rest of us even worse than the mules."

"I ain't plannin' on takin' a bath in it," Pugh replied.

Ramirez laughed. "Good! I'm not sure there is enough water in the world to rid you of your stench, señor."

"Hold on," Deadlead said. "Pugh's our friend, so we can talk that way about him, but I ain't sure I cotton to you doin' it, mister."

Ramirez sneered at him. "If you are offended, señor, you know what to do about it."

Deadlead tensed. He was good with a gun himself, and he didn't like that arrogant challenge.

"Hold on," Jamie snapped. "How many times do I have to tell you fellas we're here to fight Apaches, not each other?"

Pugh said, "It's all right. I don't want nobody squabblin' on my account. And like I said, I ain't figurin' on takin' a bath or nothin'. I'll just fill my canteen."

He did so while Deadlead and several of the other old mountain men glared at Ramirez, who ignored them.

The gunfighter wasn't through stirring up trouble. He sidled over to Clementine and said, "Perhaps this pool is large enough that you could have an uninterrupted swim in it this time, señorita. I mean, *Señora* Wylie."

"You need to stop making that mistake," Clementine told him sharply. "I'm a married woman, and I don't believe you actually keep forgetting that."

Ramirez shrugged eloquently and said, "Perhaps it is just that I know when a woman is saddled with a man who does not deserve her."

Kneeling beside the waterhole, filling a canteen, Fletch heard him even though Ramirez hadn't spoken loudly. Fletch looked up quickly with an angry scowl on his face. "Hey!" he said as he came to his feet. "You can't talk to my wife like that, and I don't appreciate you talking about me that way, either."

Ramirez gave him a cool, contemptuous glance. "You believe that I care what you appreciate or not, Wylie? Why would I do that?"

Jamie saw the way Fletch stiffened and could tell the young man was about to lose his temper. Before that could happen, Jamie allowed his own anger to boil over. "By the great horn spoon, Ramirez!" he bellowed as his big left hand fell on the gunfighter's shoulder. He hauled Ramirez around and gave him a shove that made him stagger several steps backward.

Ramirez caught his balance and his hands darted toward his guns.

Jamie waited until Ramirez started his draw, but he cleared leather first anyway. Ramirez's guns were barely out of their holsters and still pointed at the ground when Jamie's Walker lined up on the Mexican's face and the hammer clicked back.

"I'm sick and tired of you trying to start a ruckus, mister," Jamie said in a flat, hard voice. "I started out thinking we needed every man we had, but now I'm not so sure you're worth it. You just go ahead and tip those hoglegs up if you want to. Won't bother me a bit to squeeze the trigger."

For a second, it seemed that Ramirez was going to go ahead and try it. He had no chance of beating Jamie, but he might believe he could get off a shot or two before he died.

But then, with another eloquent shrug, he let the guns slide back into their holsters. "I am no fool, Señor MacCallister. And I am patient. I can wait for a better time."

"You give me your word that so-called better time won't come until after we're finished with the job that brought us here?" Jamie cocked his head a little to the side. "Or should I just go ahead and put a bullet through your brain right now? With all the other trouble I have to keep an eye out for, I don't feel like watching over my shoulder for you, too, mister."

Ramirez's lips thinned. After a couple of seconds, he said in a voice that showed the strain of keeping his hot-blooded emotions under control, "I give you my word, MacCallister. You will have no more trouble from me until we are done with the Apaches."

Jamie studied him, narrow-eyed, for a moment before he carefully lowered the Walker's hammer. "All right," he said as he pouched the iron. "I'll accept your word, Ramirez. And if I get even a hint that you're not going to keep it, I'll go ahead and kill you right then, no questions asked."

Preacher added, "And if you make *me* even a mite suspicious, I'll kill you, too. I ain't as patient as Jamie here." He paused. "One more thing. Keep your distance from Miz Wylie and don't talk to her less'n you got a good reason, too. Comprende?"

"I understand," Ramirez said. His gaze flicked toward Fletch and Clementine for a second. "But my opinions are still my own."

"As long as we don't have to listen to them," Jamie said, "and these two young folks don't, either."

Stone-faced, Ramirez turned away. He went to his horse, got his canteen, and walked over to the water-hole to fill it. After a moment, the hubbub of making camp resumed, although at a more subdued level than earlier.

Smiling a little, Preacher said quietly to Jamie, "Ol'

Ramirez looked plumb surprised when he saw the way you outdrew him. You'd figure that even down yonder in Mexico, a *pistolero* like him would've heard about how slick on the draw Jamie Ian MacCallister is."

"Well, I won't be taking him by surprise again," Jamie said. "I don't believe he's the sort to do any back-shooting—no fame or glory in that—but I don't think he'll forget what just happened here. Sooner or later, I may have to face him."

"Yeah," Preacher said, "unless Dog Brother kills him first. Or them 'Paches wipe us all out."

Jamie chuckled. "Yeah," he said with a note of grim humor in his voice. "Maybe we'll be lucky."

CHAPTER 26

They had a cold camp that night, which caused some grumbling about the lack of hot food and coffee. Despite the fact that Jamie *wanted* the Apaches to know they were in the vicinity, he didn't believe it was wise for them to draw too much attention to themselves just yet.

"I think it would be a good idea for us to have a better look around first," was all he said by way of explanation. He wasn't in the habit of justifying his decisions or actions.

Guards were posted at the three spots he had mentioned to Preacher. The guard shifts rotated among the experienced fighters. Fletch and Noah Stuart had both volunteered to stand watch, but Jamie told them it wasn't necessary. To spare their feelings, he didn't go into detail, but he just didn't have the confidence in them that was necessary to assign them to a job where the lives of the entire group might be in their hands.

The next morning, Clementine kindled a small fire to prepare breakfast.

While the group was eating, Jamie announced, "Greybull, Pugh, Dupre, the three of you are going to stay here in camp today while the rest of us do some scouting. I don't want any complaints about missing out on the action, because somebody else will be staying here tomorrow. Besides, we may not run into any trouble today at all."

"I suppose we were chosen at random?" Dupre asked.

"That's right," Jamie replied with a nod.

Actually, he had picked the three mountain men for what he believed to be a good reason. They were three of the oldest and steadiest in the bunch. They could be trusted to remain alert and not pick any fights with Fletch or pay any undue attention to Clementine. On this first day at the main camp, that was what Jamie wanted.

He had devoted considerable thought to how he was going to split up the group and had discussed the matter with Preacher. They'd agreed that Ramirez and Dog Brother couldn't be trusted to be in the same scouting party. There was too much chance of trouble between them.

"I'll take Ramirez with me," Preacher had said. "He's already got a grudge against you because of the way you showed him up. Besides, I'll have Audie and Nighthawk with me, and those two won't tolerate any shenanigans. And if it's all right with you, I'll take them two Scandahoovian brothers with me. Them and Nighthawk have become pretty good friends."

Jamie had grinned at that. "With those three along, none of the rest of you will be able to get a word in edgewise."

"Oh, we'll manage, I reckon. That leaves you with Dog Brother, Edgerton, Powder Pete, Tennysee, and

Deadlead, who's carryin' a little grudge against Ramirez, too."

"That'll work. I'll go east along this escarpment for a ways with my bunch and then cut south. You head west and do the same."

Preacher had nodded his agreement with that plan.

After telling who would be remaining in camp, Jamie announced who would be going with him and who would be part of Preacher's scouting party.

Edgerton asked, "If we run into any Apaches, do we fight or do we try to avoid them?"

"We didn't come all the way down here to duck trouble," Jamie said. "If the odds aren't too high against us, we'll fight."

Satisfied looks appeared on the faces of most of the men. Several of them nodded in emphatic agreement.

After breakfast, Noah Stuart went over to Jamie and asked, "Are Chester and I supposed to stay here in camp today?"

"It's too dangerous for you fellas to be out roaming around on your own."

"Isn't it also dangerous just to be in this region?"

"It is," Jamie admitted. "We all knew that before we started down here. But the Wylies can fight, and I know from what happened back in Santa Fe with Clementine's brothers that you've got some sand. Greybull, Pugh, and Dupre have a lot of experience at staying alive. Unless a mighty big war party happens along, you should be all right."

"I hoped to set up my instruments and actually take some readings today, as well as doing some more preliminary cartographic work."

"Mapmaking, you mean."

"That's right," Stuart said.

"Like I told you before, we'll probably be shifting camp in a few days. Maybe you can do some of your work then."

As a matter of fact, Jamie wasn't convinced that they *would* need another base camp. They might not be able to find one as good as this. It all depended on how much luck they had finding the Apaches they were supposed to drive out of the territory. Whether or not Noah Stuart and Chester Merrick would be able to carry out their jobs didn't really matter that much to him.

"All right," Stuart said with obvious reluctance. "I'd like to explore this escarpment and do some more sketching, though, if there's ever time for something like that."

"We'll see," Jamie said.

A short time later, the two groups of men who would be leaving mounted up. They were taking enough supplies with them for a couple of days, because it was impossible to predict what they might encounter. They might get involved in a running battle with the Apaches and have to stay out that long.

As they headed in opposite directions from the camp, Jamie lifted a hand in farewell to Preacher. He was confident that he couldn't have picked a better cocommander for this mission. As each bunch followed the ragged lines of the escarpment, it wasn't long before they were out of sight of the camp and each other.

* * *

"As barren and empty of human life as this region appears to be, it must bear a definite resemblance to the surface of the moon," Audie remarked later that morning as he rode alongside Preacher.

Preacher jerked a thumb toward the sky and said, "You mean the moon that's up yonder?"

"That's the only one of which I'm aware," Audie replied with a smile. "No, wait, actually, that's not true. I've heard that some men steeped in the astronomical sciences believe there may be moons around the other planets, as well. As telescopic devices continue to improve, I've no doubt that sooner or later we'll be able to tell for sure."

"Other planets?" Ramirez said from behind them. "What are you talking about, little man?"

Audie looked back over his shoulder. Preacher could tell that his old friend was trying not to sound disdainful as he said, "I'm talking the other worlds orbiting our sun. Mars, Venus, Neptune, Saturn, and the others. You're not one of those people who believe that everything in the heavens orbits around the earth, are you, Señor Ramirez?"

"No, of course not," Ramirez replied quickly, but despite that denial, Preacher thought the gunfighter sounded like maybe he *had* believed that. "My only schooling was at the mission," Ramirez went on, "and the priests, they were more interested in saving my soul than anything else." He laughed. "They failed spectacularly, no?"

"Umm," Nighthawk said.

Both Molmberg brothers chuckled dryly.

For a second, Ramirez looked like those responses were going to make him angry, but then he shrugged them off. That was good, because a moment later, they had something more important on which to concentrate.

"Look up yonder," Preacher said. "About a thousand yards, at the edge of the escarpment."

"I see him," Audie said.

"So do I," Ramirez put in.

Nighthawk, Lars, and Bengt didn't say anything, but Preacher was confident that they had spotted the lone figure on an Indian pony, too.

They all reined in and watched as the distant Apache suddenly put his mount down the slope and rode out onto the flats, moving fast enough that the pony's heels kicked up a thin curl of dust. The rider headed due south.

"Where is he going?" Ramirez asked.

"Don't know," Preacher said, "but he wanted us to see him. Otherwise he never would've been just sittin' there on the rim like that. He was waitin' for us."

"And now he expects us to follow him," Audie said. "Why would he take off like that as soon as we came in sight if he didn't?"

"Umm," Nighthawk added.

Audie nodded. "Yes, it seems the same way to me. That gentleman is the bait in a trap."

"Well, shoot," Preacher said, "if them 'Paches have gone to that much trouble, we sure don't want to disappoint 'em, now do we?" With that he heeled Horse into motion again and turned the rangy gray stallion to the southwest, on a course that would allow him to follow the distant, galloping figure.

The others all fell in behind him, and the chase was on.

CHAPTER 27

After angling southwest for several minutes, the pursuers were behind their quarry and hurrying due south after him. Preacher deliberately held Horse's speed down, not because he didn't want to catch the Apache but because he knew how quickly the mounts would wear down if they were run flat out in the heat, which was already growing worse even though it wasn't midday yet. The other men followed his example.

The Indian pony was fast, but soon its rider had to slow down, too, to spare the animal. Being set afoot out in this wasteland was a slow death sentence. The chase settled down, considering it might be a long one.

Preacher didn't think so, and when some large rock mounds came into sight a few minutes later, that confirmed his hunch. The fleeing Apache appeared to be headed straight for them.

Those mounds were far from tall enough to be called mountains and couldn't even be considered hills. They looked more like the Good Lord had simply dropped divine handfuls of boulders here and there. Some of the rocks had scattered, while others piled up on each other.

Audie's horse drew alongside Preacher's. "They're probably waiting in there to ambush us," the former professor called to the mountain man over the rattle of hoofbeats.

"I'm countin' on it!" Preacher replied with a reckless grin. With that expression on his face, he looked more like a youngster than the man in late middle age that he actually was.

The Apache reached the mounds and disappeared around one of them.

Preacher waved an arm and shouted to his companions, "Spread out! We're gonna surround the place!"

Six men couldn't completely surround the large cluster of rock mounds, of course, but neither were they charging in a group to be slaughtered, if that was what the Apaches had hoped for.

One at a time, the men veered off, heading right and left in turn. Preacher took the middle position, riding straight toward the rocks on the same path their quarry had taken. He didn't see any men or horses around the boulders, but he felt sure they were there, just waiting to attack.

As he got closer, he expected to see arrows suddenly start flying out at him, but that didn't happen. The Apaches were being cagey about it, trying to lure him on, he thought. Either that, or they weren't really holed up in the rocks after all.

As Preacher rounded the mound where the man they'd been chasing had disappeared, the ambush finally came. Figures sporting bare chests and colorful headbands around their long black hair popped up from behind some of the rocks and opened fire with their bows.

"Dog, hunt!" Preacher shouted to the big cur who

had followed him into the cluster of mounds. At the same time, the mountain man pulled Horse sharply to the left and drew his right-hand Dragoon.

The gun roared and bucked against his palm as he fired toward one of the Apaches. The bullet struck the man in the throat just as he loosed an arrow. The shaft sailed far wide of Preacher. The warrior who had fired it jerked back with crimson flooding from his wound down over his chest. He pawed futilely at the flow for a second, then pitched forward lifelessly over the rock where he had been hidden.

Preacher twisted in the saddle as another arrow cut through the air not far from his head. He spotted the man who had fired it. The Apache had been bold enough to climb on top of the mound to get a better aim, and he still stood there as he tried to nock a second arrow.

The man's attempt from that vantage point hadn't been good enough, unfortunately for him. Preacher's Dragoon blasted again with the same deadly accuracy. The slug punched into the Apache's belly and doubled him over. He toppled forward and bounced off a couple of the boulders before disappearing into a tangle of smaller rocks that had scrubby brush growing up between them.

Preacher hauled Horse into a tight turn around the mound to his left. Somewhere in the other direction, Dog snapped and snarled and a man screamed as the big cur's fangs tore into his flesh. Guns boomed elsewhere in the field of boulders as the rest of Preacher's group got into the fight.

A high-pitched war cry jerked the mountain man's head around. He caught a glimpse of a knife-wielding warrior diving toward him from the top of a boulder.

Preacher didn't have time to get out of the way, but he swung the Dragoon around and metal rang against metal as the gun barrel clashed with the knife and deflected it.

A split second later, the Apache's shoulder rammed into Preacher's chest and knocked him sideways out of the saddle.

Preacher tried to twist in midair so he wouldn't land on the bottom, but he was only partially successful. As he struck the ground, enough of the Apache's weight came down on him that it drove most of the air out of his lungs. The back of his head hit the hard-packed dirt with stunning force. Most men would have dropped the gun and passed out, but Preacher hung on not only to consciousness but also to the Dragoon.

Hot, foul breath blew in his face as the Apache tried to get a better hold and pin him down. Preacher drove his left elbow up under the man's chin and levered his head back. At the same time, the mountain man arched his back and twisted, throwing the Apache off to the side. He rolled the other way and came to a stop on his belly as he gasped for air to replace the breath he'd lost.

A couple of yards away, the Apache sprawled on his stomach as well. Preacher snapped a shot as the man started to surge up. The blow to the head must have made Preacher's vision a little fuzzy. Normally he wouldn't have missed at that range, but the Apache kept coming as the bullet whipped past him.

Preacher rolled out of the way as the warrior flung himself at him. Drawing back his right leg, Preacher straightened it and drove his boot heel into the Apache's ribs as the man went past him. That kick knocked the man away from him and gave Preacher the chance to come up on his knees. The Apache rolled over, caught himself, and came up throwing the knife.

Preacher dived to the right. He felt the blade touch the left sleeve of his shirt, but it didn't slice into the flesh underneath. The Apache, a stocky, barrel-chested warrior with a face twisted by hate, sprang to his feet and charged again, evidently intent on throt-tling Preacher to death with his bare hands since he didn't seem to have any other weapons.

Preacher fired twice as he lay there propped up on his right elbow. Smoke and flame spurted from the Dragoon's muzzle. The Apache stopped short for a second as the bullets hammered into his chest, then he stumbled forward another step before collapsing.

As Preacher shoved himself up onto his feet, more Apaches came into view, seeming to appear as if by magic from the rocks around him. He was sur-rounded, facing at least half a dozen enemies. He had one shot remaining in the revolver he held, but the Dragoon on his other hip still had a full wheel. He might not be able to draw the weapon and gun down the rest of the attackers before they overwhelmed him, but he was going to try.

He didn't have to. At that moment Ramirez ap-peared, racing on horseback around another of the rock mounds. He guided his horse with his knees while the guns in both hands spat flame. Some of the Apaches tried to turn to meet this new attack, but the bullets from Ramirez's guns ripped through them before they could do anything.

Preacher lifted the Dragoon in his right hand and

shot another warrior in the head. At this range, the slug blew off a good chunk of the man's skull.

At the same time, Preacher drew the other Dragoon with his left hand and brought it up. He thumbed off a couple of rounds that knocked another warrior off his feet.

Instinct warned him, and he spun around to see an Apache leaping at him from behind. He leaped to the side to avoid a sweeping slash of the knife the man held, then lashed out with the empty revolver he held in his right hand. The heavy Dragoon crashed into the Apache's head with a crunch of shattering bone. The man's knees buckled and he pitched forward as blood ran from his ears, nose, and eyes.

A scream made Preacher look over his shoulder. Ramirez had ridden down one of the warriors. His horse's steel-shod hooves slashed and pounded the man into insensibility. But the last of the Apaches who had surrounded Preacher was drawing a bead on Ramirez's back with an arrow. Preacher fired the left-hand Dragoon past Ramirez, who looked startled, as if he thought Preacher's shot was aimed at *him*.

Then the arrow that would have skewered him from behind flew past his head, and he turned to see the Apache who had fired it folding up with Preacher's bullet in his guts. The warrior dropped to his knees and pressed both hands to his belly. Blood welled between his fingers. His mouth opened and closed. Preacher knew he was trying to sing a death song, but the spirits caught up to him too quickly for that. He fell forward onto his face and didn't move again.

Preacher looked around and saw that all the other Apaches were either dead or too close to it to be a threat anymore. A few more shots blasted from other areas around the cluster of rocks, then an echoing silence fell. Dog padded into sight, his muzzle bloody from the havoc he had wreaked.

One by one, Audie, Nighthawk, and the Molmberg brothers appeared, too. They appeared to be unhurt.

Preacher asked, "Got this hornet's nest cleaned out?"

"Indeed we have," Audie replied. "We can get a more accurate count later, but right now I'd estimate that we killed somewhere between fifteen and twenty Apaches."

"Any get away?"

"Umm," Nighthawk said curtly. He shook his head in disgust.

"One, but only that one," Audie said. "He appeared to be wounded, but perhaps not fatally."

Preacher rubbed his chin. "Jamie won't mind that one of the varmints lit a shuck. He'll rattle his hocks back to the others. They already knew we were here, but now they know why we came."

"We came to kill," Ramirez said as he slid his re-loaded guns back into their holsters.

"We sure did," Preacher said.

CHAPTER 28

Jamie took the lead as his group rode east along the base of the escarpment. Behind him in single file came Edgerton, Powder Pete, Deadlead, and Tennysee. Bringing up the rear, about twenty yards behind the others, was Dog Brother.

Jamie hadn't told the half-breed to hang back like that. Dog Brother was doing it on his own, probably because he just didn't like to associate with the others.

That seemed to be all right with the rest of the group. Dog Brother was a surly varmint—but he had a reputation for being good in a fight. As long as he was close by in case the Apaches jumped them, nobody gave a hoot if he was friendly.

Other than the ragged-edged bluff that formed the escarpment, the country in that direction seemed featureless. Jamie spotted a few mesas and rock spires far to the south, but closer there was nothing to be seen except flat, sandy ground and the occasional rock, clump of hardy grass, or stumpy greasewood bush.

Then Edgerton, riding a few yards behind Jamie, said, "Hey, look over there, MacCallister. Is that a cave?"

"Yeah." Jamie had spotted it just before Edgerton spoke up.

Powder Pete said, "We'd better check it out. Might be some Apaches hidin' in it."

Jamie was already turning his horse toward the dark opening in the side of the bluff. "Not likely to be any Apaches in there, but I don't suppose it'll hurt anything to take a look."

"More likely a den o' rattlesnakes," Tennysee said. "I'll let you boys go in there iffen you want to. I don't like them scaly critters myself."

The lanky mountain man might be right, Jamie knew. Rattlers loved rocky areas like this. He reined to a stop while he was still several yards from the cave mouth.

And it wasn't *exactly* a cave, he saw now that they were closer. A large, rugged shelf of rock extended outward from the bluff, and the overhang created a cavelike area underneath it. That area extended *into* the bluff, and as Jamie studied it, he decided that at some point in the past, it had been hollowed out to make it bigger. Not by the elements, but by human beings. Someone *had* lived there.

Nothing moved in the shadowy gloom, at least as far as Jamie could see—and his eyes were pretty good. He swung down from the saddle and motioned for the others to do likewise. "Gather up some of that dry greasewood and make a little fire," he told Edgerton. "I want to fashion a torch before I go in there."

Edgerton grunted and set about the task.

"There ain't no Apaches in there," Powder Pete said. "If there was, they'd be shootin' at us by now, I reckon. So why do we need a better look?"

"Maybe we don't *need* it, but I want to see what's

in there," Jamie replied. "I think somebody used to live there, and I'm curious about them."

Dog Brother gave him a disdainful sneer, as if that was the most ridiculous thing he had ever heard. Jamie saw the look but ignored it.

Using flint, steel, and tinder, Edgerton got the small stack of dried greasewood branches burning. Jamie gathered more branches, bundled them together in his left hand, and held the other end of the bundle in the flames until it caught. Then he walked quickly into the cave underneath the beetling rock outcropping. He drew his Colt with his other hand in case any rattlesnakes were lurking.

He didn't hear the telltale whirring sound that the rattles made when one of the snakes was ready to strike. The flickering light from the makeshift torch reached out to the edges of the roughly circular area and didn't illuminate anything except sandy ground and curving rock walls. Then Jamie spotted something else on the rocks and stepped closer.

A smile touched his lips as he looked at what the light revealed. Crude figures and designs had been painted on the stone. Time had faded the painting, but he was able to make out marks intended to depict humans, animals, maybe some mountains and a river, the sun, even a scattering of stars. Whoever had lived here hundreds of years ago—perhaps even longer than that—had attempted to leave a record of their lives. They were long dead, but their paintings remained, creating a bond that stretched back from Jamie's time all the way to theirs.

He looked at the fading marks for a moment longer, then dropped the torch to the sandy ground before the curling flames reached his fingers. He backed away from the stone wall, turned, and stepped out into the light of morning, holstering his gun.

"No Indians in there, I reckon?" Edgerton asked.

"Not now," Jamie replied. "But there were a long time ago. Not Apaches, though. The folks who lived here were around these parts while the Apaches were still over in West Texas and hadn't been run out yet by the Comanches." He glanced at Dog Brother, whose features remained impassive.

Clearly the half-breed didn't take any pride in how his father's people had chased the Apaches out of Texas, for the most part.

"There are some paintings on the wall in there," Jamie went on. "The old-time Indians left them there. If any of you want to take a look at them, go ahead."

None of the men budged.

Edgerton said, "If those paintings don't get us any closer to the varmints we came here to kill, I don't reckon they matter much."

"Suit yourself," Jamie said with a shrug. It was too bad Audie wasn't here, he thought. The former professor would be interested in the cave paintings, he was sure of that. Maybe he would tell Audie about them later. "The horses got to rest a few minutes, anyway."

They mounted up and moved on, staying close to the bluff as they headed east. After a while, Jamie reined in again. He leaned over in the saddle to study the ground.

"Hoofprints from unshod ponies," he announced as he straightened. "Looks like about a dozen of them."

"An Apache huntin' party, more 'n likely," Tennysee said. "Iffen I recollect rightly, there's one o' them little mountain ranges five or ten miles north o' here. They must've gone up there hopin' to get 'em a sheep or an antelope."

Dog Brother had ridden forward. He slid down from his horse's back and dropped to one knee to take a better look at the hoofprints. After a moment, he looked up at Jamie and said, "These tracks are only a few hours old."

"I thought the same thing," Jamie replied with a nod. "And they're all headed north."

Edgerton grunted. "That means they haven't come back yet. They'll be heading this way."

"Unless they went back to their camp by some other trail," Jamie pointed out. "But it's more likely they'll return on the same trail they used going north."

"Likely enough for us to wait an' see?" Tennysee asked.

Jamie nodded again. "That's what I'm thinking."

The rest of them dismounted. Jamie sent Deadlead up to the top of the bluff to keep an eye out for the Apaches if they returned. The rest of the men checked their weapons and took little sips from their canteens. There was no telling how long they might have to wait. It might be late in the day before the hunting party rode back this way—if, indeed, it actually did.

In the meantime, there wasn't much shade to speak of, and the sun was almost overhead. The heat grew uncomfortable and would get considerably worse before it started getting better, Jamie knew.

Luckily, only half an hour had passed before Deadlead came to the edge of the bluff and waved his hat over his head to attract the attention of the men below. Once he had it, he put the hat on again and cupped his hands around his mouth to call, "Riders comin'!"

"Apaches?" Jamie shouted back.

"Don't know! They're still too far out to tell for sure! But who in blazes *else* could it be?"

Jamie didn't know. It wasn't likely that any other groups of white men would be wandering around in this dangerous wasteland. He supposed the riders might be a Mexican army patrol. He wasn't sure exactly where the border was, and he figured the Mexicans probably didn't know, either.

He told the other men to stay where they were and climbed up the rocky slope to have a look for himself. He had a telescope in his saddlebags, but he didn't take it with him. Too great a risk the sun might reflect off the lens and warn the approaching riders that someone was here. He would have to depend on his own eyes.

When Jamie reached the top, Deadlead pointed out the distant figures he had spotted. At this point, they weren't much more than tiny black shapes making their way across the sun-blasted wilderness.

Jamie shaded his eyes with a big hand and squinted at the approaching figures. "Can't get an exact count, but there seems to be about a dozen of them. That matches up with the hoofprints we found down there."

"It's the Apaches," Deadlead said confidently.

"We're going to get ready like it's them, anyway," Jamie said. He rubbed his beard-stubbled chin and went on. "Get down low so they won't spot you and keep an eye on them. Let us know if they veer off one way or the other."

Deadlead nodded. He stretched out on his belly at the edge of the bluff while Jamie went back down the slope to rejoin the rest of the group. He told them what was going on, then asked Powder Pete to take the horses back along the bluff to the west until he found a spot where they would be out of sight.

"You can lead them into the cave underneath that overhang," Jamie suggested.

"But I'll miss all the excitement," Pete protested.

"Next time, somebody else can handle the horses," Jamie said. "The rest of you, take your rifles, go on up, and find good positions along the rim. Keep the guns below the edge for now so the sun won't reflect off them. With any luck, those Apaches will ride right up to us before they know we're here."

"Good luck for us, you mean," Tennysee said. "Howsomever, I don't reckon it'll be all that fortunate for them if they do."

"No," Jamie said, shaking his head. "Not good luck for them at all."

CHAPTER 29

Jamie went up to the top of the slope and motioned for Deadlead to move back until he was below the rim. Jamie knelt beside him and peered across the flats at the riders, who were still coming steadily toward the escarpment. They had closed the gap enough that Jamie was able to distinguish the men on horseback.

"I'm pretty sure they're Apaches, all right," Deadlead commented. "You can make out those bright-colored headbands and sashes they like to wear."

Jamie agreed, having already spotted a few splashes of red and blue himself. He nodded and said, "You're in a good position, so you can just stay right here. I'll move off over there to the left. The rest of the boys are spreading out along the rim. When I figure the Apaches are close enough, I'll start the ball. The rest of you open fire then."

"Gonna be a little like a turkey shoot," Deadlead said.

With a grim note in his voice, Jamie said, "Except the turkeys never fought back. These Apaches will."

Staying low so they wouldn't spot him moving along

the rim, he made his way to a good place where he could crouch just under the edge and bring up his Sharps when the time was right. He looked along the rim in both directions and saw the other men readying their weapons.

A grimace pulled Jamie's lips away from his teeth for a second. An ambush like this was very much like cold-blooded murder, and that rubbed him the wrong way. Unlikely though it might be, the possibility existed that some of the warriors in that hunting party had never slaughtered any innocents. But they would be cut down, too, either in the opening volley or the fighting that would follow hard on its heels. True, it was the job of him and his companions to kill Apaches and force any survivors out of the territory, and in the long run that would save many innocent lives . . . but some things were still hard to swallow.

Jamie was thinking about that when two of the mounted figures suddenly moved out in front of the others, pushing their ponies to a considerably faster pace. They rode hard toward the rim.

Instantly, Jamie realized what was going on. Whoever was in command of that party didn't want to ride up to the edge blindly, without knowing whether any enemies might be lurking out of sight just beyond it. The hombre was smart, Jamie thought. He would have done the same thing if he were in charge.

Jamie ducked low so he wouldn't be spotted and signaled urgently to his men, trying to let them know that they needed to hide as best they could. A number of boulders littered the slope and provided potential cover. If the men could manage it, they would let the scouts ride down the slope without noticing them, then jump the two men and try to take care of them without any shots to give away their presence. Jamie slid over behind one of the rocks and tried to make himself as small as possible, but for a man of his size, that wasn't easy.

The ponies' hoofbeats got louder as they approached, then stopped. Jamie couldn't see the riders from where he was, because he didn't want *them* to see *him*, but he guessed the two Apaches had come to a halt near the rim to look over the landscape. He was glad he had told Powder Pete to take the horses back along the bluff until they were out of sight.

After a minute or so that dragged by with maddening slowness, the ponies *clip-clopped* closer. Jamie held his breath and stayed absolutely still, knowing that movement attracted the eye quicker than anything else. About twenty feet away, two young Apache warriors on horseback appeared at the edge of the bluff and started slowly down the slope.

When their heads were turned, Jamie eased his knife out of its sheath. He waited, letting them continue descending so they wouldn't be as visible to the other members of their group they had left up on the flats. When he judged they had gone far enough, he carefully drew back his arm and then whipped it forward as he threw the knife.

The blade flashed through the air and then landed with a solid *thunk!* in the side of the nearest Apache. The young man cried out and twisted around on the back of his pony as he grabbed reflexively at the knife.

At the same time, Deadlead leaped up from behind the rock where he had taken cover, on the far side of the scouts from Jamie, and charged toward them. The second Apache, who carried an old flintlock rifle, tried to swing it toward Deadlead, but the frontiersman grabbed the barrel, wrenched the rifle out of the Apache's hands, and rammed the stock upward into his jaw. The sudden attack spooked the pony and made the animal lunge forward. The impact of the blow Deadlead struck with the rifle flipped the man backward off the pony.

The same speed that made Deadlead dangerous with a gun served him well now. He darted in and slammed the rifle's butt in the middle of the fallen man's face, crushing his nose and shattering bone. The Apache spasmed and then sagged back into the stillness of death.

The man with Jamie's knife in him was still mounted. He managed to get a hand on the weapon and yanked it free. Blood flowed out thickly from the wound. Jamie charged at him and ducked as the Apache flung the bloody knife back at him.

Edgerton rushed in from the other side, and the wounded man didn't see him coming in time. Edgerton reached up, grabbed the Apache, and hauled him off the pony. He heaved the man farther down the slope where Dog Brother was waiting with a knife clutched in his own hand. Almost too swiftly for the eye to follow, the half-breed bent over and slashed the blade across the Apache's throat, then straightened and stepped back as blood shot up from the gaping wound. The dying warrior flopped his arms and legs for a couple of seconds before going still. Blood still welled from his throat as his heart pumped out its last feeble beats, then that stopped as well.

Dog Brother took off his hat and tossed it to one side. He pulled off his vest and then ripped the crimson headband from the dead Apache to put it on his own head.

Jamie had figured out what the half-breed was doing, so he wasn't surprised when Dog Brother ran over to one of the Indian ponies, grabbed its rope hackamore, and leaped onto the animal's back. He rode back up to the rim and waved an arm to let the rest of the Apaches know it was all right to come ahead.

"Hate to say anything good about that varmint because he's surlier 'n an ol' possum," Tennysee drawled, "but that's a pretty smart move."

"It is," Jamie agreed, "but there's a chance that's *not* the signal they agreed on. If it is, we've still got a chance to spring this trap. Everybody spread out and take your positions at the top again."

While they were doing that, Dog Brother turned the pony and rode back down the slope. He dropped off the animal's back, tore off the headband, and flung it away from him with a look of disgust. He picked up his own hat and put it back on, then shrugged into his vest as he joined the others just below the rim.

Jamie had taken off his hat so he could look over the edge. The rest of the Apaches had started moving again. They came on toward the rim at a leisurely pace and didn't seem concerned about anything.

"Looks like your little trick worked," he said to Dog Brother. "They thought you were one of those scouts they sent ahead."

"I thought they might," Dog Brother said. "I'm bigger than either of those two, so I knew they might notice that, but evidently they—"

Suddenly, with strident, angry whoops, the Apaches jabbed their heels in their ponies' flanks and the animals lunged forward. The warriors were in bowshot range, and as they charged, they unslung their bows and sent arrows flying toward the rim.

Tennysee ducked a shaft that went right over his head and exclaimed, "Looks like the joke's on us, boys—and it's a corker!"

CHAPTER 30

With the Apaches already aware of their presence and attacking, there was no need for stealth. Jamie lifted himself a little higher, raised the Sharps to his shoulder, took aim, and squeezed the trigger.

He was used to the loud boom and the heavy kick. He looked through the pall of powder smoke that had gushed from the Sharps' muzzle and saw that the man he had targeted was down. The riderless pony galloped on. Jamie reloaded as more shots blasted from the men concealed along the rim.

From the corner of his eye, he saw two more Apaches topple from their horses. Others may have been hit but were able to stay mounted; he couldn't tell about that. He closed the rifle's breech and lifted it again to draw another bead.

When he fired, the pony being ridden by the man he targeted chose exactly the wrong second to throw its head high. Jamie's shot hit the animal, killing it instantly. The pony went down as if its legs had been jerked out from under it, and the yelling rider flew through the air, arms windmilling, as momentum flung him forward.

He hit the ground hard and rolled over several times but was able to spring back to his feet—just in time for a bullet fired from Jamie's Walker Colt to crash into his chest and drive him backward. The Apaches were in revolver range, so Jamie didn't take the time to reload the Sharps. He thumbed back the Walker's hammer, swung it to the right, and triggered again. This shot shattered the shoulder of another Apache and dropped him howling to the ground.

Although several of the warriors were down, the rest had reached the rim and dived from their ponies, hitting the ground running as they closed with their enemies to do battle hand to hand.

One screeching warrior came at Jamie with a lance and tried to ram the weapon through him. Jamie twisted aside. The lance's sharp-pointed flint head raked along the side of his buckskin shirt. The Walker boomed again as he fired a round into the middle of the Apache's face. The warrior's features disappeared in a red, powder-scorched smear.

The dead man fell against him, getting in his way for a second and threatening to get tangled up with his feet. Jamie shoved the corpse aside and looked up to see another warrior aiming an arrow at him. Before the Apache could turn loose of the bowstring, a rifle blasted. The bullet slammed into him and turned him halfway around. The arrow flew off wildly. As the Apache collapsed, Jamie glanced to the right and saw Tennysee lowering a rifle with smoke curling from the muzzle. The two men exchanged curt nods. There was no time—or need—for anything else. For fighting men, that brief look conveyed all that needed to be said.

His instincts warning him, Jamie whirled and shot another warrior closing in on him with a knife.

Gun-thunder rolled along the rim for a minute or so, and a gray cloud of acrid powder smoke gathered to make noses sting and eyes water. The battle seemed longer than it really was.

As the shots died away, an eerie silence took their place. That silence lasted until one of the wounded Apaches began to chant his death song.

That ended abruptly when Dog Brother cut the dying man's throat.

Jamie was breathing a little hard as he looked around. He was getting too old for this, he thought. Even though he was only in his early forties, that was a pretty advanced age for a fighting man. Preacher was ten years older, Jamie reminded himself—but Preacher seemed nearly ageless and probably always would.

Dog Brother, Tennysee, and Deadlead were all on their feet. The Apaches were down, either dead or dying, and the ones who still moved were stilled quickly as Dog Brother stalked among them, finishing them off.

"Where's Edgerton?" Jamie asked as he realized he didn't see the dour frontiersman.

"Over here," Edgerton called from behind one of the boulders. Jamie circled it quickly and saw Edgerton sitting there with his back propped against the rock. His legs were stretched out in front of him. The left one had an arrow embedded in the thigh.

"Doesn't look too bad," Jamie said as he hunkered on his heels next to the wounded man.

"No, it didn't go in very deep," Edgerton agreed. Despite the calmness in his voice, his face was pale from the pain. "The varmint fired it just as I ventilated him, and his grip on the bowstring slipped a little, so the arrow didn't have full force behind it. Bad enough, though." He paused. "You know what's got to be done now."

Jamie grunted. "Sure. We'll tend to it once I've made sure everybody else is all right and sent one of the others to fetch Pete and the horses."

"What about the Apaches? Are they all dead?"

"Dog Brother is seeing to that," Jamie said.

Edgerton nodded slowly, understanding exactly what Jamie meant.

Tennysee, Deadlead, and Dog Brother had come through the fight without a scratch. Tennysee volunteered to walk back and let Pete know it was safe to return with the horses.

"How bad's Edgerton hurt?" Deadlead asked.

"He caught an arrow in the leg. I'm fixing to take it out of him."

Tennysee had started to walk off. He stopped, turned around, and reached inside his buckskin shirt to take out a small silver flask. As he held it out to Jamie, he said, "Give him this. I reckon he'll need it more 'n I do. Sorry there ain't more."

"This'll help me clean the wound, once I get the arrow out."

"Yeah, that, too," Tennysee said. "Just don't waste too much of it on that."

Jamie took the flask and he and Deadlead went back to Edgerton. He let Edgerton swallow a slug of the whiskey and then told him to give the flask to Deadlead for the moment. Deadlead tucked it away in his pocket and took hold of Edgerton's wounded leg, getting a good grip on it as Edgerton rolled onto his right side.

Jamie grasped the arrow with his left hand and shoved as hard as he could. Edgerton yelled in pain as the bloody arrowhead emerged from the back of his leg. Jamie stopped pushing as soon as the head protruded enough from the flesh for him to cut it off with his bowie knife. Edgerton's breath hissed between his teeth as Jamie drew the shaft back through the hole. That method did less damage overall than trying to withdraw the barbed arrow.

Deadlead took out the flask and dribbled the fiery whiskey on the entrance wound until it started to trickle from the exit wound. Both holes bled freely for a few minutes, but the crimson flow slowed and then almost stopped.

"Soon as Tennysee and Pete get back with the horses, I've got some cloth in my saddlebags we can use to bandage that leg," Jamie told Edgerton. "We'll do a better job of patching you up once we get back to camp."

"That's fine," Edgerton rasped. "Right now, just gimme that flask."

"It's Tennysee's," Deadlead said as he handed it over. "Reckon you ought to thank him for it."

"I will." Edgerton tipped the flask to his lips and his throat worked as he took a long swallow. "Later."

With nothing really to do, Noah Stuart was bored as he sat around the campsite. Chester Merrick, whose mind wasn't as active as Stuart's, was more than happy to nap most of the time. Like a sleeping cat, the heat didn't seem to bother him.

Pugh had posted himself at the top of the bluff behind the camp. Dupre stood watch on the rocky outcrop to the west, Greybull on the one to the east. Stuart supposed they were accustomed to passing the time in such fashion, too. Knowing that there might be a horde of bloodthirsty Apaches out there, eager to slay all of them, was enough to keep a man alert and occupied with the task of watching for them.

Fletch and Clementine Wylie were inside their wagon most of the time. Stuart didn't know what they were doing in there and didn't want to speculate. The actions of the young married couple were certainly none of his business.

That left him to pore over the sketches and rough maps he had made on the way down there. He sharpened them up, tracing the lines darker and bolder. When he had done all of that he could, he took his pencil and pad of paper and walked away from the campsite, heading south.

From the rim to the west, Dupre called, "*M'sieu* Stuart, where are you going?"

Stuart stopped and tipped his head back to look at the French frontiersman. "I'm just going far enough to get a better look at the escarpment. I thought I'd start mapping it."

"*M'sieu* MacCallister said for you to stay with the wagons!"

"I'm only going a few hundred yards!" Stuart replied without bothering to hide the exasperation in his voice. He waved his free hand toward the flats to the south. "There are no Apaches out there! We can see for miles—"

As he spoke, he turned his head in the direction he was waving, and he stopped short as something out there, several miles away, glinted in the sunlight. Just a flash of reflected light, there and then gone, but he was sure he had seen it.

He turned back toward the camp and lifted his voice to ask Dupre excitedly, "Did you see that?"

"See what?"

Stuart waved his hand again. "Something flashed out there. Reflected off metal. That can't be natural."

"How far away?"

"A couple of miles. Maybe more."

Dupre stood stiff and straight on the rim as he peered southward with great intensity. After a few moments, he shook his head and called down to Stuart, "I saw nothing, but I believe you, *m'sieu.* You had best come back to the wagons."

Fletch and Clementine heard them shouting back and forth, and emerged from their wagon.

Fletch asked, "What's going on?"

Stuart noticed that the young man had his hand on the butt of his revolver, and Clementine held the rifle he had seen her use skillfully during target practice.

"I thought I saw something out there," Stuart told them. "A flash of light." He glanced nervously over his shoulder, seeing nothing now but sure that *something* had been there a few minutes earlier. Maybe it would be a good idea to go back to the wagons, he decided. Just in case. He began trudging toward them.

When he got there, Fletch said, "Could've been the sun reflecting on a knife, I guess. Or a gun barrel. Those Apaches have a few old rifles, Preacher and Jamie said."

Chester Merrick climbed out of the surveyors'

wagon, yawning. "What's all the commotion about?" he wanted to know. "Trouble?"

"Not really," Stuart told him. "But there may be someone lurking a few miles to the south."

Merrick immediately looked more nervous than Stuart felt. His eyes got big and he licked his lips. "It must be the savages. Who else would be down here in this godforsaken wilderness?"

"Well, we know one thing," Clementine said. "It can't be my brothers. If they're anywhere around here, they're behind us."

CHAPTER 31

"Blast it!" Clete Mahoney yelled as he jerked the spyglass out of his brother Jerome's hands. "What did I tell you about keeping that thing in your saddle-bags?"

"Sorry, Clete," Jerome said quickly. Like his other two brothers, he didn't want to risk Clete's anger. The oldest of the Mahoneys had a fearsome temper.

Clete closed the telescope and tossed it to Harp, who fumbled it for a second but caught it.

"Put that away, and don't let this idiot have it again," Clete said as he jerked his head toward Jerome.

Even as wary of Clete as he was, that insult rubbed Jerome the wrong way enough to make him say, "Hey, you got no right—"

"To call you an idiot?" Clete interrupted him. "Why not? Just what sort of good thinking have you con-tributed, Jerome? *I'm* the one who came up with the idea of circling around them so we could get ahead and wait for them to come to us."

"I know, I know," Jerome muttered with his eyes

downcast now. "I just don't cotton to bein' called names, that's all."

"Then use your head for somethin' besides hangin' your hat on," Clete snapped. He looked around at all three of his brothers. "I swear, if you boys didn't have me around to handle all the brain work for you, you'd be wanderin' around at loose ends, not even sure when it was time to feed yourselves."

He could tell they wanted to argue, but they didn't dare. They were too afraid of him. Good, he thought. It was better all around if they were scared of him. It would be better if *everybody* was so scared of him that they let him be the boss.

If Clementine hadn't been so stubborn and defiant and had gone along with what nature intended, none of them would be out here under that burning sun, in the middle of a wasteland not fit for human critters, only lizards and Apaches.

When it came right down to it, if it had been up to the others they wouldn't be out here, either. After what had happened in Santa Fe, Lew, Harp, and Jerome would have turned tail and gone running back home. They were too worried about that old mountain man who, for some reason Clete couldn't even begin to understand, seemed to have appointed himself as Clementine and Fletch's protector. According to the stories his brothers had heard about Preacher, the old-timer was supposed to be some sort of ring-tailed roarer.

Well, nobody roared like Clete Mahoney, and the sooner everybody knew that and accepted it, the better.

After they had served the seven-day sentence they'd gotten for disturbing the peace, Clete had started rounding up supplies and extra horses for the pursuit. He hadn't asked the others what they wanted to do, and only Harp had been bold enough to say something about how maybe Clete shouldn't be getting in such a big hurry.

Clete didn't put up with any mouthing off like that. He had walloped Harp so hard that a little blood trickled out of his ear as he lay on the ground where Clete had knocked him, and after that none of them dared to sass their older brother or try to talk him out of his plans.

They rode out of Santa Fe well aware that they were a week behind their quarry, but Clete insisted they could make up that time. With extra horses and no wagons, they could move faster.

That was exactly what had happened. They had spotted the wagons and riders far ahead of them a couple of days earlier. After closing in as much as they dared, they had swung wide and circled to the south, getting ahead of Clementine and the rest of that sorry bunch. It was just a matter of waiting for the right opportunity for an ambush to come along.

Earlier, they had stopped to rest their horses next to a small mesa with a thick growth of cactus around its base. The bluff they had descended early that morning was still visible as a low, dark line back to the north, a couple of miles away. That was where the group they were after had made camp, and it appeared that they intended to stay there for a while. Smaller groups had ridden off to the east and west.

Clete wasn't sure what was going on, but they had heard rumors back in Santa Fe that the party was coming down here to hunt Apaches. That sounded to

Clete like such a blasted fool thing to do that he had a hard time believing anybody would even attempt it.

The rumors were nerve-wracking to his brothers, though.

In fact, Harp chose that moment to say, "I don't like just sittin' here. Some of them savages could be lurkin' around. This is their country, not ours."

"Well, then, what do you think we should do, Harp?" Clete asked.

"We could find a better place to hole up—"

Clete interrupted him by waving an arm at their surroundings. "A better place?" he repeated. "Why don't you tell me where that'd be? There's *nothin'* out here. A few little mesas like this, and that's all. Right here's the best we can do."

"There's no water," Lew said.

"Maybe not, but look at all that cactus. We can get water from them. All you have to do is cut 'em open and suck it out. We'll do that and save what's in our canteens for the horses. Anyway, there are bound to be some waterholes around here somewhere. It's just a matter of findin' 'em. We'll have time for that . . . once Clementine is back with us where she belongs." Clete glared at his brothers. "Or maybe you don't care about that no more. Maybe you want to let her get away with disrespectin' and defyin' her family!"

None of them responded to that. After a moment, Lew muttered something about hacking off a piece of that cactus like Clete was talking about.

"Mind you don't get the needles stuck in your fingers," Clete warned him. "The stuff's mighty thorny."

Lew muttered something else too quietly for Clete to understand it. Clete didn't mind. He was feeling generous again. His brothers were scared of him, and that pleased him.

As long as they were more scared of him than they were of any cactus needles—or Apaches—or old mountain men—everything would work out just fine.

Both groups got back to the camp late that afternoon, driving Indian ponies ahead of them. That was a grim indication in itself that their search had been successful.

"What do you plan on doing with them, Jamie?" Preacher asked. "There ain't enough grass and water here for these critters and our horses, too. And we don't have a good place to keep 'em."

"We're going to push them up the bluff and then haze them off to the north," Jamie replied. "We'll scatter them as much as we can. They'll head for some of those little mountain ranges where they can find water. At least the other Apaches down here in these parts won't get any use out of them for a while. It'll take time to round them up again . . . if they ever do."

While some of the men tended to that chore, Greybull and Nighthawk carried Edgerton over to the Wylie wagon and set him down on the lowered tailgate.

Edgerton didn't like being fussed over, and he said as much in no uncertain terms. "If anybody's got any more whiskey, just pour some on those arrow holes and call it good," he insisted. "I'm fine."

"I don't know about that," Audie said. "Let me take a look at the injury."

Preacher said, "Audie's a pretty good sawbones. You best listen to what he says."

"I'm an amateur physician, at best," Audie said, "but I do have a considerable amount of practical experience with all sorts of wounds. I suspect most of us here do. Let's see, shall we?"

Several of the men gathered around to watch while Audie examined the wound. So did Fletch and Clementine and Noah Stuart. Chester Merrick started to, then turned a little green at the sight of the angry-looking wounds on Edgerton's leg and walked away.

"Jamie and Deadlead appear to have done a good job," Audie announced after a few minutes. "I'll clean the wounds a bit more and then replace this dressing with a fresh one. You'll have to stay off that leg for a day or two, my friend, and it'll be sore for quite some time, but you should be fine."

"A day or two!" Edgerton said. "I can't be laid up. I came down here to work, and nobody'll ever say I don't earn my wages."

"You'll earn 'em," Jamie said. "You'll stay here and help guard the camp. Somebody's got to do that anyway, so you might as well be one of them. In a few days, when you're able to ride again, we'll probably move farther south . . . unless we've got all the business we can handle right here where we are."

Nobody had to ask Jamie what he meant by that. After today's bloody clashes that had resulted in the deaths of more than two dozen Apache warriors, they might not have to go hunting for trouble anymore.

It might come to them, ready and willing to massacre the whole bunch.

CHAPTER 32

That evening, Noah Stuart sought out Jamie and Preacher to tell them about the flash of reflected sunlight he had seen off to the south earlier in the day.

"Any of the others see it?" Preacher asked.

Stuart shook his head. "No, I seem to have been the only one. I'm absolutely certain about it, though."

"It's not that we don't believe you, Noah," Jamie said. "But if one of the sentries had seen it, too, we might be able to get a better idea exactly where it was."

"You intend to go down there and have a look?" Stuart asked.

Jamie shrugged. "Seems like the thing to do. Not this evening, though. It's too late in the day for that. We'll check it out first thing in the morning."

"Will it be all right if I come with you?" Stuart's voice had a note of eagerness in it.

Jamie and Preacher exchanged a glance.

"Liable to run into trouble," the mountain man warned.

"Perhaps, but it would give me a chance to have a better look around the territory along this escarpment, as well as the bluff itself. I need some distance to get the proper perspective."

"All right," Jamie said. "Make sure you bring your rifle and pistol, though, along with that sketch pad of yours, in case we run into any trouble."

"Leave the scattergun here for Merrick," Preacher added. "If there's need of gunplay, he's more likely to be able to get some use out of it."

If it came down to relying on Chester Merrick to put up a fight, they really *would* be in trouble, Jamie thought.

Nobody did any fighting that night. It passed quietly except for Edgerton's snoring. Normally he wasn't that raucous while he was asleep, but he had guzzled down enough tanglefoot to deaden the pain of his wound that he slumbered more deeply than usual.

The next morning, Jamie announced over breakfast, "Preacher and I are going to do some scouting today, at least starting out. I want to have a look at that area where Noah saw something yesterday."

They hadn't tried to keep Stuart's claim a secret, since Dupre, Greybull, Pugh, Fletch and Clementine, and Merrick already knew about it.

"Noah's coming with us," Jamie went on, "and I figured we'd take Audie and Nighthawk, too. Lars, Bengt, Deadlead, Tennysee, you boys drive those Indian ponies up on the flat and haze them off to the north, like I told you about last night. The rest of you stick close to camp here until we get back." He directed a hard look toward Ramirez and Dog Brother. "Everybody try to get along while we're gone."

Ramirez opened his mouth as if he were going to

say something, then thought better of it and shrugged. Dog Brother's face remained as stony as ever.

A short time later, the five men who were going to scout to the south mounted up and rode off in that direction. Jamie and Preacher took the lead, while Audie and Nighthawk flanked Noah Stuart behind them. Audie and Stuart talked about surveying and mapmaking. As with most subjects, Audie knew enough about them to carry on an intelligent conversation, and Stuart seemed quite engaged by their talk.

Up ahead, Preacher said quietly, "You reckon we're gonna find anything?"

"I don't know, but it's possible," Jamie replied. "We're not the only ones in these parts. There's really no telling what Noah saw."

"If he saw anything."

Jamie nodded and said slowly, "I reckon I believe him. Or I believe *he* believes he did. But he seems like a pretty sharp young fella, not the sort that would go imagining things or making them up."

"He's had sense enough not to cause any trouble betwixt Fletch and Clementine. I wasn't sure at first if he would."

"Yeah, I was worried about that, too," Jamie admitted. "Glad it hasn't happened."

They hadn't ridden more than half a mile when they spotted the low mesa ahead of them. Jamie and Preacher reined in and let the other three riders catch up to them. Jamie pointed at the mesa and asked, "Is that about where you saw something, Noah?"

"Well, it's hard to say for sure . . ." Stuart turned his head, looking back and forth between the camp and the mesa. "But it seems to line up right. Yes, I think that's the area." He squinted toward the mesa. "What is that?"

"Just a little mesa," Jamie said. "They pop up here and there in this part of the country."

"Would you be likely to find Apaches there?"

"You can find Apaches just about anywhere in these parts," Preacher drawled.

Jamie heeled his horse into motion again. "Let's go see what we can find out."

"Take the horses around on the back side—fast!" Clete Mahoney ordered his brother Harp. "Lew, Jerome, go with him!"

"Ain't we gonna bushwhack those fellas, Clete?" Lew asked.

"They're ridin' right into our gunsights," Jerome added.

"Let me think about this, blast it," Clete snapped. They had been waiting for an ambush opportunity, but he wasn't sure this was the right one. There were only five men riding toward the mesa right now, and when he sprang the trap, he hoped to be able to wipe out more of the party than that before they knew what was going on.

Even if he and his brothers killed these five, the rest of the bunch likely would figure out what was going on and be warned that they were in danger.

On the other hand, he couldn't tell yet who those riders were. If Preacher and Jamie MacCallister were among them, it might be worth alerting the others just to get rid of those two old ripsnorters.

As the others were leading the horses around the

mesa as Clete had ordered, he turned and ran over to them. "Where's that spyglass?"

"You told me to put it away yesterday afternoon, remember?" Harp said.

"I know I did, blast it! And for good reason, too. Why do you think those fellas are ridin' in this direction this morning? Somebody spotted a reflection off that glass!" Actually, he didn't know that, but it seemed like a reasonable assumption. "Gimme it!"

"What? The spyglass?"

"Yes, the spyglass!"

Grumbling, Harp dug out the instrument and handed it over. Clete opened it and used his hat to shade the lens as he lifted the spyglass to his eye with his other hand. He peered through it, and after a moment the two big men riding in front of the approaching group sprang into focus.

"Preacher and MacCallister," Clete breathed. A chance like this might not fall into their laps again, he thought as he lowered the spyglass, braced one end against his thigh, and closed it. As he tossed it back to Harp, he barked, "Picket those horses and get your rifles. We're fixin' to have us a turkey shoot!"

The group led by Jamie and Preacher was within half a mile of the mesa. Jamie's keen eyes could make out the deep cracks and seams in the reddish sandstone walls, and he also saw the low clumps of cactus around the base. Nothing appeared to be moving around the mesa—but they couldn't see what was on the other side of it.

Jamie was about to suggest that they split up and

circle the mesa to check it out before approaching any closer, when Preacher suddenly said, "Listen! You hear that?"

Jamie reined in and motioned for their companions to do likewise. As the horses came to a stop, Jamie listened intently and after a few seconds heard what Preacher had noticed first.

In the distance to the southwest, a gunshot sounded. Not a flurry of them, just a single report.

"Fella's got hisself a single-shot rifle," Preacher said. "He's just about had time to reload it once, and now he's let off a second round. Let's wait a bit . . . Ah, there it is again!"

The third shot drifted faintly to their ears.

"Someone hunting?" Audie speculated.

"Ummm," Nighthawk said.

"Yes, the shots *do* seem to have a regularity to them . . . There it goes again."

"Somebody's loading and firing just as fast as he can," Jamie said. "Whoever the fella is, it seems like he's got a battle on his hands."

"But nobody's shootin' back at him," Preacher said. "To me, that says Apaches."

"Umm," Nighthawk agreed emphatically.

"If the Apaches have somebody pinned down, we have to go see if we can give him a hand," Jamie declared. He turned to Noah Stuart. "Noah, you light a shuck back to camp. Tell the boys I want four or five of them to come after us, just in case *we* need help. The rest of the group needs to stay there until we get back."

"You don't care which of the men follow you?" Stuart asked.

"No, any of them are fine. But not you, in case you're getting any ideas."

Stuart shook his head. "No, I plan to stay out of any fights that I can."

"That makes you and me just the opposite," Preacher said with a grin. He turned Horse's head to the southwest and put the stallion into a run as he added over his shoulder to the big cur, "Come on, Dog! The fight's a-wastin'!"

"Where in blazes are they goin'?" Harp exclaimed as the five men on horseback suddenly split up, one turning to gallop back toward the camp, the other four pushing their mounts hard to the southwest.

Clete didn't know the answer to that question, but the realization that he and his brothers were about to lose a prime opportunity to strike a hard blow against their enemies tasted bitter in his mouth. He was kneeling behind some of the cactus at the base of the mesa, using it to conceal himself even though it wouldn't have stopped a bullet. His brothers were close by, also kneeling and holding their rifles.

"I heard somethin'," Jerome said. "Sounded like a gunshot over yonderways." He waved a hand vaguely toward the southwest, the same direction Preacher, Jamie, and two of their companions were heading.

Clete thought he'd heard the shot, too, although it was mighty faint. That explained why Preacher and the others had lit a shuck in that direction instead of riding on toward the mesa. They were going to check out that shot.

"Blast it," Lew said. "I thought we were gonna get to kill some of those fellas."

"We'll get another chance," Clete said. "And maybe sooner than you think."

An intriguing idea had started to form in his head. They would have to wait and see what happened . . .

But their little sister and her no-account husband and their newfound friends might be getting some unexpected company this morning.

CHAPTER 33

That country might have appeared flat and feature-less at first glance, but it really wasn't. Little ridges and valleys were scattered throughout the region, and after riding hard for a mile or so, Jamie, Preacher, Audie, and Nighthawk came to one of those valleys that couldn't be seen until the ground abruptly sloped down under their horses' hooves.

About two hundred yards ahead of them, a tiny stream meandered, with a thread of green vegetation marking its course. That verdant patch widened out in one spot to an actual field where crops of some sort were growing. The plants didn't look all that healthy as they struggled to live in the hot, arid climate, but they were hanging on—the same as the man who likely had planted them. He was inside a tiny adobe hut surrounded by Apaches who hunkered in the brush and fired arrows at the hut's windows and through the open doorway.

The four men reined in at the top of that little rise to take in the scene being played out along the creek.

Nighthawk said, "Umm."

"I agree," Audie told him. "Anyone who would

attempt to farm in such a dangerous, inhospitable place is either a lunatic or an incurable optimist."

"Same thing, ain't it?" Preacher growled. "I ain't all that surprised, though. I've seen some o' them Mexican peons try to scratch out a livin' in places you'd never dream of. They're the stubbornest varmints you ever seen."

Jamie was trying to get a count of the attackers. After a moment he said, "Looks like there are eight or ten Apaches down there, and they don't act like they know we're here."

"They'd hear us comin' if we went poundin' down on 'em, though," Preacher said.

Jamie pulled his Sharps from its scabbard. "That's why I was thinking we'd hit them first from up here, then charge the ones who are left."

"We could wait for the other fellas that Noah was gonna fetch to catch up to us," Preacher pointed out.

Jamie thought about that and shook his head. "I've never been good at waiting around when there's a fight going on. Especially when the odds are no worse than they are here. I think we should go ahead and hit them now."

"Sounds like a good idea to me," Preacher said with a grin as he reached for his own Sharps.

Audie and Nighthawk carried the same old-fashioned, long-barreled flintlock rifles they had used during their fur-trapping days, when they had first met Preacher. Those weapons were accurate and reliable, although not as powerful nor with as much range as the Sharps.

As all four men dismounted, another shot came from inside the hut. As far as they could tell, it didn't hit any of the Apaches. Nor were any warriors' bodies lying on the ground where they could see. It seemed that the man in the hut was trying to put up a determined fight, but apparently he just wasn't very good at it.

These four men, however, were *very* good at what they did.

As they started lining up their shots, one of the Apaches leaped to his feet and darted forward. The defender in the hut didn't get a shot off. The Apache reached the hut and put his back against the wall, then began edging along it toward the door.

"Jamie . . ." Preacher said.

"I see him," Jamie replied as he shifted his aim. "And I've got him."

"Figured you would. We ready?"

"Ready," Audie said, and Nighthawk chimed in with his usual response.

"All right. Let's start the ball," Jamie breathed just before he squeezed the trigger.

The familiar boom and kick of the Sharps came just as the Apache beside the door poised himself to leap through the opening. The heavy round smashed into his chest and pinned him to the adobe wall for a second with his arms flung out in shock and pain. Then he toppled forward on his face.

At the same time, Preacher, Audie, and Nighthawk fired, too. Their bullets scythed through the brush and struck the Apaches they had targeted. Two of the warriors simply fell, knocked to the ground by the impacts. The third one bounded high in the air, like a fish jumping out of a lake, and then dropped back down in a boneless sprawl of death.

While the roar of the shots still hung in the air, the four men were already back on their horses. They rammed rifles in scabbards and charged down the gentle slope toward the hut and the remaining attackers.

The Apaches who had been concentrating on the hut leaped up and turned to meet the new threat. As they did, the defender inside the hut finally scored with one of his shots. A warrior pitched forward on his face with blood welling from the hole between his shoulder blades where a bullet fired from the hut's window had smashed into him.

Jamie drew his Walker as he galloped into battle. Preacher filled his hands with both Dragoons and guided Horse with his knees. Dog raced alongside them. Audie and Nighthawk weren't far behind. Audie gripped a flintlock pistol while his big Crow friend fingered the tomahawk stuck behind his belt.

Jamie ducked as an arrow flew over his head, then thumbed off two shots that pounded into the chest of the warrior who had fired the shaft. The Apache sailed backward.

The Dragoons played a roaring symphony in Preacher's expert hands as he fired them—left, right, left, right—and two more warriors tumbled off their feet. Responding instantly to the slightest pressure from Preacher's knees, Horse veered to the right as an arrow whipped past the mountain man's left ear. The left-hand Dragoon spoke again, its speech punctuated by smoke and flame spurting from the barrel, and another Apache screeched and slewed around as a bullet ripped through him.

Audie's flintlock pistol slammed a ball through a warrior's throat and dropped him to his knees as he started to choke on his own blood.

A few yards away, Nighthawk left the back of his horse in a diving tackle, spread his arms wide, and crashed into two of the Apaches. His momentum and great weight carried them all to the ground. The tomahawk in Nighthawk's hand rose and fell in a swift blur and split the skull of one attacker wide open.

The Crow backhanded the gory tomahawk across the face of the other Apache, shattering the man's jaw and almost shearing it right off his face. The Apache could only lie there, thrashing and burbling blood for a second before another stroke of the tomahawk sundered his skull, too.

Dog had another man down, ripping the Apache's throat out as he snarled. Jamie and Preacher wheeled their mounts and swung their guns as they searched for more targets. However, it appeared that the warrior Dog was savaging the last of the Apaches. The rest of the attackers were sprawled around in various limp attitudes of death. Nighthawk was going from body to body, checking just to make sure. He held his knife ready for a swift stroke across a throat if such was needed.

Jamie turned his horse toward the hut and called, "Hello, the house!" Referring to the little adobe *jacal* as a house was a bit of a stretch, but he figured there was no reason to insult the farmer's dwelling. "You can come on out now. It's safe."

Nighthawk nodded and said, "Ummm," to confirm that.

A short, slender figure in the white, pajama-like clothing of a peon emerged from the hut carrying an old muzzleloader. The man's dark, weather-beaten face was set in lines of gratitude. He looked like the sort of hombre who would try to carve a farm out of this desolate landscape.

Jamie wasn't expecting the four figures who followed the man. The first was a woman with a few streaks of gray in her black hair and the same lined features that showed she, too, spent most of her time out in the elements, trying to coax those plants to stay alive and produce a crop.

Around her long, dark brown skirt clustered three children—a boy about eight years old and a couple of girls who were younger. They were already starting to show the signs of premature aging that this hard life had carved onto the faces of their parents, as Jamie assumed the man and woman were.

"*Hola,*" he said, not knowing if any of these people spoke English. He went on in Spanish. "You're safe now. All the Apaches are dead."

"*These* Apaches are dead, señor," the peon replied mostly in English. "But they are far from being the only Apaches in this region."

"Yeah, we know that, amigo," Preacher said. "We've been tusslin' with 'em for a few days now."

The children were staring in horror and awe at the corpses strewn around the place. Kids that young having to see such things was bad, Jamie thought, but what they would have gone through if he and his friends hadn't come along would have been much worse.

Their father noticed, too, and spoke sharply to them in Spanish, sending them scurrying back into the hut. Then he turned back to the visitors. "My name is Armando Sandoval, señors. This is my wife Honoria. Welcome to our home, humble though it may be. I extend to you our hospitality and ask that you come in and dine with us."

Jamie exchanged a glance with Preacher and figured the mountain man was thinking the same thing. That hut was so small it was surprising that five people could fit in it, even when three of them were little ones. If four more men tried to crowd into it—especially hombres as big as Jamie, Preacher, and Nighthawk— the place would be busting at the seams.

Not to mention the fact that these people obviously had very little. They didn't need to be sharing what they did have, even though the visitors had saved their lives, no doubt about that.

"*Muchas gracias*, Señor Sandoval," Jamie said. "We appreciate your offer of hospitality, but I believe there's a chore out here that needs to be taken care of."

"The bodies of these Apaches," Sandoval said grimly.

"That's right. We'll tend to them, and then we'll be on our way back to our camp." Jamie jerked a thumb over his shoulder, aiming it northeast. "It's back that way a few miles, where that long bluff drops down from one stretch of flats to another."

"*Sí*, I know the place," Sandoval said, nodding. He spoke to his wife in Spanish, and she went into the hut to be with the children. Turning back to the men, the farmer went on. "I will help you with the bodies. We can drag them into the brush, well away from the creek." He shook his head. "These savage heathens do not deserve proper burials."

"Can't argue with you there," Preacher drawled. "Anyway, buzzards and coyotes got to eat, too."

From the back of his horse, Audie said, "Riders coming, Jamie. Looks like half a dozen or so, from the amount of dust they're kicking up."

Jamie turned and looked, then nodded. "That'll be some of our boys, the ones Noah sent after us. Why don't you and Nighthawk go meet them and let 'em know everything's all right here now? Then you can head back to camp and Preacher and I will catch up to you in a little while."

"All right," Audie said. "Come on, Nighthawk."

The two old friends rode away while Jamie and Preacher dismounted. With typical efficiency, they each grabbed the ankles of a dead Apache and hauled the corpses toward the brush, heading for an area well away from the stream as Sandoval had said.

The way they handled the bodies might have seemed callous to some observers, but it really wasn't. Both of these men had seen enough violence in their lives—had taken part in enough violence—that their experiences had hardened them in some ways. But they didn't take death and killing lightly. At the core of Preacher and Jamie Ian MacCallister was a huge humanity that made such a thing impossible. They knew full well that if no help had arrived for the Sandoval family, the Apaches would have killed Armando in the most brutal and painful way possible, would have raped and probably killed Honoria, and would have enslaved the three youngsters, if they hadn't decided to go ahead and kill them, too.

No, the Apaches would have shown no mercy, and that was exactly what they had received from their enemies.

Sandoval joined in the grim work, and when the chore was done, he again invited Jamie and Preacher into the hut.

"We really need to be getting back to our camp,"

Jamie said, "but before we go, Señor Sandoval, do you mind if I ask you a question?"

"Of course not, Señor MacCallister." Sandoval called him by name since Jamie and Preacher had introduced themselves to him while they were dragging off the bodies for the scavengers. "What is it you wish to know?"

Jamie gestured toward their surroundings. "Why do you stay out here in the middle of nowhere? You have to know it's not safe for your family."

"It is my land," Sandoval replied with an eloquent shrug. "And the creek, she never runs dry. At least, she has not in the time we have been here, almost three years. Each year, I work a little more land and grow a few more crops. In time, I will cultivate this entire valley and be a rich man . . . or at least, not a poor one."

"If the blamed Apaches don't wipe you out first!" Preacher exclaimed.

Jamie could tell the mountain man was feeling some of the same exasperation he was.

"But you have to understand, señors, the savages were not always as bad as they are now. Most lived in the mountains farther south and were content to remain there. It was only a year or so ago, after Perro Blanco rose to power, that they began to raid more."

"Perro Blanco," Jamie repeated. "Who or what is that?"

"The new war chief of the Apaches. There are farms such as this one here and there, and an old trader travels among them in his wagon. He brings rumors of the raids led by Perro Blanco and how he tries to bring all the scattered bands together. He claims that when he does, he will drive out all the *Mejicanos*, along with any gringos who dare come down here, and this land will belong only to the Apaches."

Jamie rubbed his chin. "That's what he's got in mind, does he?"

"So it is said, Señor MacCallister."

"Then it sounds like this hombre Perro Blanco is somebody we need to meet up with," Jamie said, and Preacher nodded in grim agreement.

Armando Sandoval stared at them in confusion. "You wish to meet the war chief of the Apaches?"

"We'll introduce ourselves with lead," Preacher said.

CHAPTER 34

When Noah Stuart reached the camp and delivered Jamie's message, Tennysee grew serious for a change. He took charge and said, "Pete, Greybull, Deadlead, you fellas come with me. We'll give Preacher and Jamie a hand if they need it. The rest of you stay here."

"And be left out of the action?" Ramirez said. "I'm coming with you!"

Tennysee pursed his lips and looked like he was going to argue, but then he said, "All right. Just don't go rushin' in all recklesslike. We'll see how the ground lies before we take a hand in whatever's goin' on."

Ramirez nodded his agreement, and within a very few minutes, the five men were mounted and riding off to the southwest, following the direction Stuart had indicated.

Fletch said, "Maybe I should have gone, too. It's not fair to all the other fellas that I just stay here in camp all the time."

"Your job is here," Clementine told him, "making sure the wagon stays safe. And me, too."

Fletch blew out a breath. "The way you handle a rifle, I'm not so sure you even need me around anymore."

"Don't you ever think that, Fletcher Wylie!"

Edgerton, who was sitting on the lowered tailgate of the surveyors' wagon to rest his heavily bandaged leg, grimaced and said, "If you want to talk about something not being fair, it's me being laid up like this. I'm a fighting man. I can't abide just sitting around."

"In a few more days, you'll be up and around more, Mr. Edgerton," Clementine told him.

"In the meantime, we have your sparkling company," Dog Brother said with utter solemnity. The half-breed's expression never changed as the others stared at him in the shocked realization that he had made a joke.

"Yeah, sure," Edgerton grumbled.

Dupre brought out his fiddle and suggested, "Perhaps some music is what we need to pass the time." He tucked the instrument against his shoulder and under his chin and lifted the bow, poising it to scrape across the strings.

Before he played a note, a shot blasted somewhere not too far away, and the fiddle seemed to leap out of Dupre's hand as a bullet tore through it and sent splinters flying in the air.

Dupre howled Gallic curses, but an instant later more shots shattered the morning air and drowned them out. Fletch grabbed Clementine and dived underneath the wagon with her. Everyone else in camp scrambled for cover as well. Edgerton threw himself backward between the wagon's sideboards. Bullets whipped through its canvas cover.

Noah Stuart and Chester Merrick had been standing next to one of the front wheels on their wagon. Stuart dropped to his knees and brought Merrick down with him by tugging on the other man's arm. They crawled underneath the wagon with Fletch and Clementine. Merrick lay on his belly and covered his head with his arms, as if that would stop a bullet.

"Where in tarnation are those shots comin' from?" Pugh yelled.

"Up in the rocks to the east!" Dupre called back. Normally, a guard would have been posted up there, but the sentries hadn't taken their positions yet since most of the group was still in camp.

These weren't the sort of men to hunker in fear. They began firing back, even though they couldn't see the ambushers. They spotted little puffs of powder smoke among the rocks and aimed at those, knowing that their shots would be coming close to the bush-whackers, at least.

During a lull in the firing, Dupre called, "Is anyone hurt?"

From under the surveyors' wagon, Fletch answered, "We're all right down here, me and Clementine and Mr. Stuart and Mr. Merrick."

Dupre and Pugh were crouched together behind the Wylie wagon, at the back end of it. The Molmberg brothers were at the vehicle's front end. None of them had been hit.

Dog Brother replied from some brush on the far side of the little pool. "I'm all right."

No response came from Edgerton.

Dupre noticed that and said, "Hey, Edgerton! Are you hit?"

Still nothing.

Grimacing, Dupre looked at the four people huddled underneath the other wagon and asked, "Can one of you see about him?"

"I'll go," Fletch said immediately, but Noah Stuart put a hand on his shoulder to stop him from moving.

"No, let me," Stuart said. "You've got your wife to worry about."

Fletch looked like he wanted to argue, but Stuart had a point. After a second, the young man nodded. "All right, but be careful."

"I'll try to keep the wagon between me and those gunmen."

Over at the Wylie wagon, Pugh said to Dupre, "Those are modern rifles the varmints are usin'. You can tell by the sound of 'em. That ain't Apaches."

"I was just thinking the same thing, *mon ami*," Dupre replied. "We have been ambushed by white men." He glanced at the other wagon and saw Clementine's bright blond hair underneath it. "The girl's brothers, perhaps?"

"More 'n likely," Pugh replied. "Preacher figured they'd try to catch up to us."

Noah Stuart crawled out from under the front of the wagon where he had taken cover and grabbed hold of the wheel to help himself get to his feet quickly. Moving as fast as he could, he clambered onto the driver's box. A bullet struck the seat not far from his hand, chewing splinters from the wood that stung his skin. He powered himself into a dive over the seat back that carried him into the wagon bed, where he sprawled among the crates of supplies and surveying equipment.

Edgerton lay just inside the wagon at the back end, not moving.

"Mr. Edgerton!" Stuart called. "Mr. Edgerton, can you hear me?"

The frontiersman didn't answer, didn't budge.

Fearing the worst, Stuart started crawling toward the back of the wagon. Bullets continued thudding into the thick sideboards, and he caught his breath at every impact. He didn't know when one of the slugs might penetrate the wood and hit him. Hearing bullets going through the wagon's canvas cover, too, he kept his head down. Those few moments were as nerve-wracking as any Noah Stuart had ever experienced.

When he was close enough, he reached out, grasped Edgerton's shoulder, and shook it. Edgerton rolled loosely onto his back. Stuart recoiled as he saw that the man's eyes were open wide but staring sightlessly up at the canvas above them.

He raised himself a little higher on his elbows and lifted his head until he saw the large bloodstain on the left side of Edgerton's shirt. One of the bullets had struck him as he was trying to reach cover inside the wagon, and judging by the blood's location, it had penetrated the left lung or perhaps the heart. Either way it had proved fatal.

Stuart flinched as he felt as much as heard the wind-rip of a bullet past his ear. He flattened out again and stayed there. He thought about trying to back up and get out of the wagon, but that would just put him at an even greater risk, he realized. The best thing he could do was lie there and wait for the ambush to be over.

But what if the shooting continued until everyone

else in the party had been picked off? Then the killers would come and find him alone. He'd have no chance of escaping death then.

Torn by indecision, Noah Stuart lay there a few feet away from a dead man and listened to the roar of guns outside.

CHAPTER 35

Jamie, Preacher, Audie, and Nighthawk were on their way back to the campsite when they met Tennysee, Deadlead, Greybull, Powder Pete, and Ramirez. The two groups of men reined in and greeted each other.

"I reckon Noah made it back to the camp all right, or else you fellas wouldn't be heading in this direction," Jamie said.

Tennysee nodded. "That's right. He said you rattled your hocks off to the southwest to check out some shootin'. What'd you find?"

"More Apaches. They were laying siege to the *jacal* where a farmer and his family live next to a little creek off that way."

Tennysee's eyebrows climbed up his forehead. "There's somebody dumb enough to try *farmin'* in this hellhole?"

"He's not just attempting it," Audie said. "He appears to be having a small degree of success. I took a look at his field while we were there, and while I doubt that he has any actual education on the subject, he's using solid irrigation techniques that go back to the ancient Romans. That's probably just instinctive on his part. He seemed fairly intelligent."

Tennysee snorted. "Not smart enough to keep from bringin' his family out here where the 'Paches can get 'em."

"Some men are born to take risks," Jamie said. "That's how civilization spreads."

"These Apaches," Ramirez said. "Did you run them off or . . . ?"

"We *dragged* 'em off," Preacher said. "Into the bushes for the buzzards and the coyotes."

"Then you did not leave any for us to kill." Ramirez sounded disappointed.

"We found out something, though," Jamie said. "The Apaches have been raiding so much in these parts because they've got a new war chief who's trying to get them to work together and run out all the intruders, white and Mexican alike. Calls himself Perro Blanco."

"White Dog," Ramirez said. The gunfighter shook his head. "These savages and their names. The half-breed is called Dog Brother, and now we have White Dog to contend with." He glanced at Preacher. "And your cur is just plain Dog."

"I believe in keepin' things simple," the mountain man drawled.

Powder Pete said, "You were goin' to see if you could find any sign of whatever it was ol' Noah saw reflectin' sunlight yesterday. Did you turn up anything?"

Jamie shook his head. "No, we got sidetracked before we could do that. We'll take up that chore again if you boys want to head on back to camp."

"Since we're already out here, why don't we just come with you?" Tennysee suggested.

"Yeah," Greybull rumbled. "That way, if there's any more excitement, we won't miss out on it."

Jamie thought about it for a second and then nodded agreement. There was still a good-sized force at the camp in case anything happened there. He wasn't expecting trouble, particularly, but out here it was always possible and the air had an unsettled feel to it this morning, as if something was going to happen but he didn't know what.

The nine men rode together, turning south again when they reached the line running between the camp and the distant mesa where it seemed like Noah Stuart's mysterious flash might have originated. The mesa was rather small, and as they approached, Jamie once again suggested that the men spread out and circle around the little tableland so they could get a good look at all sides of it before they came too close.

Nothing about the mesa seemed suspicious as far as Jamie could see, and Preacher agreed. They waved the others on in, and the circle slowly closed.

Jamie immediately noticed the hoofprints and horse droppings and pointed them out to Preacher, who had already seen them, too. The mountain man studied the tracks for several moments, then dismounted and hunkered next to a pile of droppings.

"You gonna pick 'em up and see how soft they are?" Tennysee asked with a grin.

"Don't have to," Preacher replied. "I can tell just by lookin' at 'em that some critter left 'em here earlier today." He looked up at Jamie. "Tracks are muddled enough it's hard to say for sure, but I figure there were eight horses here. Maybe nine or ten, but I don't think so."

"Clementine has four brothers," Jamie said. "An extra mount apiece would make eight."

"Yeah, but they left Santa Fe after we did. How much after us, we don't know, but we had to have a good lead on 'em."

"With extra horses and no wagons to slow them down, they could close up that gap if they didn't mind pushing hard. And shod horses left those prints, so it's mighty unlikely they belong to the Apaches."

Preacher nodded slowly. "You're right about that."

"If they are the señorita's brothers," Ramirez said, "where did they go?"

"Señora," Jamie corrected him, although he knew it wouldn't do any good. Ramirez's "slip of the tongue" was deliberate.

Nighthawk said, "Umm," and lifted a tree-trunk-like arm to point.

"My large friend is right," Audie said. "There are tracks angling off slightly east of north . . . as if the riders intended to circle around and approach the camp from that direction."

"If they've got a spyglass or somethin' like that," Preacher said, "it'd explain that flash Noah saw. And they'd know the camp ain't as heavily defended as it was because they spotted all of us ridin' away."

"Blast it. You're right," Jamie said. "We need to get back—"

He didn't get any farther than that before the distant popping of gunfire reached their ears.

* * *

The Mahoney brothers alternated shooting so they could pour a steady stream of fire at the two wagons and the people who had taken cover around them. They were careful not to target the area where Clementine had taken cover, but if they could kill everybody else in the group except her and Fletch, they could go down there and take their sister back.

They would save Fletch for some special entertainment, Clete had explained, and Clementine would be forced to watch. And when they were finished, she would never dare cross them again.

The problem was, they hadn't downed any of those other men with their first volley, and the blasted varmints were putting up a fight! The brothers had been forced to duck behind the rocks they were using as cover when the return fire came too close.

Finally, Clete called, "Hold your fire, hold your fire!" As the shooting died out, he went on. "We don't have an unlimited supply of ammunition. We can't just sit here and blaze away at 'em all day."

"Then what are we gonna do?" Harp asked.

"Maybe since we stopped shootin', they'll think we left, and then they'll come out and we can kill 'em then," Lew suggested.

Clete scrubbed a hand over his face and grimaced in frustration. His brothers had never been the brightest sorts, and once again he told himself how lucky they were to have him around to handle the thinking for them.

"That would only work once, if it even did then," he said. "We'd be lucky to get a couple of them, and then the rest would know what we were up to. What we need to do is split up. Two of us will stay here and keep them pinned down, while the other two work their way around to where that ridge sticks out from the bluff on the west. That way we can catch them in a crossfire—"

"Hey, Clete," Jerome interrupted him.

"Just shut up until I'm done, Jerome," Clete said without looking at his brother.

"But Clete—"

Swinging around sharply, Clete said, "Blast it, if you think you've got a better idea—"

"No, it ain't that." Jerome pointed. "Look."

Clete looked. To the southeast, the direction Jerome was pointing, a large dust cloud rose. It would take a good number of riders to kick up that much dust.

"Is that the rest of the bunch comin' back?" Jerome went on.

"No, they rode off to the southwest," Clete said. "That's got to be somebody different."

"Who?" Lew asked.

"Looks like quite a few of 'em, whoever it is," Harp added.

Unfortunately, Harp was right, and Clete had no idea about the answer to Lew's question. The rapidly approaching riders probably were Apaches but might be something else. An army patrol? Mexican bandits? Clete didn't know, but one thing was certain in his mind.

The Mahoney brothers had no friends down here in this wasteland except for each other. "Come on," he snapped. "We're gettin' out of here."

"But what about Clementine?" Harp said.

"We'll have other chances to grab her. Whoever that

is comin' this way, I don't want to tangle with them. From the looks of that dust, we'd be outnumbered."

"Maybe we could bushwhack them, too," Jerome suggested.

Clete suppressed the urge to wallop his brother. It wouldn't do any good. If it had been possible to knock some sense into them, he would have already accomplished that.

"There are too many of them," he explained. "Now come on. Get mounted up!"

Harp asked, "Which way are we goin'?"

Clete sighed. "Back to the north, I reckon. Any other way, we'd stand too much of a chance of running into trouble."

"So we're back where we started," Lew said.

Lew was more correct than Clete wanted to think about. Muttering bitter curses under his breath, he swung up into the saddle and led his brothers away from there.

Whoever that was galloping up from the southeast, he hoped they wouldn't wipe out the whole bunch at the wagons, Clementine included.

CHAPTER 36

Noah Stuart slowly lifted his head as he realized the shooting had stopped. Maybe the ambushers had just paused for a moment to reload or allow their weapons to cool off, he thought. He wasn't going to stick his head outside the wagon, that was certain. Just raising it to listen more closely was running a big enough risk.

A few seconds later, Dupre's familiar voice called, "*M'sieu* Stuart, you are all right in there?"

"Yes, I . . . I believe I am," Stuart replied. "But Mr. Edgerton is dead. One of those first shots must have hit him."

Grim silence greeted that announcement and lasted for a few seconds. Then Dupre said, "Stay where you are for now, *m'sieu*. I believe all the assassins are gone, but they may be trying to lure us into the open so they can try again to murder us."

"I'm not going anywhere," Stuart assured the Frenchman, even though lying only a few feet away from Edgerton's body made him extremely uncomfortable.

As the minutes stretched interminably past, he

heard some of the other men talking quietly among themselves.

Then Pugh exclaimed loudly enough for Stuart to hear, "Look up yonder! It's Dog Brother."

"He must have crawled off through the brush and circled around." That was Dupre. A moment later, he said, "You can come out now, *M'sieu* Stuart. Dog Brother is up in the rocks and has just given us a sign indicating that the ambushers are gone."

Stuart wasn't going to clamber over Edgerton's corpse. He backed away and climbed out over the driver's box. As he dropped to the ground, he saw the rest of the party emerging from the cover they had taken when the shooting started.

Stuart went over to help Merrick to his feet as his assistant crawled out from under the wagon. "Are you all right, Chester?"

Merrick's face was pale as a sheet and his hands shook as he brushed dirt off his clothes. "I'm not hurt, Mr. Stuart, but I sure do wish I'd never agreed to come along on this trip. I think it's just a matter of time until we're both killed!"

"I'm sure that won't be the case. Our companions are nearly all experienced frontiersmen."

"That won't stop a bullet. You saw how close Mr. Dupre came to being shot."

That was true. Even now, the Frenchman was picking up his ruined fiddle and looking glumly at the damage the bullet had done. "Never again will a merry tune come from you," he told the instrument as he patted it gently. "But I will avenge you, old friend. You can count on that."

Fletch and Clementine had crawled out from under the wagon after Merrick. Clementine looked at Stuart and asked, "Did I hear you say that Mr. Edgerton is . . . dead?"

Stuart nodded. "I'm afraid so. It looked like one of the shots hit him as he was trying to move farther back in the wagon where it was safer."

"You're sure he's dead?" Fletch asked.

"Yes, I could tell he wasn't breathing at all."

One of the Molmberg brothers pointed silently. Stuart looked around and saw Dog Brother trotting toward the camp. The half-breed had climbed down from the ridge where the ambushers had been concealed.

"Riders coming," Dog Brother reported as he came up to the others. He waved a hand toward the southeast. "Looks like a large group."

Pugh groaned. "What sort of woe is comin' at us now? The whole derned Apache nation?"

Dupre shaded his eyes with his hand and peered in the direction Dog Brother had indicated. So did the others. Even though Dog Brother had been able to spot the column of dust first from his higher elevation, it was coming in sight and advancing steadily toward the camp.

"At least we will not be taken by surprise this time," Dupre said. "Everyone find a good spot and get ready to fight. Whoever those riders are, if they mean us harm, they will not find us ready to surrender!"

For a minute or so, everyone scurried around getting in position. Fletch and Clementine climbed into their wagon, and Stuart and Merrick forted up inside their vehicle. Even though Merrick looked like he wanted to be somewhere else—anywhere else!—he clutched the shotgun, swallowed hard, and waited behind the driver's box. Stuart was at the tailgate, which had been raised after Dupre and Pugh hurriedly lifted Edgerton's body and placed it underneath the wagon.

"Might should've propped the old boy up," Pugh had said while they were doing that. "Would've looked like one more of us to put up a fight."

"It would take too long to make it look real," Dupre had replied. "Not to mention being disrespectful. We didn't know Edgerton for long, but he was one of us."

The rest of the group used the wagons for cover. The dust cloud was in plain sight as the unknown riders approached the camp. Dog Brother, who had perhaps the keenest eyes in the group, leaned forward and peered through the haze, then suddenly exclaimed, "They are soldiers!"

Stuart squinted through the dust and haze and saw sunlight reflecting from metal trappings on men and horses alike. It was a large group, at least thirty strong.

As they came closer, Stuart could make out the figures of two men in resplendent uniforms riding in the lead. Sporting large hats that extended to points in front of and behind the head and had feathered plumes sticking up from them, as well as bright scarlet sashes angling across the front of their blue uniform jackets, they had to be the officers in charge of this command.

The other soldiers also wore blue jackets and white trousers turned gray with dust, but they had white sashes across their chests and flat-billed black caps on their heads. The officers were armed with pistols and sabers. The troopers following them carried flintlock rifles.

In his job working for the Office of the Interior, Stuart had been around enough American soldiers to see the similarities between their uniforms and the ones these men wore, but he recognized the differences, too. These were foreign soldiers, specifically members of the Mexican army.

That made sense, he told himself. A border might be precisely drawn on a map, but out in this vast wasteland, it was much more difficult to tell exactly where that line might be. Stuart hadn't been sure for a couple of days if they were in Mexico or the United States.

It was highly likely that these soldiers didn't know for certain, either, but he expected that they would *act* like they did.

"Everyone, stay where you are," Dupre called. "These men may be soldiers instead of Apaches or whoever just ambushed us, but that is no guarantee they mean us no harm."

When the riders were fifty yards from the camp, they reined in. For a moment, the two officers appeared to be talking things over, and then one of them spurred his mount forward. The other officer turned to call a command to the troopers and waved for three of them to follow the first officer. Those men fell in behind the rider who approached the camp, holding his horse to a deliberate walk.

As he came closer, Stuart could see the gaudy gold epaulets on the shoulders of his uniform. The man had several colorful ribbons pinned to the breast of his uniform jacket, as well. Somehow, he managed to look a bit like a dandy, despite the heat and the surroundings that left everyone else sweaty and grimy.

Dupre stepped out into the open and walked slowly toward the officer.

The man reined in again when roughly twenty feet separated them. "*Buenos dias. Habla español?*"

Dupre shrugged. "Some. But I am more fluent in English. Or French, if you happen to speak it."

"English is better," the officer said. "I am Capitan Enrique Garazano, the commandant of this patrol." His words were heavily accented, but Stuart, listening from inside the wagon, could make them out. "This land belongs to Mexico. Do you have permission to be here?"

"We are on a mission representing the United States government," Dupre replied.

Captain Garazano's dark, narrow face creased in a frown. "You are soldiers?" he asked sharply, indicating that he might just consider them an invading force if Dupre answered in the affirmative.

The Frenchman shook his head. "No, we're all civilians. But we're still here on behalf of the United States."

"Doing what, exactly?"

Stuart decided that as one of the two people actually employed by the Office of the Interior, it was time he took part in this conversation. He stepped over the tailgate, dropped to the ground, and stepped forward so the Mexican officer could see him.

"We're surveying and mapping the region," he announced, causing Dupre to flick an annoyed glance in his direction because of the interruption. "My name is Noah Stuart. I work for the United States Office of the Interior."

Garazano regarded him coolly. "Do you have permission from my government to be carrying out this task, Señor Stuart? Written permission?"

Stuart tried to stay equally cool and reserved as he replied, "I don't believe that's necessary, Captain."

"Oh, but you are wrong, señor. You are very wrong. Without such written permission, you are trespassing on Mexican land." Garazano's voice took on a menacing purr as he added, "Some might even consider you invaders, to be driven out by any means necessary."

This wasn't going well at all. The Mexican army patrol vastly outnumbered their group, and technically, Garazano might be right about them trespassing. Not only that, but according to the rumors he had heard, many of the Mexican soldiers were little better than bandits, always on the lookout for loot they could grab for themselves. They might decide that the Americans' supplies and the surveying equipment ought to belong to them.

And if they laid eyes on Clementine . . . Stuart didn't want to think about the trouble *that* might cause.

"*Capitan!*" The other officer was calling to Garazano.

The captain turned, and an exchange of loud, rapid Spanish that Stuart couldn't follow passed between the two men. Garazano barked an order at the three troopers who had accompanied him and trotted back to rejoin the other officer. The troopers remained, regarding Dupre and Stuart and the wagons with cold, impassive faces. Obviously, Garazano had ordered them to stay there and guard the Americans.

The three men looked almost as Indian as the Apaches, Stuart thought. They couldn't expect any mercy from men such as this.

Stuart walked up alongside Dupre. From the corner

of his mouth, the Frenchman said, "You should have stayed out of it, *m'sieu.*"

"You told him we're working for the government," Stuart reminded him. "He already had his back up about that."

Dupre's shoulders rose and fell in a display of Gallic indifference. "These Mexicans always look for an excuse to steal," he said quietly. "I suppose it doesn't matter what we tell them. It comes down to whether they decide to kill us and take everything we have."

"We won't let them do that, will we?"

"Of course not. We will fight . . . but with their numbers, they will likely kill us anyway. Although not before we kill some of them. And when Preacher discovers what had happened, he will never rest until we are avenged. I suspect M'sieu MacCallister will be the same way." Dupre smiled faintly. "No, Capitan Garazano does not realize the hell he may be about to unleash upon himself."

"But that won't help us any if we're dead," Stuart pointed out.

"No, it will not. But . . ." Dupre's eyes narrowed as he looked at the two Mexican officers. "What are they talking about? They appear to be agitated about something . . ."

Suddenly, Dupre laughed. "See the dust out there, Noah? Riders are coming fast. That can only be Preacher and Jamie and the others. That changes everything."

"We're still outnumbered."

"But only two to one! That is nothing. The Mexicans are caught in a crossfire, too, and they know it! Look how they scurry around like ants!"

It was true. Garazano and the other officer shouted

orders. The troops began to spread out, dismount, and ready their rifles. In response to a command from Garazano, the three men who had been left to guard the Americans suddenly hauled their horses around and galloped back to join their comrades.

"Get behind cover," Dupre snapped at Stuart. "The battle is about to be joined!"

CHAPTER 37

"Looks like a bunch of soldiers," Preacher said to Jamie as they rode at a fast trot toward the camp. "And they ain't ours, I'm bettin'."

"Probably a Mexican army patrol," Jamie replied. "We knew there was a chance we might run into one down here."

"They may not be much more friendly than them 'Paches."

"No, but I doubt that they'll try to slaughter us outright."

Preacher drew his Sharps from its saddle sheath. "If they do, I reckon they'll find themselves in a heap o' trouble. Looks like there's more of them than there are of us, but we got 'em betwixt a rock and a hard place."

"Let's see if we can get through this without any shooting," Jamie suggested.

"Sure. But you know how hotheaded those varmints are."

Jamie knew, all right, and having spent some time at the Alamo before it fell, he still carried a grudge against the Mexican army, especially now that the infamous General Santa Anna was in charge of the country again. Crockett, Bowie, Travis . . . Jamie remembered them and all the other good men who had been wantonly slaughtered by Santa Anna's troops. That blood debt would never be paid in full, as far as he was concerned.

Still, he was here to do a job for his country, a job he had agreed to carry out to the best of his ability, so he turned in his saddle and said to the men with him, "I'm going to try talking to those fellas first, so hold your fire and let the hand play out. Hang back a little, and I'll go ahead and parley, if they're of a mind to."

"Take Audie with you," Preacher suggested. "He speaks Spanish better 'n anybody I know."

Ramirez let out a disgusted snort and demanded, "What about me?"

Preacher said, "Audie speaks Spanish better 'n anybody I know who ain't a hotheaded gunslinger who's liable to cause a heap of trouble. There, is that better?"

Ramirez just glared at the mountain man.

Audie moved his mount up alongside Jamie's and said, "I'd be glad to accompany you, Jamie."

"Obliged to you. Let's go see if we can find out what's going on."

They moved ahead of the others at a faster pace. From where they were, the group of Mexican soldiers blocked sight of the camp for the most part, but in the glimpses Jamie got, he didn't see any of the people he had left there. Had the Mexicans already wiped them out? They had heard shooting, after all, although it had stopped not long after they rode away from the mesa.

Audie must have had a pretty good idea what Jamie was thinking. The diminutive former professor said,

"I don't believe there were enough shots to signify a full-scale battle. If a force of that size had attacked the camp, it would have sounded worse."

"It would have been over pretty fast, though," Jamie argued. "And the shooting we heard didn't last very long." He drew his Sharps and balanced the loaded weapon across the saddle in front of him.

His keen eyes picked out the two officers, and at the first sign of trouble, he intended to blow one of those men out of the saddle. He said as much to Audie, then added, "You take the other one. Mexican troops aren't any good without somebody to tell them what to do. Despite the odds being on their side, they might just cut and run if they don't have any leaders."

"The same thought had occurred to me," Audie said. "But without commanders, they might turn into an even more ravening and rapacious horde than they would be otherwise."

"A chance we'll have to take," Jamie said. Abruptly, he stiffened in the saddle. "I see Dupre and Noah Stuart. They're still alive, anyway."

One of the officers peeled away from his companion and rode out to meet them, trailed by a trio of troopers. It looked like the man wanted to talk, and Jamie was grateful for that, even though just the sight of the Mexican soldiers had his blood up and a part of him was eager for battle.

They all reined in when they were a short distance apart. The officer nudged his horse ahead a couple more steps and asked, "Are you men part of this group of surveyors, as well?"

Had Stuart told the officer they were all surveyors? Jamie knew that claim wouldn't hold up once the man got a good look at the rest of them—nobody was going to mistake the old mountain men or Dog Brother for surveyors—but Jamie avoided a direct answer to that question by saying, "We're all part of the same bunch."

"You are trespassing on Mexican land!"

Audie asked, "Can you document that, Capitan?"

He must have been able to tell the officer's rank by the markings on his uniform, Jamie thought.

The man drew in a deep breath and pulled himself up stiff and straight in the saddle. "I am Capitan Enrique Garazano, and the word of an officer in *El Presidente*'s army is all the documentation that is needed!"

"Actually, that may not be the case," Audie insisted. "The boundary between your country and mine has shifted in recent years due to the signing of the Treaty of Guadalupe Hidalgo, and unlike over in Texas where there's a river to mark the border, here it's much more nebulous." Audie waved a hand to indicate their surroundings. "Here, it requires a skilled surveyor to determine exactly *where* we are. We may be in Mexico, we may be in the United States, in New Mexico Territory, to be precise. We simply don't know."

Jamie's eyes narrowed. "But whichever one we're in, Captain, one thing is certain. There are a bunch of Apaches out there led by a war chief who wants us all dead." It was a bit of a shot in the dark, but evidently it found its mark.

Capitan Garazano looked surprised and said, "You speak of Perro Blanco."

"You've heard of him, too?"

"*Sí*, this devil is the reason we are out here!" Garazano shrugged. "Well, that and to run any gringo invaders off Mexican soil."

"We'll have to settle that part of it later," Jamie said. "For now, it sure seems to me like we're all after the same thing."

Audie said, "There's an old proverb from the Sanskrit that stipulates the enemy of my enemy is my friend. That seems to apply to us, wouldn't you say, Captain?"

Jamie didn't know anything about Sanskrit, but the sentiment that Audie expressed was a good one. The logic of it seemed to get through to Captain Garazano, too.

He frowned and said, "You claim you have come to fight this Perro Blanco, as well?"

"We didn't know about him when we started down here," Jamie said, "but we kept running into trouble from the Apaches and earlier today we found out why. A fella told about this so-called White Dog who's trying to band all the Apaches together. That's why they're all stirred up and riding out on murder raids so often."

"And now you wish to destroy him?"

"That's the general idea," Jamie said with a decisive nod.

Garazano's frown deepened as he considered everything he had just learned. After a minute or so that seemed longer, he said, "You are still trespassing on Mexican land."

"Tell you what," Jamie drawled. "Why don't we let your government and my government haggle about that later? We'll go ahead and do the surveying we came down here to do. That's not going to hurt Mexican interests. In fact, I've heard rumors that there's some sort of business deal in the works between your president and mine, so if they knew we'd run into each other out here, they might *order* us to work together."

That seemed like a lot for Garazano to swallow, but what Jamie said made sense. Finally, the officer nodded slowly and said, "There will be a truce between us for now, Señor . . . ?"

"MacCallister," Jamie supplied. "Jamie Ian MacCallister."

"Very well, Señor MacCallister. I will withdraw my men, but we will remain nearby. Your party may continue with its work, but if you do anything that I believe threatens the interests of Mexico, I will take action to prevent it. Do you understand?"

"Clear as day," Jamie said. To emphasize that, he slid his Sharps back in its scabbard.

Garazano nodded again, turned his horse, and rode back to join his men.

Jamie motioned for the others who were with him to move on up, then said to Audie, "Ride into camp and find out what happened there. Something was going on before these soldiers showed up."

Audie headed off while Jamie waited for Preacher and the rest of the men to catch up with him. While he was doing that, the Mexican patrol mounted and moved off to the east, about a quarter of a mile along the bluff. The spring where Jamie's group had made camp seemed to be the only water within several miles, so they probably would have to let the Mexicans fill their canteens and any water barrels they might have on their pack animals.

It might be a good idea to keep Clementine out of sight while any of the soldiers were around, Jamie mused. No sense in tempting fate.

As they rode on in, Jamie watched the ones who'd been left behind emerge from inside and behind the wagons. Then he caught sight of the body lying underneath the surveyors' wagon and his jaw tightened.

"Edgerton?" he asked as he swung down from his saddle.

"*Oui*," Dupre answered. "He was hit in the first volley when we were ambushed."

"Ambushed by who?" Preacher said.

Clementine brushed back a strand of blond hair that had fallen over her face and swallowed hard. "It must have been those no-good brothers of mine. That's all we can figure out."

"They were up on the rocks to the east," Dupre explained as he gestured in that direction, "but they stopped shooting and evidently fled when they saw the dust of those soldiers approaching."

"What about those soldiers?" Stuart asked Jamie. "That captain's not happy about us being here."

"He may not be happy, but he's agreed to go along with it," Jamie said. "For the time being, anyway, he's got bigger fish to fry, and I sort of gave him the idea that we'd help him. You see, today we found out that there's one hombre who's behind a lot of the trouble down here in these parts, and Captain Garazano wants his hide as much as we do."

Preacher said, "So we're goin' on a dog hunt," then glanced down at the big cur sitting beside him, who had looked up at him and cocked his head to the side in the universal sign of canine puzzlement.

"No, not you," the mountain man said.

CHAPTER 38

They laid Edgerton to rest the same day as the ambush that had killed the dour frontiersman, digging a grave atop the bluff and then mounding it with rocks after it had been filled in. Even though Edgerton had never been very friendly or had much to do with the others, not having him around was still a loss—and a reminder of the dangers that always seemed to be lurking nearby.

But after everything that had happened, the next few days were surprisingly uneventful. Because of all the various threats, Jamie wanted to leave a larger group in camp than they had been. Instead of he and Preacher splitting up and heading off in different directions with some of the men, they searched for the Apaches together, taking half a dozen fighters with them each time. They saw no sign of their quarry, however.

It was almost as if the Apaches had given up and abandoned the area.

"You reckon the varmints headed deeper into Mexico, into them mountains south of here?" Preacher asked as he and Jamie returned to camp with some of the others after another day of fruitless searching.

"I suppose they could have," Jamie replied as they slouched along on horseback. "We killed several dozen of them. They might have decided that was too high a price to pay for staying around these parts."

"Never knew an Indian who didn't want revenge, though, when he felt like he and his people had been done wrong. And killin' them, even though they were tryin' their best to kill us, is wrong in their minds."

"But they can be practical, too, and figure that it's better to just cut their losses."

Preacher nodded solemnly. "That's true. What it comes down to is that they're a plumb notional people, and you can't ever be sure what they're gonna do." He gazed around. "They could be out there watchin' us right now."

"I wouldn't doubt it a bit," Jamie said.

Noah Stuart and Chester Merrick had been allowed to make some surveying and cartographic trips along the bluff for several miles in both directions. Stuart also rode out to the mesa with a well-armed escort and sketched it, adding it as a landmark to the rudimentary maps he had drawn. While they were there, he asked, "Can I climb it?"

Tennysee, who was in charge of the group that had accompanied the surveyor, frowned at Stuart and said, "Why in blazes would you *want* to?"

"So I can see better, of course," Stuart answered without hesitation. "It's not a terribly tall formation, but in land that's as flat, overall, as this is, you don't have to get up very high in order to be able to see for a long way."

Tennysee took off his battered old hat, scratched his thinning hair, and said, "Well, I reckon if you want to give it a try, there ain't no reason for me to stop you. I warn you, though. It probably ain't as easy as it looks. I know the sides of that mesa are pretty rough and ought to give you plenty of handholds and footholds, but if you slip, you'll fall into that cactus growin' around the base. And then you'll look like a gosh-darn porkypine!" The thought of that tickled Tennysee, and he slapped his thigh and laughed.

"I won't fall," Stuart said. "Or at least I'll try not to."

He walked around the mesa until he found a good place where he could approach the wall without getting tangled up in cactus, then tucked his sketch pad inside his shirt and started climbing. The wall leaned in slightly, so it wasn't sheer, and that made the climb easier. As Tennysee had said, there were enough cracks and knobs that Stuart found numerous places where he could hang on or plant a foot to push himself higher.

As he went up the side of the mesa, he warned himself not to look down. He didn't want to make himself dizzy and slip. He was high enough that a fall could be pretty bad, and besides, there were all those spiny cactus down there.

Finally, he reached the top and pulled himself over the edge, rolling onto his back. He lay there for a moment with the sun beaming into his eyes while he caught his breath. His shirt was soaked with sweat from the exertion of the climb. When he had recovered somewhat from the effort, he rolled farther away from the brink and pushed himself to his feet.

Mesa meant *table* in Spanish, he believed, and that was a reasonably accurate description of this flat-topped geographical feature. The top of the mesa wasn't really *flat*. It was rough and rugged and heavily worn by erosion just like the sides were. A few clumps of hardy grass grew here and there, as well as some very scrubby bushes covered with what looked like wickedly sharp thorns.

He recalled hearing Preacher make some comment about how most things on the frontier could bite you, sting you, stick you, or make you miserable in some other way. "And kill you if you weren't careful," the mountain man had added. So far on this trip, Stuart hadn't seen anything to convince him that wasn't true.

He had been right about the view. He could see a long way from up there. When he looked back to the north, he saw the shallow escarpment stretching out for miles to the east and west, much farther than he had explored so far. But from what he could tell, it looked the same in both directions, other than minor irregularities. He *thought* the bluff began curving to the north several miles away to the east, but he couldn't be sure. That might be something to look into later.

He also had a good view of the campsite and the nearby tents of the Mexican army patrol. Captain Garazano had been keeping a close eye on the so-called invaders. When Stuart and Merrick went out on their surveying and mapmaking forays, a small group of soldiers always followed them at a distance. The same was true when Jamie and Preacher went searching for Apaches, although Garazano sent a larger force to trail them. It was like the captain was afraid the visitors would get up to some sort of mischief that would harm Mexico.

The top of the mesa was roughly fifty yards in diameter. Stuart started across it, veering sharply around a pile of rocks, when he heard a distinctive buzzing sound coming from it. A rattlesnake was denned up in there, he knew, and he wanted nothing to do with the reptile. The pistol was holstered on his hip, so he wasn't defenseless, but *why seek out trouble?* he asked himself.

When he reached the other edge, he gazed off to the south for several minutes, intrigued by what he saw there. At least five miles away stretched a darker band of ground that ran east and west as far as he could see. Stuart couldn't tell for sure, but it appeared to be a several-mile-wide area of ravines and gullies, the sort of badlands that cropped up here and there. The dark color was puzzling, but it would require a closer look to solve that mystery. Beyond the badlands—if that's what they were—was a low, gray-blue line that Stuart figured marked the location of some hills.

"I wish Chester and I could bring some of our equipment up here," he said aloud, not worrying that some of the men down below might hear him and think he'd gone mad. "I wonder if we could rig a rope sling and bring it up that way."

Of course, that would mean Chester would have to climb the mesa, too, and Stuart wasn't sure that would ever happen.

He really wanted to explore and map that desolate area. Along with the escarpment and this mesa, it would make a good landmark. The area running between the bluff and the badlands might provide a passable route for the transcontinental railroad, especially if the escarpment curved to the north and out of the way as he thought it did.

To run a railroad through here, though, would require more negotiations between the United States and Mexico. As far as far as Stuart could determine—and he had shot a number of readings with his sextant—they actually *were* south of the current border, although not by much. He had gone along with the fiction that it was difficult to determine their exact location, but the truth of the matter was that for a couple of days now, he had had a pretty good idea where they were and could have pinpointed it on a map.

"Hey, Mr. Stuart!" Tennysee called. "You about done up there?"

Stuart walked back across the mesa, looked over the edge at the men gathered below, and replied, "Yes, I'm coming down right now!"

"No rush," Tennysee told him. "Take it nice and easy. You don't want to slip and fall."

With all those cactus waiting down there, he certainly didn't.

"Taking a look at those badlands will mean moving our camp," Jamie said when Stuart told him that night about what he had seen from the top of the mesa and how he wanted to explore that area. "There's probably water to be found in those hills on the other side."

"Movin' might not be a bad idea," Preacher put in.

The three men were standing beside the surveyors' wagon and keeping their voices down so the rest of the party wouldn't overhear.

"We ain't seen hide nor hair of any 'Paches for days now. Maybe we'd have better luck somewheres else."

Stuart said, "It'll also mean going farther south. Will Captain Garazano agree to that? He already doesn't like us being here. A move such as that will convince him more than ever that we're interlopers."

"I don't plan on letting that Mex dandy tell me what I can or can't do," Jamie stated bluntly. "We came down here on a job of work, and it's not finished yet."

Stuart hesitated, then told them what he thought about running the railroad between the bluff and the badlands. "Of course, I have no idea what obstacles might exist east and west of here. That's going to take a much more extensive survey, probably starting in Texas and proceeding westward along the entire potential route. But what Chester and I are doing is a start, anyway. I think we're going to be able to see enough to state that a southern route *is* feasible."

Preacher said, "Only if the crews can work without havin' to worry all the time about bein' massa-creed by a bunch of bloodthirsty Apaches. And to make sure that don't happen, we're gonna have to find that varmint Perro Blanco and put a stop to his shenanigans."

"We'll find him," Jamie said. "In fact, I've got a hunch he's waiting for us." He nodded toward the distant badlands. "Down there."

CHAPTER 39

Early the next morning, while the others were breaking camp, Jamie rode over to the Mexican camp to talk to Captain Garazano.

Several guards challenged him with lifted rifles. Jamie reined in, and while he was sitting there waiting for one of the troopers to let Garazano know he was there, he clenched his jaw and tried to keep his anger and resentment under control. He had known that being around Mexican soldiers might be difficult because of what had happened at the Alamo, but he hadn't expected his reaction to be quite so strong.

Thankfully, it wasn't long before Garazano stepped out of his tent and waved Jamie over. He called to the guards in Spanish, telling them it was all right. With surly reluctance, they stepped back to let Jamie ride past them.

"Good morning, Señor MacCallister," Garazano greeted him. "What brings you here?"

Jamie swung down from the saddle. "Just wanted to let you know that we're moving our camp. We're heading down to a stretch of badlands about five miles south of here. Mr. Stuart, our chief surveyor, noticed it from the top of the mesa yesterday and wants to explore it. He said it looks like there are some hills on the other side, so I figured we'd make our new camp over there, if we can find some water."

Garazano, who was dressed in his uniform except for his beribboned jacket and big, plumed hat, frowned at Jamie. "Such a move will take you even deeper into Mexican territory. I was willing to make an exception due to the vagueness of the border's location, but I have seen those badlands and I know they are part of my country, not yours, Señor MacCallister."

"I imagine you're right about that," Jamie admitted, "but it seemed to me those badlands might be a good place to look for Perro Blanco. And if he's not there, he may have pulled back into the hills. I don't think he's around this escarpment anymore, and if we want to chase him down, we're going to have to look somewhere else."

Garazano's frown deepened into a scowl, but after a moment he gave Jamie a curt nod. "What you say is true, Señor MacCallister. But I must draw a line. Those hills where you intend to make camp are as far into Mexico as you are allowed to go. If you try to penetrate further into my country, I will stop you."

Jamie shrugged in seeming acceptance, but in truth, he wasn't agreeing to anything. He would do what was necessary and go where he needed to go in order to complete his mission.

He mounted up and headed back to camp. By the time he got there, everything had been packed into the wagons, and the mule teams were hitched up.

Clementine looked out from the back of the Wylie wagon, making eye contact with Jamie over Fletch's shoulder. "Preacher told me to stay back here instead of riding on the seat. Do you agree with that, Mr. MacCallister?"

"I sure do," Jamie replied. "Those soldiers have probably caught a few glimpses of you around the camp, but I don't think they've gotten a good look at you yet and it'd probably be better to keep things that way."

"Am I so beautiful that I'd drive them all mad or something?"

Fletch smiled over his shoulder and told her, "That's what happened to me."

"Oh, hush," she said, but she smiled a little as she scolded him.

Jamie said, "Beautiful or not—and you *are*, ma'am, I don't think there's any point in arguing that— you're the only woman in a lot of miles. And I don't know how long those troops have been out here on patrol. Taking all that together, I reckon it's a good idea for you to lay low as much as you can."

Clementine blew out her breath in a frustrated sigh. "Oh, all right. I'll stay out of sight."

Jamie nodded his thanks and rode over to the surveyors' wagon. Chester Merrick had the reins this morning and Noah Stuart sat beside him holding their rifle.

"You fellas ready to go?"

Stuart said, "I'm eager to get a closer look at those badlands."

"There could be *anything* hiding in there," Merrick

said with a sigh. "Savages, wild beasts . . . At least here, we can see trouble coming."

"Chances are, we won't be making camp in the badlands," Jamie explained to him. "We'll just move through them and go into the hills on the other side."

"But what if we can't get through them? What if it's too rough for the wagons?"

That was a possibility Preacher and Jamie had considered, but they thought the effort was worth a try, anyway.

"I reckon we'll have to see about that when we get there," he said to Merrick.

Preacher and Dog were waiting for Jamie to join them. The rest of the party was gathered in a loose group around the wagons. Jamie looked around, got nods from several of the men to signify that they were ready to go, and turned his horse south.

Considering the desolate nature of the region, this had been a good campsite. They might not find one as favorable in the hills. But Jamie's instincts told him that they had accomplished everything they could from there. It was time to move on.

As the wagons rolled past the mesa, Noah Stuart smiled and said to the man on the seat beside him, "I considered the idea of the two of us trying to get some of our equipment up there, Chester."

Merrick craned his neck to look up at the top of the mesa. "You mean *climb* up there?"

"Well, sure. I made it to the top, remember?"

"And if I'd been here, I would have told you that you'd lost your mind," Merrick muttered.

"I didn't have any real trouble. And from up there, I was able to find our next destination."

"I'll keep solid ground under my feet, thanks. Even when I was a kid, I didn't like climbing trees and things like that."

Stuart had no trouble believing that.

Once again, appearances proved to be deceptive in the thin air. When the expedition had covered what had to be more than the five miles Stuart had estimated, they still hadn't reached the badlands, and the area wasn't even in sight yet. They pushed on through the morning and into the afternoon, stopping only for a short noon meal of biscuits and salt pork left over from that morning. They took advantage of the halt to water the mules and horses, too.

Jamie looked behind them and saw that the Mexican army patrol had stopped about a quarter of a mile away.

"Our shadows are still back there," he said to Preacher.

"*El capitan* is an ambitious fella," the mountain man drawled. "You can tell that just by lookin' at him. He wants some more ribbons and medals to pin on that jacket, and he figures he can get 'em by roundin' up ol' White Dog and the rest of the Apaches."

Jamie squinted off into the distance and said slowly, "I've been doing some thinking about Perro Blanco."

"What about him?"

"You remember the other reason we came down here? Besides surveying and fighting Apaches?"

Preacher frowned and cocked his head a little to the side, just as Dog might have. "You mean findin' out for sure that the 'Paches killed that young lieutenant? What was his name?"

"Damon Charlton," Jamie said. "The general's son."

"You reckon Perro Blanco was leadin' the band that wiped out his command?"

"Not . . . exactly."

Preacher's frown deepened. "I might have an idea what you're gettin' at, Jamie. And I got to say, it sounds plumb loco."

"Think about it," Jamie said. "You know what that farmer, Sandoval, told us. Perro Blanco has only started stirring up trouble in the past year. It's been a little more than a year and a half since Damon Charlton disappeared down here. The bodies of the rest of the soldiers were found, but his never was."

"Maybe not, but that don't mean he survived. And it sure as tarnation don't mean that a white, shavetail army lieutenant could somehow turn into an Apache war chief! That's plain crazy, Jamie."

"Not completely. White captives have been adopted into Indian tribes before. You've probably seen that happen."

"I have," Preacher admitted.

"And once a man's been taken into the tribe, he generally has the same rights as if he'd been born to it. Including the right to rise to the position of war chief if he can prove worthy of it. There's the name, too . . . White Dog. The Apaches might have called him something like that if they made him a captive."

Preacher shook his head stubbornly. "You know good and well the only reason those varmints would've taken the boy prisoner was to haul him back to their village and make him scream his guts out by torturin' him for a few days before he died. He's been dead and gone for more 'n a year now."

"Likely. But I reckon there's only one way to prove it."

"Find Perro Blanco and ask him."

Jamie nodded in agreement with that blunt statement.

Preacher went on. "Well, you said you had a feelin' he might be waitin' for us in the badlands. Reckon maybe we'll find out before too much longer."

However, it was late afternoon before the riders and wagons reached the edge of the dark-colored stretch Noah Stuart had seen from the mesa. As they came up to it, reined in the horses, and pulled the teams to a stop, the reason for that mysterious dark color became apparent. The ground itself was black rock in many places, although there were trails of hard-packed dirt winding through it.

"That's volcanic rock," Stuart exclaimed in surprise from the wagon seat. "This whole area was covered in lava at some time in the past, and the black rock is what's left."

Jamie and Preacher had stopped beside the surveyors' wagon.

"Like the *malpais* farther north," Jamie said. "Mighty rough country. Those rocks are sharp enough to cut a horse's hooves . . . or a man's feet . . . to ribbons if he's not careful."

Chester Merrick said, "I don't understand. If it's volcanic rock . . . where's the volcano it came from?"

"If it was active long enough ago," Stuart said, "it could have been one of those hills, only time has eroded it down to the point that it doesn't look impressive anymore. And sometimes a volcano's cone will collapse until it's not even a hill anymore, but a crater instead."

"All I know is that we'll have to be careful goin' through there," Preacher said. "And as late in the day as it is, might be a good idea to wait until mornin' before we try it."

"I agree." Jamie hipped around in the saddle and called to the others, "We're going to make camp right here."

CHAPTER 40

It wasn't a particularly good place to camp—no water or shade, very little grass for the animals—but they would be there for only one night. The next morning, they could start following the torturous trails through the badlands and hope that one led to the other side where the low hills waited, showing enough green to indicate that there had to be some water available.

Captain Garazano rode over, accompanied by a couple of troopers, to confer with Jamie and Preacher. They explained their plans to him, and he agreed that it was too late in the day to attempt crossing the badlands.

They weren't far from the Wylie wagon as they talked, and just as Garazano was about to mount up and return to his men, Clementine emerged from the back of the wagon, stepping over the tailgate and jumping lithely to the ground.

It was the closest any of the Mexican soldiers had been to her, and Garazano stood up straighter as he got a good look at her. She wore men's baggy trousers and a flannel shirt with the sleeves rolled up over her tanned forearms. Her blond hair was tucked up under her hat.

Despite the outfit, it was obvious that Garazano identified her as a woman at first glance.

Nor did he stop at one glance. Rather, he looked intently at Clementine until she became aware of his scrutiny and stepped quickly around to the other side of the wagon.

"You need something else, Captain?" Jamie asked with an edge in his voice.

Garazano shook his head. "No . . . No, I suppose not." For a moment it seemed as if he were going to ignore the incident, but then he said, "Some of my men told me you have a woman traveling with you. I found such a thing difficult to believe, but now I see that it is true. Tell me, Señor MacCallister, why would you bring a woman into such a country as this? Especially a woman who looks like that one?"

"Bein' a mite plainspoken about it, ain't you?" Preacher grated.

Garazano returned the mountain man's chilly stare. "I see no reason not to speak my mind, señor."

"It's a long story," Jamie said, "and it doesn't really have anything to do with why the rest of us are here. When this mission is over, Mrs. Wylie and *her husband* will be moving on, along with Preacher. He's going to help them get to California."

He wanted to make certain that Garazano understood Clementine was a married woman and therefore off-limits. The rest of the soldiers needed to know that, too, so Jamie went on. "None of us over here would take it kindly if anybody was to cause trouble for the Wylies. *Anybody.*"

"There will be no trouble," Garazano said stiffly. "I

was merely surprised. I thought perhaps you had brought an older woman along to cook for you and your men."

"Clementine's a fine cook," Preacher said, "but that ain't why she's here."

"Clementine," Garazano repeated with a slight smirk on his face. "A lovely name. It suits the señorita. I mean, the *señora*."

Preacher groaned. "Now, don't *you* start that!"

"*Que?*"

"Never mind," Jamie said. "As long as we understand each other."

Garazano nodded. "Of course." Still acting stiff-necked, he swung up into his saddle and rode away, followed by the soldiers who had come with him.

Preacher watched them go and shook his head. "You reckon that's gonna cause some trouble?"

"I don't know," Jamie said. "The captain doesn't strike me as the sort of hombre who'd go back and share what he just saw with all the others. He might tell his second in command, but that's all, I figure." He rubbed his chin. "Question now is, just how taken with Clementine was the captain himself?"

The young woman they were talking about came back around the wagon then and said, "Mr. MacCallister, I'm sorry. I didn't realize Captain Garazano was here in camp. I've been trying to stay out of sight most of the time, like you suggested."

"Yes, ma'am, and I appreciate that. Don't worry too much about what just happened. We're all liable to have other things on our mind before too much longer."

Clementine summoned up a smile, but she said,

"Somehow, that doesn't make me feel all that much better, Mr. MacCallister."

Everyone was on edge, for various good reasons. Jamie posted a heavy guard. From what he could tell, Captain Garazano did the same. Night fell suddenly, like the dropping of a curtain, as it did in that part of the country, and the darkness just made everyone more nervous.

Even though no one got much sleep, nothing happened during the night.

Early the next morning, after a hurried breakfast, the hollow-eyed travelers saddled their horses, hitched up the wagon teams, and started through the badlands as soon as it was light enough to see where they were going.

The gray and black landscape was so bleak and barren they might as well have been on the moon, Jamie thought as he and Preacher led the way. Not that he knew what the surface of the moon was like, of course, but he could imagine it, and he figured it looked something like this *malpais*.

The moon was probably as empty and deserted as these badlands, too. He hadn't seen a bird, a snake, or even a lizard moving as they made their way along the twisting trail.

The sun climbed above the horizon, but the garish red light that spread over the badlands just seemed to make the landscape even more ugly. At least it was easier to see where the trail was and not wander off it into the dangerously sharp and jagged rocks.

The path never ran straight for more than twenty

yards, and at times it was so narrow the wagons could barely travel between the mounds of ancient lava. After running into a couple of dead ends, which, luckily, were wide enough for the vehicles to turn around, Jamie and Preacher began ranging farther ahead to make sure the trail they were following continued.

On the surveyors' wagon, a tense and pale Chester Merrick handled the reins while Noah Stuart kept his pencil moving on his pad of paper, sketching not only the route of the trail they followed but also the various rock spires and other features he could see.

By midmorning, it seemed to a frustrated Jamie MacCallister that they should have come ten miles and be on the far side of the badlands by now. He had no idea how many miles they actually *had* covered, but he didn't believe they were actually that much closer to emerging from the desolation. The way they were constantly twisting and turning, they weren't making much actual headway toward the hills.

Now that they were in this maze, though, there was nothing they could do but keep going.

While they were stopped to let the mules and horses rest, a clatter of hoofbeats came from behind them along the trail. The men all rested their hands on their weapons as they turned to see who was approaching.

Captain Enrique Garazano rode around a bend in the trail between two looming boulders of volcanic rock and came toward them. He appeared to be alone for a change, with no troopers following him. Jamie motioned for his men to relax and strode out to meet the Mexican officer.

As Garazano reined in, he said, "I have decided to

join you, Señor MacCallister, leaving my patrol in the competent hands of Lieutenant Bernardo."

Jamie could have pointed out that nobody had *asked* Captain Garazano to join them, but the politeness ingrained in every Westerner kept him from doing so. He just nodded and said, "All right. We're resting and watering the animals right now, but we'll be moving on again pretty soon."

Garazano dismounted. "These badlands, they are like something out of a nightmare, no?"

"It's not the prettiest place I've ever been," Jamie said dryly. "I'm surprised you'd leave your men, Captain."

"As I said, Lieutenant Bernardo is quite competent." Garazano smiled and led his horse toward the wagons.

Preacher ambled over and cocked an eyebrow at Jamie, who said quietly, "I expect you're thinking the same thing I'm thinking."

"*El capitan* there figures on gettin' another look at Clementine," the mountain man said. "Maybe even flirtin' with her a mite. Like Ramirez, he ain't overly worried about her bein' hitched to Fletch."

Jamie looked around. "Where is Ramirez? I saw him just a minute ago."

"When he saw the cap'n comin', he got on his horse and rode out. Told Audie and Dupre he was gonna scout out the trail ahead of us. I figure he just don't want Garazano gettin' a good look at *him*. He's probably wanted by the law down here and don't plan on gettin' caught by the army."

Jamie grunted and shook his head. "I don't think Garazano would give a hoot in Hades about that.

Arresting a minor *bandido* won't get him a promotion. Capturing or killing the Apaches' new war chief might."

They kept an eye on Garazano as he loitered around the wagons, talking to Noah Stuart and Chester Merrick. Jamie knew that was just an excuse to try for another glimpse of Clementine. She must have noticed Garazano approaching, and stayed in the wagon. The canvas flap at the back was closed, cutting off the officer's view into it.

After only a few more minutes, Jamie called for everyone to mount up. They started off with Jamie and Preacher in the lead, as usual, but Preacher looked over his shoulder and said, "Garazano's ridin' next to the Wylie wagon now, talkin' to Fletch. And from the looks of things, Fletch don't much cotton to it."

"Better drop back and see if you can settle things down," Jamie said.

"Just what I had in mind." Preacher slowed Horse and pulled to the side of the trail as the Wylie wagon came closer. He could hear Fletch and Garazano talking.

Garazano was saying, ". . . an excellent driver. Give me the reins, Señor Wylie, and I will show you."

"I can handle my own wagon," Fletch replied with a scowl on his face. "No offense, Captain, but I don't need your help . . . with anything."

"Oh, but you do, señor." Garazano moved his right foot from the stirrup, placed it on the floorboards of the driver's box, and moved agilely from horseback to the wagon seat. He reached for the reins in Fletch's hands, but at the same time, he turned his head to look into the back of the wagon. "Let me—"

Fletch hauled back on the reins, bringing the vehicle

to an abrupt stop, and lunged against Garazano, ramming his shoulder into the officer's chest. "Get off my wagon!"

Taken by surprise, Garazano rocked back from the impact. He tried to catch his balance but was unable to. His plumed hat sailed off his head as he toppled off the seat and fell to the ground next to the wagon's front wheel on that side. Grayish dust billowed up around him.

Though he looked startled and shaken by the fall, Garazano stayed on the ground only for a second. He sprang up, jerked his saber from its scabbard, and charged at Fletch as he yelled a curse in Spanish.

CHAPTER 41

Fletch was already twisting around on the wagon seat and clawing at the revolver on his hip. Preacher jabbed his heels into Horse's flanks and the big stallion leaped forward. Garazano might have been outraged by what he considered an insult to his honor and his person, but that didn't matter when he was about to be trampled. He stopped short and threw himself backward, out of Horse's way.

Preacher wheeled Horse around sharply and put the both of them between Fletch and the Mexican officer.

"Hold it right there, mister!" he told Garazano. His right hand hovered near the butt of the Dragoon on that side. He didn't want to shoot Garazano, but he would if the man tried to stab him with that pigsticker.

Shooting a Mexican army officer might wind up starting a war, but at the moment, Preacher didn't much care.

Garazano's face was dark with anger. He was so mad he was trembling. With a visible effort, he controlled his emotions and lowered the saber.

Without looking around, Preacher said, "Fletch, if

you pulled that hogleg, you just go ahead and pouch it. This ruckus is over."

"No!" Garazano said. "I demand satisfaction!"

"You can demand up one way and down the other, Capitan, but you and Fletch ain't gonna kill each other. Now, why don't you get on your horse and go back to your men?"

"You cannot give me orders! This is Mexico! I am in charge!"

The Wylie wagon was in the lead, so when it had come to a halt, the surveyors' wagon was forced to stop, too. Jamie had noticed that something was going on, and he rode back hurriedly to find out what it was.

"Captain Garazano, are you all right?" he asked.

Garazano pointed his saber at Fletch and said, "That man attacked me!"

"I told you I didn't need your help, and I didn't want you on my wagon," Fletch flared back at him. "So I pushed you off. Anyway, we all know you didn't want to help me with the mules. You just wanted to leer at my wife!"

"How dare you! I demand we settle this like men—"

"We're American citizens, Captain," Jamie said, not bothering to keep the dislike out of his voice. "We may be in Mexico, but we're not under your command. And you don't have any right to come between a man and his wife. If you were a gentleman as well as an officer, you'd know that."

Garazano's lip curled at Jamie's scathing words. It was even money whether he would be able to control his temper, but before the matter could be decided one way or the other, a burst of gunfire came from somewhere back up the trail.

Garazano exclaimed something in Spanish as he jerked around in that direction. The other members of Jamie's party, who had been watching the confrontation with interest, stiffened in their saddles and looked toward the shooting, as well.

"Sounds like a little war done broke out," Tennysee said.

"My men must be under attack." Garazano glanced back and forth between Fletch, Preacher, and Jamie, and back up the trail toward the spot where he had left the patrol. The anger he felt warred with loyalty to his men.

Loyalty won. Garazano rammed the saber back into its scabbard and ran toward his horse, which shied away from him. He cursed again and tried to grab the dangling reins.

Another sound made the men turn and look ahead toward the south. Ramirez galloped around the next bend in the trail. The Mexican gunslinger was bent low over his horse's neck as he urged the animal on.

Shots came from that direction as well. Powder smoke jetted from behind outcroppings in the wasteland of lava sloping up on both sides of the trail. No ambushers were visible, but they were there, the volley of gunfire left no doubt of that.

As Ramirez neared the wagons, he jerked in the saddle and almost toppled off, maintaining his grip at the last second. But as he came on, he slumped instead of leaning forward deliberately. He swayed back and forth, indicating the precariousness of his position.

Preacher could tell the gunslinger was wounded but not how badly. He kneed Horse into motion again and rode hard to meet Ramirez. Preacher might not like the man, but Ramirez was one of them.

Garazano finally brought his horse under control and mounted, swiftly but awkwardly. He wasn't too steady in the saddle, either, as he raced back in the direction he'd come from.

Meanwhile, Jamie shouted, "Take cover!" at his companions.

Fletch dived into the back of the wagon with Clementine, while Noah Stuart and Chester Merrick scrambled over the seat into the back of their vehicle. The mountain men, the Molmberg brothers, and the half-breed Comanche all left their saddles in a hurry and sought shelter behind rocks or the two wagons.

As Jamie turned his horse in a tight circle, he drew his Walker Colt and thumbed off a couple of shots into the rocks on both sides of the trail. He didn't figure he would hit anything unless he was incredibly lucky, but at least maybe he would make the attackers keep their heads down.

Those hidden riflemen had to be Perro Blanco's men. Jamie wouldn't have thought the Apaches had that many rifles among them, but evidently they did. And they were putting the weapons to good use.

One of the Molmbergs grabbed his right leg and toppled over. Blood spread darkly on his trouser leg as his sibling grabbed hold of him and dragged him underneath the surveyors' wagon. Jamie didn't know how badly the wounded man was hit, but both brothers were out of the fight.

He had known they were running a risk when they'd entered the badlands. This wild, rugged stretch was a good spot for an ambush, and sure enough, the Apaches thought so, too.

Preacher and Ramirez reached the Wylie wagon. In a display of agility unusual in a man of his age, Preacher dropped off Horse's back while the stallion was still moving. He caught Ramirez as the gunslinger finally tumbled out of the saddle. Ramirez tried to stay on his feet, but Preacher had to practically carry him to the wagon and help him crawl underneath it.

The shooting from the rocks came to an abrupt stop, almost as if someone had given a signal for the ambushers to hold their fire. Maybe someone had. Perro Blanco might have done it.

That didn't mean the fight was over, though. The Apaches probably had a limited amount of powder and shot and didn't want to waste ammunition. After only a couple of seconds, arrows began to rain down on the wagons and the area around them.

One of the arrows struck a board in the side of the Wylie wagon and embedded itself there, only a few inches from Preacher's head as he straightened from helping Ramirez get under the wagon. The shaft hung there, quivering from the impact.

Preacher turned, palmed out the right-hand Dragoon, and looked up into the rocks in the direction the arrow had come from. For the first time, he caught a glimpse of one of the attackers as the man shifted slightly to get a better angle with the arrow he was aiming at Preacher.

That proved to be a fatal mistake. The mountain man's gun came up almost faster than the eye could follow and flame shot out from its muzzle. Preacher had fired by instinct, not taking the time to aim, but his eyes, nerves, and muscles were in perfect coordination, as always. The heavy ball smashed through the Apache's bow and ripped into his throat. Preacher saw blood spray high in the air as the man went over backward.

Another Apache fell forward over a rock as a shot found him, and then a third man went down as well, rolling into plain sight from behind the rocks where he'd concealed himself. The Apaches were better than just about anybody when it came to not being seen unless they wanted to be, but as dangerous as they were, the members of Jamie's group were their equal when it came to fighting. They were warriors, too.

At least most of them were. Sporadic, ineffective shots came from inside the surveyors' wagon.

Jamie rode up beside it, dropped off his horse, and called through the opening at the front, "Save your bullets if you don't have a clear shot."

"We're trapped here!" Chester Merrick squealed as he huddled over the shotgun he clutched. He hadn't fired it yet. "We have to get out of here!"

"There's no place to go right now." Jamie lifted the Walker Colt and triggered another shot. He had spotted only a few inches of an Apache's shoulder up in the rocks, but that was enough. The shoulder jerked and blood flew as the bullet smashed it. "If we want to go anywhere, we'll have to fight our way out!"

That wouldn't be easy. The Apaches knew these badlands much better than their foes. They had picked a good spot for their attack.

Jamie heard a rumbling sound over the continuing blast of gunfire and turned his head in that direction. His rugged features twisted into a grimace As he turned his head in that direction, his rugged features twisted into a grimace. The sound was unmistakable. Hoofbeats, a lot of them. A large group of riders was about to sweep around that bend in the trail and come pounding down on the defenders.

Would it be the Mexican patrol, fleeing from the ambush?

Or had they been wiped out, and Perro Blanco's Apaches were about to overrun Jamie, Preacher, and their companions?

CHAPTER 42

Capitan Enrique Garazano led the charge of riders around the bend toward the wagons. That was a relief, Jamie supposed, but not much of one. Less than half the patrol followed Garazano. The other officer, Lieutenant Bernardo, was nowhere in sight, and chances were that he had been killed in the fight.

Garazano had a streak of bright blood on his face but didn't appear to be badly wounded. A couple of the men following him looked to be hurt, though, and were barely staying in their saddles. In fact, one of them suddenly toppled off and landed in a loose-limbed sprawl that meant death had caught up to him despite his frantic flight.

The soldiers converged on the wagons. The sturdy vehicles were the best cover around. They rushed up and dismounted so hurriedly and haphazardly that several of them fell down. The scene might have been funny had it not been so deadly serious.

As one trooper struggled back to his feet, an arrow struck him in the right side of his neck and drove all the way through, the bloody arrowhead emerging on the left side. The man's eyes grew incredibly wide, and he pawed at his throat as his mouth opened and blood gushed out. He stumbled forward a couple of steps and then fell on his face.

Another man shrieked as an arrow hit him in the back. He tried to reach behind him and pull it loose but slowly twisted to the ground as his strength deserted him.

Everyone else managed to scramble to cover either underneath or beside the wagons, joining the members of Jamie's group who were already there. With ambushers on both sides of the road, it was difficult to find a place that promised even a little safety, but Jamie thought the steady and deadly accurate fire of his friends was having an effect. Fewer arrows were flying down from the rocks.

The Apaches had no stomach for long battles, Jamie knew. They liked to hit their enemies quick and hard and then fade away until the next attack. That seemed on the verge of happening.

Clutching the saber, Garazano moved alongside Jamie as they crouched next to a wagon wheel. Panting slightly, the officer said, "My men . . . so many of them dead. Bernardo went down in the first volley. We never should have come into this hellhole! This is your fault, MacCallister!"

"You didn't have to follow us," Jamie said. "That was your own choice." He thumbed off another shot but couldn't tell if it hit any of the Apaches. Then with a cold smile, he went on. "Anyway, you wanted to find Perro Blanco. I reckon there's a good chance he's up there somewhere."

"I'm getting out of here," Garazano said with a note of hysteria edging into his voice. He sounded oddly like Chester Merrick. "We have no chance if we stay here like this, pinned down."

"We can wait them out—" Jamie began.

"No! The savages will kill us all if we stay!" A cunning light entered the officer's eyes. "I will take Señora Wylie and get her to safety."

"You stay away from that woman," Jamie snapped.

Garazano lifted the saber. "You do not give me orders, you filthy gringo!"

"Don't wave that pigsticker at me," Jamie warned. He didn't want to shoot Garazano, but he would if it was necessary to protect Clementine.

The tense confrontation between the two men ended abruptly as Greybull boomed, "Here they come!"

Jamie whirled around and saw that instead of giving up, as he had hoped they would in the face of such stiff resistance, the Apaches were attempting a last-ditch, all-out attack, dozens of them swarming down out of the rocks to battle hand to hand with the defenders clustered around the wagons.

"Let 'em have it!" Jamie bellowed. The Colt roared and bucked in his hand as he fired the remaining two rounds in it. An Apache went down with each shot.

Preacher appeared at Jamie's side with a Dragoon in each fist. Shots rolled like thunder as he scythed hot lead through the attackers. Then the Dragoons' hammers clicked on empty chambers, and Preacher holstered the weapons smoothly, drawing his bowie knife instead.

"Wish I had my old tomahawk, too," the mountain man said with a grim smile and the light of battle blazing in his eyes.

Beside him, Jamie had already drawn his knife, and

to Jamie's left, Garazano stood with the saber poised. The three of them were ready when the tide of blood-thirsty Apaches rolled up to them.

A fight at close quarters was always bloody chaos.

Garazano hacked and slashed at the warriors, trying to hold them off as they clustered around him. He was good with the saber. Blood sprayed as the blade ripped across one man's throat, and then another of Garazano's swings connected with an Apache's wrist with enough force that it sheared through flesh and bone and the warrior's hand flew off, still clutching a knife. The man reeled back, waving the crimson-spurting stump, his scream cut short by Garazano's saber splitting his skull.

One of the Apaches leaped at Jamie, knife raised high to come down in a killing stroke, but Jamie caught the man's wrist and stopped it as the blade swooped toward him. At the same time, he thrust his bowie up at an angle into the man's chest, penetrating to the heart. The Apache's eyes widened in the shock of impending death. Jamie pulled the knife free and shoved the dying man into the path of two more warriors whose feet tangled with him. One of those men toppled forward out of control, unable to keep his balance, and Jamie was ready for him. The bowie sliced through his left eye, grating on the bone of the socket, and lanced on into the brain. Gray matter clung to the blade as Jamie yanked it out.

Preacher kicked a man in the groin, and as the Apache bent over involuntarily, the mountain man chopped down on the back of his neck with his bowie, cutting so deep that the blade severed the spine. The warrior flopped bonelessly to the ground. Another Apache hurtled over him, screaming in hate as he thrust a knife at Preacher. Preacher swept the blade aside with his left arm and drove the bowie into the man's wide-open mouth, all the way through to the back of the neck. He yanked the knife from side to side as he withdrew it, cutting a ghastly grin into the dying man's face.

Bodies piled up around the three men as they fought, making it more difficult for the remaining Apaches to reach them. Jamie, Preacher, and Garazano all suffered minor wounds as they battled the copper-skinned horde, but they were still on their feet, still fighting. Jamie had no idea how the rest of the bloody fracas was going. There was no time to even wonder about it. All his attention was focused on avoiding the Apaches' knives, axes, and lances and dealing out death strokes of his own.

The clamor of rage-filled screams filled the air. Shots still blasted. The scattergun boomed as Chester Merrick finally got into the fight. The sharp reek of freshly spilled blood stung the nose. It was like being trapped in a madhouse with gore-dripping walls steadily closing in.

Then the crazed cacophony suddenly fell away. Apache warriors turned and fled instead of continuing the fight. They bounded over rocks and disappeared into the wasteland of ancient lava. The price for defeating the enemy had been too high, and they weren't going to keep paying it.

Jamie and Preacher had backed against the wagon. They leaned on the vehicle as their chests heaved from the exertion of battle. Garazano was beside them. He braced himself with his left hand against the wagon while the right clutched the saber. Crimson dripped from the curved blade.

Jamie looked around. Apache bodies littered the ground on both sides of the wagons. Several of the Mexican soldiers sprawled lifelessly among the dead warriors.

"Audie! Nighthawk!" Preacher called to his long-time friends. "Are you boys all right?"

From underneath the other wagon, Audie replied, "We're here, Preacher, and unharmed, for the most part."

"Umm," Nighthawk confirmed.

"What about the rest of the fellas?"

Audie came out from under the wagon and said, "I'll check on everyone."

Captain Garazano was steady enough on his feet now that he was able to stop leaning on the wagon and straighten up. He drew his sleeve across his sweaty face, smearing the blood from a scratch on his cheek. Then he glared at Jamie and Preacher and said, "Enough of this madness! You and all your men will leave Mexico immediately—"

With a faint fluttering sound, an arrow flew from somewhere and slammed into the officer's chest. The impact drove Garazano back against the wagon. He hung there for a moment, his eyes bugging out as he lowered his head and stared in disbelief at the shaft buried in his body. His mouth opened and closed a couple of times, but no sound emerged.

Then his eyes rolled up in their sockets, and he pitched forward, dead.

"Looks like we won't have to be followin' the *capitan*'s orders," Preacher said.

A rifle boomed. Preacher and Jamie looked up from Garazano's body to see Dog Brother lowering his rifle. Powder smoke still drifted from the muzzle.

In the rocks above them, the limp form of an Apache warrior rolled down several yards before coming to a stop wedged against a boulder.

"The fool had to try one last shot," the half-breed Comanche said. "I hope killing the Mexican was worth his own life." The cold flintiness of Dog Brother's voice belied the sincerity of that sentiment. He didn't care whether Garazano's death had been worth it or not.

Audie walked over to Jamie and Preacher. "Bengt Molmberg is dead," he informed them. "The shot that wounded him hit an artery, and his brother wasn't able to stop the bleeding in time. Ramirez is gone, too. He was shot through the body while he scouted ahead of us and didn't make it. The rest of our men are all right except for minor injuries." The former professor sighed. "We were very, very lucky not to lose more of them, I'd say."

"How about the Mex soldiers?" Preacher asked.

"It appears that only three are still alive."

Jamie nodded and went to the back of the wagon. "Noah? Are you and Merrick all right in there?"

Noah Stuart stuck his head up from the among the crates of equipment they had been using for cover. "Yes, we managed to come through unharmed, except . . . well, Chester appears to have fainted."

"Fainted?" Jamie repeated. "You sure he's not dead? Maybe you missed a wound."

"No, he's alive," Stuart said. "There's not a drop of blood on him."

Jamie grunted. "All right. I'm glad to hear both of you fellas pulled through."

Meanwhile, Preacher went to the back of the Wylie wagon and said, "Fletch? Clementine?"

Not getting any answer, he stepped up and threw a leg over the tailgate to climb inside. He was back a moment later, and the look on his weathered face immediately told Jamie that something was wrong.

"What is it?" Jamie asked as he started in that direction.

"Fletch is layin' in there with his head in a pool of blood," the mountain man replied, "and Clementine is gone."

CHAPTER 43

Despite appearances, Fletch wasn't dead, but he did have an ugly gash on his head where he had bled profusely. So much, in fact, that it would have been easy to believe he had crossed the divide.

Clementine was gone, though, just as Preacher had said. A quick search of the area by Dog Brother, Pugh, and Dupre turned up no sign of her—but when Dog Brother trotted on up around the bend in the trail, he found a few scattered hoofprints made by shod horses.

Preacher told himself he would do something later about what that meant. For the moment, he waited at the back of the wagon while Audie worked on patching up Fletch.

"This wound appears to have been made by a bullet," the former professor said over his shoulder as he used a wet rag to wipe away some of the blood from Fletch's head. "However, it struck him a glancing blow instead of penetrating, which is what saved his life."

"You mean he's gonna be all right?" Preacher asked.

"It's too soon to say that. His skull could still be fractured, or he could have a concussion or some other sort of brain injury. But I don't believe that he's in immediate danger of dying."

Preacher nodded and said, "That's good. Do what you can for him, Audie."

"Of course."

Preacher went over to Jamie, who was supervising the sorting out of bodies. Ramirez and Bengt Molmberg had been placed in the back of the surveyors' wagon. Garazano and the other dead Mexican soldiers lay on one side of the trail. Currently, Nighthawk and Greybull were dragging off the Apache carcasses and leaving them on the other side of the trail.

"How's Fletch?" Jamie asked.

"Looks like he'll probably make it. That head wound was a plumb mess, but other than losin' a lot of blood, it don't appear to have done much damage."

"I'm glad to hear it. I expect he'll have a devil of a headache when he comes around, though."

"Findin' out that Clementine is gone is gonna hurt worse," Preacher said. "Those tracks Dog Brother found can only mean one thing, Jamie."

"I know. Hold on a minute." Jamie called the three surviving Mexican soldiers over to him and told them in Spanish, "It's up to you to bury your officers and the rest of the men from your patrol. We don't have time."

The men glanced at each other. Judging by their expressions, they didn't think burying Garazano and the others was all that important.

One of them shrugged and said, "We cannot bury them here. The ground is too hard. Too much rock."

Jamie nodded toward the hills. "You'll have to take them out of these badlands and find a place over there."

"But Santa Fe is that way," the man said, pointing to the north.

"You mean you're going to leave them here for the buzzards, desert from the army, and head to Santa Fe?"

One of the other two soldiers sneered. "What business is that of yours, gringo?"

"None at all," Jamie said. "I didn't plan on asking you to come with us." He added bluntly, "I don't reckon I'd ever trust the likes of you."

The third man looked a little nervous. "We might still run into some Apaches."

"Take extra horses and guns and ammunition with you. You stand a pretty good chance of making it if you keep moving. That is, if you don't mind never being able to go home."

"Home holds nothing for us except squalor and hardship," the man said, shaking his head. "We will take our chances, I think."

Jamie gave them a curt nod and turned away, dismissing them from his thoughts. Whether they made it to civilization and safety or not was no concern of his. He said to Preacher, "We'll bury Ramirez and Molmberg as soon as we get out of these badlands."

"Can't be soon enough to suit me," Preacher said. "I want to get on the trail of those varmints who carried off Clementine."

"Her brothers, you mean."

"Couldn't have been anybody else riding shod horses and comin' from that direction. They got around us again somehow, and without runnin' into the 'Paches. Those Mahoney brothers are the dad-blasted luckiest sons of guns I ever did see."

"They've got grit, you have to give them that," Jamie said. "Sneaking into the middle of a pitched battle like that just to grab her. When they saw Fletch in the wagon with blood all around his head, they must have figured he was dead."

"He sure looked like it," Preacher agreed. "They're bound to have left a trail in the hills. I intend to follow it, and I ain't stoppin' this time until all four of those varmints are dead."

Jamie rubbed his chin, grimaced a little. "I'd like to go with you, Preacher, you know that, but there's another little chore I plan to take care of."

"Followin' Perro Blanco and the rest of that war party?"

"We've hurt them pretty bad. There's a good chance their stronghold is in those hills. That's the best place in this whole area for them to be holed up, and we may never have a better opportunity to find it. If I can track them and capture or kill Perro Blanco, I have a strong hunch that'll put a stop to all the hell-raising they've been doing in these parts. *And* maybe it'll tell me the truth about what really happened to Damon Charlton."

Preacher was still dubious about Jamie's theory of Perro Blanco's true identity, but at the moment, that didn't matter. What was important to him was finding Clementine and getting her out of the hands of her no-good, degenerate brothers. He had promised to get her and Fletch to California, and he was a man of his word.

"I want to take Audie and Nighthawk with me," he said. "And if Fletch wakes up in time, I know he's gonna want to come along, too. Not so sure it's a good idea if he does, but I don't reckon we'll be able to hold him back."

"No, probably not," Jamie agreed.

From behind them, Noah Stuart said, "Preacher,

Mr. MacCallister, I heard what you're talking about. I want to come along and help rescue Mrs. Wylie, too."

They turned to look at the young surveyor.

Jamie said, "That's not your responsibility, Noah."

"I know that, but . . . well, Fletch and I have become pretty good friends, and I greatly admire Clementine . . . Mrs. Wylie." Stuart held up a hand, palm out. "Not in the way you're thinking, although it's undeniable that she's a very beautiful woman. But she's also smart and determined, and I believe she and Fletch are meant to be together. If I can help with that . . ." He shrugged. "Anyway, I want to come along."

"What about Merrick?"

"He can do what he likes, either come with me or stay with you." Stuart smiled. "Since you said you're going after the Apaches, I suspect he'll want to come with me. As bad as the Mahoney brothers are, I don't believe Chester would be as afraid of them as he is of the Apaches."

"Huh," Preacher said. "That's like askin' a fella if he wants a diamondback rattler or a copperhead stuffed down his pants. Either way, he ain't gonna like what happens."

As Noah Stuart predicted, Chester Merrick chose to accompany him and go with Preacher, Fletch, Audie, and Nighthawk after the Mahoney brothers. Some of the other men wanted to come along, too, but Preacher asked them to stay with Jamie.

"Y'all are chasin' a lot bigger bunch than we are,"

he said. "If you find Perro Blanco's stronghold, you'll be facin' high odds."

"Maybe," Tennysee said. "The way we been killin' them Apaches hand over fist, we must've whittled 'em down a mite. But we'll do like you say, Preacher, and go with Jamie."

There was no question that Lars Molmberg would be part of Jamie's group, as well. The Apaches had killed his brother, and the taciturn Swede wanted revenge. Nighthawk had been closer to the Molmbergs than anyone else in the party. He and Lars had communed in silence after the burials, which took place at the edge of the hills, right outside the badlands, as soon as they came to a place where the soil was deep enough for graves to be dug.

Audie had cleaned the wound on Fletch's head and wrapped a bandage around it. As expected, the young man had a terrible headache and was a little weak and disoriented, but those things would fade with time. Mostly he was furious that his wife had been stolen from him. He grumbled about taking the time to lay Ramirez and Bengt Molmberg to rest, but, like the others, he grew solemn as Audie recited scripture over the graves.

Earlier, when he had regained consciousness and everything had been explained to him, Fletch had confirmed that one of the wild shots from the Apaches must have struck his head and knocked him out. As far as he remembered, Clementine had been beside him in the wagon, unharmed, when the world suddenly went black.

"I don't know what happened after that," he had

said. "I don't remember anything until I woke up and you were bandaging my head, Audie."

"Well, when we catch up to the Mahoneys, we can ask 'em how they did it," Preacher had drawled. "If there's a chance, that is. If there ain't, I reckon we'll just kill 'em and take Clementine back."

That plan sounded good to all the others.

With Fletch's wound tended to and the burying done, the group was ready to split up. They would be leaving the wagons there and traveling on horseback so they could move faster. Enough of the Mexican army mounts had survived that Stuart and Merrick had horses to ride.

Jamie said to Merrick, "If you want, you can stay here with the wagons. Might not be a bad idea to have somebody watching over them."

"By myself?" Merrick practically yelped.

"You shouldn't have to worry," Preacher told him. "Clementine's brothers don't have any reason to come back this way, and there's a good chance the 'Paches won't, neither. They'll be headin' back to wherever they usually hole up, so they can lick their wounds for a while before venturin' out again."

Merrick shook his head. "No, thanks. I'll come with you. I don't want to be stuck out here by myself."

"Suit yourself."

"If I did that," Merrick said with a sigh, "I'd be back in Washington, D.C., right now."

Tennysee shook his head. "What a terrible-soundin' fate *that* is."

They had backtracked the hoofprints left by Clementine's captors and would follow them on into the hills. Jamie's party, with Dog Brother and Jamie himself handling the tracking, would have to locate the trail of the Apaches, which probably would be more difficult. But Jamie was determined to track them to their lair and finish this job, once and for all.

With a quick round of farewells, the men split up, Preacher's group angling to the southeast while the others, with Jamie in the lead, headed almost due south, deeper into the hills.

CHAPTER 44

Clete Mahoney still almost couldn't believe they had done it. Well, *he* had done it, to be honest. Lew, Harp, and Jerome had been close by, ready to give him a hand if he needed it, but he was the one who had darted from rock to rock, staying out of sight of the defenders and the attacking Apaches alike, until he was close enough to the wagon to make a run for it, leap up on the tailgate, and haul himself inside.

He'd had a gun in his fist and was ready to shoot that little varmint Fletcher Wylie, but somebody had beaten him to it, he saw as soon as he got inside the wagon. Clementine was huddled over his bloody corpse, weeping and wailing. Feeling the wagon shift under Clete's weight, she'd jerked her head around toward him, expecting to see one of those filthy red-skinned savages.

When she'd recognized him, she'd made a grab for Fletch's revolver, but she wasn't fast enough. Clete bounded forward and backhanded her, snapping her head to the side and stunning her. It took him only a second to lift her, throw her over his shoulder, and climb out of the wagon while the wild melee still raged outside. He'd held on tight to Clementine and dashed toward the rocks where his brothers waited.

An Apache had seen them and tried to stop them, leaping in front of them with a defiant scream. Clete never slowed down, just planted a couple of bullets in the heathen's face and blew his head apart like a melon. Then he was among the rocks again, and Lew and Harp were there to take Clementine's senseless form from him. They threw her on a horse, and then all of them rattled their hocks out of those blasted badlands with the gunfire and screams dwindling behind them.

They stayed close to the northern edge of the hills and skirted the badlands for miles as they put distance between themselves and the site of the battle. Clete knew the badlands would play out in a few more miles and they could turn north again. It was the way he and his brothers had come, pushing their mounts to get ahead of their quarry once again. It had almost worked once before, so he didn't see any reason not to try it again.

Clete remembered hearing somebody say something once about how fortune favors the bold. He understood that and believed it now. Stealing Clementine out of the wagon in the middle of a battle was about the boldest thing he could have done—and it had worked.

She was awake, riding double in front of him with his left arm tight around her waist. Her head drooped forward in despair and her fair hair hung over her face. Every so often she shook a little as a bout of sobs seized her.

"If you're cryin' over Fletch, you're wastin' your tears," Clete told her. "He was never good enough for you, Clem, and you know it. You're goin' back to your family where you belong."

Sullen silence was her only response. Well, she would come around once they got home, he told himself. She wouldn't have any choice about that.

Lew pushed his horse up alongside Clete's and said, "It's gonna be dark before too much longer. Hadn't we best start lookin' for a place to camp?"

"We're not gonna stop just because it gets dark," Clete replied. "We can't get lost. All we've got to do is keep those badlands on our left. There'll be time enough to stop for the night once we've gotten clear of them and headed north a ways. I want to put as many miles as we can between us and any trouble that might be followin' us."

"You mean those Apaches," Lew said.

"Or Preacher."

"I thought you said the redskins were gonna wipe out that whole bunch."

"I said I *hope* they do. That would make it a lot easier on us."

Lew looked worried. "Unless the savages come after *us* next."

"They don't even know we're anywhere in these parts," Clete snapped. "They've had their hands full with Preacher and MacCallister and the rest of those varmints, not to mention those Mex soldiers. No, we don't have to worry about the Apaches."

Lew still looked doubtful.

That made Clete mad, and he added, "Have I steered you boys wrong yet?"

"It took us until now to get Clementine back," Lew said, then he winced involuntarily as if he expected his older brother to wallop him for mouthing off.

Clete thought about it, but he decided to be forgiving for a change. "We had some bad luck, but that's over now. Before you know it, we're gonna be back home, and then everything will be like it used to be." He squeezed Clementine tighter. "Ain't that right, honey?"

Again, she didn't say anything, but a shudder went through her. Clete felt it and grinned in the gathering dusk.

Nighthawk handled the tracking and rode slightly ahead of the others. Preacher trusted the keen eyes of the big Crow warrior and hung back a little, riding next to Audie. Fletch, Noah Stuart, and Chester Merrick were behind them. Whenever Preacher glanced back, Merrick was looking around frantically, jerking his head back and forth until it looked like he was going to wear out his neckbone. He was mighty nervous about something sneaking up on them.

Preacher didn't believe that would happen as long as Dog was around. The big cur, who padded along beside Horse, would warn them if he smelled or otherwise sensed anything suspicious.

The trail led them southeast for a while, then angled north, back toward the badlands, when they were several miles away from the spot where the Apaches had jumped the wagons. Preacher knew what the Mahoney brothers were doing just as surely as if they'd written it out for him—if any of those uneducated scoundrels could write, that is.

They planned to get back to the edge of the badlands and travel along it. They weren't familiar with these parts, but the area of volcanic rock was such a distinctive landmark a blind man could almost follow it. They wouldn't try crossing for fear of getting lost and stuck in there, especially with night coming on. But the rough terrain would peter out eventually, and once around the badlands, the brothers could head north and make for Santa Fe as rapidly as possible.

Preacher discussed that with Audie, and the former professor agreed.

"They'll have to keep Clementine too frightened to say anything and give them away to the authorities, once they reach civilization again," Audie commented. "But in all likelihood, she believes that Fletch is dead, so there's a very good chance she'll be overcome by despair and just cooperate with them, thinking that she has nothing to live for."

"She struck me as bein' a mite too feisty for that," Preacher said.

"Well, that's certainly possible. But grief is very powerful. We don't know what she'll do if she's convinced she's a widow."

When they reached the badlands, the tracks turned almost due east along that desolate stretch, just as Preacher expected. They paused there to rest the horses.

"How's your head feelin', son?" Preacher asked Fletch.

"It still hurts like blazes," the young man admitted. "But I don't care. I can put up with it. All that matters is finding Clementine . . . and settling things with those brothers of hers."

"Lean over here and let me look at your eyes," Audie said. While Fletch did that, Audie studied his eyes intently, tipping his head back and forth slightly to get the best view of each orb. Apparently satisfied,

Audie finally nodded. "I don't see any sign of brain injury at this point. The eyes are clear and focus well. Your headache may continue for a day or two, Fletch, but I believe you're going to be all right. You're a very fortunate young man."

"To be shot in the head and still be alive, you mean? I can't argue with that. Whenever I think about Clementine being gone, I don't feel very lucky, though. And it's bound to be worse for her."

"They don't want to kill her," Preacher pointed out. "This whole thing has been about takin' her back home alive."

"Yes, but you don't know Clete Mahoney like I do," Fletch said grimly. "I honestly believe that if he thought Clementine was going to be taken away from him for good . . . he might kill her rather than let me or anybody else have her."

"He's that loco?"

"I don't want to risk that he's not."

Preacher nodded. He would have to keep that in mind and try to get Clementine out of Clete's hands before he had a chance to harm her.

They pushed on, and as night approached they came to a halt again so Preacher could have a council of war with Audie and Nighthawk.

"My hunch is that they ain't gonna stop and make camp just because it gets dark," the mountain man said. "As easy a trail as they've got to follow with these badlands right alongside 'em, I think they'll keep movin' at least part of the night."

"I concur," Audie said, and Nighthawk added, "Umm."

"So we can't afford to make camp, either, but if for some reason they were to veer off to the south again, we might miss the tracks in the dark, and come mornin', we'd have lost considerable ground on them."

"Ummm," Nighthawk said.

"That's true," Audie responded. "If we stop temporarily once it gets too dark to see the tracks and wait for the moon to rise, there ought to be enough light then to follow the trail if they do something unexpected. We'd lose a little time doing that, but not as much as we'd be risking if we were to lose the trail entirely and have to locate it again."

"Do I get a vote in this?" Fletch asked.

Preacher's mouth quirked under his graying mustache. "I didn't know we was votin' . . . but I reckon you got a right to speak your piece, Fletch."

"I don't like waiting," the young man said. "I'm so scared for Clementine that I just want to keep moving. But what Audie says makes sense. We have to do whatever gives us the best chance of staying on their trail."

Noah Stuart said, "That sounds like a good idea to me, too."

Preacher turned to Merrick and asked, "What do you think, Chester? You're the only one who ain't spoke up yet."

"Are there any ravines we can fall into in the dark, or anything like that?" Merrick said. "Because if there are, I think we ought to wait until morning to go on."

"Umm," Nighthawk said.

"If there are any ravines, Nighthawk'll spot 'em in time for us to stop," Preacher assured Merrick. "And as for waitin' until mornin' . . . well, that ain't gonna happen, Chester." The mountain man rubbed his chin. "It's time them dadblasted Mahoneys got what's comin' to 'em, and I aim to be the one to deliver it, sooner instead of later."

CHAPTER 45

Although Jamie and Dog Brother were the best
trackers in the group that went after the Apaches, all
the mountain men were pretty good at reading sign,
too, so they split up to search for the trail. Jamie
picked one of the hills that was fairly distinctive, with
a couple of mounds on top of it—Tennysee claimed
that it looked like a woman's bosom—and pointed it
out to them before they went their separate ways.
They would rendezvous there late in the afternoon.

Lars Molmberg didn't have much experience at
tracking, so Dupre said, "Lars, why don't you come
with me? I can always use an extra pair of eyes."

"That's 'cause you're so old you're gettin' blind as
a bat," Tennysee gibed, which helped ease a little of
the tension they were all feeling. Molmberg just
nodded his gratitude to Dupre and moved his horse
alongside the Frenchman's.

Finding tracks where the Apaches had fled from
the badlands wasn't that difficult, but they had scattered in all different directions. They probably had a
rendezvous point as well, Jamie speculated, so it was

a matter of finding that location and then following them from there to their stronghold.

The hills were rugged enough that Jamie was soon out of sight of the other men. As he rode along, he thought about everything that had happened and how he could have spent this time at home in MacCallister's Valley with Kate. Maybe it would have been better if he had, he mused. Edgerton would probably still be alive, and so would Ramirez and Bengt Molmberg. Those three lives—so far—had been spent in the service of someday uniting both sides of the country by rail. That was a worthwhile goal, and doubtless it would cost the lives of many more men before it came about, if it ever did.

Jamie wondered if he would live to see it.

His children would, he told himself. It would make a difference for them, and so *he* was making a difference. Making the world a better place for those who came after him. That was the main thing any man should aspire to.

But at the same time, he thought about how much change the future would bring. There would be no need for men such as him and Preacher and most of the others in their party. No, that world would belong to Fletch and Clementine, and to Noah Stuart, not to a bunch of rough, cantankerous old-timers.

But it would be a while before that came about. For now, Jamie and Preacher and the men like them still had jobs to do. Once the frontier was tamed, *then* it would be time for them to fade away, to be remembered for a while but ultimately to be forgotten by those who had no idea what the West had been—and in their small self-satisfactions, no desire to know that once giants strode across this land . . .

* * *

When Jamie reached the rendezvous late that afternoon, Dog Brother was already there, as were Dupre, Lars Molmberg, Powder Pete, and Greybull. Tennysee, Deadlead, and Pugh showed up soon after.

Jamie gathered them around and pointed to a saddle of land higher in the hills. "The tracks I followed led in that direction."

"The ones I found did, too," Dog Brother agreed.

One by one, the other men nodded or spoke up to say that the trails they had found converged on that gap in the hills, too.

Jamie nodded. "I reckon it's safe to say their stronghold is somewhere on the other side. No way to tell how far on the other side until we go and look. Everybody feel the same way?"

"We been lettin' them come to us," Deadlead said. "It's time we took the fight to them."

"Likely they'll still outnumber us by quite a bit," Jamie pointed out.

"Yeah," Tennysee drawled, "but there's a heap fewer of 'em than there was a couple o' weeks ago."

That comment brought grim chuckles from several of the men.

"It's too late in the day to get through that gap before dark," Jamie said, "but we can get closer and then maybe one or two of us can do a little scouting tonight." He lifted his reins. "Come on."

Now that they were together again, they rode steadily higher into the hills. Jamie was careful to lead them along a route that didn't skyline them and stuck to whatever scant cover was available. It was possible the Apaches had left guards behind to keep an eye on their back trail. Jamie wanted to take Perro Blanco by surprise if at all possible.

He called a halt when they came to a beetle-browed outcropping of rock where they wouldn't be readily visible to anybody watching from higher in the hills. "We'll stay here until dark. Then Dog Brother and I will scout up through that gap on foot and see what we can find."

"Don't get caught, Jamie," Dupre said. "Those Apaches are not known for their hospitality."

"I'm not planning to pay them a visit . . . yet," Jamie said with a grin. "But if we're not back by morning, you fellas will probably have to figure out how to proceed on your own."

Greybull said, "We'll come lookin' for you, of course."

"Durned right," Pugh added.

"And settle up with the 'Paches if they need settlin' up with," Tennysee put in.

With that, the men loosened the cinches on their saddles but didn't remove them from the horses. They wanted to be able to get moving in a hurry if they needed to. They poured water from their canteens into their hats and let the mounts drink. Their water would run low if they didn't find a spring or a stream in the hills, but none of them were particularly worried about that. There would be time for that later—if they survived their next encounter with the Apaches.

Night's curtain dropped down suddenly. When the last reddish-gold vestiges of the sun had faded from the western sky, Jamie and Dog Brother started out on their scouting mission. On foot, with both men wearing moccasins so they could move more quietly, they headed up toward the gap where the Apaches had fled.

They didn't get in any hurry. It took them more than an hour to reach the saddle formed by two large, upthrust rock masses about a quarter of a mile apart. Without speaking, Jamie and Dog Brother started through the gap.

They hadn't gone very far when the faint scrape of leather on rock warned Jamie. He twisted aside, guided by his instincts, and the warrior who lunged out of the deep shadows missed with the knife he tried to thrust into Jamie's chest. As the Apache, off balance from the missed stroke, collided with him, Jamie's arms shot out and wrapped around the man's neck. He heaved and twisted, and a sharp snap sounded as the Apache's neck broke. The man made a strangled sound and went limp in Jamie's grip.

Another scuffle was going on a few yards away. Dog Brother and a second Apache sentinel, Jamie thought as he heard shuffling footsteps and grunts of effort.

Deeper in the gap, running footsteps suddenly slapped against rock.

Jamie grimaced as he jerked out his bowie. The fleeing man had to be a third guard, trying to get away so he could warn the rest of the Apaches. Jamie tried to spot him, but not even his keen eyes could make out any movement in the thick gloom of the gap.

He had those footsteps to aim at, though, and since that was his only option, he drew back his arm, flicked it forward, and let fly with the bowie.

He didn't hear the knife hit, but the hurried footsteps suddenly broke stride. They resumed raggedly, then stopped again as a faint thud sounded. Jamie hoped that meant his throw had been accurate and the fleeing guard had collapsed with the bowie in his back.

"MacCallister!" Dog Brother whispered.

"Here," Jamie said. "You all right?"

"Yes. This man is dead. Yours?"

"Dead, too. I don't know about the one who tried to get away, though."

The two men catfooted forward. After a couple of minutes of stealthy advance, Jamie heard a quiet, wheezing sound. He followed it until one of his feet bumped into something. Stopping abruptly, he knelt and reached out.

He touched bare flesh slick with sweat and grease, moved his fingers along it until he found the bowie's handle sticking up from the body. The man was lying on his belly with the knife in his back, just as Jamie had hoped. He was still alive, though, so Jamie wrapped his hand around the bowie's grip, pulled the blade out, and struck twice more in the darkness, aiming for the heart. The Apache spasmed a little and then went still. Jamie couldn't hear him breathing anymore.

Dog Brother hunkered beside him. "Three more dead."

"That's right, but we're a long way from finished."

They slipped through the shadows again, came out on the far side of the gap, and paused to look across the rolling hills in front of them. The moon was coming up, but its silvery illumination hadn't really started washing over the landscape yet. Jamie and Dog Brother were able to spot a faint orange glow in the sky, coming from the other side of a ridge about half a mile in front of them.

"Light from fires," Dog Brother said.

Jamie didn't respond, but he knew the half-breed was right. He started toward the ridge with Dog Brother alongside him. Again they moved as quietly as possible. They might not run into any more guards, but the possibility still existed.

By the time they reached the base of the ridge, they smelled wood smoke from the fires that had cast the orange glow into the sky.

This was the main Apache camp, Jamie thought. If Perro Blanco was still alive, they stood a good chance of finding him there.

The ridge was steep and topped with stunted pines. Jamie and Dog Brother climbed it easily and stretched out on the ground underneath the trees.

They could see into a small valley with Apache wickiups scattered on both sides of a tiny stream. A few scrubby cottonwoods grew along the banks. The valley was steep-sided, and at the far end was a rope enclosure where the band's pony herd was contained.

Half a dozen fires burned, but one blaze was larger than the others and a group of warriors had assembled around it. One man in particular seemed to dominate the gathering as he stalked back and forth and harangued the other men. He was dressed like them, in boot-topped moccasins, a breechcloth, and a colorful headband—in this case blue—around his dark hair. He wore a faded blue shirt, as well, and had a gun belt and holstered revolver strapped around his lean waist.

"From the way he's reading the others the riot act, I'd guess that's Perro Blanco," Jamie whispered.

"Yes," Dog Brother agreed. "Look at the way the others stand. Some of them want to disagree with him, but they remain silent. They are afraid of him."

Jamie hadn't shared his theory about Perro Blanco's true identity with anyone except Preacher. As he watched the Apache war chief stalk back and forth, it was difficult to believe he might actually be a white man, but so far Jamie hadn't seen anything to make him think his idea was wrong. Perro Blanco was taller and leaner than the other warriors, lacking the squatty build of the typical Apache male. Of course, not every Apache was shaped the same way.

Jamie leaned closer to Dog Brother and said, "Go back to the others and tell them what we've found. Bring them here."

"We are going to attack the village?"

"Not unless we have to. I'm going to see if I can grab Perro Blanco and bring him out of there. If I can, the rest of the bunch will be liable to come after us, so I want the other fellas on hand to hold them back, maybe keep 'em pinned down as much as possible."

"I thought you were going to kill him."

"I will if it comes to that," Jamie said. "But I'd like to take him back if we can." He sensed Dog Brother staring at him in puzzlement, but after a couple of seconds the half-breed made a sound of agreement.

"Do not do anything foolish until I get back with the others, old man."

"Then don't waste any time getting back," Jamie told him. "Because if I see a chance, I plan on taking it."

CHAPTER 46

It was far into the night, long after midnight, when Clete Mahoney finally allowed them to stop. Several hours earlier, they had reached the end of the badlands, turned north, and come to the low escarpment that divided one vast tableland from the other.

"We've come far enough," Clete declared. "That bluff's not steep, but we'll be able to get up it easier in the morning when we can see. Anyway, the horses are about played out."

"So am I," Harp said. The other two brothers muttered agreement.

Clementine seemed to have dozed off a while earlier, slumping back limply against Clete as he held her on the horse in front of him, but she was awake, turning her head from side to side as she looked around. He tightened his grip on her, lifted her from the horse's back, and set her on the ground.

As soon as her boots touched dirt, she started running, heading west along the base of the bluff as fast as her flashing legs would carry her.

As tired as Clete was, and as annoyed as he was by her antics, a part of him rose to the challenge. He whooped and drove his heels into the flanks of his tired mount. The horse leaped into a gallop and thundered after Clementine.

She couldn't outrun the pursuit, of course. In the moonlight, he saw her jerk her head around to peer over her shoulder, then she started veering back and forth to throw him off. It didn't do a bit of good. He overtook her in less than a minute and leaned down to grab her again.

She fought and squirmed like a wildcat as he swung her feet off the ground, and the sheer ferocity of it took him by surprise. As he pulled her closer, she leaned in and latched on to his ear with her teeth, then threw her head back.

Clete yelled, "Ow!" and had to lean sharply toward her to keep her from tearing his ear off. His balance suddenly deserted him, and he toppled out of the saddle.

He was able to kick his feet free as he fell, so he wasn't dragged by the running horse, but he couldn't prevent himself from crashing to the ground. The impact jolted Clementine out of his grip.

As they rolled apart from each other, Clete felt a tug at his hip.

He had a pretty good idea what had happened, and sure enough, as he rolled over and came up on his knees, he saw Clementine a few feet away using both hands to lift the heavy revolver she had plucked out of his holster. At the same time, she fumbled with the hammer, trying to cock it.

Clete threw himself forward and swept his left arm up. It struck the revolver's barrel and knocked it skyward just as the gun went off. The thunderous roar almost deafened him. He shouted a curse and rammed into Clementine, knocking her over backward. His momentum landed her on top of him. He grabbed her wrists and pinned her arms to the ground above her head. The roughness of the action made her lose her grip on the gun. As she thrashed around, he planted a knee in her belly and tried to hold her down.

"Stop it!" he bellowed at her. "Stop it, you crazy little fool! I don't want to hurt you!"

"You don't?" she said through clenched teeth as she glared up at him. "You follow me hundreds of miles, steal me away from my husband, and drag me back to that . . . that evil place you call home!"

"Your husband's dead," Clete told her. "The Apaches killed him, and you know it. You got nowhere else to go, girl. Anyway, home's where you belong, takin' care of me and the rest of the boys."

She spat in his face.

Clete lost his temper then. He let go of her left wrist and used his right hand to hit her twice, forward and back, and the brutal blows left her stunned. Vaguely, through the roar of blood inside his head, he heard hoofbeats, and a few seconds later, hands took hold of him and pulled him away from her as he lifted his arm to hit her again.

"Wait, Clete!" Lew said. "You'll kill her!"

Lew and Harp held him while Jerome hurried to Clementine and dropped to a knee beside her. After a moment, he glanced over his shoulder at his brothers and reported, "She's all right. Just knocked a mite silly."

Clete's chest heaved from the rage that filled him,

but gradually the feeling subsided. "Let go of me, blast it! I'm all right now."

With obvious reluctance, Lew and Harp released him. Clete shook himself and took a deep breath. He looked around. They were still close to the escarpment. The bluff rose no more than twenty feet away.

"We might as well make camp right here," he said. "One place along this bluff is as good as another. Lew, Harp, tend to the horses. Jerome, take care of Clementine. Watch her mighty close. If she tries any tricks and gets away, she's liable to kill you. And if she don't . . . I will."

Farther south in the night, Preacher stiffened in the saddle when the distant sound drifted to his ears. He reined in and the rest of the group followed suit.

"Umm," Nighthawk said.

"Indeed," Audie said. "That was definitely a gunshot."

"But only one," Fletch said. "What does it mean?"

"Means we're on the right trail, I reckon," Preacher drawled.

They had been moving slowly. Following a trail by moonlight was a tricky business, even for wily, vastly experienced trackers like Preacher and Nighthawk. He had been confident they were still on course, but that gunshot confirmed it as far as Preacher was concerned. The likelihood of anybody else being out there in that wasteland other than the men they were after was so remote that the mountain man discarded the possibility.

"But why would they be shooting?" Fletch wanted to

know. "What if . . . what if Clementine tried to get away? What if they shot her? Clete's crazy enough to—"

"Take it easy, son," Preacher cut in on Fletch's rising hysteria. "They don't have any way of knowin' we're back here on their trail, and they sure don't know we're as close as we are. I don't reckon that shot was more 'n a mile or two off. So there's no reason for Clete to think somebody's about to take Clementine away from him. No matter how loco he is, I don't believe he'd just up and shoot her for no reason."

Audie said, "From what little I've seen of the vile miscreant, I agree. And none of his brothers would dare do such a thing against his wishes."

"No, that's true," Fletch agreed, his voice steadier. "Lew, Harp, and Jerome are bad enough, but mostly they just do what Clete tells them to do."

Nighthawk pointed and said, "Umm."

"I can't quite make it out myself," Audie said, "but I'm sure you're right. We're not far from that escarpment. There's a good chance they'll stop there for the rest of the night, instead of trying to ascend it in the darkness. It would be easy for a horse to make a misstep and fall and break a leg. They have extra mounts, but I doubt they want to risk such a thing, to say nothing of the risk of injury to themselves in such a mishap."

Noah Stuart moved his horse forward and spoke up. "I took a good look at the escarpment from the top of that mesa. We're at least five miles east of there now, from what I saw, I believe there's a good chance it curves back to the north somewhere in this vicinity. Maybe within a mile or two farther east."

"What are you getting at?" Fletch asked sharply. "What difference does that make?"

Preacher said, "I reckon maybe I see what you're thinkin', Noah. If we circle in that direction, we can get up on the higher ground and then cut across behind 'em. They've made a habit of comin' at us from unexpected directions. Might be it's time to do the same to them."

Nighthawk nodded gravely and said, "Umm."

"With the added wrinkle that we can split up and catch them between two forces," Audie said.

"Yep, just what I was thinkin'," Preacher said. "Audie, you and Nighthawk and Chester stay down here and move in on their camp. Get close, but be careful not to blunder in on 'em."

"Of course," Audie said.

"Fletch and Noah and I will flank the varmints and come in from the north. That'll mean climbin' the bluff in the dark, but I reckon the risk is worth it. It'll take us some time to get in position"—Preacher squinted up at the stars—"but I reckon we'll be ready to make our move by first light. That ought to be a good time. They'll either still be asleep or they'll be pretty groggy. I'll come down the bluff into their camp and grab Clementine. Fletch and Noah can cover me from above. I'll try to get her away from there without a ruckus, but if the ball starts, you three boys can come thunderin' in from the south. How's that sound?"

"An eminently workable plan," Audie said.

"Umm," Nighthawk agreed.

Chester Merrick said, "I think it sounds like we're all going to get killed."

Preacher laughed. "You keep sayin' that, Chester, but we're all still alive and kickin', ain't we?"

"Sooner or later, I'll be right," Merrick said glumly. He drew in a deep breath and raised the shotgun. "But maybe we can kill some of those no-good, stinking Mahoney brothers first."

"Umm!" Nighthawk said and slapped the surveyor on the back.

CHAPTER 47

Noah Stuart's prediction concerning the escarpment proved to be correct. The low bluff began to curve to the north within a couple of miles to the east, after he, Preacher, and Fletch parted company with Audie, Nighthawk, and Chester Merrick. It wasn't a sharp bend, but steady.

"We could've climbed up there 'most anywhere as long as we were far enough away that those blasted Mahoneys wouldn't hear us," Preacher commented. "But it looks like the bluff ain't as steep around here."

"That's typical of geologic formations such as this," Stuart said. "Thousands of years ago, possibly longer than that, there was probably a vast, inland sea covering this whole area, but then some of it dropped and the water drained away, leaving this peninsula extending southward."

"You mean this whole blasted place was underwater?" Preacher asked.

"Well, I don't know that for certain, but it's possible. People have found shells and fossils of sea creatures in regions where they shouldn't have been, and that's the only explanation that really makes sense."

The mountain man shook his head. "When this is all over, you need to sit down and talk to Audie. He knows all about that sort o' thing, from when he was a professor at one of them fancy colleges back east. Most of the time, he don't get to talk to folks who understand what he's goin' on about."

"I'll do that," Stuart said with a smile. "But right now I'm going to concentrate on helping to rescue Mrs. Wylie."

Fletch said, "I appreciate that, Noah. You've turned out to be a better fella than I thought at first."

"Thanks," Stuart said with a wry grin.

They dismounted and led their horses up the slope. When they reached the top of the bluff, they waited a few minutes to let the animals rest, then swung up into their saddles again and rode southwest. Preacher had a pretty good idea where the shot they'd heard had come from, and he trusted his instincts to lead him to the right area.

When he thought they were getting close, he stopped and the other two did likewise. Looking down at the big, wolflike cur, Preacher said quietly, "Dog, hunt."

Dog loped off and quickly vanished in the darkness.

"If the varmints are out there, he'll find 'em," Preacher told his companions.

They sat there waiting. Preacher could tell that Fletch was getting more antsy with every passing second. He couldn't blame the young man for feeling that way. Having your wife in the hands of perverted scoundrels like the Mahoney brothers had to be mighty nerve-wracking.

Finally, after a time that seemed longer than it probably was, Dog returned, moving at a fast trot. He stopped in front of Preacher and the others, whined a couple of times, then turned to look the other way and growl.

"He found 'em, all right, just like I said." Preacher lifted Horse's reins. "Lead the way, Dog!"

The three men followed the cur across the semi-arid plains. The horses' hoofbeats were fairly quiet on the sandy ground. It became rockier as they approached the bluff, however, and Preacher signaled another stop.

"We'll go ahead on foot now," he told Fletch and Stuart. "Keep your guns handy."

They moved forward slowly and carefully, leading the horses. After a couple of minutes, Preacher smelled smoke. The Mahoneys were confident enough they had outrun trouble that they had risked a fire.

Preacher was going to be happy to demonstrate to them just how wrong they were about that. "We'll leave the horses here," he whispered. "Let the reins dangle. Horse won't stray, and he'll keep the other two in line. We'll go the rest of the way on foot."

He went first, leading the other two toward the escarpment. Just as Preacher had predicted, the eastern sky had a gray tinge to it. Dawn was less than an hour away. Audie, Nighthawk, and Chester Merrick would be down on the lower level, somewhere not far away, waiting for trouble to erupt.

Which was exactly what was going to happen. Preacher intended to get Clementine out of harm's way first, if he could, but even if he accomplished that, the time had come to deal with the Mahoney brothers. Otherwise, Fletch and Clementine would have the varmints dogging their trail all the way to California. They would never have any peace, would never be able to stop looking over their shoulders for trouble and just live the lives they deserved.

Judging by the smell of the smoke, the fire had burned down to ashes and embers.

That was true, Preacher saw as he knelt at the edge of the bluff a few minutes later. A few orange, faintly glowing spots were visible in the shadows below, marking the location of the campfire. Nearby, several dark shapes were stretched out on the ground—the brothers and Clementine sleeping.

But not all four of the Mahoney brothers. One of them sat on a rock with a rifle across his knees, guarding the camp. That was the first man Preacher would have to deal with.

One of the sprawled forms was separate from the other three. That would be Clementine, the mountain man thought. She was probably tied hand and foot to keep her from running away. Preacher's bowie knife would make short work of her bonds if he could reach her without rousing the others.

He backed away from the edge. Fletch and Stuart waited a few yards away. "They're all down there, all right. One fella's on guard duty, and the others are asleep. I'm pretty sure I know which one is Clementine. I'll take care of the varmint who's awake, then get her and head back up here. You boys be ready to take a hand if you need to. Just don't shoot me or her while you're doin' it."

"We'll be careful," Fletch promised. "Just bring Clementine back to me."

"I intend to, son, I intend to." Preacher added, "Dog, stay," and then slipped over the edge and started making his way down to the camp.

Sneaking up on four louts from Tennessee wasn't

nearly as much of a challenge as getting into a Blackfoot village unnoticed, which Preacher had done many times back when that tribe had known him as the Ghost Killer, but he wasn't nearly as young as he'd been in those days, he reminded himself wryly.

He was still capable of greater stealth than most men, however, so he reached the base of the bluff and the edge of the camp without the man on guard duty having any idea he was there. He had already slid his knife out of its sheath noiselessly, so as he drifted up behind the man like a lethal shadow, he was ready to loop his left arm around the sentry's neck to choke off any outcry and thrust the blade between the man's ribs and into his back.

A rock suddenly bounced down the slope with such a clatter that it sounded loud enough to wake the dead.

Preacher knew instantly that one of the young men had gotten too close to the edge and dislodged the rock. Which one did it didn't matter. The damage was done.

With a startled cry, the guard leaped to his feet and whirled around. He tried to swing the rifle toward Preacher, but the mountain man didn't give him a chance. Preacher lunged forward and slashed with the bowie, swiping the blade straight across the sentry's throat from left to right. The man jerked back with a dark fountain of blood spurting from his severed arteries. Preacher felt its hot gush across the back of his hand. The man made a grotesque choking sound and then his knees buckled and dropped him to the ground.

The other three Mahoney brothers were scrambling out of their blankets. The fourth figure, the one off to the side, stayed on the ground, confirming that it was Clementine. Preacher darted in the other direction to draw any gunfire away from her. As he moved, he tossed the bowie from his right hand to his left and then palmed out the Dragoon from the holster on his right hip.

"Whoever that is, kill him!" The bellowing voice belonged to Clete Mahoney.

Booming gunshots followed the shouted order. Muzzle flame blossomed in the night like garish orange flowers. Preacher heard the wind-rip of slugs past his head.

Shots rang out from the two men on top of the bluff. Hoofbeats thundered somewhere close by as Audie, Nighthawk, and Merrick rushed to join the fracas. Preacher dropped to a knee, leveled the Dragoon, and thumbed off two rounds with a deafening roar of black powder from the revolver. One of the Mahoneys flew backward as the bullets hammered into him.

A shot kicked up dirt next to Preacher, less than a foot away. He swung his Dragoon toward the man who had fired it, but Nighthawk was already there, diving out of the saddle and swooping down on the man like his namesake. The Crow warrior's huge form crashed into the Mahoney brother and momentum rolled them both on the ground.

With a bitter curse, the fourth brother abandoned the fight, turning and racing toward Clementine. That had to be Clete, Preacher thought, and he intended to kill the girl, just as Fletch had predicted.

Before Clete could reach her, another man on horseback loomed up in his way. A shotgun's double boom and twin lances of muzzle flame told Preacher the newcomer was Chester Merrick. Clete tumbled to the ground but came back up again almost instantly, and as he did, the gun in his hand roared. Merrick cried out and went backward off his horse.

Clete hobbled toward Clementine, obviously with a wounded leg from the shotgun blast. He wasn't letting the injury stop him, though. His gun lifted toward her.

A gray shape flashed through the air and crashed into Clete, knocking him off his feet again. Dog landed on top of him, snapping and snarling. Clete yelled in pain but managed to grab hold of Dog and throw him off. The cur landed several yards away and appeared to be a little stunned.

Clete reeled upright again, driven on by his hatred.

Clementine had kicked out of the blanket that had been wrapped around her. Preacher could see that her hands were tied behind her back and her feet were lashed together. But that didn't stop her from swinging her legs and knocking her brother's legs out from under him. Clete crashed heavily to the ground beside her.

Clementine jackknifed herself up and dived onto Clete's gun arm, pinning it to the ground with her weight. He started to reach for her with his left hand, but Preacher was there and his booted foot came down hard on Clete's left shoulder, making it impossible for him to move with the two of them holding him. Preacher saw dark red blood pumping steadily from the wounds on Clete's thigh and knew the man had only moments to live.

"You got anything to say to your brother, Clementine, you best do it now," he told her. "He's goin' fast."

Clementine lifted her head, snarled as she gazed down into Clete's face, and told him, "Go to hell."

Clete's back arched and a ghastly rattle came from his throat.

"Reckon he's knockin' on the Devil's door right now," Preacher said.

Clete sagged as all the life went out of him. Clementine began to cry. As terrible as they were, they had been her brothers, her flesh and blood. But they had made the decision to follow the twisted path that had brought them all there.

Feet pounded on the ground nearby and then Fletch was there, lifting Clementine away from Clete's body and calling out her name. He clutched her to him, and Preacher severed her bonds so she could return her husband's embrace.

In a voice that shook with surprise and relief, she cried, "Fletch! I thought you were dead!"

"Never!" he told her. "Nothing could ever keep us apart!"

Preacher stepped back so the couple could enjoy their reunion. Audie rode up, and Nighthawk strode away from the huddled, broken shape that lay behind him, all that was left of one of the other Mahoney brothers.

Noah Stuart knelt next to the fallen Chester Merrick and lifted Merrick into his lap, saying, "Chester! How bad are you hurt?"

Preacher wanted to know the answer to that question, too. He told Audie and Nighthawk, "Keep an eye on things," and walked over to Stuart and Merrick.

The assistant surveyor was sitting up, opening and closing his mouth and looking a little like a fish. When he found his voice, he said, "I . . . I'm not dead!"

"Nope," Preacher told him. "And I don't even see any blood on you."

"But . . . that man shot at me . . ."

"Appears he missed," Preacher said dryly. "Which means you just fell off your horse after you shot the varmint."

"I never said I was a good rider!" Then something occurred to Merrick, and he went on. "Did . . . did you say I shot that man?"

"That's what you were tryin' to do, wasn't it?"

"Yes, but . . . did I kill him?"

"Matter of fact, you did," Preacher said. "It took a couple of minutes for him to bleed to death, but in the end, it was the buckshot from that scattergun o' yours that did him in."

"Well, I . . . I guess . . ." Whatever else Merrick was going to say was lost, because his eyes rolled up in their sockets and he started to fall backward as he fainted.

Stuart was there to catch him. "He'll be all right."

"Yeah, I reckon so." Preacher looked around. "Anybody else hurt?"

Dog had joined Audie and Nighthawk and appeared to be unharmed. That was a relief.

Audie said, "We seem to have come through the battle unscathed."

"Good," Preacher said with a decisive nod, "because we need to get back down yonder to those hills and see if we can find Jamie. He's liable to be needin' a hand by now."

CHAPTER 48

After Dog Brother was gone, Jamie continued to watch the gathering of warriors near the largest fire in the Apache village. The man he had pegged as Perro Blanco ranted for a while longer, then stalked off to stand beside the creek, apparently staring at nothing as he brooded.

The group he had left behind him broke up and the warriors drifted away, some going to their wicki-ups, others checking on the pony herd or tending to other tasks. Dogs barked here and there, but that was the only sound from the village. Any conversations going on were too quiet for Jamie to hear them.

He kept his attention focused on Perro Blanco. After a while, one of the women hesitantly approached the war chief as he stood by the creek. She looked young, although Jamie couldn't make out many details at this distance. She spoke to Perro Blanco, and he turned sharply toward her. She drew back a little, as if afraid, but then gestured stubbornly and said something else. Perro Blanco glared at her for a few seconds, then jerked his head in an abrupt nod. She turned and went toward the wickiup.

He followed.

Everything Jamie had seen was pretty plain to him. Perro Blanco was upset because once again, an attack on the white invaders had failed. He had said as much to his warriors, who hadn't taken the criticism kindly but couldn't really refute it, either. Jamie and his companions had done a lot of damage to the tribe. Perro Blanco would never be able to unite all the bands and form an army of Apache warriors as long as he continued suffering these defeats.

After the discussion with the other warriors had broken up, Perro Blanco's woman had approached him and offered to comfort him. He had resisted at first but then succumbed to her blandishments. The two of them were alone in that wickiup where she had taken him.

And the rest of the village was going to sleep.

Jamie glanced back toward the gap looming behind him. Dog Brother might have had time to reach the others, but it would still be a while before they got to him. Jamie knew he ought to wait for them, but he wasn't sure he would get such a good opportunity again. Perro Blanco didn't have any of his warriors around him at the moment, and he was distracted, too.

Jamie pondered for a moment longer, then slipped over the top of the ridge and started down the slope toward the Apache village. Despite not knowing how long this chance would last, he didn't get in a hurry. In these circumstances, stealth was as important as not wasting any time.

All the fires were burning down. As far as Jamie could see, no one moved around the village except for one old man who shuffled along with what appeared to be an equally ancient dog plodding behind him. Jamie wondered idly how the dog had managed to avoid the stewpot and reach such an advanced age, but after a second he put that out of his thoughts and asked himself were the Apaches so confident in their safety that they hadn't posted any guards?

That appeared to be the case. The old man and the dog trudged on across the village in the fading light from the dying campfires and disappeared into one of the other wickiups. The whole place was still and quiet as Jamie reached the bottom of the slope and started toward the dwelling where Perro Blanco had gone with the woman. He stayed to the thickest shadows, moving soundlessly past the other wickiups toward the one that was his destination.

Many years earlier, when he'd been a captive of the Shawnee, he had learned how to walk quietly through the woods so as not to alert the game he was stalking. If he made too much noise, *he* would be the prey. He was determined that wouldn't happen.

Reaching the wickiup, he realized a hide flap hung over the entrance. He leaned close and listened intently, barely breathing. No voices came from inside, no sounds of anyone moving around.

Suddenly, someone snored. He heard a feminine voice mutter in response, then someone stirred around for several seconds before quieting again. The snoring continued raggedly. Perro Blanco was asleep, and so was his woman, but the racket coming from him had disturbed her slumber momentarily. Judging by the sounds, she settled down as his snoring tapered off, continuing but not as loud as when it had started.

Jamie lifted the hide flap and slipped inside.

A fire had been kindled in a small, rock-lined pit,

but it had burned down to embers, too. The glowing
coals gave off enough light for Jamie to make out the
two shapes stretched out on the ground beside the remains of the fire. Perro Blanco lay on his back. The
woman was curled on her side, a couple of feet away
from the war chief.

Jamie slid his bowie from its sheath. He could kill
Perro Blanco. The man would never awaken, would
never know what had happened to him. But Jamie
would never know the truth about Perro Blanco's real
identity, either.

Maybe he really was simply another Apache war-
rior. But one way or the other, Jamie wanted to know.
He lifted the knife and dropped to a knee beside
Perro Blanco.

At the very last instant, some instinct warned the
war chief. His eyes flew open and he started to sit
up, but Jamie struck with the swiftness of a snake as
the round brass ball at the end of the bowie's bone
handle slammed into Blanco's head before he could
do anything. A faint shiver ran through him, and he
was out cold.

Jamie twisted, knowing the sound of the blow
might awaken the woman. She jerked upright into a
sitting position as her mouth dropped open to let out
a scream.

He backhanded her before she could make a
sound. Hitting a woman went against the grain for
him—but so did being tortured to death. Anyway, he
told himself, he didn't hit her hard enough to do any
real damage. The blow just stunned her and knocked
her back to the ground.

Jamie continued to act quickly. He cut strips off the
woman's long skirt and bound her hands and feet.

Another strip was wadded into a ball, wedged into her mouth, and tied in place. She probably could work her way loose eventually, but it would take her a while. Even if she wasn't able to free herself, someone was bound to find her in the morning, and the night was more than half over.

That left Perro Blanco to deal with. Jamie tied his hands behind him, but that was all. Then he hefted the war chief and slung him over his shoulder. Perro Blanco was leanly built but still no lightweight. Jamie's massive strength was renowned from one end of the frontier to the other, though. He straightened under the burden and shouldered out past the hide flap.

The fires outside no longer gave off much light at all. The village was in darkness except for the silvery glow of the moon and stars. Jamie glided past the wickiups, but he hadn't gone very far before he froze at the sound of a voice nearby.

The voice was thin and reedy and sounded like it was muttering some sort of complaint. He couldn't make out the words, but they were in the Apache tongue, he was sure of that. He stood absolutely still, cloaked in shadows, as whoever was roaming around came closer.

That blasted old man! Jamie saw him shuffling along with the dog still following him. The dog stopped suddenly and stiffened. A low growl came from the animal's throat as its hackles rose. Jamie knew the dog had smelled him and recognized the scent as that of an intruder.

He didn't want to kill either the old-timer or the dog, but he would if he had to. Seconds ticked past tensely as the dog continued to growl and the old man turned and spoke to it sharply. He motioned for the dog to follow him. Jamie couldn't understand the words, but he figured the old man was telling the dog to shut up.

After a moment, the dog did so. It let out one final chuff and then followed the old-timer, who had turned toward one of the wickiups.

As Jamie watched them go, he realized the old man was heading for Perro Blanco's wickiup.

Was that really his destination, or would he veer off in another direction again? Was he just wandering around blindly, unable to sleep?

Jamie didn't wait to find out. With Perro Blanco's still-senseless form slung over his shoulder, he headed for the ridge as fast as he could move without making a lot of racket.

He had reached the slope and started up it when a screech ripped out from the village and shattered the night's stillness. That blasted old pelican had found the woman and realized that Perro Blanco was gone!

Jamie tightened his grip on Perro Blanco and lunged up the slope, hoping that he wouldn't lose his footing and tumble back down into the hands of his enemies. He was breathing hard and his pulse pounded like a drum inside his skull by the time he reached the ridge's crest. Carrying a grown man uphill at a dead run was enough to tax any man's strength, even a veritable Hercules like Jamie Ian MacCallister.

His horse waited only a short distance down the far slope, and he was thankful for that. He spoke calming words to the animal as he slung Perro Blanco face-down over the horse's back in front of the saddle. It took only a second for Jamie to find the stirrup and swing up.

Angry shouts rose into the air on the other side of the ridge. He was sure the woman would tell the warriors that some giant had crept into the wickiup and stolen Perro Blanco, but for the moment they wouldn't know which way Jamie had gone with his prisoner.

Jamie hadn't had time to try to cover his trail, so it wouldn't take long for the Apaches to light some torches and find the tracks he'd left. They would be after him in a matter of minutes. He needed to cover as much ground as he could. Dog Brother would be on the way back with the rest of the men. If Jamie could meet up with them before the Apaches caught him, the odds of getting away would improve drastically.

Holding the prisoner in place with one hand and clutching the reins in the other, Jamie galloped hard across the rugged hills of northern Mexico. He had almost reached the gap through which he and Dog Brother had come earlier and was starting to think he might have given the Apaches the slip after all, when he heard savage whoops behind him, interspersed with his horse's drumming hoofbeats. He turned his head to look. In the moonlight he saw a large group of riders topping a hill behind him, leaning forward intently on their swift ponies as they raced after him.

Well, it *was* a race now—with life and death as the stakes.

CHAPTER 49

Since his horse was carrying double, Jamie couldn't run the animal flat out for very long at a time. Every few minutes, he had to slow down and let the horse walk. Those delays grated at his tightly drawn nerves, but he knew that if he ran the horse into the ground, that would be the end for him. He would never get away from the pursuing Apaches.

And if they did catch him, he would be lucky if he was killed in the ensuing battle. Being captured alive meant that he would wind up back in their village, suffering the torments of the damned as they had their hellish sport with him. The imps down in Hades had nothing on the Apaches when it came to torture.

Perro Blanco suddenly groaned. He didn't stir, but the sound told Jamie that the war chief was regaining his senses. That meant added trouble.

They were almost at the gap. Jamie urged the horse on, alert for any sign that the animal's strength was starting to flag.

He heard the frenzied whooping again and looked back. The pursuit had closed to within a few hundred yards. Maybe what he ought to do, he thought as he reached the opening between the two massive up-thrusts of rock, was dismount and fort. He could use some of the boulders for cover, and he knew he could pick off several of the Apaches as they tried to come up the slope.

But he only had a limited number of shots before he would have to reload, and when his guns ran dry, the Apaches would overrun his position and that would be the end of it.

Best save the last round for yourself, old son, he thought as he reined in.

He heard a sudden flurry of gunfire from an unexpected direction—ahead of him on the other side of the gap. Jamie stiffened in the saddle as he tried to figure out what that meant and could come up with only one explanation.

Those shots had to be coming from Dog Brother and the rest of his allies.

He had no idea what sort of trouble the others might have run into, but the shots were coming closer so it seemed like he would find out soon enough. At any rate, he wasn't going to continue charging through the gap when he didn't know what was going on. He turned his horse back toward the rocks clustered at the passage's opening.

Not bothering to be gentle about it, he shoved Perro Blanco off the horse. The war chief landed hard, and Jamie saw his head bounce as it struck the ground. While Perro Blanco was still stunned, Jamie dismounted quickly and wrapped a strip of rawhide he had ready for just such a purpose around the man's ankles. Lashed up like that, Perro Blanco wouldn't be able to give him any trouble while he tried to thin the ranks of the pursuers.

The hoofbeats of their horses were loud. Jamie yanked the Sharps from its sheath and ran over to a slab of rock at the entrance to the gap. He knelt, aimed by moonlight, and stroked the rifle's trigger. With the Apaches only a hundred yards away, the heavy round from the Sharps blew a fist-sized hole through the chest of one of them and flung him backward off his pony.

That slowed the attack but didn't stop it. Jamie set the Sharps aside and drew the Walker Colt. Aiming carefully, he triggered one shot. It was long range for a handgun, especially in bad light, but Jamie's accuracy was deadly. Another Apache screamed, threw his arms up, and toppled off his mount.

That brought the charge to a halt as the warriors hauled their ponies around and veered off in different directions, seeking cover along the slope leading up to the gap.

That was a mistake on their part, Jamie thought with grim satisfaction. They should have just kept on a-comin'. He wouldn't have been able to stop them. But he would have killed several more of them, and evidently none of them were all that anxious to die.

A swift rataplan of hoofbeats echoed from the gap's rock walls. Jamie swung around to see what fresh hell was about to break loose.

"Jamie!" That was Dupre. "Jamie, are you there?"

"Over here!" Jamie called back to the Frenchman. "At the other end of the gap."

He heard several horses galloping toward him. The thick gloom inside the passage made it difficult to see what was going on, but then guns began to bang at the far end and he knew some of the group had stopped there to hold off whoever was chasing them while the others hurried to reinforce his position. A moment later, with a clatter of hooves, those men reined in and dismounted.

Tennysee hunkered behind the rock next to Jamie and said, "Dog Brother told us we'd find you waitin' on the other side. Reckon that didn't work out like you'd planned."

"And I told Dog Brother that if I saw a chance to grab Perro Blanco, I was going to take it." Jamie jerked a thumb over his shoulder. "He's stretched out over there, maybe unconscious. But even if he's awake, I've got him tied up so he can't do anything."

Dupre and Deadlead joined Jamie, as well.

The Frenchman said, "We were on our way here when an unfortunate incident occurred. We ran into a group of Apaches, either a hunting party or perhaps some warriors from another band on their way here to join forces with Perro Blanco. Whoever they are, they outnumbered us and gave chase. So now we are between the proverbial rock and hard place, no?"

"Sounds like it," Jamie agreed. "Anybody hurt?"

"Not so far," Tennysee said. "Pete, Greybull, and Pugh stayed at the other end along with Dog Brother and that Scandahoovian. They said they'd hold off the bunch comin' from that direction. It's our job to deal with the varmints on this side."

"At least we've got some good cover," Deadlead said as he knelt behind another rock. Suddenly, he snapped his rifle to his shoulder and fired. "Got him! One of the varmints figured he could run from one patch of shadow to another. He was wrong."

Jamie had reloaded his Sharps while they were

talking. "Plenty of targets out there to shoot at, boys. Try to make every shot count, too. We may have to hold out for a while."

"Until we run out of ammunition?" Dupre said. "You know what will happen then, Jamie."

"I'm sort of hoping Preacher will show up before then."

A while later, when the gray light of approaching dawn had begun to filter into the gap, the warriors from Perro Blanco's village made another rush, but with help from the deadly accurate trio of frontiersmen who had joined him, Jamie turned them away again. Shots came from the other end, too, from time to time, but the standoff continued.

As the sky continued to lighten, Perro Blanco started ranting at his captors in Apache.

Jamie told his three companions, "Keep an eye out and give a holler if those varmints try anything else. I'm going to go talk to our guest."

Tennysee laughed. "I don't reckon you'll get much polite conversation outta that one, Jamie!"

Jamie walked over to where Perro Blanco lay on the rocky ground. With his ankles lashed together and his hands tied behind his back, he wasn't able to do anything except squirm around futilely. Jamie figured Perro Blanco's position had to be pretty uncomfortable. Knowing that didn't bother him the least little bit.

Jamie hunkered on his heels, staying back far enough that the war chief couldn't spit on him. Perro Blanco fell silent and glared murderously at him.

"You might as well save your breath . . . Lieutenant Charlton," Jamie said.

Perro Blanco's expression didn't change, but Jamie thought he saw a flicker of surprise in the man's eyes. Jamie frowned and leaned closer. It was light enough in the gap for him to see that those eyes were blue.

"Yeah, I know who you are," Jamie went on. "It wasn't that hard to figure out. Lieutenant Damon Charlton disappears down here after the rest of the patrol he's leading is wiped out, and not long after that, the Apaches have themselves a new war chief whose name means White Dog."

"Ligai Chinii," Perro Blanco said through clenched teeth.

"What? I don't really savvy your lingo."

"My name . . . Ligai Chinii!"

Jamie nodded. "I reckon I understand. That's Apache for White Dog, right? You can call yourself anything you want, but it doesn't change anything. You're still Damon Charlton."

Perro Blanco writhed furiously in response to that.

"My name is Jamie MacCallister. I know your father. He's the one who sent me down here to look for you. Are you hearing me, mister? Your father believes you're still alive. I don't reckon he ever dreamed that you wound up leading the very Apaches who wiped out your patrol, though. How'd you manage that? Are you just so loco, so ruthless, that the Apaches figured it would be a good thing to have you on their side instead of torturing you to death?"

Jamie's frown deepened as he looked more closely at the captive and saw the scars covering Perro Blanco's body.

"They *did* torture you," he said in astonishment. "But you didn't die." Jamie nodded slowly. "They must've figured the spirits were protecting you, and that made you special. That's how you became one of them. But the pain you'd endured . . . it must have driven you mad. Made you kill-crazy." Jamie shrugged. "So you fit right in with the rest of them, well enough that after a while they made you their war chief."

The man was breathing hard, his chest rising and falling rapidly as he glowered at Jamie. But after a moment, he whispered in English, "Damn you . . . damn you for . . . for bringing all that up again."

"You don't want to remember who you were," Jamie said. His voice was hard and flat. "Well, considering all the things you've done, if I was in your place I don't reckon I'd want to remember when I was a decent human being, either."

Damon Charlton tried to lunge up at Jamie. If he'd had fangs, he would have struck like a snake. But he was just a man, tied up, helpless, ravaged by hate and madness. Deciding to capture him and bring him back had been a mistake, Jamie realized. He wasn't going to be doing anyone a kindness, and certainly not General Owen Charlton.

"Jamie, here they come again!" Dupre called. "And there are more of them now! They've gotten reinforcements!"

Jamie grimaced and leaped to his feet. He hurried back to the mouth of the gap and dropped behind the same rock slab he had used for cover earlier. He thrust the Sharps' barrel over the rock and looked down the slope at the attacking horde of Apaches. Some of them fired old muzzleloaders up at the gap, and the balls from those rifles whined through the air as they ricocheted.

Mostly, though, the Apaches sent a swarm of arrows flying up the slope. Jamie ducked one of them that whipped perilously close to his head, then drew a bead and pressed the trigger of the Sharps. One of the Apaches sailed backward as the shot blew away a good-sized chunk of his head.

As Jamie set the Sharps aside and reached for his revolver, he heard renewed firing from the other end of the gap, as if the Apaches on the other side had just launched a renewed attack, too. He wondered if the two groups had coordinated their actions somehow, or if it was just happenstance.

Either way, they were closing in and on the verge of overwhelming the defenders.

Jamie and his companions emptied their guns in a furious volley that mowed down many of the Apaches—but for every warrior that fell, another one took his place. Sometimes more than one. The savage horde swarmed into the gap, and in a matter of seconds, the battle became bloody, hand-to-hand chaos.

Jamie rammed the empty revolver back into its holster and yanked out the bowie knife. He laid into the attackers who crowded around him, and gore sprayed like rain. With his other hand, he caught hold of an Apache's neck and squeezed until the man's windpipe was crushed. Then Jamie threw the choking, dying warrior into the path of two more men who were rushing him.

His companions battled just as desperately, but they were about to be overwhelmed and dragged down. Once they were off their feet, that would be the end for them, and they knew it. So they fought with the intensity of insane men.

From the corner of his eye, Jamie caught a glimpse

of one of the warriors bent over Perro Blanco, cutting his bonds and freeing him. Jamie kicked a man in the belly, slashed another's throat, knocked a third man away from him with an elbow. He struggled to get through the crowd of killers and reach Perro Blanco . . . or rather, Damon Charlton. If nothing else, Jamie swore to himself, the white lieutenant turned Apache war chief would die today. That would spare the young man's father more pain in the long run.

Suddenly, two massive figures strode through the melee, flailing around them with giant, clublike arms that sent warriors flying. Greybull, who had been at the other end of the gap, was entering the battle at this end, and alongside him was none other than Nighthawk. Jamie's heart leaped as he recognized the big Crow warrior. Greybull's presence meant that the battle at the other end was won, and if Nighthawk was here, then probably so, too, were Preacher, Audie, and the other men who had gone after the Mahoney brothers.

The arrival of the second group was enough to swing the advantage away from the Apaches. The re-inforcements had taken them by surprise, and the tide of battle changed within minutes. Jamie spotted Preacher with a Dragoon in each fist spewing flame, and despite the close quarters, every shot made by the mountain man was deadly accurate. Apache warriors fell like ninepins before the onslaught of hot lead.

"Ahhhhhh!"

The crazed scream came from Perro Blanco as he hurled himself at Jamie. The former lieutenant had picked up two knives, and they flashed in the light from the sun that had risen high enough to penetrate the gap. Jamie needed every bit of his quickness to fend off the maddened attack. Sparks danced from steel as the blades clashed again and again.

The rest of the battle seemed to retreat around Jamie and Perro Blanco. Jamie knew that if he took his attention off his opponent even for a fraction of a second, the war chief would bury one of those blades in him.

Nor could Jamie go on the attack. It was all he could do to block all the slashes and thrusts directed at him.

Inevitably, one of those thrusts got through. Jamie felt the bite as Perro Blanco stabbed him in the left shoulder. He grimaced and took a step back, but the rock wall was behind him and he couldn't go any farther. The arm holding the bowie sagged.

A look of savage glee appeared on Perro Blanco's face as he leaped in to finish off his hated enemy. He raised the other knife high for the killing stroke . . .

Just as Jamie intended.

Jamie's arm flashed up again. The bowie leaped from his hand in a powerful throw and drove into Perro Blanco's chest. The war chief stopped short, eyes widening in surprise. He stumbled forward and tried to strike at Jamie with the knife. But he lacked the strength, and as he moved his knees unhinged. He fell onto them and then leaned forward, slowly collapsing and pushing the knife even deeper in his chest.

Not that it mattered. The Apache war chief Perro Blanco—Lieutenant Damon Charlton of the United States Army—rolled onto his side, as dead as he would ever be.

Jamie leaned back against the wall, his chest heaving, blood trickling around the knife still lodged in his shoulder. A few more shots rang out here and there, but for the most part, the battle appeared to be over.

Preacher went toward him, a grin on his rugged face. "Just take it easy, Jamie, you got a knife stuck in you."

"Yeah, I kind of noticed that. I don't think it's too bad, but it'll need some patching up."

"Lots of fellas around here got plenty of experience at that." Preacher looked down at Perro Blanco. "He didn't make it, eh? You kill him?"

"He didn't give me much choice," Jamie replied grimly. "And I'd already figured out that was the best thing for everybody's sake."

"And that idea you had . . . ?"

Jamie drew in a deep breath. "It was a crazy notion, all the way around. Lieutenant Damon Charlton died a long time ago, when he was taken prisoner after his patrol was wiped out."

Preacher looked at Jamie for a moment, then said, "That's what you're gonna tell the boy's pa?"

"That's exactly what I'm going to tell him."

"Probably a good idea." Preacher put an arm around Jamie to help him away from the wall where he was leaning. "Let's get that knife outta your shoulder. Don't want you bleedin' to death. Kate 'd never forgive me."

CHAPTER 50

"We had extra horses we took from them Ma-honeys, so we rode like blazes gettin' back down here," Preacher explained later, while Audie was wrapping a bandage around Jamie's injured shoulder. "When we did, we hit those varmints on the north side of the gap without them knowin' we was comin', so with them caught in a crossfire, it didn't take long to clean 'em up. Then we rushed on through the gap to give you boys at the other end a hand."

"And just in time, too," Jamie said. A solemn look came over his rugged face. "Too bad about Lars. He and his brother were mighty close. I'm not sure he would've wanted to go on without Bengt."

Lars Molmberg was the only one in their group who had been killed in this battle. Everyone else who had been defending the gap had suffered some sort of injury. They were a bloody, bedraggled bunch—but alive.

Jamie had no real idea how many Apaches had survived, but judging by the number of bodies, it couldn't have been many. He believed the ones who were left wouldn't be much of a threat for a long time to come, especially since Perro Blanco's effort to unite the different bands had ended.

Sooner or later another strong leader would arise among the Apaches, and then the frontier would be ripe once again for more bloody savagery. But maybe by that time, things would be settled with Mexico, the railroad would be built, and civilization would be spreading through that part of the country.

Or maybe not. Jamie was no fortune-teller. All he knew was that he had done the job he'd been sent to do, and he was ready to go home.

Home to MacCallister's Valley. Home to Kate.

Preacher must have read his mind. The mountain man said, "I reckon you'll be headin' back to Santa Fe and then on to Colorado?"

"Pretty soon," Jamie said with a nod. "Noah wants to scout around a little more down here and map out a possible route for that railroad. I don't expect to run into any more trouble from the Apaches, though. The ones who are left will be holed up in the hills and licking their wounds for a long time. So if you want to start on out to California with Fletch and Clementine . . ."

"That's what I was thinkin', all right. After everything they've gone through, those youngsters need a new start. I wouldn't mind helpin' 'em get it."

"You buried her brothers, back up there along that bluff?"

Preacher nodded. "Yep. Said proper words over 'em and everything. Probably more 'n they deserve, in fact, but . . . well, family's still family, I reckon, no matter how sorry they are. Sometimes folks need to grieve for what never was, as much as for what they lost."

That seemed sensible to Jamie. The past was always there, branching into more trails than any man could ever follow, and all too often, ghosts walked those trails, crying out for what might have been, cries that could never be answered. The best a man could do was turn his eyes and his heart toward the infinite paths that still waited in front of him . . .

And keep moving forward, answering the call of the frontier.

CHAPTER 1

"You two old scalawags stop that wagon and throw your guns down, or we'll fill you so full of lead, they'll need an ore dray to haul you to Boot Hill!"

The shout had vaulted down from somewhere on the forested ridge jutting on the right side of the old wagon trail. The words echoed around the narrow canyon before dwindling beneath the crashing rattle of the freight wagon's stout, iron-shod wheels.

Jimmy "Slash" Braddock turned to his partner, Melvin Baker, aka the Pecos River Kid, sitting on the freight wagon's seat to his left, and said, "Whose callin' us old?"

Driving the wagon, handling the reins gently in his gloved hands, Pecos turned to Slash and scowled. "Who . . . *what*?"

"Someone just called us old."

Pecos lifted his head and looked around, blinking his lake-blue eyes beneath his snuff-brown Stetson's broad brim. "I didn't hear nothin'."

"You didn't hear someone call us old from up on that ridge yonder?"

"Hell, no—I didn't hear a damn thing. I think you're imaginin' things, Slash. It's probably old-timer's disease."

"Old-timer's disease, my butt." Slash's brown-eyed gaze was perusing the stony ridge peppered with lodge-pole pines and firs, all cloaked in sparkling, smoking gowns of high-mountain sunshine. "I heard someone insult us way out here on the devil's hindquarters."

A rifle cracked on the ridge. The bullet punched into the trail several feet ahead of the two lead mules and spanged shrilly off a rock. Instantly, the mules tensed, arching their tails and necks. The off leader loosed a shrill bray.

"Whoa!" Pecos said, hauling back on the reins. "Whoa there, you cayuses!"

As Pecos stopped the mules, Slash snapped up his Winchester '73, pumping a live round into the action. He'd started to raise the rifle, to aim up the ridge, when another rifle barked—this one on his and Pecos's left. The bullet cracked loudly into the wagon panel two feet behind Pecos. The sound evoked a low ringing in Slash's ears; it made his heart kick like a branded calf.

Pecos flinched.

As men who'd spent over half their lives riding the owlhoot trail, robbing trains and stagecoaches and evading posses and bounty hunters, they were accustomed to being shot at. That didn't mean they'd ever gotten comfortable with it.

"You were told to throw your weapons down, buckos!" said a man with a British accent from the pine-clad slope on the trail's left side, on the heels of the rifle crack's dwindling echoes. "You won't be told a third time. You'll just be blasted out of that wagon boot to bloody hell an' gone!"

Slash glanced at Pecos, who sat back on the hard wooden seat, holding the reins taut against his chest. Pecos returned Slash's dark look, then lifted one corner of his mouth, clad in a silver-blond goatee that matched the color of his long, stringy hair, in a woeful half-smile.

Slashed cursed. He eased the Winchester's hammer down against the firing pin, then tossed the rifle into some soft-looking brush to his right. Pecos set the wagon's brake, wrapped the reins around the whip-sock, then tossed away his Colt's revolving rifle, which had been leaning against the seat between him and Slash.

Crunching, scraping footsteps sounded to Slash's right. He turned to see a man descending the steep, talus-strewn ridge on the trail's right side, weaving through the scattered pines. He held a Spencer repeating rifle in one hand, aiming it out from his right hip while he used his free hand to grab tree trunks and branches to break his fall.

"Now, the hoglegs!" he shouted as he approached the bottom of the canyon.

He appeared to be a young man—whipcord lean and wearing a shabby black suit coat coppered with age over a ragged buckskin shirt unbuttoned halfway down his bony, hairless chest. A badly mistreated opera hat sat askew on his head, from which a tangled mess of lusterless, sandy hair hung straight down to his shoulders.

An old-model Colt jostled in a soft brown holster hanging loose on his right leg.

He stopped near the bottom of the trail, sidled up to a stout pine, and aimed the rifle straight out from his right shoulder, narrowing one coyote eye down the barrel at Slash's head. "Ain't gonna tell you old tinhorns again. Just gonna drill you a third eye. One you can't see out of!"

He gave a crow-like caw of laughter, obviously pleased with his own joke.

"More insults," Slash said, staring at the coyote-faced youngster. He couldn't have been much over twenty. The scars from a recent bout of pimples remained on his cheeks and forehead. "First we're old scalawags. Now we're tinhorns."

"You fellas are startin' to hurt our feelin's," said the Pecos River Kid, looking from the younker on the right side of the trail to the Brit now descending the slope on the trail's left side.

"We'll hurt more than that, old man," said the limey as he dropped down even with the kid, on the opposite side of the trail. He was older but not any better-looking. "If'n you don't shed those shootin' irons I can plainly see residin' in your belt sheaths, you're gonna be snugglin' with the diamondbacks. The knives, too. Nice bowies, they appear. Might have to confiscate those. I'm a knife man, myself. Had to be in the Five Points. I have quite a collection, and an ever-growin' one, I might add."

He smiled, showing large, horsey teeth the color of old ivory. "I keep 'em sharp enough to split hairs with, don't ya know." The smile grew more suggestive, menacing.

Slash exchanged another dark glance with Pecos. Slash carefully slid his two matched, stag-butted Colt

.44s from their holsters—one positioned for the cross-draw on his left hip, the other thonged on his right thigh—and tossed them away, again aiming for a relatively soft landing. As a man who'd lived his life depending on his guns to stay alive, he didn't like mistreating them.

Pecos wore only one pistol—a big, top-break Russian .44—in a holster tied down on his right thigh. He pulled the big popper free of its holster with two fingers and heaved it into some brush on the trail's left side, near where the limey stood aiming his Winchester at him.

When he and Slash had both gotten shed of their bowie knives as well, the two ex-cutthroats and current freighters sat in uneasy silence, hands raised shoulder-high, palms out. Slash didn't like this position. He wasn't used to it. He was usually the one calling the shots and facing men staring back at him, warily, with their own hands raised shoulder-high.

He hadn't realized what an uneasy feeling it was, having guns held on you, your life almost literally in the hands of someone else. Someone who might just have an itchy trigger finger, like the scrawny kid in the opera hat, for instance. The kid not only looked like he had an itch to sling some lead, but the maniacal glint in his coyote eyes told Slash he had a fondness for killing.

Or at least of inflicting fear.

The kid and the limey continued on down the slope, keeping their rifles aimed at Slash and Pecos. As they did, two more men appeared, stepping out from behind boulders on either side of the trail, thirty and fifty yards beyond, respectively, where the trail doglegged to the left.

One was a big, beefy Mexican in a shabby suit that was two sizes too small for him. He'd probably stolen the garb off some hapless wayfarer now feeding buzzards in a deep mountain ravine. He wore a bowler hat and two sidearms, and was wielding a Winchester Yellowboy rifle. A thick, black mustache drooped down over the corners of his mouth.

The other man was almost as big as the Mexican, but he was older, maybe in his forties. He had red hair beneath a black slouch hat. He was dressed in a paisley vest and sleeve garters, like a pimp or a gambler, and he carried a double-barreled shotgun at port arms across his chest—a grim, angry-looking gent with a large, wide slab of a face outfitted with small, gray eyes set too far apart, giving him the look of a demented mongrel. All four were likely riding a bout of hard luck in these remote mountains, probably having followed gold veins to nowhere. They'd probably thrown in together to make do, which meant haunting lonely trails for pilgrims to plunder and send nestling with the diamondbacks.

The redheaded mongrel's thick lips were set in a hard line. His ratty string tie blew back over one shoulder as he caught up to the Mexican, and they stopped about ten feet out beyond the two lead mules, who shifted uneasily in their hames and traces.

"How much you carryin'?" asked the red-haired man, giving his chin a belligerent rise and shoving it forward.

"I'll do the askin', Cord," said the Brit.

"Get on with it then," Cord said, an angry flush blazing in his nose.

The Mexican grinned as though nothing thrilled him like dissension.

The limey turned to Slash and Pecos. "How much you carryin'?"

The kid squealed a little laugh. The Mexican's grin broadened.

Their demeanors told Slash that they weren't professionals, and that they hadn't been together long. Sure enough, they'd merely thrown in together to try their hands at highway robbery for a stake that would take them to the Southwest before the first winter snows. Their types were a dime a dozen on the western frontier.

"What're you talkin' about?" Slash said.

"Don't let's chase the nanny goat around the apple orchard," the kid said, canting his head and twisting his face angrily. "We seen you comin' up this trail two days ago. You had a good load on ya. You came up from Fort Collins. We followed you out of town. Now, your wagon bed is empty, and we're thinkin' you mighta made a tidy little sum for deliverin' them goods up to one o' the minin' camps in the higher reaches."

Pecos glanced at his partner and said, "Slash, I think they're fixin' to rob us of our hard-earned wages. What do you think of that?"

"I don't like it, Pecos. I don't like it one bit."

Pecos looked at the limey and then at the kid standing on the opposite side of the trail from him, aiming his rifle out from his right hip. "Why don't you four raggedy-heeled vermin get yourselves some honest jobs? Try workin' for a livin'!"

Given his and Slash's shared past, Slash glanced at him skeptically. Pecos caught the glance and shrugged it off.

"Wait, wait, wait," the kid said, scowling again, again canting his head to one side and staring at the two former cutthroats through skeptically narrowed eyes. "Did you say *Slash* an' *Pecos*?"

Slash winced.

Now that he and Pecos had given up their outlaw ways and had bought a freight company in Fort Collins and become honest, hardworking, and more or less upstanding citizens, he and his partner had tried to forget their old handles and call each other by their given names instead. Slash was now Jim or Jimmy, and Pecos was now Mel or Melvin.

Old habits died hard.

The kid grinned like the cat that ate the canary and slapped his thigh. "I'll be damned!"

"What?" asked the Mex.

The kid glanced at each of his long coulee-riding partners in turn and said, "You know who these two old coots are?"

"Who?" asked the limey.

"Why, they're Slash Braddock and the Pecos River Kid, that's who!" The kid threw his head back and laughed, showing that he was missing one of his eye-teeth.

"You mean," said the Brit, dubiously, "you think these two old men sitting here in this freight wagon are Slash an' Pecos?" He stared at the two freighters and shook his head. "No. No. Nonsense. You're gettin' soft in your thinker box, Donny boy."

"We ain't that old, fer chrissakes!" Slash said, scowling angrily at the younger men, all four of whom were now laughing at him and his partner. "We ain't but fifty or so . . ."

"Give 'er take," put in Pecos.

"Whatever," Slash said. "That hardly makes us old men. Besides, were you fellas raised by wolves? Don't you know you're supposed to respect your elders, not rob and belittle 'em?"

The limey shook his head again and stared in disbelief at the two middle-aged freighters. "Damn, you two sure have changed. I've seen pictures of you both in the illustrated newspapers, an', an', well . . ."

"Yeah, well, we all get older," Slash said, indignant. "Just wait—it'll happen to you, amigo."

"What's Slash Braddock an' the Pecos River Kid ridin' a freight wagon for?" Donny asked, keeping his rifle aimed at the two former cutthroats. "You mossy-horns get too stove up to sit a saddle? Your peepers dim so bad that you can't shoot?"

He smiled again, mockingly.

"As if it was any of your business," Pecos said, "which it ain't, we was both pardoned by none other than the president of the United States his ownself. So we got no more paper on our heads, and we're free to live honest lives workin' honest jobs, which is exactly what we're tryin' to do."

That wasn't the entire story. The agreement was that they'd be pardoned for their many sundry sins in exchange for, under the supervision of Chief Marshal Luther T. "Bleed-Em-So" Bledsoe, working unofficially from time to time as deputy U.S. marshals, hunting down the worst of the worst criminals on the western frontier. Between those man-hunting jobs, they were free to run their freight business, which they'd been doing now for six months, having bought the small outfit from an old man in Fort Collins who'd wanted to retire and live with his daughter in Denver.

"You're also free to get robbed by blokes like us," said the Brit, narrowing his eyes threateningly again, clicking back his rifle's hammer. "Now . . . back to how much money you're carryin', which, by the way, we'll be relievin' you of."

CHAPTER 2

Pecos turned to Slash and made a face. "Ah, hell. How much we got, Slash?"

Slash sighed as he reached inside his black wool suit coat, which he wore over a pinto vest and suspenders.

"Slow, now," the limey warned, steadying the aimed Spencer in his hand.

Slowly, Slash reached into the breast pocket of his chambray shirt and withdrew the manila envelope in which he'd collected his and Pecos's pay after delivering an organ to a canvas dance hall up in Boulder and sundry dry goods and whiskey to a mercantile in Estes Park.

He ran a thumb over the slender stack of bills, making soft clicking sounds. "One hundred and fifty dollars."

"What?" the kid said, shocked.

"You heard me."

"You mean you two old cutthroats ran a load of freight all the way up there into them mountains and are only bringin' down *one hundred and fifty dollars* for your trouble?"

Slash felt the flush of embarrassment rise in his leathery but clean-shaven cheeks. Pecos glanced at him. He, too, looked sheepish. It used to be they'd done jobs for thousands of dollars. They never would have done a job—taken down a train or a stagecoach—unless they were sure they'd take home at least three times what they were carrying today for a whole lot more work.

Now, here they were busting their backs several days on the trail for a measly two hundred and fifty.

"That ain't so bad," Slash said, indignant.

"And it's honest," Pecos added, defensively.

"Jesus Christ!" said the limey, glancing at the kid. "From now on, I reckon we'd best keep our sights on whole freight trains instead of single wagons."

"And on younger men," said the redheaded mongrel, Cord, mockery flashing in his eyes.

Slash said, "You could try makin' an honest livin' your ownselves."

"We tried that," Donny said. "We been bustin' rocks for two summers. The winters damn near killed us. We found a little color, all right, but not enough for a stake. Hell, this is easier." He moved toward Slash's side of the wagon, keeping his rifle aimed straight out from his hip. "Throw it down."

"We need that money more than you do," Pecos said.

"You don't need it." The kid stopped and looked up darkly at the two former cutthroats, his mouth lengthening, though the corners did not rise. "You ain't gonna need a dime from here on in."

"What're you talkin' about?" Pecos said.

Quietly, the kid said, "Throw the money down, Slash Braddock. Just toss it down here by my right boot." The kid tapped the toe of his boot against the ground.

Slash glanced at Pecos. Pecos looked back at him, expressionless.

Slash glanced at the limey, then turned to the kid. "If you're gonna kill us anyway, why should I turn over the money we worked so hard for?"

"You never know," the kid said with quiet menace, dark amusement glinting in his cold eyes, "I might change my mind . . . once I see the money. It's enough to buy us all whiskey and girls for a coupla nights, anyway. We haven't had neither in several days now.

"Throw it down, Slash," the limey ordered.

Pecos turned to his partner, his eyes wide with fear. "Oh, hell—throw it down, Slash. Don't give 'em a reason to kill us." He glanced at Donny. "You wouldn't kill two old codgers in cold blood, would you, boy? Throw it down, Slash. Throw it down, an' let's go home!"

"Yeah," Cord said, moving slowly toward the wagon, stepping around the mules and striding toward Slash's side of the driver's box. The Mexican was sidling around toward Pecos. "Throw the money down, Slash . . . so you old cutthroats can go on home. Looks like one of you has lost his nerve in his old age."

He stopped and blinked once, smiling.

"Oh, lordy," Pecos said, throatily.

Slash glanced at him. "What is it, Pecos?"

"My ticker."

"What?"

"My ticker. It's . . . it's actin' up again." Sweat dribbled down the middle-aged cutthroat's cheeks.

"Ah, Jesus, Pecos—not now!"

"What the hell's happening?" Donny said.

"Ah, hell," Pecos said, leaning forward, dropping a knee onto the driver's boot's splintered wooden floor. "I can't . . . I can't breathe, Slash!"

"What the hell is going on?" asked the limey, striding down the slope, letting his rifle hang nearly straight down along his right leg.

"Can't you see the poor man's havin' ticker trouble?" Slash said, dropping to a knee beside his partner.

"He's fakin' it," said the kid. "He ain't havin' ticker trouble."

Slash shot an angry look at him. "Yes, he is. It started a couple months back. We were hefting heavy freight down from the wagon box, and his chest tightened up on him and his arm went numb. He said he felt like a mule kicked him." He turned back to Pecos, who was really sweating now, face mottled both red and gray. "Fight it, Pecos. Fight it off . . . just like last time!"

"I'll be damned," said the limey, leaning forward over the wagon's left front wheel and tipping his head to one side to stare up into Pecos's face. "I think he really is having ticker complaints." He chuckled at glanced at the kid. "I think we done made the Pecos River Kid so nervous, his heart is givin' out on him!"

They all had a good laugh at that.

Meanwhile, Slash patted his partner's back and said, "We need to get him down from here. We need to get him off the wagon and into some shade. Anybody got any whiskey? The sawbones told him he should have a few swigs of who-hit-John when he feels a spell comin' on."

"Yeah, I got whiskey," the limey said. "But I sure as hell ain't sharin' it with him."

They all had another good round of laughs.

"Just hand the money down, you old mossyhorn," the kid said, extending his hand up toward Slash, who'd stuffed the envelope into his coat pocket. "Then you can be on your way and get that poor old broken-down excuse for the Pecos River Kid to a pill roller . . . if he lives that long." He snapped his fingers impatiently. "Come on, hand it down, Slash. I ain't gonna ask you again!"

"Oh, hell!" Slash said, drawing the envelope out of his coat pocket. "Here, take the blasted money!" He threw the envelope down. In doing so, he revealed the small, silver-chased, pearl-gripped over-and-under derringer he'd also pulled out of his pocket and that was residing in the palm of his right hand.

He flipped the gun upright. He closed his right index finger over one of the two eyelash triggers housed inside the brass guard. He shoved the pretty little popper down toward the kid, who blinked up at him, slow to comprehend what he'd just spied in Slash's hand, his mind still on the money beside his right boot.

There was a pop like a stout branch snapping under a heavy foot.

The kid flinched as though he'd been pestered by a fly. His eyes snapped wide. Instantly, the rifle tumbled from his hands as he lifted them toward the ragged hole in the right side of his slender, lightly freckled neck.

A half an eye wink after the derringer spoke, Pecos, recovering miraculously from his near-death experience, shoved his right hand beneath the driver's seat just off his right shoulder. He closed his hand around the neck of the twelve-gauge sawed-off shotgun housed there in the strap-iron cage he'd rigged for it, constructed to resemble part of the seat's spring frame.

He pulled the short, savage-looking gut-shredder out from beneath the seat and swung it in a broad arc toward the limey, who'd just turned to stare in shock toward where the kid's precious bodily fluids were geysering out of the hole in his neck. As the Brit's eyes flicked toward Pecos, dropping his lower jaw in sudden exasperation as he began raising his rifle once more, Pecos tripped one of the double-bore's two triggers.

The limey's head turned tomato-red and bounded backward off the man's shoulders. Even as the limey was still raising the Spencer in his hands, his head bounced into the brush and rocks beside the trail.

As the head continued rolling and bouncing, like a child's bright-red rubber ball, Slash slid the smoking derringer toward Cord, who shouted, "Hey!" and lunged forward, raising his Henry repeater. The gray-eyed Cord didn't quite get the butt plate snugged against his shoulder before Slash squeezed the pretty little popper's second eyelash trigger.

Having only one more round with which to save himself from St. Pete's bitter judgment, Slash decided to play the odds. He aimed for the redheaded mongrel's broad chest and curled his upper lip in satisfaction as the bullet nipped the end off the man's string tie as it plowed through his shirt into his breastbone and then probably into his heart.

"Oh!" the redhead said through a grunt, looking down at his chest in shock as he staggered backward, the Henry wilting in his arms.

At least, it appeared to Slash that "Oh!" is what the

man said as the bullet shredded his ticker. He didn't know for sure, for the man's exclamation, whatever it was, was resolutely drowned out by the second, dynamite-like blast of Pecos's twelve-gauge on the other side of the wagon.

That fist-sized round of double-ought buck punched through the chest of the Mexican, who, just like his cohort on the other side of the mules from him, was bounding forward as he realized he and his brethren had just found themselves in dire straits. He didn't get his rifle raised even halfway before the buckshot picked him two feet off the ground and hurled him straight back into the brush already bloodied by the limey's disembodied head.

Meanwhile, Slash looked at the redheaded mongrel who'd stumbled backward to sit down against a boulder a few feet off the trail. He sat there against the rock, his chest rising and falling sharply as blood continued to well out of his chest and turn his shirt dark red.

He stared at Slash in slack-jawed, wide-eyed shock and said, "I'll be damned if you didn't kill me."

"If I hit your ticker, then you'd be correct," Slash said. "Do you think I hit your ticker? There's a chance it might have ricocheted off your brisket and missed your heart. If so, I'd better reload."

Cord shook his head once, his gray eyes glazed with deepening shock and exasperation. "No, no. You got my ticker, all right." He paused, staring at Slash, then added simply, "Hell," because in his shock and mind-numbing realization that he was teetering on the lip of the cosmos, he couldn't think of anything else to say.

Slash couldn't blame him. He didn't know from personal experience, of course, but he was sure that the place where Cord was just now entering was hard for a mere mortal to wrap his mind around. Slash would know soon enough. Every day, he was a little closer and more and more aware of that bitter fact . . .

Slash looked at the kid, who was rolling around on the ground, squealing like a stuck pig and cursing like a gandy dancer, clamping his hands over his neck, for all the good it did him. He was losing blood fast.

Slash looked across the wagon to see the carnage Pecos's shotgun had left in the brush over there. He glanced at his partner, who was just then breaking open his twelve-gauge and plucking out the smoking, spent wads.

"How's your ticker?" Slashed asked him.

Pecos grinned. "Better."

Slash chuckled as he climbed down off the side of the high, stout wagon, a Pittsburgh freighter he and Pecos had bought along with the business. He walked over to the brush where he'd tossed his weapons and picked up one of his .45s.

"I need help," the kid croaked out, sitting up against a rock, holding his hands over his neck.

"You're askin' the wrong jake, kid."

"Please don't kill me! Please don't kill me!"

"Kid, even if you weren't already a goner, I'd still kill you. Think I'd leave a little demon like you alive to sow your demon seed? What this world does *not* need is more of you."

The kid's eyes appeared ready to pop out of their sockets. "Please don't kill me! Please don't kill me!"

Slash killed him with a neat, round hole through the middle of the kid's forehead.

The demon spawn fell back against the ground and lay quivering.

"Kid," Slash said, flicking open his Colt's loading gate and shaking out the spent round, "I've come to know that what we want in this life and what we get are very rarely the same damn thing." He glanced at Pecos staring down at him from the driver's boot. "Ain't that right, partner?"

Pecos laughed and shook his head as he shoved his shotgun back into its cage beneath the seat. "Partner, sometimes your wisdom astounds me. Purely, it does!"

Connect with Us

Visit us online at
KensingtonBooks.com
to read more from your favorite authors, see books
by series, view reading group guides, and more.

Join us on social media

for sneak peeks, chances to win books and prize packs,
and to share your thoughts with other readers.

**facebook.com/kensingtonpublishing
twitter.com/kensingtonbooks**

Tell us what you think!

To share your thoughts, submit a review,
or sign up for our eNewsletters, please visit:
KensingtonBooks.com/TellUs.